PRAISE FOR NATI…
TWO TIME RITA AW…

JODI T… MAS

"Jodi draws the reader into her stories from the first page. Her stories are gripping, poignant, and just plain good reading."
—Debbie Macomber

"Jodi Thomas will render you breathless!" —*Romantic Times*

"Jodi Thomas's writing is breathtaking . . . her name should be at the top of everyone's favorite author list."
—*Affaire de Coeur*

TEXAS LOVE SONG

"A warm and touching read full of intrigue and suspense that will keep the reader on the edge of her seat." —*Rendezvous*

FOREVER IN TEXAS

"A winner from an author who knows how to make the West tough but tender. Jodi Thomas's earthy characters, feisty dialogue, and sweet love story will steal your heart."
—*Romantic Times*

"A great Western romance filled with suspense and plenty of action. It is the two tremendous lead characters . . . who will have the audience forever reading *Forever in Texas.*"
—*Affaire de Coeur*

TO TAME A TEXAN'S HEART

WINNER OF THE ROMANCE WRITERS OF AMERICA
BEST HISTORICAL SERIES ROMANCE AWARD OF 1994

"Earthy, vibrant, funny, and poignant . . . a wonderful, colorful love story." —*Romantic Times*

"Breathtaking . . . heart-stopping romance and rip-roaring action." —*Affaire de Coeur*

The Texan and the Lady

"The woman who made Texans tender . . . Jodi Thomas shows us hard-living men with grit and guts, and the determined young women who soften their hearts."

—Pamela Morsi, bestselling author of *Something Shady* and *Wild Oats*

Prairie Song

"A thoroughly entertaining romance." —*Gothic Journal*

The Tender Texan

Winner of the Romance Writers of America Best Historical Series Romance Award of 1991

"Excellent . . . Have the tissues ready; this tender story will tug at your heart. Memorable reading."

—*Rendezvous*

"This marvelous, sensitive, emotional romance is destined to be cherished by readers . . . a spellbinding story . . . filled with the special magic that makes a book a treasure."

—*Romantic Times*

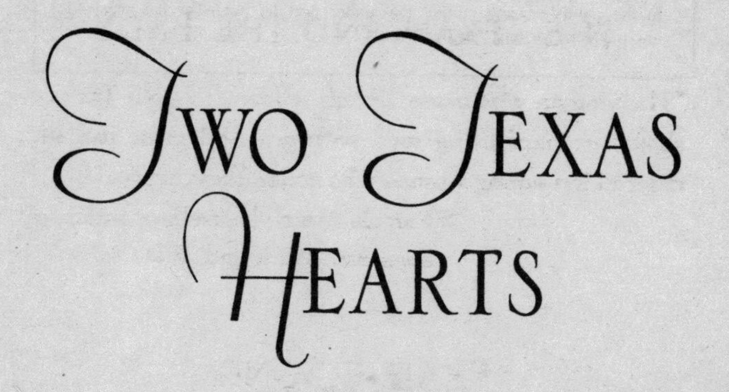

Jodi Thomas

TWO TEXAS HEARTS

A Jove Book / published by arrangement with
the author

PRINTING HISTORY
Jove edition / July 1997

The Putnam Berkley World Wide Web site address is
http://www.berkley.com

ISBN: 0-515-12099-5

A JOVE BOOK®
Jove Books are published by The Berkley Publishing Group,
200 Madison Avenue, New York, New York 10016.
JOVE and the "J" design are trademarks
belonging to Jove Publications, Inc.

PRINTED IN THE UNITED STATES OF AMERICA

10 9 8 7 6 5 4 3 2 1

This book is dedicated to

George and Maxine Koumalats

50 years together

May your love live forever.

PROLOGUE

WINTER MCQUILLEN PLANTED HIS BOOTS FARTHER apart and adjusted the brim of his worn gray Stetson against the glare of the late afternoon sun. He stared down into the six-foot hole, dry-eyed and angry.

"Lower the coffin," he ordered, feeling the words tighten in his throat. "Let's put the captain to rest before sundown."

"Yes, Boss," Logan Baker mumbled, around a wad of tobacco.

Winter didn't move as several of his ranch hands followed his instructions. Then, hesitantly, each stepped away, allowing their boss room to say goodbye to Captain Russell for the last time.

Only Logan remained within the boundary of the small wrought-iron fenced cemetery with Winter. "He was like a father to you, Win," Logan said. "We'll all miss the old man, but he's where he'd want to be, next to his Miss Allie."

Winter realized Logan hadn't used the shortened version of his first name in more than a year. He'd been Winter as a boy, but as his height passed six feet, his name had been shortened to Win. Last year, when the captain's health began to fail, Win had taken the reins of one of the biggest ranches in Texas without anyone saying a word. Logan, the oldest hand, had stood by his side and began calling him simply "Boss." Everyone in Armstrong County knew the ranch would be Winter's when the captain passed on. Everyone but Captain Russell, it seemed.

"My father, an Irish trapper, died before I had more than a handful of memories of him." Winter forced each word out as if needing to state the facts before rumors and legends got started. "My mother was killed in one of Custer's raids into Indian Territory a few years after the War Between the States."

His words drifted across flat, frost-hardened land colored in shades of brown. "I ran away from the good people who'd offered to finish raising me, thinking I was old enough to make it on my own. Captain Russell found me in the back of one of his supply wagons coming in from Dallas a few months later. I thought he'd skin me alive for eating a bushel of his apples."

"But he took you in and gave you a home." Logan nodded as if proving some unspoken point. Logan had been around in those days, but paid little attention to the skinny half-Indian kid the captain spent most of his day issuing orders to.

Winter lowered his gaze, not wanting the other man to see the anger in his eyes. "If you call letting me sleep in the coldest corner of the bunkhouse and working me from dawn till dusk six days a week giving me a home, I guess he did."

Looking back at a time twenty years ago, Winter stared at the horizon. "I used to live all week for Sundays, when I'd get to go up to the big house and study all day from mail-order books with Miss Allie. She'd even insist that I eat meals with them, like I was somebody. But the captain never let me forget he thought I was nothing but half-breed trash who came in with the supplies. Once a month he'd pay me a man's wages, then sell me an acre of land for the money.'' Winter tightened an already rock-hard jaw as he continued, ''About dark, he'd play me a game of checkers for the land, double or nothing. I was twelve before I won.''

He pulled a checker from his leather vest pocket and tossed it on top of the casket. ''I won all but the last twenty acres of this place. The captain never would play me for the square with the house on it. He always told me, 'Don't bet more than you're willing to lose.' I think the captain was never sure what I'd do if I won the house.''

''All the boys are guessing he left it to you in his will,'' Logan mumbled. ''You may not have noticed, but there wasn't another human alive the captain cared about but you. I remember back in the blizzard of seventy-nine, he had everyone including the cook watching for you to come in off the open range. He was about ready to send every hand back out if you hadn't come riding in when you did.''

Winter shook his head. ''He never cared about me, or gave me anything in life. Chances are he won't in death, either. He was a hard, cold man who never cared about anyone, except maybe Miss Allie. He never gave me an inch. But don't worry, whoever he willed the ranch house to, I'll deal with—even if it's the devil himself. Whoever it is couldn't be any harder than the captain.''

Logan watched in silence as Winter walked away. Somewhere inside the tall, powerful man was the little boy Logan had seen the captain shaking that night so many years ago. Winter had yelled that he was only seven, and the captain had shouted back for him never to tell folks what he ''was only.'' Winter had never given excuses after that night, or backed down from anyone, including the old man.

Lifting the shovel, Logan leaned against it. The new boss was wrong about one thing. There was a man harder than the captain. He was walking down the hill now toward the big house to hear the reading of the will. Not yet out of his twenties, Win McQuillen was harder than Captain Russell had managed to get in eighty years of rough living.

Logan shook his head, thinking of the will he'd witnessed one night over a year ago. Win was going to be madder than a rattler when he found out the captain left the twenty acres not to Winter McQuillen, but to his wife . . . a wife Win didn't even have yet, but according to the will, had better find within a month.

ONE

"I CAN'T JUST WALK INTO THE WIDOWS' MEETING LIKE a beggar looking for a handout.'' Winter shifted in the saddle and glared down at Logan, who was already hitching his horse to a rail. The banty rooster of a man had been pestering him all month, and now Logan had dragged him halfway across the county to a meeting.

"This was a damn fool idea,'' Winter mumbled. "They'll laugh us into the next state.''

Logan folded his spider-thin arms and waited for his boss to quit complaining.

Frustrated, Winter said, more to himself than the suddenly deaf Logan, "I've got diseased cattle from down south to worry about. This whole area is fixing to break into a battle. I don't have time to go courting. Seems like blocking any herds to keep half of mine from dying is more important than dropping in on some ladies' tea party.''

"You want to give up the prettiest twenty acres on your place, Boss?''

"I've never given up anything in my adult life!'' Winter growled. He'd been hell-raising angry for a week after they'd read the will. Win had thought all he'd have to do was ride over to Tascosa and ask that pretty Mary Anna Monroe to marry him. She'd given him enough signs every time she was here visiting her kin. During the few socials he'd attended in the past five years, she'd made it plain she was interested in getting to know him better. Plus, the woman could talk ranching as good as any man he'd met when she wasn't batting her eyes and acting coy.

But flirting was obviously one thing to Mary Anna, and marrying another. He would never forget standing in her aunt's parlor like a greenhorn as Mary Anna not only turned him down but told him that she didn't care how many miles of land he owned because everyone in the country knew he didn't own a heart.

"Well, if you're not giving up"—Logan spit a long line of brown fluid—"then you'd best get off that horse. Because according to the will, come sunup, if you ain't married, the First Methodist Church gets that house and the twenty acres smack-dab in the middle of your spread."

"The old man did this to me just to get the last laugh from the grave. He knew I never wanted a wife, any more than I'd stand for some preaching farmer living on my land." Winter swung his long leg over the saddle, shoved his dark brown hair out of his eyes, and stepped to the gate. "Let's get this over with, Logan. I'll marry the devil's sister to keep what's mine. I swore once that no one would ever take anything from me as long as I live, and it's time to make good on that promise no matter who I have to partner up with."

The two dust-covered cowmen walked to the side of the huge window of Widow Dooley's home and looked in at the circle of women, mostly dressed in black. They were having tea, and though Armstrong County had little society, it was plain these ladies all considered themselves gentlewomen just by the way they held their china cups. Leaving a widow was a hard fact of life in this country. The society had started up about the same time as the cemetery.

"Unless you're looking for a schoolgirl, these are the only pickings for a hundred miles."

"I'll be twenty-eight this spring, and the last thing I want is some giggly girl running my house. A woman no more than five years my junior seems a good range. And a widow would be practical because she'd already know her duties."

Win stared into the room with the interest of a condemned man asked to choose a rope. Half the women looked old enough to be his mother. Two others he couldn't imagine ever being lucky enough to find one man to outlive. One was young, but outweighed him by double, at least, and the last was tall, well-proportioned . . . and toothless.

"Well?" Logan's bushy eyebrows danced up and down. "Which one will it be, Win?"

"I had no idea the devil had so many sisters." Winter squinted hard, as if he could improve the looks of the group. "Are there no others?"

"None." Logan shook his head. "Every widow in Armstrong County is here tonight except Mrs. Adams. She keeps to herself out on that little farm by Saddleback Ridge. It wouldn't even be proper for her to make the widows' meeting for at least another month . . . not that she'd likely come anyway, being new in town and all. Most of the farmers' wives don't get into town much. She'd be about the right age, though, if you had the time to wait for her to finish grieving."

"How'd he die? Not poisoning, I hope."

"Who?" Logan carefully looked over each woman in the room as if the choice were his.

"Mrs. Adams's husband."

"He was killed in a stage robbery, I heard. Not too long

after they was married. She's been trying to run the place, but without money to hire help, she's not having much luck. Talk is, he wasn't much of farmer. I remember seeing him a few times. Didn't seem like much of a man, either. Since his place is between ours and town, he used to run deliveries for us once in a while. Folks wondered why he even wanted a wife, unless maybe he thought she'd come with a little money to help get his place going. He always seemed long on lazy and short on sense, but he did all right picking a wife."

"What does she look like?" Winter started moving toward his horse, already making up his mind. "Does she have all her teeth?"

Logan tried to stop him, but the little man's arm wasn't quick enough, so he hurried to catch up to his boss. "She's just a mouse of a woman I've seen a few times. Not so pretty you'd remember or so ugly you'd need to forget. But you can't ride out there. Pick one of these, Boss. These are ranchers' widows. They know the life better. I doubt Mrs. Adams would marry a man this soon after her husband's death even if the fellow were a farmer and someone she'd known for years. It wouldn't be right."

Winter swung into the saddle. "I'll take a slip of a woman before I'll be strapped to any one of those crows for life. And she'll say yes if I have to promise her the moon."

"But, Boss?" Logan spat a stream of tobacco as though just the thought of approaching a newly widowed woman left a bad taste in his mouth.

"Get the preacher and meet me at the ranch in an hour." Winter didn't give Logan any more time to argue as he rode off toward Saddleback Ridge. He'd talk Mrs. Adams into marrying him, then he'd live with a shadow roaming around the captain's huge house. If she was as mousy as Logan thought, he'd hardly notice her. And as far as Winter was concerned, that would make her the perfect wife.

TWO

KORA ADAMS FOLDED AWAY THE CLOTHES SHE'D FOUND in Andrew Adams's trunk. "Six months," she whispered. Six months since she'd read another woman's letter at the mercantile and decided to meet a stage. Six months since she'd watched them lift Andrew Adams's bloody body out of the coach. He'd thought he was coming to Bryan to meet a woman he'd married by proxy. Instead, a stage robber had put four bullets in him, and the woman was long gone with another.

Pushing away the tears, Kora whispered again, "We were meant to marry, Andrew Adams and I. We have the same bad luck." She hadn't even known the man, but she had the proxy letter and he had a farm. It was so simple to step forward as the bride of a dying man. No one questioned. No one checked the name on the paper. Her luck hadn't changed, though. The farm wasn't Andrew's, but the bank's. She'd brought her brother and sister across Texas to starve. Jamie once said they were nothing but weeds in life's garden. Nothing but weeds.

Kora glanced at her brother, Dan, sleeping in the chair by the fire, and wished as she had a million times before that he had really come back to them from the war. He'd been only fourteen when their father was killed. He had enlisted all excited and ready to fight. Only two years later they brought him home in the back of a wagon. He hadn't said a word since.

"I promised Mother I'd take care of you and Jamie," Kora whispered, knowing he didn't hear her. "I promised and I'm doing a terrible job."

Her great idea of marrying and running the farm after Andrew died seemed insane now as she looked around the shabby little one-room cabin that no amount of scrubbing could ever make clean. She'd always been the planner, the organizer, the leader who sacrificed for the others. She had always done whatever was necessary to keep them together, but this time the witchin' luck that her mother said followed her seemed to be smothering them.

The sound of an approaching rider pulled Kora from her worries. She shoved Andrew Adams's clothes back in the trunk and quickly added her cigar box full of keys to the chest before closing it. The keys inside the box fit nothing. Just as she seemed to. Even her mother thought the world was over because of Dan. It never mattered that she had two other children. She'd given them nothing, not even her love after Dan returned.

That was when Kora began to collect keys. They were her only treasure for as long as she could remember. Once in a while she found another in the dirt and built the room it would fit in her mind. She cleaned the key up carefully to add to her collection, as though someday she might stumble across the lock her key would fit.

Quickly Kora moved to the door.

But before she could reach the latch, someone pounded loud enough to shake the walls of the small cabin that had been half built, half dug from a rise in the ground.

"Yes?" Kora asked as she opened the door, expecting to see one of the neighbors.

"Mrs. Adams?"

A tall man removed his hat. He was dark-headed with sharp features and a mustache that hid his upper lip. The smell of leather and dust seemed layers thick between them. She could hear the heavy breathing of his mount only a few feet behind him and the soft jingle of his spurs as he shifted impatiently. He wore a jacket of wool, but his vest was leather. Leather was also strapped around his lean, powerful legs all the way past the top of his muddy boots. Kora stepped backward, trying to hide her fright. She'd seen the cattlemen in town. They always wore Stetson hats, leather, and spurs on their boots. But they'd never looked quite so frightening as this one, with his wide shoulders and gun strapped low across his hip. He seemed born to wear a holster.

"Mrs. Adams?" he asked again in a voice that rumbled like echoing thunder.

"Yes," she whispered and tried to pull her terror under control. If he'd come to kill her, he'd have little trouble doing so. She barely reached his shoulder, and he looked strong enough to snap her bones in half with one twist. She didn't dare scream for Jamie, or they might both die. Dan would be no help even if he awoke—which was unlikely.

"May I come in?" The stranger slapped his dusty hat against his leg.

Kora let out a breath. If he were going to murder her, he'd hardly be asking permission to enter. A man whose Colt was worth more than everything in her dugout cabin wouldn't need to rob her.

Moving to the table, Kora turned her back to the stranger as she lit the lantern, burning precious oil. "If you've come about the horse and wagon for sale, you'll have to return in the morning. I have no way of showing them to you in the dark.''

Winter stooped slightly and moved into the cabin. Her face had been in shadows when she'd answered the door, and now she had her back to him.

''I didn't come about the horse,'' Winter said, wishing she'd turn around. ''You're small. Logan didn't say anything about you being so tiny.''

She turned to face him then, her pale blue eyes huge with fright as her hands knotted around her black shawl. ''I'm not tiny.''

Forcing her voice not to shake, she added, ''You're the one who doesn't fit through the door.'' He was so tall his hair almost brushed the ceiling.

''I guess I am,'' Winter answered as his eyes adjusted to the cavelike shadows. Her hair reflected in the firelight as it hung to her waist. ''Your hair,'' he mumbled. Most of the women he knew looked as if they'd spent hours burning curl into their mass of ringlets piled atop their heads. But hers reminded him of his mother's, straight and thick. Only his mother's had been as black as midnight while this woman's was the color of sunshine.

Kora pulled her shawl over her head as though ashamed. ''I wasn't expecting anyone, so I'd already unbound it for the night.'' She felt like a fool explaining her actions to a stranger. What did she care if he thought she ran completely wild in her own house?

''I'm sorry to call so late, but time is vital at this point.'' He tried to stand still as she seemed to shrink before his eyes, folding into her huge shawl and moving away from the light.

Winter had never backed away in his life. He'd always silently enjoyed the fear he'd seen in most folks' eyes since he'd reached his full height. But he backed down now, not wanting to frighten her. He put as much distance between them as the tiny cabin allowed.

''I'm Winter McQuillen, Mrs. Adams. Most folks call me Win for short.''

She was so far into the shadows, he couldn't even tell if she was looking at him as he spoke.

''I'm sorry I frightened you. I just have to talk to you, and it can't wait till morning.''

Kora took a step toward the rifle Andrew Adams had left beside the fireplace. She knew it wasn't loaded, but it was her only weapon.

Winter widened his stance, wishing they were outside. This half-dugout seemed little more than coffin-size. It wasn't easy to propose twice in as many weeks, but at least now no one was watching. ''I'd like you to hear me out before you answer, Mrs. Adams.''

''Agreed,'' she whispered.

''I've got a ranch not far from here. Good land with enough grass and water to run all the cattle I can handle. Square in the middle of my land is a house. I'm hard-working, twenty-seven years old, and healthy. Couldn't swear I never take a drink, but I've never downed so much I couldn't get up at dawn and do a full day's work.''

Kora watched him closely. He showed no signs of a man who'd been tilting the bottle, but he was certainly making no sense.

''I'd see that no harm came to you by my hand or by any other.'' Winter recited the words he'd practiced all the way from town. ''I've never gone to church, but if you've a need, I'll do my best to take you every Sunday, weather permitting.''

Kora began to shake her head. Somehow this cowboy must be mad and think he was talking to another. ''I'm sorry,'' she whispered, not knowing how else to respond.

"I'd give you whatever you needed. When I'm on a drive, my credit's good at every store in town." Winter took a step toward her. She couldn't be turning him down! He wouldn't lose, not this time. Not when all that had ever mattered to him in years was the ranch, and part of that ranch was the house, his house. He'd sworn years ago after losing his mother to Custer's butchering never to turn loose of anything that was his ever again.

"Name your price, Mrs. Adams!"

The hollow click of a gun cocking was his answer. For a second Winter wasn't sure where it was coming from, then Kora stepped out of the shadows with an ancient weapon in her hand.

"I don't know what you're talking about, mister." She tried to keep both her voice and her hands from shaking. "But I don't want anything you're selling. I think you'd better leave."

Winter slowly moved his hands to the front of his holster and unbuckled his gunbelt. He propped his foot on a chair by the table and pulled the string holding the weapon against his leg, then lifted the Colt, holster and all, toward her.

"If you're going to shoot me for asking you to marry me, would you mind using a weapon that will do the job and not some antique that looks like it might blow off your hand if you pulled the trigger?"

Kora lowered the rifle slightly and took another step forward. "You're asking me to marry you?"

"I am." Winter didn't take his eyes off the barrel.

"But why? You don't even know me." Curiosity outweighed fear for the first time.

"I have to have a wife by sunup or lose part of what is mine." He could tell she was intrigued, if not interested in the proposal. "If you marry me, the house in the middle of my land is yours forever."

"I don't believe in *forever*," Kora whispered.

"Then stay for six months and I'll buy it from you. Then you can leave. I won't try to stop you." A touch of hope made him smile and he slowly began restrapping his gun-belt. "The place will be yours the minute you're my wife."

Kora tilted her head slightly. "Is this place large enough so that my brother and sister can live with us?"

"It is," he answered soberly. If she had a little brother and sister she wanted to bring along, that would be no problem for him. They'd probably be company for her when he was on a long drive. He hadn't expected a widow to come without baggage.

"And the price at the end of six months? Is the house worth enough to buy three tickets to California?"

"That and more," Win answered with a raised eyebrow.

Kora laid the gun down on the table between them and pressed her palms against her closed eyes. "This is insane. I can't marry you."

"Why not?" Winter leaned closer.

"I don't know you. I hadn't planned to ever marry and even if I did, I've another half year of mourning." She couldn't explain to this stranger how all her life she'd been invisible. No man had ever given her a glance. He'd be sorry within hours.

"Did you know Mr. Adams well when you wed him?"

"No," Kora admitted. She wasn't about to go into detail about how she didn't know Andrew Adams at all. This stranger, or anyone else for that matter, would never understand.

"I'll tell you about me." Winter straightened slightly. "My mother was Cheyenne, my father Irish. But no man's ever given me trouble about being mixed blood, at least not more than once.'' Winter knew he had to be honest now for he'd not have her saying she was tricked. ''If you ask my men, they'll tell you I'm a tough boss but fair. I don't ask a man to do something I wouldn't do myself, and I work as hard as any. If you ask women''—he thought of Mary Anna's words—''they'll tell you I don't have a heart, so don't go expecting any affection from me. I've no time for things as foolish as love. I'm offering a fair bargain of marriage, for a lifetime if you like, or six months. By the time you've finished mourning Mr. Adams, you'll have enough money to go wherever you like.''

''Are you saying you're asking for a marriage in name only?'' Kora felt her face redden from the neck up. She couldn't believe she was asking such a thing of a stranger.

Winter hesitated, knowing what he was about to say might very well end his chances. ''No, Mrs. Adams. If I'm going to have to marry, I want a wife.'' He knew he was embarrassing her, but there could be no misunderstanding. ''I expect us to live together as man and wife. I'll not sleep with another while we're married, and I'd expect the same of you.''

He could tell his words frightened her, but she seemed to be fighting gallantly not to allow her fear to show. Logan had told him there would be bargaining in marriage, so he'd better start before she bolted.

''I know you're newly widowed, so there'd be no rushing you on my part.'' He backed down guessing she'd be in California long before she climbed into his bed. ''You can take your time to grieve one husband before you bed another. But as far as the world will know we're to be truly married.''

The woman's face paled so much beneath the black shawl Winter feared she might faint, but she didn't say a word.

"Marry me, Mrs. Adams, and I'll do my best to see that you're never hungry or cold." He could tell by looking around the place that she'd be both soon. "If all you want in the bargain is to be in California, I'll see you set up there by summer if you don't want to stay married."

She stared at him and smiled as though he'd just sketched her hopes in the air between them. He wanted to yell at her for wanting so little. Hell, he'd give her a fat bank account if she asked, or trips to Dallas to buy clothes, or horses and a proper buggy.

"Name your terms," he said again. "But marry me to-night."

To his surprise she lifted her chin and stood taller. "I can't be bought," she said simply. "I'm sorry. You'll have to look elsewhere."

"I'm not buying you, I'm offering a bargain we both need. A marriage, right and proper as any. And I'm not saying being my wife will be easy. I won't promise to make you happy, but I will keep you safe. You'll own the house and the land around it outright. You can kick me out if I get difficult to live with. I'll stay in one of the line shacks if I must. I swear the house will be yours and you can come and go as you like, but the ranch is mine."

A thousand refusals ran through her mind. Even if she'd wanted another husband, which she swore she never would, the man before her wasn't what she'd look for. He seemed hard and cold and not even overly friendly when he was proposing. He was too covered in dust to sit at a table in a dugout, and the weapon he wore looked like it never came off.

But he just might be the solution she'd been hoping for. He was offering her a place to live, a refuge for a while. Then, by summer, she'd be in the warm sunshine of California. She'd taken a husband once to find a home. It hadn't worked, but this time it might, if only long enough for Dan to grow strong enough to travel. Nothing lasted forever, not jobs, or homes, or husbands.

She could survive alone, Kora told herself, but she had to think of Jamie and Dan. They were the reason she'd signed the paper to marry Andrew Adams, and they were her motivation now. "I'd ask one thing," she whispered, realizing she was demanding a great deal of this stranger.

Winter watched her closely, knowing that she was considering marriage for the first time since he'd suggested it. "Agreed." He felt his body relax. "Pack what you need tonight. I'll send one of the hands for the rest tomorrow. I'll hitch your horse to the wagon."

Kora looked up at him. "But you haven't heard what I want."

"It doesn't matter. I said name your price." Winter saw no point in trying to bluff when she'd won. Whatever she asked, he'd give.

"One thing I think you should know. I'm left-handed." Kora felt she had to be honest, he'd find out soon enough. "My mother did everything she could to change me, but nothing worked."

The corner of Win's mustache lifted. "I can live with that." Among his mother's people being right- or left-handed hadn't mattered. He'd always thought it strange that others seemed to care.

"Some say being left-handed is bad luck," she whispered.

"I believe a man makes his own luck."

Kora bit into her bottom lip for a long moment, then offered her right hand. "Then I'll marry you tonight, Mr. McQuillen. And I'll hold you to your word."

"Thank you, Mrs. Adams." Winter closed his fingers around her small hand. She seemed so fragile, he wondered how she'd survived in this harsh country. After tonight she'd have it easier, he'd see to that. He might be offering her safety, but she was giving him his dream—all of the ranch.

Before he could release Kora's hand, a knife flew past his face at bullet speed.

Winter swung with pure instinct, pulling Kora behind him as he raised his Colt and turned in the direction of the door.

"Touch my sister and I won't just brush your nose next time, cowboy." A high voice sounded from the shadows.

Lowering his weapon only slightly, he answered as he loosened his grip on Kora's hand, "I wasn't hurting your sister."

The shadow in the doorway came closer.

"Jamie!" Kora moved in front of Winter. "Stop trying to slice up my future husband. I've just told Mr. McQuillen I'll marry him, and that is exactly what I plan to do if you don't kill him first."

Winter couldn't stop the grin that widened his mustache. All Kora's shyness was gone as she scolded her brother, making him hopeful that she might prove stronger than he'd thought.

"You weren't married to the first husband long enough for me to see him before he died." Jamie moved into the light. "And judging from the way this place was run down when we got here, he wasn't much of a man. Now you're thinking of going and making another mistake? Well, you're not rushing out in the wrong direction again, Kora. I'm old enough to stop you from marrying another bastard."

"We'll not speak ill of the dead!" Kora ordered, as though speaking ill of husband number one was worse than offering to cut up husband number two. "And put away those knives."

"Knives?" Winter mumbled, wondering what this sibling of Mrs. Adams might also carry. Jamie was Kora's height, but younger by several years. The youth's face was dirty, but the buckskins he wore appeared fairly clean.

Kora turned to Winter and pointed toward Jamie. "Maybe before we marry, you'd best know my condition. I want you to find Jamie a mate. I promised my mother."

"What!" both Winter and Jamie yelled.

"I'm not getting hitched," Jamie added.

"I'm no matchmaker," Winter grumbled. He'd had a hard enough time getting married himself. "Let your brother find his own wife."

Kora faced Winter squarely now, and he saw the determination in her stance. "First, you've already promised and we've shaken hands on the bargain, and second, Jamie is my *little sister*, not my brother. She'll be twenty this spring and near past the marrying age. By summer I want her to at least have been asked." Then at least Jamie would have been asked and could make her own decision to go to California or marry.

If Winter had thought the knife surprised him, Kora's words cut through the air sharp as a blade. He glanced over at the dirty, half-wild kid in buckskins. She was small, like her sister, but no child. Her eyes were the hard chilling blue of a full-grown woman who'd battled through her share of sorrow and pain.

He folded his arms over his chest. "You're right, I have already agreed." He'd find the wildcat a husband if he had to beat, bribe, and bind one to get him to the altar. Once he gave his word, Winter never broke it.

Kora moved around him, lightly touching his arm as if

getting used to the fact that he was now a part of her life. "Then it's settled. I'll marry you."

As Kora moved away, Jamie leaned across the table toward Winter. "You're wasting your breath, 'cause I'm never going to marry no matter how bad Kora wants me to. She thinks she has to settle me down. She thinks her bad luck won't follow me if I marry, but I'm dead set against it. No one, including my sister, is saddling me with a husband. Have you got that?"

"Yes, you are," Winter whispered back, wondering how two women so different could be from the same bloodline. "I've given my word. I'll find you a husband. Have you got that?"

"Like hell, cowboy! This is one promise you ain't keeping to her. But if you break another, I'll quarter you and cook you for stew. I know she's just marrying you 'cause she ain't got any other out. I'll be coming along to make sure you treat her right till she decides it's time to pack up and leave." Jamie pulled a knife from her boot and played with the point. "And she will leave you, cowboy, 'cause we ain't settled in one place long enough to watch the seasons change since I can remember."

In silence, Winter watched her toy with her knife. He thought briefly of having the girl kidnapped and dumped into the nearest coyote den before she became his sister-in-law. But he decided he could never do that to the coyotes.

As Kora climbed up the ladder to the loft and Jamie glared at Win, a thin man stood from a chair almost hidden in the corner of the room. Before Winter could speak, the man walked past them as though he didn't see anyone and went out the door. Win heard him coughing as he stepped out into the night air.

"Who was that?" Winter looked at Jamie.

"That's our brother, Dan," she answered, as if daring

Win to say anything against him. ''He fought in the war, but not all of him came home.''

''What's he do?''

''Nothing,'' Jamie answered, ''except every morning and night, he walks. And sometimes he screams. We think the ghosts in his mind are coming to get him.''

Kora stepped down the ladder. ''He comes with me,'' she said with granite determination. ''Ghosts or no ghosts.''

''Another promise?'' Win asked.

''No, a fact,'' she answered. ''He's my responsibility.''

Win smiled slowly. He'd take the brother and help get the sister married off as long as Kora would say yes. For suddenly she was the woman he wanted for a wife. She was a woman who kept her word, and that was quite a dowry to bring to a marriage.

THREE

KORA WALKED INTO WHAT WAS TO BE HER NEW HOME trying not to stare as she and Winter passed through the foyer to the foot of a wide staircase. The place must have once been grand, judging from the thick rugs, heavy velvet draperies, and hand-carved molding. Now a layer of dust, topsoil-thick, covered everything in aging neglect. Lacy cobwebs hung from corners as if each web were an antique doily caught in midair. The smell of stale disregard dampened the room.

"This is your home?" she whispered to Winter, wanting to be closer to the living in this dead place. The lean cowboy beside her didn't fit in these surroundings. Only the layer of dust he wore seemed to match.

"No." He put a firm palm on the small of her back and directed her down the hallway, stopping only briefly to toss his hat on one corner of the stairs' railing. "This is *your* home. Or it will be as soon as we're married."

He paused just outside closed double doors made from a solid oak piece so that the very grain of the wood seemed to bar the entrance. "I live in here and run the ranch from this office when I'm not on horseback. But I want it clearly understood that you're the mistress of this place and free to do whatever you like. I want no part of it except to know my wife is here.''

He looked around the rooms behind them as if for the first time in a long while. ''When I was a boy I used to visit this place every Sunday. It was something to see back then. The captain might have managed the ranch, but everyone knew Miss Allie ran the house. I'd like the same rules to apply now. I'd appreciate a meal now and then that isn't served from the bunkhouse kitchen or a chuck wagon, and a bed other than my bedroll.''

Kora didn't meet his gaze as she realized he meant *her* bed. ''I'll try to be considerate.'' His request didn't seem so outrageous; husbands usually slept with their wives. But the thought that she might very soon be sleeping with him made her add, ''And patient.'' If he were patient, she'd be gone before he assumed his husbandly rights.

''So will I,'' Winter answered honestly. This marriage was more than he'd hoped for. If she was willing to wed after only knowing him an hour, he would wait until she invited him into her bed. Except for asking him to find her wild sister a husband, Kora Adams seemed agreeable enough. And when she wasn't curling into that shawl, she looked prettier than most women. ''I've more important things to think about than sleeping arrangements.''

''I see.'' Kora stared at the floor, remembering how her mother always said she had more important things to worry about than raising girls. She'd add like a chorus, ''Boys are a mother's blessing, girls are a mother's hands.''

Kora raised her gaze to him. If all he wanted was a hard working pair of hands, she'd offer him that in exchange for a roof and food. When Dan was stronger, she'd trade this house for tickets to where the sun always shown. Six months, she almost whispered aloud.

"There's extra bedrooms upstairs for Jamie and Dan." He bit back his lie, knowing he had to make the offer. "She's welcome to stay until she marries. And Dan can stay as long as you like."

Silently he hoped Jamie would be leaving soon. She'd threatened him while they hitched Kora's one horse to the wagon and loaded Dan's ladderback chair, along with an old chest and a few bundles of clothes. Then the girl had continued to rant as she helped Dan into the back of the wagon without a word to her brother about where they were going. She hadn't stopped talking while Winter rode beside the wagon through the darkness. The only reason his ears were getting a rest now was that Jamie seemed more interested in his horses than seeing the house or watching her sister's wedding.

He'd gladly left Jamie with one of the hands. When he'd looked back, Dan was still sitting in the back of the wagon looking completely uninterested in his surroundings and Jamie was picking out a mount.

Kora seemed to match his thoughts. "That was kind of you to offer Jamie a horse."

He opened the doors to his office, thinking that she was the first person he could ever remember who thought of him as kind.

As the heavy oak doors parted, three men turned toward them.

"There they are!" Logan yelled. "I told you they'd come."

As he recognized the bride, the reverend frowned. "Mrs. Adams?" He looked over his glasses at her. "I didn't think I'd see you as a bride. Your first husband is hardly cold in the ground."

Kora knew she should probably feel guilty. Everyone over the age of six knew a woman mourned a year before even going out in mixed company, much less thinking of marrying. But Kora lifted her chin slightly and stared at the reverend in silence. She hadn't any more time to wait. Judging from the reverend's width, he'd never known hunger or the kind of fear that closes in around you in the night so thick you can't breathe. She'd been asked by Winter, and for better or worse, she'd stick by her decision. At least he'd been practical and straightforward, unlike Andrew Adams, who'd lied about his wealth in his letters. Not that she could say much since she'd also lied by answering under another woman's name.

"Kora"—Winter said her name slowly for the first time—"do you still wish to marry me? I'll not go against your will in this no matter how much I want a wife. I'll not ask you to do what you believe is wrong."

She leaned close to his shoulder. "Are you sure you want to marry me? I come with more responsibilities than most new brides." She thought briefly that if the man had any sense, he'd run.

"I'm sure."

"Then I wish to continue." She looked at the minister. Winter's words helped ease her fears. He'd given her the choice. "Tonight or a year from now makes no difference to me." He offered her a fair bargain and for as long as it lasted, she'd stay.

Winter spoke directly to the preacher. "Then let it be known that it was I who insisted this wedding take place right away. Anyone who has any objections or raised eyebrows best turn them my way and not my wife's."

The preacher swallowed hard. "I understand, Mr. McQuillen. I'll be happy to join you two in wedlock."

Staring down a nester's widow was one thing, but facing a rancher like Winter was quite another. Smiling for the first time in days, Win turned slightly, nodding once toward both cowhands. "Kora, I'd like you to meet Cheyenne and Logan."

Kora faced the two men, fighting the urge to pull up her shawl.

"Logan spends most of his time telling me what to do," Winter said, "and Cheyenne gets me out of trouble when I'm foolish enough not to listen."

Logan's face wrinkled into a thousand lines as he smiled, but the younger man only lowered his head slowly in a nod much as Winter had done earlier. Cheyenne's stare was direct and cold. Kora wanted to move away. He reminded her of someone who saw everything in life and liked very little of what he saw. In build, the two men Winter called friends were as opposite as they were in welcoming. Logan was average in height and weight for his fifty years, reminding Kora of old jerky. Cheyenne was as tall as Winter but rawhide thin.

"These are the two men I trust completely." Winter didn't give the compliment lightly. "I'd be honored if you'd both witness this marriage."

The men agreed.

Winter offered his arm to Kora. "Are you ready?"

Kora glanced at his Colt still strapped to his leg. "Are you planning to wed wearing a gun, sir?"

"Does my answer affect your decision to become my wife?" Winter's voice was gruff. The gun was a part of his life. He saw no need to remove it now. He'd already unstrapped it once tonight for this lady. He figured once was enough.

"It does not," she answered, realizing that trying to change a man while standing at the altar was probably not the best time.

"Then, if you've no further objections, I'd like to get this ceremony over with."

When she placed her fingers atop his forearm, Winter said simply, "Begin, Preacher."

Kora had never seen anyone command so much power with little more than a whisper. As the minister spoke, she studied Winter, wondering who this man she was marrying could be. He was so dusty, he could have been little more than a cowhand. But his Colt looked custom-designed, and he'd made the point that it was a part of him. The horse he'd ridden was the most powerful animal she'd ever seen. The house he kept insisting was hers looked as if it had been totally neglected for years, yet somehow it was a part of him. And his eyes, now staring ahead with a faraway look, as though even during his own wedding he had something more important to worry about than her. She could see a strength in the brown depths and wondered if it would be there when she needed him. Or would he turn away and not even see her as her mother had after Dan's return?

"I will," Winter said, startling her.

"And you, Kora Adams?" The minister waited.

"I will," she answered.

"Then I pronounce you man and wife." The minister closed his Bible with a sigh of exhaustion. "You may kiss your bride, Mr. McQuillen."

Winter leaned down and lightly kissed her cheek. "Thanks," he whispered.

Kora smiled, wondering if she should kiss him, or whisper back, "You're welcome."

While Logan and the minister took care of the paperwork, Cheyenne stood a few feet behind Winter as if on guard.

Winter thanked them, then insisted on showing Kora the rest of the house. A big kitchen, a dining room, parlor, and sunroom helped the study make up the downstairs. Upstairs, she found four bedrooms, none of which looked as if they'd been lived in for years. They were all furnished with heavy oak and mahogany, and the beds had been covered with tarps.

"Where do you sleep?" Kora asked as Winter climbed the stairs to the third floor.

He paused as he reached the top and set the lamp down on the stair post. One huge empty room welcomed them with starlight from all four sides shining through dusty windows. "Until a month ago I lived in the bunkhouse. When the captain died, I started sleeping in the study, trying to catch up on all the paperwork. Logan said the captain liked to sleep in the sunroom, and from the day his wife died six years ago, never climbed the stairs to the second floor again."

Win looked around the room lined with trunks and boxes packed away long ago. "Miss Allie told me once she'd built the attic with lots of windows to use as a quilting room. But by the time I knew her, the extra flight of stairs was too much for her."

"I thought I'd make Dan's bed in the sunroom. Then he can slip out for his walks without waking anyone."

"Will he get lost?"

"No," Kora said as she studied the huge attic. "We've moved several times since my mother died and he never does. I think he just walks in a circle, never looking at anything along his way, never stopping. He's no trouble. He seems to live more with his ghosts than with us. All we have to do is put his chair in the wagon, and he goes with us."

She didn't want to talk about her family. There would be time later to tell Winter of all the treatments they'd tried to help Dan. Right now, she wanted to know more about this man and his house. "You inherited this place a month ago?"

Kora walked around the room, loving the way the moonlight played across the wood flooring. All the windows were framed into the roof line, making the ceiling high in places and low in others.

"No." Winter's voice hardened slightly. "I worked, or won, every inch of the ranch. *You* inherited the house the minute you married me. I imagine Logan will have the papers in order by the time we go downstairs." He stared out into the midnight of his land, not seeing the stars above. "The old man we all called 'Captain' left my wife the house in his will, not me. The house will be fully yours on our six-month anniversary."

She wanted to ask more, but she could feel the tightness of Win's stance, as though she'd reached out and touched him and he'd pulled away from her. He had his forbidden topics as well.

Stepping off the room in wide steps, Kora decided to ask about the captain later, when Winter's wounds were less raw. "Did you mean it when you said I could do anything I wanted with the house?"

"Of course," he answered as he leaned against the windowsill, only half listening as he looked out over his land. "I'll even move back to the bunkhouse. Or I'll sleep in the study if you like. It doesn't matter to me."

"Could we have our bedroom up here?" she whispered, afraid to hope such a thing was possible.

Winter turned from the darkness outside to her. Though the moonlight was strong enough to highlight her hair, he couldn't see her face. They'd moved too far away from the lamp for its light to be more than a yellow glow several yards away. But her hair seemed to have lights of its own. Or perhaps the strands had stolen the starlight.

He almost laughed aloud at the foolishness of his thoughts. "It's cold up here in the winter and hot in the summer,'' he said, folding his arms and moving toward her slowly. His words were meant to put an end to the discussion.

''But we'll have the stars,'' she countered unexpectantly. ''And the moon. I love seeing the moon. With these huge windows we can watch the sun rise and set and see storms coming in from miles away.''

Stopping his progress, he tried to see her face once more; but she was looking about the room, as though already moving furniture in her mind. Kora had done it twice more, casually—she'd used the plural to the room as though it were understood that it would also be his. Was she making him a part of this house when the captain never had? Was she offering more than an occasional hour in her bed?

''I'll have the men move up anything you ask,'' he said, still not believing she meant to include him. ''If you want this room for a bedroom, you'll have it.'' She'd challenged in such a gentle way, he'd surrendered without defense. ''I said I'd give the moon for a wife. You might as well be able to see it.''

Kora whirled, her hair flowing like a cape around her. ''Thank you.'' She laughed. ''Finally I'll be able to sleep without the smell of dirt surrounding me.''

Winter couldn't help but laugh as well and was surprised at how much pleasure seeing her happy brought him. ''I take it you're tired of the dugout?''

''Yes, but I never dreamed I'd have such a room. We'll survive the heat in summer by opening the windows and the cold in winter with quilts. You'll see.''

Win watched her, wondering if she had any idea what she'd just said. She'd done it again. She'd invited him to be a part of this room, this house. She was honoring their agreement to be husband and wife to the world.

''Boss!'' Logan's voice carried up from the stairwell.

"The riders are in from the south pasture, and you'd best come down."

"I'll be right down, Logan!" he yelled, not wanting anyone to come up. This was their room. "If this place is going to be a bedroom, I'll have to build a door."

He turned to Kora as he lifted the lamp. "I didn't have time to tell you that we've got our share of trouble on the ranch."

Kora crossed to the stairs, knowing that he was waiting for her to join him.

"There's cattle from down around San Antonio that are heading this way. Talk is the owners are trying to get them to market up in Kansas before they all die of yellow fever. If they run the sick beeves through the Panhandle, every rancher in these parts stands to lose half his herd, maybe more. And my range is their only clear path to market."

They walked down the stairs, Winter two steps ahead of her with the light. Kora rested her hand on his shoulder for guidance. "What can you do?"

"We're riding a blockade. One rider along every five miles of land where they could cross the Palo Duro Canyon."

"But if they come, one man can't stop them."

"One Winchester can. As long as the rider gets off a shot, others will respond. We'll drop every last head at the canyon wall if we have to, but they'll not climb and cross while I've bullets left. I may not be able to stop them from getting to market, but I can stop them from crossing my land, and that will cost them dearly."

Kora listened to the anger in his tone and felt once more the power of this man. His talk of killing frightened her, making her aware that the man she married might not be as reasonable as their bargain suggested. Her hand tightened slightly on his shoulder.

He'd said he didn't believe in luck, but she hadn't spent a night in his house and already trouble was echoing. This wasn't of her doing, she told herself. The problem had been there before she came. It would pass. Then, maybe for a few months, or weeks, she could pretend this house and this man were really hers.

Winter slowed, too lost in his own thoughts to realize she might be afraid. "I've had riders out for three nights now, and tonight's my turn to take a shift, wedding or no wedding. I've a job to do."

"Boss!" Logan met them halfway up the last staircase. "We got trouble for sure!"

Before Winter could answer, Kora glanced at the foyer, where several men waited with guns strapped to their legs and rifles resting on their shoulders.

"Two men are late reporting in down by the south fence." Cheyenne said in a low emotionless voice as Winter approached.

"All hell's fixing to break loose!" another man yelled.

Winter took his hat from the stair railing and combed his hair back with his hand before fitting it low across his forehead. Logan handed him a leather coat, and Winter glanced up at Kora, as if he'd forgotten she was there. "Gentlemen"—he cleared his throat and silenced the cowhands below—"my wife."

All the men looked up at once as Kora moved down until she stood on the second step just behind Winter.

One man near the steps removed his hat. "Mrs. McQuillen, I'm mighty glad you're here. Sorry about the language earlier, ma'am. I didn't know there was a lady present."

All the others seemed to remember their manners and removed their hats.

Kora placed her hand on Winter's shoulder for strength.

In all her life she'd never been paid such respect. She'd always been poorer than trash, with most folks not even noticing she was around.

Several of the others mumbled introductions, but Kora knew she couldn't remember them all. First, they all looked alike in their leather and hats, and second, their voices were blurred with a southern drawl.

"We didn't even know the boss got married," one said louder than the others. "But we're mighty proud he has. It's plain to see he's a lucky man."

Smiling, Kora looked down at Winter. With the step's height, she was just above eye level with him. He stared up at her with one raised eyebrow and a question in his gaze. She wasn't sure, but she guessed he was seeing her, really seeing her, for the first time. Judging from his expression, he liked what he saw.

"I've got to go," he said slowly, as if testing her reaction and very much aware that the men were listening. "I won't be back till after dawn."

Kora leaned and touched her lips to his cheek with no more emotion than he'd kissed her earlier at their wedding. "I'll have breakfast ready," she answered as she looked at the men, "for everyone."

Winter touched his first two fingers to the brim of his hat and backed away. He had to give the lady credit, she must have read a book somewhere on how to be a wife. The kiss had been almost believable. The invitation to breakfast sounded just like what Miss Allie would have said in her day.

He'd about decided he'd made a good bargain when he and Cheyenne entered the barn to saddle fresh horses.

A moment later he reconsidered as they pulled his buckskin-clad sister-in-law out of the hay and out of a young man's heated embrace. She cursed worse than he'd ever heard a man swear, and the boy looked scared as he fought to slow his breathing to normal and straighten his clothes to presentable. But neither of the young folks, much to Winter's disappointment, looked as if they had given even a passing thought to marriage.

FOUR

WINTER RODE ALONG THE SOUTH BORDER OF HIS land with Cheyenne half a length behind him. The two men rarely talked, not seeming to have the need. Cheyenne was a few years older and had shown up at the ranch soon after Winter arrived. The captain used to say Cheyenne was the best man with a horse or a gun who'd ever ridden into Texas, but a smile never broke the hard line of his mouth.

To be honest, Winter could never remember Cheyenne being overly friendly to anyone. He didn't eat with the others in the bunkhouse and had never invited Winter or anyone else to share his campfire while they were on the ranch. Even though Winter had told Cheyenne his mother was of the Cheyenne people, it didn't seem to matter. Most of the hands had no idea where Cheyenne slept or if he had another name other than that of his people. They only knew he could usually be found a few feet behind Winter, standing at attention as though silently waiting for trouble.

Sometime over the years, Winter had learned to trust the man as he did no other. The lessons came in a hundred small ways. Winter trusted Cheyenne with his back . . . with his life. Now Winter could feel two facts seeping clear through to his bones. Trouble was coming and, when it did, Cheyenne would be the one he could depend on.

Winter pulled his hat low against the icy wind. It was good to have the man on guard with him tonight, for he was having trouble concentrating on his turn at watch. The face of the woman he'd married kept slipping into his mind.

She wasn't ordinary as he'd first thought. When he'd taken the time to look at her, she'd been pretty. Not the kind of beauty like a saloon girl all made up, but a kind of quiet pretty that was easy on a man's eyes. She had a grace about her that made him want to shelter her. Even now, after hours in the cold, he could still feel the weight of her touch on his shoulder. For the first time in all the years he'd ridden the land, he was in a hurry to get back to the ranch house. Kora would be waiting for him. He wanted to know more about this woman who shared his name.

Pulling his collar up against the first few drops of rain, Win swore beneath his breath. Who did he think he was fooling? She wouldn't be waiting for him. She'd married him for a house to live in and the promise of tickets to California. He'd better get any thought of the possibility of more out of his mind. She seemed to be playing her part, acting as though they were true husband and wife, but that was all he could expect. If he let himself hope that they'd become lovers, mates, or even friends, he was only setting himself up for a fall. Men like him didn't have time for foolish things like love.

Besides, something in the way Jamie only glanced around gave him the impression she thought they wouldn't be staying long. For all he knew they'd be packed and on the road by the time he got back.

Kora had told him she didn't want a husband. She only wanted a place to stay. That was all he cared about also, the house, he reminded himself. And as of tonight, it was all his . . . the ranch, the house, everything he'd ever wanted. The dream of a little boy twenty years ago, with nothing to claim as his own, had come true.

"Want to head back?" Cheyenne broke through Winter's thoughts. "The weather's turning bad. No cattle drive will be moving tonight."

Winter slowed so he wouldn't have to yell. "No. If I was going to cross another man's land, I'd want a night just like this when everyone would be around their fires or in bed. The wind would muffle any sound of a herd. If they're near enough to cross, they'll cross tonight."

"My guess is everyone will be in bed but us," Cheyenne mumbled. "Even that sister-in-law of yours is probably back in the hay by now."

After what he'd seen in the barn just before they left, Winter agreed. She didn't seem the type to wait long. "Put the word out that the man who gets her pregnant marries her. That should keep all but the serious bridegrooms away."

"Anyone who gets her with child will probably run for the territories," Cheyenne said pessimistically.

"Got any other ideas of how I could get her married off fast? She's more irritating than a rattler in a well. My new brother-in-law is invisible, and she's the town crier and a bossy hooker rolled into one."

Cheyenne touched his Colt. "I could shoot her. Or we could toss her in a sack and throw her in the river like the runt of the litter she is. She'd be so far downstream within a few hours that we'd never hear about who found the body."

Winter laughed, not completely sure the man was kidding. "No. I don't want to upset Kora." He took a long look at the cowhand who rode at his side. "I don't suppose you'd consider marrying her?"

Cheyenne shoved his hat back and let the rain hit his face as he stared directly at Winter. ''I'd rather shoot myself.''

''She's not that bad-looking.'' Winter's hope was fading. Cheyenne had been with him when he'd pulled Jamie out of the hay and off the young cowhand. He'd heard her swearing and threats. ''She'd settle down after a while. She might clean up fine, and judging from the bite she took out of my hand, she's got all her teeth.''

''When we were dragging her back to the house, she kicked me''—Cheyenne paused—''in a place no one should kick a man. Any woman who will do that when you first meet her . . . there's no telling what she will do once she knows you better.''

''Well, help me find the woman a husband. Preferably one who's on the move and planning to settle down at least a few states away.''

''No''—Cheyenne shook his head—''I don't have that many enemies. Just let me know if you reconsider shooting her.''

The rain worsened, ending one of the longest conversations Winter could ever remember having with the man.

Kora pulled the dusty curtain aside and stared out into the rain for the tenth time in less than an hour. The ranch was like a small town made up of a huge bunkhouse, a barn, and several other smaller buildings. The center ground was starting to look like one big mud puddle.

''He ain't coming back in this storm,'' Jamie complained as she set the table. ''You might as well stop cooking. If that cowboy you married last night is dumb enough to try to ride home in this rain, he deserves to be struck by lightning.''

Jamie laughed to herself. ''Knowing that crazy witchin'

luck you have, he probably won't live any longer than the last husband. You could make a habit of changing from wedding dress to mourning clothes if he's no heartier than Andrew Adams.''

''There's no such kind of luck,'' Kora corrected her little sister.

''Well, Mother sure used to believe in it. She said she was hated by a witch of a neighbor before you were born. That's why you're left-handed and that's why trouble follows us like a slow-moving cloud. If we ever light one place too long, it's bound to catch us.''

''The only thing that followed my birth was yours, and I don't want to talk about Mr. Adams!'' Kora snapped. After staying up most of the night cleaning, she was in no mood to be teased. ''He was already wounded when he rode into town in the bottom of that stage.'' The sooner Andrew Adams was forgotten the better. ''My luck didn't have anything to do with him dying.''

''What if it follows us here?'' Jamie asked.

''Then we'll move on as we always do,'' Kora answered quickly. She couldn't tell Jamie about the tickets Winter had promised because she'd agreed to look to all the world as if they were truly husband and wife until the six months ended.

Jamie faced her sister. ''You did tell Win about how you married Mr. Adams after he died, didn't you?'' Jamie turned to two chairs and nodded as if ghosts sat in them. ''Dear Mr. Dead Adams, do you take my sister to be your lawfully wedded wife? What, no answer? That must mean you do.''

''Stop!'' Kora tried to sound stern. ''That's not how it happened.''

''But you did tell Win how it was?'' Jamie turned back to her sister. ''About how Andrew came to marry another, but she tossed his proxy in the trash, and you picked it up and answered Adams's call only after he'd been shot four times and you knew he'd die before dawn? You did tell Win that you didn't even think of marrying Adams before you saw them lift him off the stage. Then, he didn't seem so bad.''

''No!'' Kora answered. ''I didn't think it was important. Why would Winter need to know about my first marriage? What difference could it make? It wasn't a marriage and I knew it. It was just an open door. The only opening we'd had since we left New Orleans.''

Kora glanced out the window once more. ''I thought we'd be better off up here in the Panhandle where maybe Dan could get over his cough. I never guessed that most of Mr. Adams's letters about his farm were fiction. I was just looking for a place the three of us could live. I'd do anything it took to keep us from starving, including marrying a dead man.''

''Well, this man seems very much alive, though his eyes are hard as coal. There's no love in him, Kora. He's not the type you should start with when learning about loving. I'd guess the man has a rock for a heart.''

''He didn't seem that cold.'' Kora found him a little frightening simply because he towered over her by a foot. But she saw strength in Winter, not hardness. ''I'm sure he'd understand about Adams if I told him—which I'm not planning to.''

Jamie shrugged. ''I don't guess Win probably cares. It was legal after all. Andrew Adams had already signed the proxy before he even reached town and managed to bleed all over everyone. Once there, he was too near dead to care if he was leaving a wife, and he'd said in his letter he had no other family. I guess you did the poor man a favor by volunteering to mourn.'' Jamie lowered her voice. ''But new husband Winter is bound to notice you're a virgin, so you'll have to tell him something. Widows usually know what a man likes, or at least when to be quiet."

Kora reddened. "How could he guess? I know how to kiss. And I know all about the act of mating. It can't be that much different from animals." Her mother had said once that it was a wife's duty not to make a fuss about it if Kora was ever lucky enough to find a man who wanted her.

Jamie giggled. "You might be surprised, big sister. Men can tell if a woman has never lain with a man."

Kora didn't want to have to ask. It was not a subject people talked about, but she couldn't help herself. "How?"

Jamie laughed again. "Just trust me, they can."

Before Kora could ask more, the door flew open with a pop. Thunder seemed to roll in with the storm of men dressed in rain slickers.

She looked up as her new husband raged into the house like an angry warrior. His dark face was brushed with stubble and splattered in mud. He crossed the room in filthy boots without noticing she'd washed the floor. When he saw her, he slowed, his measured gaze sizing up the sight before him as if he'd never seen her before. There was something dark and angry about him, and something more. Something very lonely. Would he understand? she wondered.

Kora fought down the urge to run. Everything about this man spoke of his power, even the way he moved. She wouldn't have been surprised if he ordered her out of his house and told her the marriage was a mistake.

But he only stared at her with dark searching eyes. Jamie was right, Kora thought, there was an animal wildness about him.

Glancing at Jamie, Kora drew in courage with a long

breath. She'd play the part of this man's wife as best she could. He might be more than she could handle. Or he might explode when he learned she wasn't what she claimed. But she had to try or she, Jamie, and Dan would likely starve. This was her house if only for a while, and it was time to take control over what he'd given her.

"Breakfast will be ready by the time you wash, sir." Kora tried to keep her voice from shaking. Marrying a dead man was certainly a great deal easier than marrying Winter McQuillen. "And I'll thank you to leave your muddy boots on the porch in the future." She guessed he'd respect her more for advancing than if she ran in retreat.

Kora braced herself. If he was going to be the kind of man who hit his wife, she might as well find it out now. There was no use living in fear.

The cowhand at Winter's left whispered the word *wash* as though it were a new language and he'd never heard the term before.

Winter straightened slightly, like a general preparing for a battle. The fingers of his gun hand opened and closed as tired muscles fought down anger. No one had spoken to him as she dared since he'd been a child. In the year since he'd taken over the running of the ranch, his word had been law and no one had ever questioned anything he did. Now this tiny woman faced him as if she had an army to back her.

Kora refused to move as he took a slow step toward her. She could see Dan out of the corner of her eye sitting at the kitchen table picking at his breakfast. Her brother wouldn't even turn to look in her direction if she screamed. He saw no world but his own.

Jamie stepped to Kora's side protectively, blocking Winter's path to his wife. "We moved a washstand up to the third floor, and I hauled water up for you. But don't bother to thank me, or expect it again.'' When her new brother-in-law continued to stare at his wife and gave no reaction to her, Jamie looked past him to the others. ''The rest of you can clean up out on the back porch. But don't take long or the gravy will have to be cut.''

Winter turned suddenly and took the stairs three at a time without saying a word. Both sisters let out a breath as the rest of the riders followed Jamie to the back porch.

For a moment Kora didn't know what to do. She felt as if she'd just won a battle in what promised to be a long war. She looked around at the table. Except for the biscuits, everything was ready. Her first day, or night, of marriage had gone quite well. The only problem now was she had a husband.

She smiled to herself. She'd faced him straight-on. Since the day she'd been brave enough to step up and claim to be Andrew Adams's wife, she'd felt herself growing stronger. Jamie had always been the fighter. But Kora saw something in this man she'd married—a strength, a need. If it took fighting to pull him out, then she'd fight. For in the end, even if she lost, she'd be a stronger person when she left him.

''Watch the bread!'' she called over her shoulder as she hurried up the stairs. ''I have to talk to Winter for a minute.''

FIVE

WHEN SHE STEPPED ONTO THE THIRD FLOOR, KORA almost tripped over a pile of muddy clothes. Winter must have stripped as he climbed. Slowly she leaned and picked up the garments, thinking of how tired he'd have to be after riding all night. Maybe she should have just offered to let him sit down to breakfast instead of insisting he wash first.

The sunrise was still shades of purple light, but she could see the outline of Winter as she moved into the attic room. He'd removed all his clothing, except his jeans, and was standing with his back to her. Somehow, leaning over the basin, bare chested and wearing so little, he didn't seem all that invincible. After placing the clothes in a basket she'd brought up linens in, she stood at the top of the stairs watching him.

Her new bedroom was cluttered with things she and Jamie could carry up, but it still looked more like an attic than a bedroom. Only the man before her seemed to belong in this huge room framed in windows with only miles of sky for curtains.

As she watched, he poured a pitcher of water over his head and scrubbed away the dirt. Water splashed around the washstand, making a plopping sound on the hardwood floor below. Kora let out a cry as moisture spotted the wood, already badly in need of polishing.

Winter's body stiffened at her outburst. He grabbed a towel and turned to face her. A worried frown darkened his already stormy expression.

When he saw where she stared, he said in a tone more of explanation than apology, "I'm sorry about the water. I guess I'm used to washing in the tub at the washstand. This little basin is pretty, but it doesn't hold much. I could scrub up—"

"I'll move a larger one up," she whispered more to herself than him. "And maybe I'll put a rug beneath the stand."

"Don't go to any trouble." Winter wasn't sure what to say. She was doing her best to be a wife, but he didn't know how he was supposed to act. Did he thank her for doing what she thought was her job? Or did he get angry at the way she'd ordered him around downstairs like he was a guest who didn't know how to act inside the house . . . Her house, he reminded himself . . . at least for six months. He'd told her she was the one to set the rules; the least he could do was follow them and not start a war over the first one she laid down. He could clean up before sitting at her table, and he could use the porch like the others from now on. It was foolish to bring water up two flights of stairs when he'd washed outside all his life.

He widened his stance and waited for her to look up. Win knew his voice hadn't sounded kind, but she should at least realize he was trying. Marriage was probably like getting a new horse; they'd both have some adjusting to do. He watched her, wondering how long it would be before they'd be comfortable with each other. He was a good provider; she seemed to be a hard worker. What more did they need to make the marriage seem real?

Slowly her gaze climbed from the floor up his body. He noticed she reddened slightly as she focused on the top of his jeans where he'd left the first button undone. Her breathing quickened as she looked over the flat line of his stomach and the wall of his chest. If he hadn't known better, he would have sworn she'd never seen a man barechested, up close. Her blue eyes sparkled with curiosity.

Not knowing what he should do, Winter rubbed the towel over his chest and continued to watch her. Her gaze followed his action as though her eyes and the towel were connected. He'd never given much thought one way or the other to his body, but now he felt himself wanting to grab his shirt. He suddenly felt exposed before her. What bothered him most was that he couldn't tell if she liked what she saw. Her expression more resembled one of a woman observing a freak at the circus for the first time than a wife looking at her husband. Everything about her seemed to want to turn away, but she continued to stare.

He looped the towel around his neck and straightened slightly, as he buttoned the top button of his pants. Her eyes followed his actions closely. Winter gripped the towel ends with his hands and waited for her to make the next move. If she wanted to look, he'd allow her the time. After all, she had a right. He found himself wondering if she'd offer him the same opportunity.

Slowly her gaze reached his eyes, and she drew in a sudden breath as though what she saw frightened her even more than the sight of his body. Before he could react, she'd stepped away into the blackness of the stairs.

"Kora," he almost yelled. "Kora, what is it?"

Only her voice reached him. A hesitant voice that seemed to be making up words even as she spoke. "I came up to

. . . ask you where . . . you store your shirts.''

Winter took a step toward the open stairwell. ''In the study,'' he answered. ''But I can get one as I go down.''

''No, I'll bring a shirt up.''

Just as she moved down another step, Winter's hand reached out and closed around her arm. ''Wait!'' he ordered as he joined her in the darkness. ''Don't be frightened.''

He could feel her trembling. Her skin was soft, but icy with terror.

''What is it, Kora? Why are you so afraid of me?'' He felt like the freak had just broken through the ropes and jumped into the crowd. ''You've no need to be.''

She reminded him of a trapped animal, afraid to move, afraid even to cry out. She pulled away, not enough to break the hold, but enough to let him know that when he opened the trap, she'd be gone.

He loosened his grip and stepped closer. ''You don't have to be afraid of me, Kora. I'm your husband. I swear I'll never hurt you.'' Could she really think him some kind of monster? Surely she wouldn't have married him if she had. He would rather have Jamie's threat of knives than Kora's sudden fear. Maybe she was afraid because she knew Jamie wasn't near enough to step between them. Didn't she know if he'd wanted to be close, Jamie couldn't stop him?

He guessed it wasn't uncommon for men to strike their wives, but it wasn't in his nature. If only she'd believe him.

''Kora, I—''

''Let go of my arm,'' she whispered so low he wouldn't have heard the words if there had been another foot between them.

Winter didn't want to let go. He knew she'd back away. He wanted to face whatever problem or fear she had. But he couldn't frighten her more. He could almost hear her heart pounding and taste her panic in the air between them. Slowly his fingers loosened. He let his hand brush the length of her arm before he released her.

She darted down the stairs. ''I'll bring you a clean shirt.''

Winter stared long after he'd heard her footsteps hurry away. All night, when he'd thought of her, he'd never thought of her being so afraid of him. She'd been shy at the wedding, but not this. After all, she was a widow. She'd already had one man in her life. Surely he couldn't be all that different?

He was waiting for her on the landing when she returned. With a silent nod, he thanked her and pulled on the shirt as he followed her down.

The cowhands were already seated at the table. Jamie was smiling at each one, reminding Winter of a pickpocket sizing up the wealth of each man's purse. Most of the hands were too tired and hungry to pay much attention. They were far more interested in the food she carried than the invitation in her eyes.

Walking to one end of the table, Winter pointed to an empty chair next to the one he chose. ''You'll join us?''

Kora hesitated, then took the seat. ''Only if Jamie does also.''

He looked up at his sister-in-law. ''Will you?'' He silently hoped she'd take one of the empty places at the opposite end.

''I will if you'll make that man you call Cheyenne sit down, too!'' Jamie shouted over all the others. ''I want him where I can see him. The man's got murder in his eyes every time he looks at me.''

Turning, Winter knew that Cheyenne would be standing near the door. ''Will you join us?''

Cheyenne didn't move. He stared at Jamie, waiting for her to attack at any moment. His dark eyes sparked with annoyance as if he'd just witnessed a plague talking.

"Please," Kora said. "We'd be honored if you'd join us."

Winter watched as Cheyenne looked from Jamie to Kora and the Indian's eyes softened. Winter may have been making the offer because it was a condition Jamie insisted on, but Kora's invitation was real and as rare in Cheyenne's life as an eclipse.

Nodding once, he took his place at the far end of the table, as many chairs away from Jamie as possible.

Winter stood behind his wife's chair for a moment, too shocked to move. In the years he'd known Cheyenne, the man had never sat at a table with him. But, in all honesty, Winter could never remember him being invited. Could it be possible that Cheyenne had waited all this time simply for an invitation?

Gently he touched Kora's shoulder. "Thank you," he mumbled as he took the seat beside her.

She smiled proudly as she passed him a platter of eggs. "It was fun to cook with a kitchen so fully stocked. As I organize everything, I'll be much faster."

He hadn't been talking about the food when he'd thanked her, but Winter didn't want to correct her. He realized he probably should have thanked her for the meal. As he looked around at all the platters, he guessed she must have gone to a great deal of trouble.

Win also noticed she hadn't shied away when he'd touched her shoulder in public. Just as she hadn't seemed shy when Jamie was around. Was that the way it was going to be? He could touch her, even kiss her on the cheek when others were near, but when they were alone, she would back away from him as if in fear? The woman acted as though she had some terrible secret he'd discover if he got too close. Or maybe she saw Jamie as her guardian angel, just as she knew Dan, her older brother, could never be.

As he tasted the food, he suddenly realized how hungry he was. Everything was warm and freshly baked. To Winter's surprise, he ate as hardily as all the hands. Only Cheyenne hesitated over each bite, as if testing it for poison before swallowing.

The men talked of the blockade and the days ahead. As spring approached, the chances of herds trying to cross grew greater. If even a small herd passed over the pasture land, it could mean death for hundreds of cattle.

Finally the platters were all empty, and each cowhand thanked Kora greatly for the fine meal.

Winter noticed Cheyenne also thanked Jamie, who denied doing any of the cooking. When all the men were gone, the house fell quiet.

Jamie stretched like a child. "Well, it may be morning, but I've had a long night. I'm picking one of those rooms upstairs and going to bed. Those dishes will wait a few hours."

Kora waved her out, then lifted the first stack of plates. "I think I'll set out Dan's clean clothes. He always takes his morning walk, then dresses for the day. He's already picked out a rocker on the front porch. I imagine after he dresses, he'll sit in it until dark."

Winter reached for her hand, then stopped, remembering what had happened upstairs. "You did a fine job getting everything organized," he said, wishing he knew how to talk to her. They were alone now and he could feel the coldness returning. She wore fear like an armor.

"I made your bed in the study," Kora said without looking at him. "And washed your clothes."

Winter nodded. She'd just answered all his questions. This might be their wedding night, or morning, but there was to be nothing between them. He told himself he expected nothing. Win didn't even know the woman. He wasn't in the habit of sharing a bed with a woman he hadn't spent time getting to know. Besides, he'd never be attracted to someone who feared his touch.

Give it time, he thought. Wait and see what happens. He'd got a fair bargain. Kora would be a good wife even if she only stayed the six months. She was proper and polite, a good cook, and from what he could tell, a hard worker. He had no right to ask for more. If she were one of those females who hated a man's touch, so be it. He'd lived without a woman in his bed all his life, and he could continue to do so.

"I think I'll turn in," he informed her, in a hurry to get out of the room before he said or did something foolish, or worse, something that frightened her more.

A few minutes later as he stretched out on the long couch in the study, he smiled. The clean sheets felt good. He closed his eyes and tried to sleep, but Kora's memory kept creeping into his mind, keeping him awake long after he should have been resting. How could the two sisters look so much alike and be so different? He should have been attracted to Jamie. She was more his kind, half-wild, stubborn, strong. But Winter found himself fascinated with Kora. Fascinated to the point that not even sleep could push her from his mind.

When his breathing finally became slow and regular, Kora silently slipped into the room. She'd allowed plenty of time for Winter to be asleep before even listening at the door. She tiptoed across the carpet without a sound and added a log to the fire. With the rain continuing, the study would grow cold long before Winter awoke if she didn't add wood.

He was stretched out on his back. Kora couldn't help but watch him. Asleep, he wasn't nearly as overwhelming and all-powerful as he seemed awake. He looked peaceful, younger. His hair was a mess and the blanket twisted across his body.

She moved to his side and pulled the blanket over more of his bare chest. She'd always thought men slept in nightshirts, but this one didn't. His chest bore the bronze hue of his Indian blood. The skin seemed stretched over muscles made of wood. Too hard to be human, she thought. A man made of oak.

Hesitantly she brushed her fingers over his shoulder, surprised at the warmth beneath her touch.

He didn't move.

Kora grew bolder. Her fingers lightly brushed across his chest, feeling the curve of his skin as a sculptor feels his wood carving. He was magnificent. She rested her palm over his heart, feeling the strong, steady pounding against her hand.

Kora smiled, fighting down a giggle. She felt terribly wicked touching him while he slept. She'd wanted to touch him when she'd seen the water dripping off his chest earlier, but she never dared. He hadn't looked at her with eyes burning with fire as Jamie said a man should look at a woman. He didn't reach for her and demand something of her she'd never given any man. She was just useful to him, nothing more.

She let her finger run over the short whiskers along his strong jaw. Hesitantly she brushed back the dark brown hair off his forehead. He was her man, she thought, if only for a while, and she'd touch him, if only in his sleep. He might not see her, but she saw him. For the first time she wished for a man like him to love. He was everything she admired and dreamt about. But it would hurt too much if he were special to her and she was just somebody, anybody, to him.

When he moved slightly, turning his head, her fingers

brushed the fullness of his slightly opened mouth. The mustache tickled her fingertip. Kora felt a fire race through her arm and warm her entire body.

She knelt beside him, careful not to touch him anywhere else as she leaned slowly forward and brushed her lips over his. She told herself she only wanted to feel what a man's lips would be like against hers, but she knew it was more. Kora wanted to taste him. He might be stronger than she'd ever be. But he was also beautiful in a way she'd never thought a man could be.

From the first, even through her fear, she was fascinated by him.

Her lips gave slightly against his. She could feel the warmth of his face and smell a wildness that blended leather and campfires and lye soap . . . and the wind and the rain of a great storm together into a smell that was only his. His skin had been hard with the muscles beneath, but his mouth was surprisingly soft, yielding to the pressure of her lips.

Pulling away suddenly, Kora was shocked at her own boldness. Touching a man was something Jamie might do. She was the one who always followed her feelings and desires, not Kora. Kora always followed duty.

Silently she slipped from the room, thankful Winter had been asleep and would never know of her actions. She'd never done anything so insane or so bold. He'd wanted a marriage because of the house. He'd shown no interest in her, and if he had, he would have probably frightened her to death. But despite what they'd agreed on, he belonged to her now. Legally this wild, powerful man was hers.

Running up the stairs, Kora felt her face redden with embarrassment as her heart pounded wildly. What if he had awakened? Or what if he'd thought her mad? She'd always been the logical one, always done what had to be done, never letting her feelings interfere. But when she looked at Win, she thought of what might be.

She had to keep her distance. He'd shown no sign of wanting to be near her. He was wealthier than anyone she'd ever known. He commanded an empire built on strength and honesty. Jamie was right. If they did sleep together, she'd have to explain about how she had never lain with her first husband, and Winter would find out what a lying, conniving opportunist she was. No honest man like Winter would want a wife who fooled the world into believing a dead man had married her.

Kora reached the attic and took a long breath, determined never to do anything so foolish as touching him again. She would keep her distance from Winter McQuillen. For her own sake, she could never afford to touch him as she had again. Fate and her past seemed to have stacked the deck against her, and the ante for a love that might not be returned was too high a price to pay.

SIX

KORA LAY DOWN ON THE PILE OF COLORFUL QUILTS she'd brought up to the attic. The blankets were beautifully done in rainbow colors and smelled of the cedar chests she'd found them in. She curled into a ball and smiled at the warm sun shining through the windows. There was a time that Kora thought they'd never see the sun again. The year they'd first been on their own, Kora managed to get work in a bakery just a bottle's throw from New Orleans' Bourbon Street. She had gone to work before dawn and never left until after dusk. She hadn't hated the work, only the city. Dan's ghosts were bad back then. Many nights she walked home after work only to find him and little Jamie asleep on the step of what had been their apartment when she'd left at dawn. The memories chilled her now with a cold reality that not even the quilts could keep at bay.

After an hour she gave up trying to sleep, washed carefully, and fixed her hair in a neat bun. Since she only had one dress other than the one she'd been married in, she put it on and hoped she looked presentable. The blue once matched her eyes, but the material was now faded to a gray color.

The house was quiet, sleeping like a lazy cat in the morning sun. Last night's rain made the air crisp and clean. She tiptoed down the stairs, smiling at the unbelievable possibility that she might be allowed to live in such a place even for a little while.

As she reached the bottom of the stairs, someone rapped on the door with an impatient sound, startling her.

Kora glanced around, unsure of what to do. Slowly she walked to the front entrance. The rapping came again, more impatient this time. Her hand touched the knob.

Winter bolted from the study, pulling his shirt on as he moved. "Hands come to the kitchen door," he said as he lifted his gunbelt from the rack. "And I'm not expecting company."

As he buckled on the gunbelt, he nodded once, telling her to turn the knob.

She pulled, intending to open only slightly, but the door suddenly flew toward her with a shove and Kora found herself pushed backward by the force.

A woman in her mid-twenties hurried in with white lace and red ruffles flying. She was tall with raven hair and ivory skin. Pretty, in a staged way.

"Winter!" the intruder shouted, lifting her arms in greeting.

When he didn't move toward her, she slowed and touched him on the shoulder, as if trying to brush away his coldness.

"I know I'm late and this is the last day, but I couldn't stay away. I had to come to you in your hour of darkest need."

He seemed to be made of stone as the woman in frills wrapped her arms around one of his like fast-growing ivy. She moved against him, pressing his sleeve between her breasts.

"I know I was cruel to you, but I thought you'd care enough to try harder." Her voice rose to a cry and her body rocked against him. "Then I decided you were too broken to ask again and I'd have to be the one to come to you. How could you believe I'd be so heartless as to let you down?"

Winter looked over the woman's hat to Kora. There was no emotion in his stare, making Kora wonder if he'd ever seen the intruder before. For an instant, Kora wanted to laugh, for this strong man she'd married flashed her a "help me" expression she'd thought she would never live to see.

"I'll make it up to you, darling." The woman backed a step away from him and pulled off her white kid gloves. "While I was riding out here, I thought I'd go to Dallas as soon as possible after we're married and buy all new furnishings for this place. If it were fixed up, it could be livable." She glanced around. "Of course, we could always build another house. A far bigger one and let a foreman have this. As soon as we're back from our honeymoon, I'd make the house twice as grand as Miss Allie ever thought about it being."

Winter stared at her as though she spoke in an unknown tongue. "I don't have a foreman," he mumbled.

"Oh, but we will," the woman said matter-of-factly. "But that man on the porch will have to be fired. He acted as if he didn't even notice me or hear me when I spoke to him. Honestly, Winter, the ranch is yours, but a hand like him simply can't be tolerated."

"Mary Anna," Winter finally found his voice, "the will said a month from the captain's death, not his funeral. You're a day late."

Mary Anna shrieked in horror. "That can't be! Oh, that can't be! You've lost the house. Oh, Winter, how dreadful!"

"No, I didn't lose anything." Winter folded his arms in blockade. "And the man on the porch isn't a hand. He's a guest."

"That's the way to stand tall, dear." Mary Anna seemed very near tears. "It can't be all lost. There's some way around that will. The captain was a crazy, bitter old man and everyone knew it. We'll hire a lawyer. Or we can sell off some of those cattle you've got and buy the house back."

"I won't be selling any cattle," he whispered between tight lips. "I don't want to buy the house away from its present owner."

Kora saw something new in him then, an Irish temper blended with a warrior spirit. The mix of his ancestry was disquieting. She knew it was time to move before she witnessed more than a hint of his fury. She could almost see the anger in his voice crackling the air like dry lightning. His eyes narrowed and the muscles beneath his sleeves tightened.

"He won't have to buy back the house." Kora could see that she startled Mary Anna with her words. "The current owner would give it to him if he asked."

The woman seemed thrown off balance as she realized someone else was in the foyer. She whirled, staggered slightly, then appeared to brace herself for something horrible.

Mary Anna glared at Kora with first fear, then disgust. She lifted her nose, as though being forced to talk to the help. "I wasn't aware we had company." She moved closer to Winter. "We prefer to have our discussions alone, miss."

Kora knew Mary Anna thought her the housekeeper. She recognized the look . . . that blank stare folks who think themselves above others give their help. A look that seems to see through someone they think of as unimportant.

Kora swallowed hard and faced Mary Anna. "I said he won't have to sell cattle or buy back the house."

"And why is that, Miss . . .?"

Kora smiled, knowing she should feel at least a tiny bit of guilt for enjoying the woman's sure-to-come shock. But she'd taken a great dislike to Miss Mary Anna. Everything about the lady, from her dress with one too many ruffles to her overblown speech, told Kora that Mary Anna made self-centeredness a life's calling.

"Not Miss," Kora said quietly as she leaned and picked up the gloves Mary Anna had tossed aside. "Mrs." She glanced at Winter and caught the hint of a smile. "Mrs. Winter McQuillen."

Color drained from Mary Anna's face so completely her patches of rouge looked like warpaint.

"No!" She shook her head and directed all her rage toward Winter. "You didn't marry another!"

All the anger vanished from his eyes as he winked at Kora. "It appears I have, Mary Anna. Kora became my wife before midnight last night."

Mary Anna glanced from Kora to Winter and sighed. The back of her hand covered her eyes as she melted slowly with practiced grace.

Winter caught the unwelcomed guest and lifted her unconscious body into his arms, then looked at Kora for instructions.

"Put her in the study." She moved ahead of him to open the door wider. "I'll get some water and a cool cloth."

"Brandy would do more for bringing her around," Winter mumbled as he dropped her on the study couch that had only minutes ago been his bed.

Kora ran to the kitchen. She searched the cabinets for brandy or any spirits. After a few minutes, she gave up and filled a bucket with water. Dropping the dipper inside the pail, she hurried back to the study.

Mary Anna was sitting up with one arm draped around Winter's neck. He knelt in front of her with a decanter of brandy in one hand and her fingers pressed against his chest with his other hand.

Looking over his shoulder, Mary Anna didn't remove her arm as Kora entered. "Not a bucket and dipper!" she scolded. "I never drink out of anything that isn't china or crystal."

Kora thought of tossing all the water at her at once, but she guessed that probably wasn't proper.

"Honestly, Winter, where did you find this girl?" Mary Anna glared. "And left-handed, too. My aunt says left-handed women and redheaded men are an abomination against heaven."

Kora was glad she couldn't see Winter's face, for she wouldn't have wanted him to see her. She knew better than to offer company a drink from a bucket, but she'd been in a hurry.

"I'll take it back," Kora whispered as she turned.

"Since you're going back to the kitchen, dear"—Mary Anna's voice dripped honey—"would you mind brewing me some hot tea? The ride out here this morning was dreadfully cold."

Without a word, Kora ran back to the kitchen. Not allowing tears to fall, she put the kettle on and searched for any china. But the kitchen had been run by men for years, and china must have long ago been packed away or broken.

It appeared whatever she served tea in would look as plain as herself. She sat down at the table in front of her half finished grocery list and tried to think.

Just as the kettle boiled, Winter opened the kitchen door.

"We won't be needing any tea," he said as he folded his arms and leaned against the counter.

"Good." Kora wiped her hands nervously on her skirt. "Because I couldn't find any china."

Winter shook his head. "She's one picky lady, isn't she?"

Kora nodded.

"I guess that's why I find it so unbelievable she chose me. Mary Anna Monroe could marry anyone in the county, yet she rode out here to offer to marry me. After the dressing down she gave me a few weeks ago at her aunt's home, I figured I'd be her last choice for a husband."

Kora didn't want to hear more. He'd said enough. She opened the back door and walked out. With long strides to nowhere, she crossed the backyard. Chickens darted around her, but she ignored them as she passed the outbuildings, then the barn, then the corral. Finally, at the edge of an orchard, she stopped and took a long breath.

The morning was sunny but cold, and the trees were still dormant in winter as Kora took in the fresh air. She would manage, she told herself. She'd managed before, she'd do so now. All her life, fate had been slapping her down, pulling the rug from under her so many times she was almost afraid to try and stand. But stand she must, before another blow of life's fist hit her and she was lost. She could take Winter's bragging on the other woman. She could take anything she had to in order to survive.

"Having a nice walk?" Winter whispered from just behind her.

Whirling, Kora almost bumped into him. "You followed me!" Her heart jumped to her throat, and she widened her stance in preparation for whatever was to come.

"Seemed like the only thing to do if I planned to continue the conversation.'' Winter backed away slightly as if uneasy with closeness.

''Shouldn't you be in the study with your fiancée?''

''She left before I came in the kitchen.'' Winter shrugged. ''Must have been something I said.''

Kora looked at him closely. He was almost impossible to read. She couldn't tell if he was happy or sad.

''You asked her first.'' Kora straightened, prepared to face what would come. ''If you like, I'll leave.''

Pulling a scrap of paper from her pocket, she handed it to him. ''I wrote down that the house was yours. You can date it in six months and say I mailed it to you. Sorry all I had was a piece of butcher paper, but I scratched out the grocery list. I signed it, so everything should be legal.''

She swallowed her pride. ''If you could give me money for the tickets, I'd pay you back since I didn't stay the agreed length of time.''

Win turned the paper over in his hand. ''Want to walk into the trees? There's a little stream that runs through them. That's why the captain planted the orchard here. No matter how long we go without rain, I've never seen this stream run dry.'' He folded the paper and put it in his pocket.

Without another word, they moved into the line of apple trees. Finally, after several minutes, Kora realized he wasn't planning to say more. Maybe he was waiting for her, but what else could she say? Mary Anna was prettier and had all the social standing any man could want. A farmer's widow must look like what she was . . . a poor faded second choice compared to Mary Anna.

Yet he'd said something to make Mary Anna leave. Kora stopped walking and waited for him to turn. When he did, she lifted her hand and placed it on his chest in the spot she'd seen Mary Anna's hand. He might only be her husband for a short time longer, but it surprised her how much she resented another woman touching him.

"What did you say to her?" She had to know how much time she had left before Mary Anna was packed and back.

He looked at Kora as if he'd been deep in thought about something else and had to pull himself back to the topic. Slowly his hand left where it had been resting on his gun-belt and covered her hand, pressing her fingers into the hard wall of his chest.

"Not much." He didn't decrease the pressure. "I just said if it were yesterday and she were here with her offer, I'd still want to marry you." He held her fingers tightly, as if wanting to say more with his touch than he could with his words.

"But—"

"I didn't add any *buts* when I helped her on her horse. It doesn't take much to know that you're ten times the woman she'll ever be. China, or no china. Left- or right-handed."

He pulled her hand from his chest and held it tightly as he put the scrap of paper into her palm and curled both their fingers around it.

Kora smiled. "So we stay married and I can stay in the house?"

He looked down at her with dark searching eyes. There was a stubbornness in him from the hardness about his jaw to the tightness of his lean frame.

"We are married, truly married forever, as far as the world knows," he corrected. "I'm never backing out, so you might as well unpack, Mrs. Winter McQuillen. The choice to end our agreement will be yours, not mine. As I said last night when I asked, be it six months or forever, I only plan to have one wife."

His words left her reeling. Kora knew life's blow would

be coming to knock her down again as it always had before, but for one moment she wanted to believe that what he said was true.

"I can't promise I'll stay." Kora studied this man who held her hand so tenderly. "I've never stayed anywhere long."

"Stay as long as you can." His voice sounded hoarse. "But I promise always if you choose. I'm not a man who goes back on his word."

"But you haven't even known me a day." Kora moved an inch closer.

"I know you love your family. I know you're a hard worker." Win cleared his throat and shifted. "And I know how I feel when you touch me."

Kora pulled her hand away and Win straightened. Suddenly neither could look at the other.

SEVEN

THEY WALKED BACK TO THE HOUSE WITHOUT ANOTHER word. Kora smiled at the warmth of the morning sun on her face, and the easy low sound the wind made in the grass. Everything on the ranch smelled fresh and clean, and untouched, as if God just made it this morning for them and no one had ever seen this land before today.

She slipped the paper into her pocket remembering what Winter had said to her. No one had ever made her feel special. His words had been choppy and hard for him to say, making them all the more powerful.

Winter also watched the horizon, only he appeared to be looking for something, not enjoying anything around him. The hardness in his eyes was back, and Kora couldn't help but wonder if there had ever been a time when he'd cared or thought of anything except his ranch. Maybe Jamie was right, maybe he was dead inside with a stone for a heart. Maybe he'd only said what he did to make her stay.

He'd told her not to expect love. If Winter tried to be a good husband, that would be enough, more than she thought she'd ever have. Her mother used to say that a life has chapters in it and maybe this could be a quiet chapter for Kora. For the first time since she could remember, she wasn't worried about how she'd keep food on the table tomorrow. For giving her that one peace, she owed Winter greatly.

"I meant what I said about giving you the house." She broke the silence.

"I know you did," he answered. His words were low, but his mood had turned dark.

Kora took a chance; it was time to learn about the demons in this man's past. "What are you thinking?" It was a very personal thing to ask, and she regretted her curiosity.

Win's eyes never left the horizon. "I was thinking, if trouble comes and I'm not here, run for the apple trees. You could hide there."

Kora watched him closely. "Do you always think of escape routes?"

"Just remember," he answered in a tone that ended the discussion. "I'll find you in the trees."

When she reached the top of the back porch steps, Kora turned, realizing Winter was no longer following her.

He stood in the dirt, his feet wide apart, his hand resting lightly on his Colt. "I've got things to do. It would be useless to go back to sleep now. You rest. I'll be back by sundown."

Kora nodded, noticing how tired he looked for a man who thought sleep useless. They were doing it again, tiptoeing around each other as strangers do. Talking without talking.

"Would you like me to make a pot of coffee to keep us both awake?" Kora grasped for something to say that sounded right. "I don't think I can sleep any longer, either."

"I'd appreciate that," he said as he turned toward the barn. "I'll come back for a cup after I saddle up."

Winter didn't glance over his shoulder as he heard the back door open. Hurrying across the yard and into the barn, he saddled his horse in record time. He told himself he wasn't in a hurry to get back to her. He cared nothing for the woman. He told himself no one would ever mean anything to him. Especially not someone who didn't hold on to something that she'd been given. She'd offered to give the house back like it was nothing of importance to her. He'd made a fool of himself by mentioning that her touch affected him. Yet, he'd told her where to run if there was trouble. He hadn't thought of an escape plan since he'd lost his family twenty years ago.

Logan asked if he'd be riding out soon and Winter snapped at the man. He guessed the boys were watching his movements from the bunkhouse kitchen, but he didn't care. None of them would put his job on the line by saying a word. By the time Winter reached the porch once more, he was almost running.

When he stepped into the kitchen, she turned as though startled to see him. She looked so tiny. Like she'd snap in two if he held her tight. How could he have married a woman who didn't even reach his shoulder? Mary Anna had been only a few inches shorter than him. Maybe that was why he'd always asked her to dance at the socials. Realizing he'd married a woman he probably would have never asked to dance bothered Winter. After all, marriage should take a little more thought than a reel. Only in his case, it hadn't seemed to.

''Coffee ready?'' he asked in almost a yell.

''Yes,'' she said so softly he guessed he'd frightened her again.

Hell, he thought, *she's going to spend the next six months jumping every time I'm in the room.*

They sat down across the kitchen table from each other with a pot and two mugs between them.

"I forgot to ask you how you like your coffee," she said as she poured.

"Strong," he answered, watching her closely. *This is marriage,* he thought. If she decided to stay, this was how it was going to be every morning for the rest of their lives, and already he couldn't think of anything to say. It might prove a long, long lifetime. He tried to think of the kind of things he talked about with the saloon girls in town, or the mercantile owner's wife, or even Mary Anna after he'd asked her to dance. Nothing he could think of sounded right.

Letting the first few swallows burn his throat, Winter decided he'd probably have little use for speech from now on. Kora seemed as quiet as her sister was chatty. He couldn't imagine how two women from the same parentage could be so different. Jamie looked as if she'd never worn a dress, and he guessed Kora was always a lady.

Finally she broke the silence. "I like a little sugar in mine."

For a second her words made no sense, for he'd forgotten all about the coffee. She was trying to help make it easier, he guessed. The least he could do was try also. "In a china cup?"

Kora smiled. "No, I've always like the feel of a mug in my hands. That way the coffee warms my fingers." She stared down at the cup.

That's it, he thought. *That's as far as the conversation will go.* What else could he say? They might be married, but he didn't feel he knew her well enough to comment on her hands now hugging the cup, or ask her why she'd touched him last night. Or why she'd chosen to sleep in the attic on the floor and not in one of the beds downstairs.

Or why she was already dressed this morning. Shouldn't she have been in her nightclothes? He wasn't about to inquire.

Hell, he swore again to himself, *I could spend a lifetime thinking about what not to talk about with this woman.*

"I have to ride out to the south pasture this morning," he said between sips. "I'd invite you to come along, but it's not as safe as usual."

"I don't ride," she answered.

"Never?" Winter couldn't imagine a woman never riding. Being able to handle a horse was a part of life, like walking, or breathing, or swimming.

"I never learned." She smiled suddenly. "Maybe you should have asked me that last night before you married me."

Winter frowned. "Most definitely. I might have changed my mind. A rancher's wife who doesn't ride, now that's something to consider. I've never heard of that." Even Miss Allie could ride when she was in her sixties.

Kora laughed suddenly. "You're kidding!"

"Of course." He liked the way she laughed. "Whether you ride or don't is up to you."

"If you'll wait until I get the house in order, I could get Jamie to teach me. I've always been afraid of horses, but if you've got a gentle one, I'll try."

"No." He stood and downed the last of his coffee. "I'll teach you to ride. I wouldn't trust that sister of yours to be safe."

She followed him to the door. Before he could reach for his hat, Kora lifted it from the peg and handed it to him. She was doing it again, he thought, playing the part of a wife as though she'd read a book on what to do.

"If there's trouble, I may be late." He wished he could think of something else to say. There were a thousand things he didn't know about her. Like where she came from and how her parents died. How did she get the ribbon of calluses on her palms?

"I'll wait up."

"It isn't necessary."

Nodding, she didn't look up at him. He had the urge to ask her to let her hair down again like it had been last night, but it seemed a very personal thing to request of a woman. She might be a mouse afraid to talk to him, but her hair was magic, all shiny white gold.

Winter didn't want to leave. Maybe if they spent some time together, they'd finally stop being as jumpy as spring colts around each other. "Kora?" He tried to say her name without sounding like he was snapping an order, but his voice had rusted from lack of conversation.

"Yes?" She raised her gaze.

He saw it then, the fear he'd seen before. Here they were standing in the kitchen in broad daylight, and she was looking at him as if he might try to murder her at any moment. Without thinking, he said the only thing that came to his mind. "Are you sorry?"

"For what?"

"For marrying me," he answered. She was the one who'd come into this marriage with nothing. The marriage had made her a wealthy woman, for even if she left, he planned to offer her far more than train tickets. But he was the one who felt like the beggar. He'd taken advantage of her impoverished situation. He knew the moment he'd seen what little she had in that hole she called a home that she'd have to agree to marry him or face starvation.

"No," she answered. "I'm not sorry."

Winter dragged his fingers through his dark, straight hair and let out a long breath before lifting his hat. "Will you promise me if you ever are, you'll tell me?"

Kora tilted her head slightly. "I promise."

"I'll tell one of the men to have a wagon ready to take you into town. I'd like you to buy anything you need to settle in here. Anything. Just put it on my account."

"All right."

"And take Logan along with you. Until this trouble's over, I'd feel safer if you had him along if you leave this area."

He wasn't sure if she agreed or was too frightened to argue. "Try to get some rest today. Logan will see that the men move one of the beds up to the attic and anything else you want hauled up there."

She didn't answer.

Winter opened the door, angry with himself for ordering her. The woman had no idea how desperate the men were to break the quarantine. A man who'd kill another man's herd with the fever was just one step away from killing the man. Later, he'd try to make her understand that his ranch was in the dead center of the only logical crossing. Which made him, and now her, the most likely targets.

He walked out onto the porch, almost colliding with Cheyenne. "Shouldn't you be asleep? We were up all night," Winter growled at the Indian.

"No." Cheyenne didn't bother to say the obvious. "Logan says you're saddled up. I thought I'd join you."

Checking his Colt, Winter lowered his voice. "I can almost smell trouble in the air."

Cheyenne glanced over Winter's shoulder to make sure Kora wasn't listening. "So can I. They're coming. I can feel it beneath my boots."

"Like a man feels a stampede coming even before he sees it," Winter added. "Well, let's ride. I'd rather go out to meet it than have trouble come knocking at my door. We've got a lot of ground to cover before dark."

"It wouldn't knock twice in one day at your door," Cheyenne mumbled as he walked to the hitching rail. "Yesterday you had no wife. Today you almost had two."

Winter sighed, knowing that if Cheyenne was mentioning it, the other hands were probably joking about Mary Anna's visit by now. "You saw the lady?"

"She was riding out in such a rage, she'll whip her poor horse to death before she reaches town."

"Maybe he'll buck her off."

"Some women aren't as easy to be rid of." Cheyenne swung into the saddle without another word, leaving Winter to wonder if Cheyenne was talking about Mary Anna's horse being rid of her or him being rid of Mary Anna.

They didn't talk for several hours as they rode back and forth across Winter's land, making sure all the lookouts were in place. Miles of range stood with open pasture, but each rancher knew where his land ended and his neighbor's began. As the weather warmed, the chances of a herd trying to cross grew greater. A few of the small ranchers had suggested barbed wire to close off the land, but most of the older ranchers were dead set against it. Some of his neighbors were even talking about hanging any man who tried to drive a sick cow over their property, but Winter thought shooting the infected cattle was as far as he'd go.

By nightfall every bone in his body ached from exhaustion. Cheyenne left him at the barn, and Winter walked slowly to the house. He could see a light on in the kitchen and found it strangely welcoming. For most of his life he'd never felt a sense of home. Before this house, the only place he'd called home had been a village along the Washita. His last memory of it had been the screams of his mother's people as soldiers rode in.

No one was around as he washed on the porch and entered the kitchen, but he found a meal on the table with a cloth covering it. He downed the glass of milk and tasted a leg of chicken with one hand while he tried to remove his coat with the other.

The chicken tasted better than any he'd ever had. Before he realized it, he'd downed another two pieces and poured himself a third glass of milk. Ten minutes later he'd cleaned the plate and eaten half a pie.

Finally Winter paused and leaned back in his chair. Married life was great. As he relaxed, he looked around the kitchen. Tiny changes were everywhere. She'd moved things, organized them differently. And there were new things, too. Towels on the bar beside the sink, jars with matching lids on a shelf, a blue bowl on the table filled with shining apples.

Winter picked up one of the apples, remembering how the captain had yelled at him for eating all the apples when he'd been a boy. But that had been all he could get to when he'd been hiding in the supply wagon. He thought the captain was going to kill him over a handful of fruit. But that next spring the captain had ordered trees all the way from Dallas and made Winter work until after dark, planting them down by the spring. In a few years they'd had more apples than they could eat.

Wandering to the study, Winter stretched out on the sofa and tossed the apple in the air. If Kora could make that good a pie with apples left in storage for months, he could hardly wait to taste the pies she'd make come summer. Closing his eyes, Winter let the piece of fruit drop to the floor from his open palm as he fell asleep.

Much later he felt someone gently tugging off his boots and spreading a blanket over him. Without opening his eyes, he heard soft steps walk to the fire and put on another log. Fighting down the desire to look up, he remained still as she crossed to him once more and lightly touched his cheek. Then, so softly he could almost swear he was dreaming, she kissed him and vanished before he could think of the way he should react.

His exhausted mind told him it was only a dream as he drifted deeper into sleep.

Dawn was just seeping into the study when Winter was jolted fully awake by the slamming of the front door.

He reached for his gun and ran toward the foyer, wondering if every morning of married life was destined to start the same.

Jamie collided with him as he rounded the study door.

He took one look at her and lowered the weapon, then saw the anger in her eyes and reconsidered.

She shoved him hard, almost knocking him off balance. "Get out of my way, cowboy!"

Winter opened his mouth to answer her just as he saw Kora come from the kitchen. All the anger left him when he saw her.

"What is it?" she asked, looking from Jamie to Winter. "What's wrong?"

"Win's given orders that we can't leave!" Jamie stomped toward her sister with a look that dared Winter to say a word. "He's planning to keep us prisoners here. I told you the man was one half wild and the other half crazy. What kind of man rides up after dark demanding you marry him before dawn, then takes us to his house and holds us prisoners?"

"I've done no such thing!" Winter shouted as he rubbed his scalp trying to awaken his brain. "I just said if you leave, someone has to go with you."

"Well, I like riding alone!" Jamie snapped.

"You'll go with a rider, or not at all. At least until the trouble's over."

Jamie took a step toward him. If she'd have been his

height, he might have considered backing down. She had the same blue eyes and blond hair as her sister, only her eyes were filled with anger and her hair tied with rawhide at the nape of her neck. He felt as if a painter had used the same model to sculpt both an angel and a devil.

"I don't have to listen to you. You're not my father or brother or husband. You're not even my sister's husband, sleeping down here on the couch. What kind of man are you anyway?"

Winter balled his hands into fists at his sides, making himself remain still. He'd never been talked to like this, and the image Cheyenne had suggested of tossing her into the river flashed through his mind.

Before he was fool enough to act or even speak, Kora stepped between them. She turned toward Jamie, almost touching Winter with her back.

"Winter's right, Jamie. If he thinks there is too much danger for you to go alone, then there is." She stood firm.

To Winter's surprise, Jamie backed down. She hadn't seemed the least hesitant to face him, but Kora's gentle voice drained her fury.

"And another thing"—Kora raised her chin as she faced Jamie and leaned slightly to touch Win's chest with her back—"our married life is none of your concern, just as yours will be none of mine once you've said 'I do.' "

"Don't hold your breath for me to ever say those two words." Jamie stomped halfway up the stairs, then turned around, her smile fixed on her face. "When you ride out, dear brother-in-law, I'm going with you. I'm not spending another day cooped up, and Cheyenne and you are the only two men on this place that look like you could keep up with me. So when you ride, I ride."

Winter opened his mouth to argue but reconsidered. Jamie would be safer with them than with anyone on the ranch, and at the pace they kept, she'd be glad to stay home for a few days after.

He took a deep breath, letting his chest press against Kora's back.

She didn't move away.

Win lifted his hands slowly, to rest them at her waist. "Don't worry," he whispered against her ear. "I'll look after her."

Kora leaned her head back. By not looking at him, she could ignore logic and enjoy his nearness. His hands were warm at her waist as he turned his face into her hair. He took a deep breath, pushing closer as his chest expanded.

"And another thing!" Jamie yelled from the second floor, shattering the moment. "Tell that Indian to stop watching me!"

Kora moved away as Win yelled back, "Tell him yourself! I'm not Western Union."

He turned and walked back into the study. The memory of Kora in front of him, touching him so slightly, was as thick as liquor in his mind. Win forced the thought aside, deciding he was being foolish. He wasn't the kind of man to waste time thinking about the way Kora felt. It wasn't as if he'd never been with women before; she couldn't be all that different. He would be far more practical to worry about how Cheyenne was going to react when he found out they'd have company today.

Kora was folding his blanket when he approached. She didn't look as if she'd been up long. Her hair was still down and she wore a white cotton gown and wrapper. Smiling, he realized they were new. He was glad she'd bought something for herself yesterday. He only wished he'd thought to tell her to.

"That's not necessary," he said as he tucked his shirt in. "I usually don't bother to fold it up."

"I'm not just folding it up, I'm putting it up." Kora didn't look at him as she worked. "Jamie's right. We're married. We should at least sleep in the same room."

He watched her closely, trying to read her meaning.

"I'll move your clothes to the attic today, and tonight you'll sleep in your own bed in our bedroom."

"Where will you sleep?" He remembered how small she'd looked all curled up in a ball on the floor that first night. She hadn't noticed that after she'd kissed him, he'd followed her upstairs. He'd watched her remove her dress, then lie down on the quilts like an orphan without a home.

"I'll sleep beside you." She said the words solid, as if she'd thought about them a long time. "After talking to Logan all day yesterday, if there was one thing I've learned, you are a man of your word. I know I'll be safe, and you'll ask nothing of me until I'm through grieving, as we agreed."

Winter fought not to groan aloud. He wished she hadn't said what she did. Now he was feeling guilty for even thinking what he'd thought when she'd mentioned him moving upstairs. "I'll hold to my word," he reminded himself more than her.

EIGHT

BY MIDAFTERNOON THE SKY WAS BOILING WITH DARK gray clouds heavy with rain. The wind whipped around through the breaks, debating a direction. Winter slowed his horse and let Cheyenne pull up beside him as he watched a dust devil dance along the ridge just south of where his land ended.

"She's still with us," Cheyenne mumbled.

Winter laughed. The man had spent half his day trying to lose Jamie and the other half worrying about her being able to keep up. To the woman's credit, she could ride as well as any of his cowhands, and better than most. Cheyenne had pointed out all her shortcomings as a horsewoman, and she'd repeatedly told him where he could ride to and back with his advice.

"We'll have to cross onto McLain's land if we go any farther. You think we should turn around and call it a day?" Winter twisted to watch Jamie approaching.

He was surprised at the expression on Cheyenne's face, then he realized he'd probably never asked for advice or turned toward home early. But for a reason he couldn't explain, he wanted to get back.

''It would probably be best for your sister-in-law,'' Cheyenne answered. ''This wind will turn cold at dusk.''

Both men nodded. For her sake was reason enough.

As Winter signaled with a wave for her to turn around, a bullet flew past his hand so closely he could feel the air tumble. A moment later the sound caught up with the lead, rattling the silence with a pop. For a second both men were stone, listening, judging direction, thinking before reacting. Then the second shattered with another pop, and their reaction was lightning fast.

They glanced at each other, then at Jamie. ''Ride!'' Winter shouted as they flanked the woman and kicked their horses into action. Though she opened her mouth, nothing came out as her horse jerked into a full gallop.

The thunder of the hooves almost drowned out the sounds of more gunfire. They leaned into their saddles, moving as one with the animals. There was no time to guess who or why, only survival. The land flattened out before them, making speed their only ally.

A hundred thoughts darted into Winter's mind. Who was firing? He'd expected trouble, but not a sudden ambush. What if Jamie were killed? How could he explain it to Kora? What if a bullet hit one of the horses and it fell? At this speed the rider would die. He had to do something fast to protect Jamie. He'd chosen this life, but she was just a bystander.

''Cheyenne! Take her toward home. I'll slow them down!''

The Indian didn't hesitate. He rode beside a frightened Jamie as Winter turned left to circle back. With the reins in one hand, Winter jerked his rifle from its sheath and swung it through the air to cock the weapon. The Winchester made a mighty clicking sound in a formal call to arms. He wrapped the reins around the saddlehorn and raised the weapon to his shoulder.

Far into the distance three men cleared a rock rise in pursuit. They were seasoned riders able to handle rifles at full gallop. From a distance all were in black with horses bearing no outstanding markings. As the smoke cleared their rifles, Win lowered his aim. Their volley sailed past him. A heartbeat later his shot knocked the center man back, almost unseating him. Win heard Jamie's scream as he cocked his rifle once more and took aim again.

The two remaining men tried to hold the center one on his saddle as they fought to control their own horses. Win squeezed off a second bullet.

The man on the left grabbed his upper arm, but didn't lose his balance as he turned his own horse and pulled the reins of the middle rider's mount back over the hill.

Win fought the urge to follow. He wasn't sure if it was because he'd been taught as a boy never to leave a wounded animal, but to make sure he was dead, or if it was a need to see who was trying to kill him.

Only Jamie's cries for help kept him from kicking his mount in chase.

Instead, he swung back toward Cheyenne and Jamie and rode to where they had stopped, well out of what he thought would have been harm's way.

As he came near, he could hear Jamie crying in huge gulps of terror. Ten feet away he saw the blood on her hands. Five feet from her he could smell the warm sickening smell of flesh ripped open by gunpowder.

''Jamie!''

She looked up at him with wide frightened eyes. For all her hard language and rough ways, she looked very fragile now.

''Jamie, where were you hit?'' The only positive thing

he saw was that she was still in the saddle, her horse close to Cheyenne's.

"I'm not!" she cried. "It's Cheyenne. He's bleeding bad."

Winter looked at his friend for the first time. Cheyenne sat his horse as if nothing were amiss. Only his face was ashen and the lines around his mouth carved of granite.

After jumping off his mount, Winter moved between their horses to Cheyenne. The man's leg was soaked in blood.

"Just below my hip," Cheyenne said softly. "The bullet's still in. I can feel the fire of it against my bone."

Winter pulled his bandanna from his neck and tied it around the leg where blood was pulsing out. His hands and shirt where splattered with crimson by the time he finished. "Can you ride?"

"I can."

For a moment Winter debated. If they took the time to make a travois to hold Cheyenne, the man would bleed to death. If they rode too fast, he might pound more blood out. The bandanna was already soaked. If they stopped on this open plain to try and remove the bullet, Cheyenne might die or they might all be picked off by the men hiding in the rocks.

"Set the pace," he said to Cheyenne. "For as long as you can, ride as hard as possible."

Jamie stayed on one side and Winter on the other as they moved toward home. Halfway, Cheyenne slumped forward and Winter stopped the horses. He ran his hand over Cheyenne's pant leg and wiped the blood across his own saddle, then turning, unbridled his horse and slapped it toward home. He knew his horse would make it in long before they could, and the blood on the saddle would send an army coming.

Winter pulled Cheyenne's feet from the stirrups and climbed up behind him. He wasn't easy to hold in the saddle, but Winter managed.

"Jamie!" He needed help and she had to stop crying long enough to do what had to be done. "Cut a strip of leather from your saddle strings and tie Cheyenne's legs to mine."

She pulled her knife and cut the thin piece of leather from the back of the saddle. "Why?" she whispered.

"I'm not sure I can hold him and travel as fast as we need to. This way we both ride or fall."

She did as she'd been told, first on the right, then on the left side. The leather cut into the back of Win's leg, but he needed it tight. "Now, take my rope and wrap it around us both."

Cheyenne was dead weight now, fighting with gravity to slide from the saddle.

As soon as Jamie was finished, Win pushed his heels into the horse's side, knowing Cheyenne's animal was finely trained and needed no spur to follow even slight commands. They rode as fast as he could and still keep his balance.

Winter's horse arrived back at the barn, sweaty and wild. Logan caught him. The moment he saw the blood on the saddle, he yelled for Kora, then stood back in surprise as she began issuing orders as though Winter had taught her.

It was almost dark when several of Winter's men found them half a mile from the ranch. They surrounded Jamie and Win and acted as guard for the rest of the journey. No man offered to take Winter's load, and he wouldn't have passed it on. Whether Cheyenne was still alive, or not, he'd ride home sitting a saddle and not across it like a season kill of beef.

When they stopped, Logan stepped beside Win and cut

the straps binding the two men. Then Winter gently lowered Cheyenne into a dozen waiting hands.

"Send for the doctor," Winter said as he touched ground.

"I already have, boss," Logan answered. "Miz Kora ordered a man out as soon as we told her about your saddle having blood on it."

Winter followed as the others carried Cheyenne into the house. Kora held the door open while Jamie rattled on about what had happened. He couldn't help but take a long breath as he stepped through the threshold. He was finally home.

Kora led them up the stairs to the first room. Winter followed, allowing exhaustion to seep into his body for the first time.

Dan sat silently in a cane chair by the door as if nothing were happening. When Win was halfway up the stairs, Dan stood and lifted his chair without looking at Winter, then slowly began to follow.

Winter held the door open as Dan moved past him into the bedroom. He didn't seem to see anyone, not his sisters or the ranch hands, or even Cheyenne lying on the bed. Dan simply carried the chair to the corner of the room and sat down, then turned so that his face was in shadows looking away from everyone.

Winter had too much on his mind to try and contact this brother of Kora's who seemed to have given up on living. He tossed his hat on a dusty dresser and looked around the room. The bed was already made out, a fire roared in the fireplace, and a kettle steamed on a rack. Towels and buckets were in ready along with a stack of bandages and the old medicine kit the captain kept nailed to the kitchen wall downstairs.

Winter glanced at Kora in question.

"When I heard of the blood on your saddle, I prepared," Kora said simply.

The other men who'd helped carry Cheyenne backed away, leaving the room silently. They all looked worried and thankful Kora seemed willing to take charge.

"Thanks," Win answered as he unstrapped his gunbelt and chaps. He was glad she was calm and not near hysterics like her sister. "We'll have to cut his pant leg off and do the best we can until the doc gets here."

"Not me!" Jamie shouted from the doorway. "I've seen all the blood I can handle for one day." She was rubbing at her hands, trying to get all the red stain off.

"Go wash, Jamie," Kora said calmly. "I'll help Winter."

Jamie hesitated. "He is going to live, isn't he? I mean, I hate the man, but I wouldn't wish him dead. There's so much blood. He couldn't have much left in him."

"He'll live," Kora responded as if she were certain.

Without another word, Jamie vanished, leaving Winter and Kora to work together. He was amazed at how skilled she was. With a gaping wound that would make most seasoned cowhands turn away, Kora's hands were steady. She cut the leather of his pants and mixed cool water in with the boiling to wash away layers of blood.

By the time the doctor arrived, they'd cleaned the wound. Cheyenne was very pale and he hadn't said a word. His shirt and the sheets were stained in varying shades of drying blood. Winter knew he was very near death, but somehow Kora's statement about him living eased Winter's worries. She did all the right things, forcing water down him when he moaned and turning his head sideways when he passed out in pain so that he wouldn't choke. She covered him in layers of wool to keep him as warm as possible.

Winter sat at the head of the bed and held his friend's

shoulders down as Doc Gage dug for the bullet. Kora was kept busy fetching more towels and water as needed. Cheyenne didn't fight the pain, but took it silently, only tightening once when the bullet was pulled out.

Finally, after Gage's nod, they stepped out into the hallway to wait. Winter lightly put his arm around Kora's shoulder, silently thanking her for everything. She was a woman who must have learned very young to do what had to be done. Despite all Jamie's yelling, she hadn't had Kora's strength. And Win couldn't even imagine Mary Anna being by his side.

To his surprise, Kora moved into his embrace, circling her arms around his waist and holding tightly.

He felt her sobs against his side more than heard them. Deep, lonely, silent sobs. Winter didn't know how to react to her sudden need. She'd proved herself strong, so it made no sense that she'd fall apart now.

"It's all right," he finally whispered, knowing he should say something. "We did the best we could."

After a long while, she looked up, her blue eyes liquid with tears. "I thought it was going to be you," she whispered. "When it was your horse, I thought it would be your blood. I was afraid my bad luck had rubbed off on you."

"I told you, I believe a man makes his own luck." He didn't know if she cried because she still grieved and didn't want to lose another husband so soon, or because she cared that he was alive. With her in his arms, it didn't matter. For the first time since they'd met, she was letting him close and didn't seem to be frightened of him. He liked the smell of her hair and the softness of her at his side. He'd never thought he needed a female except once in a while for the night, but a man could get used to Kora quickly. She was a habit already forming, and to his surprise, he had no desire to break away.

"I'm not that easy to kill." He tried to sound light. "I promised you I'd be home before dark and I almost made it."

"In my life, it seems everyone around me is easy to kill," she whispered.

Without thought, he pulled her full into his embrace and held her. She felt so good. After all that had happened today, nothing seemed more right than leaning his face against her hair and holding her so tightly he could feel her chest rise and fall with each breath against his own.

He told himself he was a man that needed nothing, but he wanted her by his side. He admired the way she took care of her siblings, the way she faced him even with fear in her eyes, and the way she took charge making arrangements in details he'd never thought about. He liked her leaning against him now, letting him be her strength if only for a moment.

"Don't be afraid of me," he whispered. She seemed so frightened of not just him, but of life. How much heartache had she borne?

"I'm not," she answered. "Sometimes I'm afraid to blink because this will all end. I never figured I'd have a home, or a husband. I'm afraid I'll awaken and be back in the dugout. Or on the streets of New Orleans without a place to sleep."

He turned her face to his. "What do I have to do to convince you that we'll stay married for as long you like?"

Before she could answer, a shadow moved in the foyer downstairs and Winter stiffened. "Who's there?" he shouted as he reached for the weapon he'd left in Cheyenne's room.

"Wyatt, ah, Wyatt Mitchell, sir," a deep voice answered nervously. "I was in the doc's office when he got the summons, and I thought if there was trouble I'd best ride out with him.''

The man stepped into the light, and Winter relaxed as he recognized a young gambler from town. Wyatt was a friendly enough fellow, always willing to relieve a man of his extra money at the gaming tables. As far as Winter knew, he was honest, or as honest as any gambler. Which wasn't saying much.

Winter moved down the first few steps. ''Thanks for tagging along with the doc. You're right about there being trouble.'' Win felt Kora's hand touch his shoulder. ''You're welcome to stay the night, Wyatt. There's plenty of room in the bunkhouse. Doc Gage said he plans to sit up with my man until he's out of danger.''

The gambler twirled his short-brimmed hat. He was of average height with the kind of polished good looks that only come when a person stays out of the weather. ''Thanks, Mr. McQuillen,'' he said. ''I'd be much obliged. I wouldn't want to interfere with you and the new missus, but I don't much care for riding half the night to get back to town.''

''You're not interfering.'' Kora stood on the step behind her husband with her hand still on his shoulder. ''In fact, you're welcome to breakfast, Mr. Mitchell. I'll send Jamie out to fetch you in the morning.''

The gambler smiled. ''Jamie wouldn't be that vision in buckskin I saw run through here a while back?''

''Vision in buckskin?'' Winter raised an eyebrow.

''Yes, sir. She looked like she'd just washed her hair and face.'' The gambler laughed, a rich laughter that comes easy to those who laugh a lot. ''She had more water on her than she must have left in the tub. Her garments were wet and clinging to her like second skin. The clothes might be buckskin, but the lady was all woman beneath.''

‘‘Jamie is my sister-in-law,’’ Winter interrupted the man’s memory before it got out of hand.

Wyatt sobered. ‘‘Sorry, no disrespect intended.’’

Now it was Winter’s turn to smile. ‘‘None taken.’’ He glanced at Kora, then back at the gambler. ‘‘You are a single man, I take it?’’

‘‘Yes.’’ Wyatt rocked back on his heels. ‘‘I never thought much of settling down.’’

Winter took Kora’s hand and moved back up the stairs. ‘‘Neither did I until recently. Who knows, Wyatt? The thought may cross your mind sooner than you think.’’

NINE

"YOU CAN'T BE SERIOUS!" KORA SAID AS SHE MOVED around the attic room lighting the lamps. During the day she'd brought up several pieces of furniture and three rugs, but the room was far too big to ever be a cozy bedroom.

"I'm dead serious." Winter pulled off his shirt and stepped in front of the washstand. The little bowl had been replaced by a large basin, and a rug now circled the floor within splashing distance. "What's wrong with the man?"

Kora moved behind a screen that blocked off one corner of the room. The panels of thin wood had been painted years ago with flowers that had faded into echoes of their former beauty. "He's a gambler!" she yelled over the wooden wall separating them.

"Any man who lives in this country is a gambler. If disease doesn't kill the cattle in the summer, snow freezes them before spring." Winter watched in the mirror as her dress lapped over the screen. "Had you rather your sister find a farmer? Now, they're *real* gamblers."

She was silent for a moment. A white petticoat floated over. "No," she finally answered.

He could hear her moving as she continued, "I only want

her to be happy. She needs to get away from Dan and me and make a life of her own. You can introduce him and see what happens. If Jamie likes him, then I'll be happy to see them married."

She stepped from her paneled blockade, her cotton gown buttoned to her throat. He stared at her in his mirror. The sleeves of her gown were too long, almost swallowing her hands, but the hem seemed an inch too short, for he could see her feet and ankles.

Winter suddenly felt the need to be interested in lathering the soap. He tried to watch what he was doing, but she kept moving past his line of vision in the mirror. The gown was thick cotton, but it still revealed the line of her body when she moved, as a dress would never do.

It was most distracting having this woman around, he thought. If she didn't light somewhere, he'd slit his throat trying to shave. Another man in the room never bothered him. He'd shared quarters with sometimes as many as twenty in the bunkhouse. But this woman was different. A fellow could look at a man once a year or so and remember him. But not Kora. Every time he looked at her, she seemed to change. He felt a need to stare just so he could catch her in the act. One minute she was all prim and proper, the next all soft, like now, with her hair down and lace brushing against her throat.

He almost ordered her to stop walking back and forth behind him so he could get on with his shave. But when she crawled up in the center of the bed and tucked her feet beneath her, he found her no less interesting. He shaved slowly as she brushed through her hair and braided it into one thick braid.

When he finally leaned to wipe the soap from his face, he glanced back in the mirror to find her watching him. She'd raised her knees beneath the cotton gown and rested her elbows on them, reminding him of a child.

"Do you always shave at night?" she asked.

"Never have," he answered honestly.

"Then why tonight?"

Winter turned toward her, forcing himself not to react to the sight of a woman sitting in the center of his bed. "Logan told me yesterday that a married man always shaves at night. I figured if he knew something like that, him not even being married, then it must be some kind of rule."

"But why?"

"You're a widow, you must know," he answered as he moved toward the bed.

Kora appeared suddenly nervous. "Oh, yes." She looked around her as if trying to find something, anything, to focus her attention on besides him. "But, I mean, there is no need for you to shave at night. Logan must have meant men who are fully married."

He didn't like being reminded of their agreement. He wasn't likely to forget. "I thought I'd get in practice," he said roughly, "for when your mourning time is over."

Without another word, he sat on the side of the bed and stripped off his jeans.

Kora moved to the edge as far away from him as she could. "Don't you sleep in a nightshirt?"

"I never have," he answered. "I usually just sleep in my long drawers in winter. Sometimes an undershirt if it's really cold."

"And in summer?" She moved off the bed.

"Nothing," he answered as he slipped beneath the sheet and leaned back. He didn't pull the covers past his waist. She might as well get used to the look of his bare chest, because he wasn't wearing one of those lacy nightshirts for the next thirty years.

She grabbed her wrapper. "I think I'll go check on Cheyenne to make sure the doctor doesn't need anything before I go to bed.'' She glanced at the rafters. ''And I'm not sure I laid out the things Dan will need after his evening walk.''

''Kora?'' Winter stopped her with a word.

''Yes?'' She turned toward him as she tied her wrapper.

''I'm not going to touch you. You can come to bed. Whether I have on a nightshirt or not will make no difference in my keeping my word.''

''I understand.'' She moved away. ''I'll be back as soon as I check on things.''

Winter closed his eyes and leaned against the pillows. Why had the woman insisted on him sleeping up here if she was still scared to death of him? If he hadn't been so tired, he would have followed her and tried to talk to her. Maybe he should move back to the couch. He was starting to believe that two floors between them might help him remember his promise.

But the long day caught up with him and Winter fell asleep in his own bed, in his own room, for the first time in his life.

Late into the night, with the moon passing overhead, Winter rolled over and opened his eyes. For a moment he wasn't sure where he was. There were no sounds of other men sleeping nearby in their bunks, and his body was stretched out as it could never be on the couch in the study. Then he saw the stars through the windows and smiled. Kora had been right, it was a grand place to sleep beneath the sky. The cool of the night was around him, but the huge room, with its tall windows, gave him a feeling of sleeping outside while he had all the comforts of a home. Miss Allie's quilts added color to the room even in shadows. Kora had draped them over chairs and hung several on boards around the room.

He raised to one elbow and looked over to her side of

the bed. She wasn't there. Glancing up, he knew by the look of the sky that it was long past midnight.

For a moment he thought she might be gone, disappearing from his life as quickly as she'd entered. Or she might still be downstairs. Cheyenne could have taken a turn for the worse. Winter grasped a handful of cover and swung his leg from the bed.

Then he saw her. The moonlight danced off the golden rope of her hair. She was curled up on the floor ten feet away. She'd circled a blanket in the moonlight, and huddled in it like a street orphan.

Slowly, soundlessly, Winter moved from the bed. He knelt beside her and gently lifted her in his arms, blanket and all.

She moved in her sleep, but didn't awaken.

He carried her to the side of the bed and laid her slowly down against the pillows. She looked so fragile as he pulled another blanket over her.

Returning to his side, he tried to sleep, but the woman beside him kept him awake. He could hear her soft breathing and feel her move as she nestled deeply into the covers. She was getting under his skin, he thought. If he didn't watch himself he'd be caring for her, and he'd learned a long time ago that to care for someone was to invite pain.

She's just a wife, he reminded himself, *bought for the price of a house. Just someone to cook and clean. Nothing more.* To expect more was just asking for disappointment. He had enough trouble without making anyone in his life a necessity. He'd treat her with respect, even kindness if needed, but she had no right to ask for anything beyond their bargain. And he told himself he had no heart to give it.

• • •

Kora awoke just as the sun lightened the sky to a velvet gray. She felt warm and rested as she stretched beneath the covers. Opening her eyes, she stiffened, suddenly realizing that she was in the bed and not on the floor. Winter lay beside her, his back to her. She could hear his low breathing and feel the warmth of him only inches away.

His shoulders looked so broad beneath the blanket. She almost giggled as she fought the urge to reach out and touch him to see if he really was made of granite. He seemed to take little interest in the house, even agreeing to their room being in the attic. But in matters about himself, there was no compromise. He hadn't even paused a moment to consider sleeping in a nightshirt. Kora didn't want to think about what he'd do if they ever faced each other head on.

She knew he thought she was afraid of him. She could see it in his eyes, the question, the uncertainty of how to handle her. If he only understood that the fear was of the dream shattering, not of him, he might relate to her differently. Kora wasn't sure she wanted that yet. She'd learned nothing good lasted and decided it was better not to get too attached to Winter. Jamie was right, they'd have to move on before the bad luck that always followed them caught up yet again.

Kora stretched beneath the warm covers, remembering that when she returned and found him asleep, she'd kissed him good night and considered curling up beside him. But kissing a sleeping man was far different that lying beside one. She'd opted for the floor. In truth, it was more normal for her. From the time her father died, she'd spent most of her nights curled on a blanket in the back room of wherever her mother had been able to find work.

She thought that maybe she'd grown cold during the night and moved to the bed, but Kora had no memory of doing so, and to her knowledge she'd never walked in her sleep.

Slipping from the covers, Kora moved to the screened dressing area. This was her private space. She'd seen an area screened off for a lady in one of the homes she'd cleaned. When she found the old wooden screen in one of the bedrooms downstairs, she'd been delighted. Now one corner of the huge attic room would be hers.

Inside the small area was a dressing table made from a board and two crates and a stool with a padded seat. Kora had rigged a broom handle across one side of the enclosure to hang her few clothes. She'd felt wealthy buying two dresses, a nightgown with wrapper, and a new jacket all at one time. Winter hadn't said a word about anything she bought, except to mention that if she needed more to let him know and he'd see that she got it. How rich he must be to be able to buy anything he needed without checking his account.

She hadn't shown anyone the one thing she'd bought with her own money. A tiny, nickle-plated perfume bottle. It had cost her all she had: a dollar twenty. But that price had included the perfume inside, so the store owner told her she was getting a bargain. It had been crazy to spend so much on a bottle, but she'd wanted something fine-looking on her homemade dressing table. Now the deep blue bottle with its casing of metal rested on a white linen handkerchief. The handkerchief bore Winter's initials and looked as if it might have been a gift from someone years ago that he'd stuffed into a side pocket of his chest and forgotten. She'd found it in the study along with Winter's other clothes when she'd moved them upstairs. The bottle and the linen made her feel very grand.

Inside the opening of one crate she kept a comb and small cracked mirror. Beneath the table, she'd hidden her cigar box of keys. The box was the one real thing she owned. It had traveled with her from her father's house to the hundred places she'd lived. She had no pictures of family, no handed-down jewelry, no treasured keepsakes. But she had her keys, most found without locks, all worthless to anyone but her. Yet Kora knew the location of where she'd found each treasure. Sometimes she'd polish them and remember the good and bad of everywhere she'd ever been. When she'd cleaned this house, she found a key that no one seemed to know what it had ever been used for. It was added to her collection with a silent promise that if anyone asked, she'd give it back.

The keys were something she'd never show anyone, but just knowing the box was there made her smile.

Quickly she dressed in one of her new dresses and tied her hair up in a bun. Blood seemed to rush through her veins as she thought of how close she'd slept to Winter. He could have reached out and touched her, or she, him. But he hadn't. Maybe he was worth the trusting. She'd made up her mind yesterday, after Jamie's remark, that she had to give him a chance. Over and over she'd told herself that being suspicious of a man who simply growled didn't make sense. She'd hold to her agreement, at least until she knew he'd bite.

If anyone had broken the bargain so far, it had been her. She'd kissed him every night they'd been married. In some strange way, her action made Winter hers and their marriage almost real. For a while she could pretend she was married just as she sometimes pretended her keys fit all the locked doors in the world.

As she stepped around the screen, Winter turned from the window. He was standing at the far corner of the room looking south. He'd pulled on his jeans and shirt, but hadn't bothered to button either. In the early light, before the day began to weigh on him, he looked younger.

"Morning." His voice sounded even lower than usual. "Have you checked on Cheyenne yet?"

"I was just going down," Kora answered, thinking she probably should have checked before dressing.

Winter buttoned his jeans. "I'll go with you. I told the doc to call me if there was any change. Since he didn't, I'm guessing no news may be good news."

Kora reached in the top drawer of the dresser and handed Winter a clean pair of socks from the stack she'd organized.

"Thanks." He stared at her as he sat on the corner of the bed and pulled on the socks. "You don't have to do that, you know."

"Do what?" she said, thinking that he needed a haircut.

"Hand me my stuff," Winter answered. "You don't have to wait on me, I can take care of myself. I've been doing it all my life."

"I wasn't waiting on you," Kora answered, surprised he'd even think such a thing. "I was helping you."

Winter pulled on his boots in silence. Finally, when he stood, he said, "I'm new at the marriage thing. I'm not sure how to react to this pampering you call help. I'm not complaining. The meals you leave out, the way you helped last night, everything. It's something I think I could get used to if you want to continue helping."

Kora smiled. "I'm glad. Just say thanks now and again. That's all you need do."

Winter took the first step down out of their room. "Kora?" He turned to meet her gaze. "This may prove a long day. After the ambush yesterday, I'm not sure you'll be safe on the ranch. If you like, I could move you and Jamie into the hotel in town until it's over."

"Are you staying on the ranch?"

"I'm staying."

"Then so am I." She moved to his side. "I'm not leaving my home unless you order me out."

"I'll never do that," he grumbled as he started down the stairs.

Kora followed, wondering what had made him seem so grumpy. Was it because she'd called it her house, or because she'd said she'd never leave? She hurried, but barely caught up with him before he opened the door to Cheyenne's room.

They entered silently as Dr. Steven Gage unfolded from a chair beside the bed. He still looked like a young man, early into his thirties, with a kindness in his eyes few men let show.

"I was just coming to wake you, Win." The doctor smiled. "Cheyenne's fever broke about half an hour ago. It's too early to tell if the wound will stay free of infection, but it looks good."

"What can we do?" Winter asked as he stared down at his sleeping friend. The room smelled of medicine and blood. Dan still sat silently in the cane chair by the windows. Winter wasn't sure if he'd been there all night, or merely returned this morning. He wasn't looking at them or giving any indication he knew they were in the room.

"Keep him warm and quiet mostly," Gage answered. "Get as much liquid and food down him as we can. He lost a lot of blood. It'll take time to build back up. Right now, he's peaceful enough, but we've got to keep him in bed longer than he's probably going to want to stay."

"I'll put a man on guard, Doc. He'll stay down if I have to stake him."

Steven Gage laughed. "I hope you won't have to go that far. I'll stay another day"—he glanced at Kora—"if your wife doesn't mind having a guest?"

"You're welcome to stay, Dr. Gage."

"Thanks, ma'am. Your sister's already been up with coffee this morning. She told me you wouldn't mind if I stayed. She also told me about how the ambush happened and how she helped get Cheyenne back. That's quite a woman, your sister."

Kora smiled. "Thank you."

"You still single, Doc?" Winter got the question out just before Kora jabbed him in the ribs.

"Yes," Steven answered. "Why?"

Winter cleared his throat. "I just wondered if I needed to send a rider to let your wife know you were staying."

Kora took Winter by the arm. "I'll start breakfast."

She pulled at his elbow until he followed her. As soon as the door was closed, she faced him, fighting anger. If Jamie had a chance with the doctor, Winter might ruin it by pushing.

Winter didn't see the anger in her gaze as he rubbed his side. "I never realized you were so strong. A little harder and I'd have a busted rib."

"Do you have to ask every man in the county if he's married as soon as they mention my sister?" She put her fists on her hips. As always, she was willing to fight for Jamie.

"Seemed like a logical thing to do. I wouldn't want to waste any time." Winter liked the way she fired up. Her blue eyes sparkled.

"You make it seem like we have to sell her off fast before she molts."

"I'll try to refrain from asking for a few more minutes." Winter held his hands up in surrender. "Just don't hit me again." He was choking down the laughter.

Kora turned to leave.

"One other thing, wife."

Winter's words stopped her and she turned, realizing how forward she'd been to hit him. He couldn't know that she'd been standing up for Jamie forever. Even when Kora didn't stand up for herself, she'd fight her sister's battles.

Winter folded his arms over his chest and waited until she looked up at him. "I just want to say, you're beautiful when you're angry."

A fire spread up Kora's throat and across her cheeks. Compliments were for others, not for her. She was always the mouse no one noticed.

"I don't know what to say," she whispered, fighting the desire to run.

"Just a thanks, now and then. That's all."

Before she could react, he leaned down and kissed her on the cheek, then disappeared, taking the stairs two at a time.

TEN

KORA COOKED BREAKFAST AND CARRIED IT UPSTAIRS to the doctor and Cheyenne. They worked together to get a few bites down the injured man, then Kora cleaned the room as the doc sat back and enjoyed his breakfast.

She caught Doc Gage's questioning glance when Dan silently picked up his chair and moved out of the room.

''The war,'' she said as she collected discarded bandages.

Gage almost dropped his fork. ''But that's been twenty years! Has he been like that since then?''

Kora nodded. ''My mother took care of him while she was alive, then I started. He's really no trouble as long as you lay everything out that he needs and don't try to talk to him or make him eat with anyone.''

''Does he wander off?''

''No.'' Kora dusted the dresser. ''He takes walks but always returns where his things are, even if we move from one house to another. Sometimes he curls up in the back of a wagon to sleep. We've almost lost him a few times because of that habit. When we move all we do is put his chair in the wagon bed and he climbs right in.''

"Can he talk?"

"I don't know." Kora faced the doctor. "My mother tried everything to make him come out of his prison. When first my father died and then Dan came home like this, the light went out of her eyes."

"But she still had you and your sister?" Gage reasoned.

"Girls weren't as important as a son. I tried everything to please her and Jamie rebelled, but in the end all she saw was Dan. The night she died, she cried for her son, saying over and over how much she loved him. She never said a word to the two daughters at her bedside."

"There are homes for veterans like him."

"He has a home with me!" Kora answered sharply.

Gage looked down at his food, embarrassed by his boldness. He shoved a biscuit in his mouth and mumbled after a minute, "If I could find a woman who could cook this good, I'd be a married man. Winter is a lucky fellow to have found you."

"There is more to being a wife than cooking," Kora said, hoping Jamie's chances wouldn't be zero when the doctor tasted her meals. Coffee was the limit to her skills in the kitchen.

"I know what you mean." The doc leaned back and downed the last of his breakfast. "I was married once, about ten years ago while I was still in school. She was an angel God called home far too soon to my liking. I've thought of tying the knot again a few times since, but somehow I'm still married to her. Even now, after all these years, when folks ask me if I've got a wife, I have to think a moment before remembering. Being married is a feeling that doesn't wash away with the tears at the funeral."

He looked at her with kind eyes. "You were a widow, I understand. You must know what I mean."

Kora reddened and looked down. She felt like an impostor. How could she tell him she'd married a stranger on his deathbed just because she'd read his letter and thought he had a farm? Anyone who heard the story would hate her for being so selfish. She hadn't even stayed for the funeral, but left when the sheriff told her Andrew was beyond hearing anyone but the angels.

Kora had tried to do the right thing. She'd paid the doctor and the undertaker from Andrew's money. Even leaving enough for a headstone to be made. Then she packed Jamie and Dan and left on the first stage heading north. Andrew's letters said he had no family, so she wasn't taking from anyone, and she thought she was giving them all a chance.

"I didn't mean to cause you pain, Mrs. McQuillen." The doctor stood. "I'm terribly sorry."

Before she was forced to answer, Jamie opened the door.

"Kora," Jamie whispered instead of shouting for once. "May I have a word with you?"

Thankful for the distraction, Kora excused herself and hurried to her sister. "What is it?"

"That husband of yours has every man on the place marching double time. He's even stationed Logan in the foyer with enough weapons to hold off a small army." Jamie looked frustrated. "There's not a soul to go riding with me. I even asked the gambler eating his way through a month's worth of groceries, and he claims he hurt his shoulder and can't ride."

"You could sit with Cheyenne," Kora suggested. The one thing Jamie never allowed herself to be was bored. If they didn't think of something, she'd find trouble. She always did.

"Oh, Kora, you know how I'd hate that." Jamie glanced over at Cheyenne. "If he's asleep, it will be so boring and if he's awake I'll probably kill him within an hour if I have to talk to him. Let Dan bring his chair back up and sit with him. He'll offer as much conversation as the man needs."

Kora stepped out in the hallway and started down the stairs. "I don't see how I can solve your problem. I know better than to suggest cooking or cleaning."

"We've got an idea," Jamie followed her down. "Wyatt and me."

"Wyatt?" Kora glanced at her sister.

"The gambler. He's really a nice sort." Jamie was suddenly bouncing with excitement. "We could take the doc's buggy into town. Wyatt said he'd show me around, and we'd be back long before dark. I could handle the reins so he could baby his shoulder."

Kora looked at Logan, who'd been eavesdropping from the foyer. The old man shrugged.

"But Winter said—"

"Winter said I couldn't leave alone. I wouldn't be alone. Besides, Wyatt says he's an excellent shot. But trouble won't come. Wyatt and I aren't involved in this range fight. Why would anyone want to bother us?"

Kora watched at Logan again. The old man raised his gaze to her and shrugged once more. He was offering no help.

"All right, but be careful."

Jamie and Wyatt left as soon as he could hitch the team and Kora could pack a lunch for them. She didn't feel right about her sister going, but she couldn't think of a reason to say no.

After they left, the day passed in a maze of work. She helped the doctor take care of Cheyenne, cooked, and tried not to worry. Logan talked constantly, trying to convince her that all was well, but the uneasiness in the back of Kora's mind would not leave. The "witchin' luck" Jamie always teased her about was drawing near. Every time she settled down and thought life would smooth out, something happened.

It was long past suppertime when Winter rode in, muddy and tired. He'd just stepped on the back porch when Kora met him at the door.

"Jamie's not back," she said as his "evenin' " died in the air.

Winter took a deep breath. "Where'd she go?"

Kora didn't want to tell him. She could feel the anger in his stance rippling the air between them. He'd probably think it all her fault, as it was. Jamie might think she was full grown, but she didn't have the common sense of a jackrabbit in a thunderstorm. Kora was always the logical one.

"She left for town hours ago with Wyatt. They promised they'd be back by dark." Kora twisted her hands together in near panic. Jamie was always late and unpredictable, but this was different. Someone was shooting at riders on Winter's ranch. This time she could get hurt, and Kora had given in against her better judgment just to avoid a fight.

Suddenly his large hand covered hers, stilling them with his grip. "I'll find her."

Without another word, he turned and signaled several men to follow him. Silently the tired men swung back into their saddles.

Kora stood on the porch and watched him adjust his hat as he moved toward his horse. His stride was long and powerful, filled with anger. The soft jingle of his spurs did nothing to lighten the mood as he led his men back out into the night.

The cloudy night had turned ink black without moon or stars. She watched until the last rider disappeared, then listened in the silence, straining to hear them returning.

Only the sounds of the night greeted her.

"He'll be all right." Logan startled her with his words from the kitchen door. "You've no need to keep watch. Win's a survivor, no matter what."

"I know," she whispered, wanting to believe. "I thought he'd yell at me for letting Jamie go."

"He knows you did what you thought was best. And he knows Jamie." Logan bit into a brown square of tobacco. "I'd be surprised if he ever yelled at you."

Kora tried to see the old man clearly in the darkness. "Why do you say that?"

"You're his wife. For Winter that means you're a part of him." Logan smiled and mumbled as he moved back into the kitchen. "Like bone and blood."

Kora paced for an hour. Every little sound made her jump. Finally she heard horses approaching and ran for the door.

Logan stepped in her path. "Hold up there!" he warned. "Best let me take a look first. Might be trouble riding in for a visit."

But as he opened the door, Jamie stormed through kicking at invisible blockades in her path. Her hair was wild and her clothes windblown.

Before Kora could say a word, she yelled, "That wild, half crazy husband of yours ruined my evening!" She attacked the stairs. "I should have known he was short on brains when he introduced us to his horse. Most men introduce a bride-to-be to the family." She stared down at Kora, as if blaming her for marrying Winter. "For a man promising to help me find a mate, he's certainly doing his part to see that I become an old maid. Keep him out of my sight, or I swear, I'll cut him up so small he'll be good for nothing but chicken feed."

Kora followed as fast as she could, but Jamie's pants made maneuvering the stairs far easier than Kora's dress.

"What happened? You said you'd be home before dark. Jamie, I was worried."

Jamie reached her bedroom door. "Ask that bossy bully you married what happened. I'm going to bed!"

Slamming the door, she ended Kora's questioning.

For a moment Kora stood at the door waiting for her sister to answer. Jamie had always been high-strung and wild, but usually she was able to talk to Kora at least. Whatever Winter did must have been pretty bad.

Suddenly the old fires flamed up. Someone was picking on her little sister. Kora couldn't stand by and allow that to happen no matter how much Jamie had asked for it. She ran down the stairs and past Logan before the old man could say a word.

The night was cold and the wind whipped at her skirts almost knocking her down, but Kora marched straight to the barn. By the time she was inside, the weather had taken the edge off her anger.

Winter had unsaddled his horse and was putting the gear up when she found him. He'd shoved his hat far back on his head and smiled as she approached.

"What happened?" Kora forced herself to give him the benefit of a doubt. Maybe Jamie had overreacted. It wouldn't be the first time.

Winter looked at her closely. "I found her," he said simply. He wasn't about to tell Kora in what state he'd found Jamie and the gambler.

"But she's very upset. Did you embarrass her?" Kora asked as they moved to the tack room.

"I reckon I did," Winter answered. "But I didn't lay a hand on her, so don't look at me that way."

"I didn't say you did," she countered, embarrassed that he'd guessed what she'd been thinking.

"You were worried, and I brought her back. If I have

any more words about tonight with anyone, I think it'll be with the gambler.'' He turned to Kora. ''Right now all I want is a meal and bed.'' Before she could step away, he caught her wrist and pulled her to him.

''And this,'' he whispered. ''I've been thinking about you all day. If you're going to be angry with me, you might as well have reason.''

His head lowered slightly as his hand moved into her hair at the back of her neck. He cradled her head as his lips brushed hers.

Kora was so shocked she didn't move. She'd tasted his lips before, but only when he was asleep. Now they moved against her mouth, making a kiss completely different from the ones she'd stolen.

His arm tightened around her waist as he drew her into the length of him.

Logic told her she should pull away. They were in the middle of a discussion. They'd agreed to wait. If she let him too close, he might learn her secret and hate her for the impostor she was.

But logic didn't win the battle raging in her body. She didn't want to stop. The hunger in his kiss fascinated her. She hardly knew this man, yet somehow she understood his need.

The kiss deepened as he met no resistance. He dropped the bridle he still carried and almost lifted her off the ground with his hug. His mustache tickled her cheek as his warm mouth moved over her lips.

A low, longing sound rumbled from his chest to his throat as if the taste of her filled a need he'd been starving for.

Hesitantly she touched his shoulders and felt the power of this man she'd married. Despite the bands of muscle around her, she had the feeling Winter was holding back.

She guessed that if she pushed on his chest, he'd let her go, just as she could turn her head and break the kiss. But his lips were soft against hers and his arms felt more like protection than chains.

Her fingers slid over the soft leather of his jacket and touched his throat. Day-old stubble tickled her fingertips as she brushed her hands along his jawline.

Winter straightened slightly, ending the kiss but not the embrace. "I need a shave and a bath."

She timidly slid her fingers over his cheek, trying to get used to the feel of him.

He moved her an inch away, his hands firm around her waist. "That was inconsiderate of me, Kora. I've got a layer of trail dust on me and probably smell like my horse. I had no right to grab you and kiss you like that, but it's been on my mind."

His words might be an apology, but there was none in his eyes. Kora had the feeling he might repeat his actions once more before he could finish apologizing. This was a side of Winter she hadn't seen.

She couldn't help but smile. He was trying to be considerate even though she could see the hunger in his eyes for more. "I didn't mind." The words were out before she thought to stop them.

"You—" Winter started.

"Well, I did!" A low voice cracked like thunder from the darkness beyond the tack room. "I happen to mind a great deal!"

Winter pulled Kora close as he lifted his Colt and pointed it into the blackness. "Step out!" he ordered. "Identify yourself."

A man stepped into the shadowy light of the barn's lantern. He wasn't very tall and even in several layers of clothes looked thin. He raised his hands to shoulder height.

"Don't shoot. I ain't got a gun. Didn't figure I'd need one to come a-callin'."

"Mister, you'd better give me a good reason for being on my land, and make it fast." Win didn't lower his Colt. "Any stranger that comes sneaking in after dark had better be quick on explaining."

"First, I didn't sneak in and second I ain't a stranger. I made deliveries here all last summer. I could find my way around this place on a moonless night. I came in a few hours ago and decided to wait for you. I must have fallen asleep over there in the hay." He made a hacking sound as though something were thick in his throat. "I hadn't planned on going up to the house until morning, but you two came out to me. I couldn't very well just stand around and watch you handle her, not once I heard her name."

The fellow moved a step closer in an awkward gate that nursed an injury.

Kora could smell whiskey on him. She pressed a fraction closer to Winter as she looked into the dirty face of a man who seemed vaguely familiar. Though his eyes were dark brown like Winter's, his were lifeless and cold, not full of fire and anger. His hair might be blond, if washed, but now hung around his face in straight hunks of brown.

"I'll thank you to let go of the lady." The stranger lifted his chest as if to make himself more powerful. "In fact, step away from her all together."

Win didn't move. "What do you want?"

The stranger took another step closer, and suddenly he looked determined. "I want ta talk to Kora alone."

"I don't think so." Win widened his stance. He glanced at Kora. She held her head high, but she slipped her hand between his rib cage and elbow. "My wife doesn't seem to wish a conversation, sir, so I have to ask you to leave."

"Not without her!" The stranger's words were angry.

"And she knows me well enough. She's *my* wife."

Kora screamed and the man's image found its place in her memory. The stage robbery, the dying man, Andrew Adams!

ELEVEN

WINTER SHOVED A CLEAN SHIRT INTO HIS SADDLEBAG. "What else?" He said the words with such controlled anger, his hand shook slightly. "Or should I say *who* else? A husband who's still alive seems a little more important than telling me you're left-handed."

Kora didn't answer. He continued to fill his bag and mumble to himself. "I'd kill this one, but another one might turn up next week. Who knows how many ex-husbands you've got wandering around?"

"I didn't ask you to marry me," Kora answered from where she stood by the windows. She'd followed him from the barn without saying a word. She knew he needed, he deserved an explanation, but she wasn't sure what to say. Anything she said would only make him think less of her. She moved farther away but didn't leave the room.

Win's gaze scanned the area. Her face was in shadows as it had been the night they met. He remembered what a mouse he'd thought she was. He was surprised she wasn't hiding away somewhere now. She'd always seemed so afraid of him, yet when she finally made him furious, she was sticking as close as a newborn calf.

"That's right," he said more to himself than her, "you didn't ask me to marry you. I've no one but myself to blame. I walked into this mess sober and plenty old enough to know what I was doing."

He made another trip to his dresser drawer. "I took on playing matchmaker to that hot-blooded sister of yours and agreed to having a mute brother wandering my house at all hours. I even agreed to the in-name-only part for a while, thinking I was being kind. But this I won't stand for. I won't put up with a man walking onto my land and demanding my wife go home with him."

Kora pressed her cheek against the window. "I didn't go, did I?" She felt suddenly ages old and very tired.

"No, you didn't. Which surprised me after all the mourning I thought you were doing for the man." Win swung his saddlebag over his shoulder and took a step toward her. "And even in the poor light I don't think you recognized him until he said his name. What kind of marriage did you two have, anyway?"

She couldn't explain without telling the whole story. If she told him of how she'd signed a proxy Andrew Adams had offered by mail to another woman, he'd think her mad. If Winter knew she waited until she thought Adams was an hour from death before she stepped forward as his bride, he'd think her a greedy, dishonest gold digger. There was no way she could win. She'd already lost. The cloud of the witchin' luck had caught up to her once again.

"Tell me the truth, Kora. How long was he your husband? Long enough to kiss you? Long enough to sleep beside you? Long enough to earn a train ticket, or did you stay long enough to . . ." He couldn't say the words. He'd thought of making love to her all day. Of how it would be between them when she was no longer shy. Of how it would feel to hold her all night.

"What difference does it make?" she answered. All she had left was a thimbleful of pride. She'd walk away with that if nothing else. "There's no use in your leaving. I'll pack. Jamie, Dan, and I will leave for town tonight. I knew this would never last, nothing good ever does in my life. I'm sure the gambler will drive us, and there must be somewhere to stay."

Win shook his head. "You're not leaving. It's dangerous enough on the road at night without there being men out ambushing folks." He looked at the ceiling and let out a long breath. "Besides, I need you here," he admitted. "Someone's got to help the doc with Cheyenne. I've got my hands full with the blockade. I'm already pushing every hand to the breaking point." He hated the idea that he had to depend on her, but all the men were needed to ride the blockade, and even if he could spare one, none would be worth much in a sickroom.

Kora turned toward him for the first time. She saw all the anger she'd expected to see in his tan face. His entire body seemed to be granite, unmoving, uncompromising, unforgiving. But in his eyes she saw something else. A tiny flickering of the pain she'd caused. Somehow, despite all his claims and all his strength, she'd hurt this man deeply, perhaps beyond forgiveness. This man who swore he'd never care, cared enough to be hurt.

She was thankful he turned and ran down the stairs, for she felt herself crumbling.

Winter knew he needed sleep, but he couldn't shut off his mind. All his life he'd been alone and told himself he wanted it that way. Yet, he could still taste the kiss he'd shared with Kora in the barn. It angered him that he needed her—he needed her for more than to help with the house and Cheyenne. Somehow, in just a few days, she'd become a part of him, and even the rage he felt couldn't drive her out.

When he'd been a boy, his father died of illness and his mother took him to live with her people in the Indian Territory. The village had been attacked one morning by soldiers when Winter was six. He remembered his mother yelling for him to run and not look back. Those were her last words to him, and it seemed he'd been running all his life. If he forced himself not to care, then no one could hurt him. But somehow, Kora had gotten to him. It was more than the need he felt to protect her, he'd grown to admire her. She had a quiet strength and a deep-water kind of touch that washed over his scarred soul.

Twisting uncomfortably on the sofa, he told himself that as soon as this blockade was over, he'd tell Kora to go back to Andrew Adams. He'd lived without a wife for years, and he could again. If the man's paper was valid, then Win wasn't married to Kora. "And the house isn't hers," he mumbled silently, vowing to burn the place if she left. Then he would pay the church for the damage.

The door to the study slowly opened, pulling Winter fully awake. He studied her in the firelight as Kora tiptoed into the room. Pretending to be asleep, he watched her move silently about. She put another log on the fire, then picked up his dirty clothes and placed clean folded ones on the chair.

She turned to go, then hesitated before crossing the rug to where he lay. Very slowly she leaned over him and lightly touched her lips to his. It took all Winter's strength not to pull her to him. He made his body remain still as she kissed him, then vanished a moment later.

"The deep water may drown me," he mumbled to himself as he rubbed two fingers over his bottom lip.

• • •

Win finally gave up even trying to sleep and pulled on his jeans. He opened one of the tall study windows and stepped out onto the long dark front porch. The captain had built the back of the house to face all the activity of the ranch and the front to face the prairie. For as far as he could see in the moonlit sky was his land. Only tonight it failed to bring him the joy it always had.

Hardly noticing the cold air, he took a deep breath, trying to clear the thought of Kora in another man's arms. He knew she'd probably be leaving by summer, but that seemed a lifetime away. Until then she'd promised to be his wife. Adams's appearance had changed all that.

He moved silently across the wooden boards toward the steps. Win was almost atop Kora before he saw her sitting on the first step wrapped in a quilt.

"Excuse me," he grumbled, hating that he wasn't alone.

Turning to leave, he almost didn't hear her whisper, "Don't go."

He thought of ignoring her request. He owed her nothing. She'd lied to him and made a fool of him. But she'd also been kind. "What is it?" He didn't turn to face her.

For a long moment she was silent and he wasn't sure she was going to say anything.

Then softly her voice drifted on the breeze. "I like to come out here. The back porch is always so busy, but around here you can almost believe you're alone on the land."

Win turned slightly, but all he could see was her outline on the steps. "If you've got something to say, say it."

"I don't know where to start," she whispered.

"With the truth would be a new spot," he answered. "And at the beginning."

He watched her head lean forward as she tucked her knees to her chin. She looked so tiny. It was hard to believe she'd come up with such a whopper of a lie.

"My first memory of my father was when he died early in the war. Mama came from a family who had a little money, and Papa had already sold all his land trying to keep her happy even before the war. When he died, we had nothing. Dan was tall enough to run off and fight, leaving me with newborn Jamie and Mom."

Kora wasn't looking at him but out at the darkness. He could tell the words came hard.

"We made do until Dan returned. Mom just gave up trying after that, not caring about anything but being with him. I'm not sure how long she lived after he came home all shot up and silent like he is now, two winters, maybe three. Then we were alone."

She leaned her head back against the wood of the porch brace and took a deep breath. "For a while we lived by me gathering food from other folks' gardens at night and from the garbage bins in winter. Finally I was old enough to work, and Jamie could watch Dan."

Kora laughed suddenly without humor. "I guess you didn't mean so far back."

Win moved to the other side of the porch steps and folded his arms. "Continue."

"There were months, years that I didn't see sunlight. I worked at any job that would pay, sometimes two, and Jamie ran the streets. Several years ago we heard about a land where the sun shines every day of the year—California. So we saved enough to get to Galveston and from there to Houston, then Bryan. We planned to work our way across the West.

"But Dan got sick a year ago, and the doctor's fee put us in debt. I started working at the mercantile, and Jamie ran the mail."

Win shifted. "What does this have to do with Andrew

Adams?'' He had the feeling she was stalling.

''Everything,'' she whispered. ''A woman who picked up her mail at the mercantile started writing him and agreed to marry him by mail. But she found another a few days before he arrived and tossed his letters in the trash. Just out of curiosity, I read them and decided to meet the stage, wondering what such a man would look like.

''The stage was late. When it came in, all were dead but Adams. He had four bullet holes in him and the doctor said he'd never live the night. I'd read the letters, I knew he had no relatives, and he'd already signed the proxy. All I had to do was sign the paper, and I'd be a widow with a farm somewhere northwest.''

''So you lied.'' Win's words were hard. ''About him and then to me.''

''The lie to him only moved us to another place to starve.''

''But you thought the lie to me would get you to your sunshine in California,'' Win snapped as he stood.

''That's right,'' Kora whispered without looking up.

''If the paper is legal, there's not much you can do. The law wouldn't step between a man and wife.''

''And if it's not?''

''Then you stay till full summer with me. I'll see that you don't break this agreement.'' He looked away from her. ''When the six months is over, I want you gone.''

The sound of him walking away was all she heard.

TWELVE

"How about I kill them both?" Jamie offered as she leaned against the counter watching Kora cut out the morning's biscuits. "Then you'd have no husbands and we could start over fresh."

Kora smiled, thankful that her sister was speaking to her once more. She had all the problems she could handle without Jamie's anger. "I'll think about it."

"It wouldn't be that much trouble. We've already paid for Andrew's funeral, and Win's got enough land around for burying. After what he did to Wyatt and me last night, I'd slit his throat without a second thought." Her eyes danced with excitement. "Then, of course, I'd have to become an outlaw. I could branch off into bank robbery and be a gun-for-hire, that kind of thing. And I'd still see Wyatt, of course. We'd be the gambler and the outlaw everyone makes up legends about."

Kora smiled at her sister's outrageous daydream. "You'll not start your life of crime on one of my husbands. But as for the gambler, what did happen between you two last night?"

Jamie raised her eyebrows up and down, then shook her head. "You wouldn't understand."

"Is he interested in marriage?" Kora asked as she agreed with Jamie about not understanding. Except for the kiss she'd shared with Win in the barn, she'd never found men as fascinating to be around as Jamie seemed to.

"He's interested in me," Jamie offered. "As for marriage, I think he feels about like I do concerning that black curse."

"It's not a curse."

Jamie laughed. "It's a curse by which you've been doubly blessed, dear sister. I'd call that witchin' luck for sure."

Both women grew silent as Winter entered the kitchen. He was dressed in the clean clothes Kora laid out, but he didn't look as if he'd slept at all. His hair was still damp from the washing, and a touch of shaving soap brushed the corner of his mustache.

"Mornin'," he mumbled as he pulled a cup from the rack. "Any coffee yet?"

"I'm not speaking to you!" Jamie shouted as she folded her arms.

Kora wrapped a towel around the pot handle and filled his cup. Her hand shook slightly, but if he wanted to pretend nothing was wrong, she would, also.

Only a foot stood between them as she poured. He leaned a little closer. "How about you?" he whispered. "Are you speaking to me?"

"I'm not angry with you," Kora said as she turned and put the pot down. "None of this mess was your fault." Lightly she brushed the soap from his face as she spoke. "I wouldn't wish the man dead, but I'm thankful I was with you when he appeared last night."

Win's gaze watched her closely as though bracing himself for another lie. The corner of his mouth lifted slightly at her action. A crack so small in the granite that no one but Kora saw it. She touched the edge of his lip again even though the shaving soap was gone.

"Well, I'm angry," Jamie said from behind him. "What makes you think you have any right to ruin my life?"

"I thought you weren't speaking to me." Win looked over his shoulder at Jamie. In the few days Kora and he had been married, he'd seen Jamie undressed more often then he'd ever see his wife.

"I'm not as soon as I finish yelling at you! You're not my kin or husband. You're probably not even my brother-in-law!"

Winter looked over the brim of his coffee at his almost sister-in-law. "Talking to me or not, the gambler goes," he said between sips of coffee.

"Brother-in-law or not, the gambler stays!" Jamie answered.

"But he's nothing but a low-down—"

"You won't speak ill of the man I may decide to love."

Winter sat his cup down. "You don't know the first thing about love and marriage."

"And you do?" Jamie shot back. "You're the one who married a woman already married. That's at least one rule I know." Jamie smiled at the anger building in his face. "And you didn't even love her, so I guess that really makes you an expert on love and marriage."

They both ignored Kora as though she weren't in the room as they squared off to take their anger out on each other.

"I know that love is more than what you were doing in the grass last night." Winter's voice was low and cold.

"I wasn't doing anything you wouldn't like to be doing to Kora," Jamie said loud and hot tempered. "I've seen the way you look at her. But you can forget any fantasies you have because, despite her marrying habit, Kora is too frightened of men to enjoy loving one."

"You don't know her as well as you think, she—"

A loud pounding on the door ended his planned threat.

"I've come for my wife!" Andrew Adams yelled from the back porch. "She damn well better be ready to leave this morning, or I'll drag her home screaming."

Winter glared at Jamie. "We'll finish this later." He turned to Kora. "Have you changed your mind since last night about going with him?"

"No," Kora answered. "I'll never go with the man. No matter what his paper proves, please don't make me go with him."

Winter gave a nod. "Then stay here. I'll be back for breakfast in a few minutes."

He opened the back door and stepped out before Andrew had a chance to poke his head inside.

Kora could hear their voices but couldn't make out what they were saying. They moved from the porch to the hitching post in the yard. Andrew Adams sounded angry, but Winter's tone was low, almost calm.

Glancing out the window, she saw Andrew Adams waving a sheet of paper at Winter's face. Win took the paper and looked at it a long moment while Andrew pointed over and over again to the house. Then, to her shock, she saw Winter reach in his pocket and pull out a roll of bills. He peeled off a few and handed them to Adams. The little man took the money greedily. Winter turned slowly and headed back to the house, dismissing Adams with his action.

"What do you think's going on?" Jamie asked as she leaned over the sink.

"I don't know, but we're not going back to the dugout with that man," Kora said. "We were better off in Bryan with me working at the mercantile and you riding the mail runs. If I'd known he wasn't going to die, I never would have signed that paper Karen Noble threw in the trash."

"Looks like he's leaving, which I'd say was a real good

plan if he wants to stay healthy. Win must have bought you lock, stock, and barrel from husband number one.'' Jamie lost interest as Andrew Adams climbed into his wagon. ''I was hoping for a fight, though it wouldn't have been much of one. Win would probably just knock him down and Adams would crawl off. He's a sorry pick for a husband, Kora. Even bleeding and dying, Adams wouldn't have attracted me.''

''I wasn't attracted to him. I simply saw a way out,'' Kora answered.

''Appears you went a ways too far.'' Jamie giggled. ''It's costing old Win dearly. But when you said 'please don't make me go,' I could tell by Win's eyes that he'd die before Adams made you go. Or more likely kill the man.''

Kora didn't want to discuss what Winter had done or might have done. She needed to talk to him alone, but Jamie seemed to be settling in as if waiting for the second act. Kora had to get rid of her or risk hearing about everything she should have said for days. ''Go ask the gambler to breakfast.'' She tried the first thing she could think of to be rid of her sister.

''Are you kidding? Win will shoot him on sight!'' Jamie shouted. ''You think he dislikes your first husband, you should see how he feels about Wyatt.''

''I'll talk to Winter. Go.''

Jamie rushed past Winter when he opened the door. For a moment he just stood in the entrance staring at Kora. ''What's your name, your real name?''

Kora swallowed. ''Kora Anderson. My mother didn't think it was important to give girls middle names. I'm just plain Kora Anderson.''

He stared at her as if weighing every word. ''Don't lie to me.''

''I'm not.''

She wished she could follow Jamie, but she had to face Winter and all his anger. She asked, "Is he gone?"

"He's gone. At least for now. He seemed more interested in getting the money you took than in having you return home."

"You paid him?"

"I did."

"I'll pay you back, I swear." She couldn't believe after all the pain she'd caused this man she was now in debt to him.

"You don't have to pay me back, Kora." Winter moved a step closer. "My guess is Andrew Adams is the drifting kind. He'll probably move on and you'll never see him again. If you do, he'll have a hard time proving a proxy made out to Karen Noble and signed by Kora Anderson is legal. The way he was waving it in my face I doubt he could read the difference."

"But by law am I married to him?"

Winter laid his hand on her shoulder, and she fought not to pull away. His eyes were guarded now, unreadable. The granite man was back.

"I don't think so, but I have to know something more important than what the law will say," he said with the formality of a judge. "Do you love the man? Or did you ever love him?"

"No."

"Does he love you?"

"I don't see how he could," Kora answered. "If it turns out that I'm his wife, I'll leave, but I won't go back to him. I'll run. I never want to see the man again as long as I live."

Winter gripped her other shoulder and turned her to face him directly as he lowered his voice. "I still expect you to hold to our agreement. At the end of six months from our marriage I'll buy your tickets to California."

Kora looked confused. "Our bargain still stands?"

"It does." His grip loosened.

"All of it?"

Win refused to act as if he misunderstood what she was talking about. "All of it. As far as I'm concerned you're my wife, just as before; but the marriage bed doesn't have to be part of the bargain. I'll stay in the study. But as far as everyone knows, you're still my wife, my true wife."

"But I lied to you."

"I figure you had your reasons."

The lines in his face were hard and unyielding, but he'd settled her toppling world once more with his words. It didn't matter that he couldn't love her; he was offering her a harbor, a solid ground she'd never known. A shelter from the witchin' luck if only for a while.

"Thank you," she whispered, wondering how a man so kind could seem so cold. She'd never love him, or any man, but she'd be his wife if he wanted. She'd stay here until the house was legally hers forever, and then she'd give it to him. Not because he paid Andrew, but because he was willing to fight for her. No one had ever done that. "I was so frightened," she whispered. "Not of Andrew Adams, but that you'd make me leave."

Winter's arms closed around her shoulders and pulled her suddenly against him. He should have, he told himself. The one thing he couldn't stand was a liar. But he couldn't make her leave, and he didn't even want to think about why.

She hugged his waist as if holding on for life. Neither said a word as they held each other.

Closing her eyes, she pressed her cheek against the wall of his chest. With her lie, she'd ended what they'd started between them, but he would still stand at her side.

THIRTEEN

"MORNIN', WYATT." WINTER DROPPED HIS ARM FROM Kora's shoulder as Wyatt Mitchell stepped through the back door. His greeting was short of friendly, but Kora's nearness managed to take the edge off his anger. He couldn't very well start swearing at the gambler when Kora's arm still rested around his waist.

Dear God, he thought, *does the woman have any idea of the effect she has on a man?* Just as she'd misjudged the amount he'd offer for marriage, she'd mismeasured on how much he'd forgive to keep her. He'd been angry with her lie last night, but all it took was one look at her eyes this morning, and he knew he wanted her to stay.

He told himself she belonged to him. She'd made the deal for six months, not him. And he never gave up anything that was his. But Win knew it was far more. Just the thought of Andrew Adams getting close enough to touch her made Win furious. He'd keep her from the man even if he had to send her out of Texas.

"Mr. McQuillen." Wyatt nodded nervously as he twisted his hat in his hands. "Mrs. McQuillen." His expression left no doubt that breakfast was the last thing he thought he'd be doing with Win McQuillen after last night. "I'd like to apologize, sir. I assure you the stop Jamie and I made on our way back from town wasn't planned. We just thought to rest the horses a few minutes and enjoy the stars."

Winter fought the urge to say that he didn't know it was necessary to remove one's clothing to enjoy the night sky. But, again, Kora's nearness stopped him. She probably had no idea of what went on with Jamie and, it appeared, any man Jamie could hold still long enough to undress.

As Wyatt and Jamie moved to the table, Kora stepped away from Winter. She gave him the "be nice" glance males learn to recognize from a woman's eyes by the time they walk until they've settled into their graves. Winter wasn't going to be fool enough to ignore the look.

Kora lifted the platter of bacon and eggs from the warmer above the stove. "I'm glad you could join us for breakfast, Wyatt. Since it's only the four of us this morning, I thought we'd sit in the kitchen, like family."

"Thank you," Wyatt said, nursing his arm.

"That shoulder still bothering you?" Kora asked. "I could take a look at it."

"No!" Wyatt almost shouted. "It's doing fine."

Wyatt smiled at Kora with a mouth that looked to Winter as if it had a few too many teeth. The gambler made a grand effort of helping her with the platters and pulling out her chair while Winter watched. It didn't take much thought to know what Kora was doing. Winter knew she hoped the gambler would marry Jamie. But Winter wouldn't bet a cat-house token on that possibility.

Reluctantly he took his place at the table. He knew he should probably do something like offer to let Wyatt call him by his first name. After all, the man was probably only five years his junior and he might be in the family soon.

Assuming *he* was still "in the family," Win thought.

Winter ate without tasting the food as Jamie rattled on about her trip to town, and Wyatt divided his time between openly flirting with Jamie and subtly flirting with Kora. Winter frowned, thinking he seemed to be the only one at the table aware that a range war could break out at any point.

Suddenly he jerked and shoved himself away from the table. "I have to go," he mumbled. "It's time I was in the saddle."

Looking at Wyatt, Winter offered his hand. "I assume you'll be going back with the doc now that Cheyenne is out of danger."

Wyatt stood and took the offered hand. "I will. But I may be back if I'm welcome." His gambler's polish gave little away.

Glancing at Kora, Winter said, "You're welcome here."

Kora winked at her sister.

"I'll be back a little after dark." Winter reached for his hat.

Kora walked with him to the door. "I'll keep supper warm no matter how late and don't worry about Cheyenne. I'll look in on him often."

Thanking her with a nod, he walked out of the house. She was doing it again, he thought, playing the perfect wife. He fought the urge to reach for her. She had a kind of quiet strength that fascinated him.

The next few days passed in a maze of work. He had a fresh horse brought to him by midafternoon so he could stay in the saddle sixteen hours or more. Kora was up each morning by the time he dressed and had a huge breakfast ready for him, but he'd ride in so late at night that the evening meal was usually waiting for him on the kitchen table. He'd eat alone and fall asleep most nights without even undressing.

Winter wasn't aware of her coming into the study every night, but he couldn't help but notice the signs that she'd been there. Clean clothes were always on the chair. An extra blanket appeared the night it turned colder than usual. The fire never died as it would have if not tended.

At breakfast she was formal. She told him of Doc Gage's visits every few days and of how Wyatt always accompanied him. Cheyenne was getting restless, but strangely didn't seemed to mind her brother, Dan, dragging his chair up the stairs and sitting in the corner of his room each day. The two men had one thing in common. Both liked to be alone, and somehow that bonded them.

During the third week of Kora's stay, the weather turned warm. No more reports of riders or shootings happened and Winter began to relax. He even started to believe that the ranchers south might have killed their infected herds, or found another way besides crossing the Panhandle to get them to market.

Winter decided to ride in early and have supper with Kora. He'd sent a man over to Adams's farm and learned that Adams had spent half the money he'd gotten from Winter to stall the bank's foreclosure and the other half on supplies, including a large share of whiskey.

Logan had checked around enough to know that Andrew Adams would not make a fit husband for any woman.

The lawyer in town told Logan that since Kora hadn't signed the same name to the proxy it was worthless. The old man had been dead set against Winter picking Kora, but somehow she'd won him over.

At sunset when Winter walked through the back door, Kora was in the kitchen. She glanced up at him with those bluer than blue eyes and smiled. For a moment it was hard for him to imagine himself ever being without her. She looked so much like she belonged not only in the house, but in his life.

"I was hoping you'd make it in early tonight." She wiped a strand of hair away with a floured hand, leaving a white streak across her cheek. "I made a special dinner. Cheyenne thinks he can make it down to the table. He'll be happy you're here."

"And you?"

"I'm glad, also. I hoped to have a chance to talk to you tonight." She paused and pulled a pie from the oven. "Supper will be ready by the time you wash up."

Winter took a step back out the doorway. "I'll only be a minute."

"Win?"

It was the first time she'd said his name, and he liked the way she used his nickname, as Logan and Cheyenne did. "Yes?" He waited.

"The washstand's ready in our room if you want to use it. I could bring you up clean clothes."

He started to say "don't bother." He could wash on the porch. She didn't have to wait on him. But instead he nodded, silently agreeing with her, and walked across the kitchen and up the stairs to the attic.

He took his time dressing, enjoying the room. When she'd suggested moving a bed up to the attic, he'd thought it was a fool idea, but now it seemed like home. She'd made some changes since he'd seen the room. A low shelf of books lined one wall between the north windows, and she'd made nightstands out of boxes. He noticed the books were all ones he'd read as a child. They started with his McGuffy Readers and went all the way to Mark Twain and Jules Verne.

Win smiled as he looked around. He could send to Dallas

for a real bedroom set and buy leather-bound books finer than any in the study. The room could have all matching wood like they advertised in the Dallas paper with bookshelves as high as the rafters between each of the windows.

Surveying the room, he thought she sure didn't look like a woman ready to pull up stakes. She'd even brought up the little writing desk the captain's wife had in the sunroom. Kora had placed it in a corner so she could look out the windows in two directions.

He moved over to her dressing area and peeked behind the folding panel. Everything was in order. Her clothes, her comb, a perfume bottle. He moved closer and lifted the corner of the hankerchief she used to cover her dresser. Miss Allie had given him the fancy hankerchief one Christmas years ago, and he'd forgotten where he put it. Now it seemed to have found a home.

Kora's soft footsteps only gave him a moment to move before she was on the landing.

"I brought you clean clothes, but they've been mended several times. Would you mind it if I picked out a few new shirts for you the next time I'm in town?"

"I wouldn't mind." He took the shirt. "But I'll be in town tomorrow for a meeting. Make a list and I'll pick up anything you need."

Their words were natural, things any husband might say to any wife, but Winter was very much aware she didn't think of him as truly her husband. He was just another way, like Adams, to survive. Every morning when he rode out, he wondered if she'd be waiting for him when he returned. Or would she load up her sister and brother and the few things they'd come with and leave? Could she swear never to return to him as easily as she had Andrew Adams?

The possibility had turned over in his mind again and again. He'd told himself that if she left he'd close the house and never open it or think of her again. But he knew he'd probably go after her. Something about this woman fit him as perfectly as kid leather. Just as he would have offered far more to get her to marry him than she'd thought, he'd do more to keep her than she might imagine.

They drifted through the meal with talk of the ranch. Cheyenne rapid-fired questions until he grew tired and declined dessert in favor of bed. Jamie had gone back to town with Dr. Gage when he'd visited that morning, and so the room seemed suddenly empty.

"Would you like dessert on the porch?" Kora asked when Winter returned from helping Cheyenne up the stairs. "I made apple pie."

He followed her to the long porch running the length of the back of the house. They moved away from the side where the sunroom's light shone across the porch. Dan sat in his room beside a half-eaten meal.

Kora hugged herself, as if cold, as she looked in on her brother. "He'll start his night walk soon, then turn out the light. Sometimes he sleeps in the chair, sometimes in bed. Once in a while he even goes to the barn and curls up in the back of a wagon. But he'll be up by dawn for his morning walk. If I don't have his breakfast waiting for him when he returns, he won't eat a thing until dark."

"Has it always been like this?"

"Pretty much. I don't remember what he was like at first. I was too young. He and Mother somehow worked out the pattern, and it hasn't changed no matter where we move or what the weather. I'm not even sure he knows Mama died. During the day he takes his chair places to sit . . . usually where the least people are. I was surprised when he moved it upstairs to Cheyenne's room."

"What happened to him?"

"We have little idea. Mom said once he was just a boy

when he left, and for a while he wrote of battle after battle. Then not a word for over a year. The man who brought him home said someone told him they just found him sitting in a battlefield among the bodies.''

''There are hospitals for people like him, Kora. Doctors who might help.'' Winter sat on the porch railing and shoveled a large piece of warm apple pie into his mouth.

''Would they have clean clothes laid out every morning in the same place where he left the dirty ones? Would they only feed him things he'll eat like eggs and bread? Would they let him walk, never interrupting his path?''

He couldn't see her face, but he guessed the things she didn't say and suddenly he was voicing them aloud. ''Would they check on him every night? Would they put a log on the fire so it wouldn't go out? Would they cover him with an extra blanket?'' Winter set the pie down forgotten. ''Would they kiss him good night in his sleep?''

''I don't kiss him good night!'' Kora snapped as she walked farther away from the window's light.

Winter was suddenly angry. All the special attention he thought she was paying him was nothing more than she was doing for her war-scarred brother. She'd made the pie for him because she knew he loved apples. She laid out his clothes. She kept him warm.

He looked across the wide yard to the barn and bunkhouse. Several lights were still on. More than likely a few of his men were in the dark on the porch of the bunkhouse smoking one last cigarette before turning in for the night.

Glancing at Kora in the dim light, he knew this was not the place for private talk. Their voices could drift on the breeze too easily.

He leaned against the porch banister and pushed all emotion aside. ''You said you wanted to talk to me?''

Kora was as far away from him as the porch railing would allow.

"If we're to get through the next few months, you have to stop avoiding me," she whispered.

"What?"

She moved a few feet closer. "I said, you're avoiding me."

"What?" he answered again.

"You heard me," she said as she came closer. "You're not as deaf as Dan."

Winter smiled. "I'm glad you recognize some difference."

Kora was within three feet of him now. "Jamie says you're sorry you married me with all the trouble over Andrew Adams, and you're trying to ignore me away."

"That doesn't work." Winter laughed. "If it did, Jamie would be weeks gone." He unfolded his arms. "Are you aware you always call the man Andrew Adams?"

"Answer my question first," she replied.

"All right. No. I'm not avoiding you. I've got a lot of work to do. With spring comes a great deal of work on top of watching for sick cattle." He knew even as he said the words that they were a lie not only to her, but to himself. He had been avoiding her. Not with much success. Logan always managed to find him and give him a rambling report of all she'd done. In the old man's eyes, Kora was becoming a saint.

She moved to the railing a foot away from him now and stared out into the night. "Jamie says you don't want to get used to me being around. She doesn't know about our bargain, but she's guessing."

"Jamie's only rattling," Winter said, very much aware of her nearness. "I'm not much interested in what Jamie says."

Kora leaned on the railing, arching her back slightly. "I'll try to be considerate."

Win was starting to hate that word.

The far-off sound of a horse and buggy chimed through the night. Winter slipped his arm around Kora's waist as they both watched the darkness. There were a hundred things that needed saying between them, but the feel of her back resting lightly against his chest was enough for the present.

After a few minutes a buggy pulled up to the back and Jamie jumped out and broke into a dead run until she spotted them on the porch. She slowed to a stroll.

Moving off the porch toward her, Win yelled, "I thought you were staying in town."

"I thought you died!" Jamie shouted angrily. "I guess that's what we both get for thinking."

He laughed, guessing her anger was directed at someone else other than him. He looked into the darkness of the buggy.

"Evenin', Doc." Winter tried to hide the surprise from his voice. He'd have bet ten to one on the gambler.

"Evenin'," Steven Gage mumbled with controlled anger. "Wyatt was out of town tonight, so I thought I'd bring Jamie home."

"Is that why she's so mad? The gambler's out of town?" Winter thought about shouting to his sister-in-law that the gambler was probably running for another state after knowing her for days.

"No," Gage mumbled with uncharacteristic rage. "She's upset because we stopped a while back to look at the stars."

Running his fingers through his hair, Winter tried to listen without laughing. He'd heard this before. Stargazing seemed to be Jamie's favorite pastime. ''She didn't like that?''

''Oh, she liked it fine until I went and did a foolish thing like asking her to marry me.'' The doc's voice rose. ''Then she called me every name she could think of and accused me of trying to put her in chains. She says she's never speaking to me again as long as she lives.''

Win almost felt sorry for the doctor. He was a good man who didn't know how lucky he was. ''Don't worry, Doc. It won't last. I can almost promise you she'll be talking to you sooner than you'd like.''

Gage shrugged. ''Guess I'm out of practice when it comes to women.''

''I'm not sure practicing helps.'' Winter laughed. ''You're welcome to spend the night if you like.''

''No, thanks. I've got a man to check on in the Breaks Settlement. I promised the old woman they call Rae that I'd take a turn sitting with him tonight. But thanks for the offer. I'll stop by tomorrow and look in on Cheyenne before I head back to town.''

Winter waved the doc off. ''Be careful.''

When he looked back at the house, Kora was inside. He could hear Jamie shouting about how the gambler had left her for some sudden business and she was never speaking to him again.

From the corner of the house Dan walked out of the shadows. Winter fell into step with the silent man, and they walked in a wide circle without either seeming to notice the other.

When Dan finally returned to the sunroom, Winter went to his study. As he closed the door, he noticed a large slice of pie and a glass of milk by the fire. Part of him wanted to scream at the top of his lungs that he wasn't Dan, then run up the stairs and prove to Kora just how alive he was.

But the reasonable part told him to sit down and eat the pie, then close his eyes and try to sleep. Yet Kora wouldn't leave his thoughts. Somehow, she'd tiptoed into his life. Her soft words and gentle ways had passed through the barbed wire around his feelings. If he believed in luck, he'd say all his luck was riding on her staying in his life.

FOURTEEN

KORA SNUGGLED INTO HER WARM COVERS AND watched the night sky. In a few minutes it would be time to get up and start the day, but right now was a quiet time when she listened to the music of a sleeping world. She could hear coyotes howling, horses moving in the corral, the house creaking slightly as it shifted in the wind. A few clouds threatened rain, but only managed to deliver enough moisture to occasionally cause a few drops to fall from the roof.

Rising and walking to the window, Kora watched the apple trees slow dancing in the shadows and the windmill beside the barn turning in time as it pumped water.

Far into the night a light flickered like a firefly who hadn't yet found its mate. Kora watched as the light drew closer.

From the shadows of darkness, came a rider dressed in black.

Alarm brought Kora full awake. Three men in black had shot at Winter and Jamie and wounded Cheyenne! Why would one of Winter's men be coming in now? Everyone knew the shift changes came at full dawn.

The man came closer. The tiny light became a huge torch.

He didn't slow as he reached the center ground of the ranch, but raised in his saddle like a black knight preparing to fight. He swung the torch in a mighty arc and let it fly.

"No!" Kora screamed as the fire hit the stack of hay beside the barn and seemed to explode.

She ran down the stairs, stopping only a moment to bang on Jamie's door. "Fire!" she screamed. "Fire!"

Win met her in the hall. "Stay back!" he yelled. "Until I know it's safe."

Kora was right behind him as he reached the barn. Men were dressing as they poured out of the bunkhouse.

"Wet the barn!" Win yelled. "Let the hay burn."

Within minutes, like a colony of ants, everyone had found a job. The well, though closer to the barn, was much too slow a way to get water. A line was formed from the windmill trough. Jamie and Kora both took a link along with the men swinging buckets as fast as they could toward the flames. The wind made the splashing water icy, and almost everyone stood barefoot in mud. Jamie was probably warmest in her buckskins with a rifle strapped on her back.

"Take off that rifle, Jamie!" Win yelled from closer to the fire. "It'll bruise your shoulders the way it's swinging back and forth."

"No!" Jamie shouted in return. "If that rider comes again, I'll be ready."

Win jerked his head toward the house, where Cheyenne sat on the porch, his wounded leg propped up on the railing. A rifle lay across his lap; another rested beside his chair.

When Jamie glanced at Win, he winked. "We're covered," he said, "but thanks for the offer to protect my ranch."

Jamie laughed but didn't slow the line down as she answered. ''I'm not protecting this place, I'm planning on shooting the fellow for waking me up so early.''

Several of the men voiced similar feeling toward whoever started the fire.

Within minutes the fire was under control, burning only the hay and leaving the barn and corral safe. The flames were high, lighting the night sky. Kora and Jamie moved toward the house as Win kept watch. The men milled around guessing the identity of the rider Kora had seen.

Just as Kora reached the steps, a scream shattered the air. A horrible cry of someone in great agony.

''Dan!'' both women said at once.

''The fire must have frightened him.'' Jamie looked across the smoky night for her brother.

''I'll get the blanket!'' Kora shouted as she darted to the house.

Jamie ran as fast as she could toward the open field, screaming Dan's name as though she believed he might answer her.

Dan was kneeling a few hundred yards from the house. He covered his ears and closed his eyes as he screamed. The fire from the haystack still danced behind him and black smoke bellowed, choking the dawn.

''Dan!'' Jamie knelt beside him. ''It's only a fire, Dan. It's only a fire.''

Kora joined her in seconds. ''It's no use calling him,'' she said. A slow rain began to fall. ''You know when he's like this, the only thing to do is wrap him tight and carry him back.'' Tears ran down her cheeks. How many times had she and Jamie found him like this and carried him back, kicking and screaming, to his bed? Sometimes he would have spent all his energy and fall asleep. Sometimes they'd have to tie him down until the madness passed.

Dan pushed them away as they tried to cover him with

the blanket. Their efforts only brought louder screams. As he fought his demons, he lashed out, knocking Jamie to the ground without even seeing her.

Jamie jumped up when Kora touched her shoulder. "Maybe we should let him scream until he's exhausted."

"No," Jamie answered. "He'll only make himself sick."

Both women moved closer to their brother. His movements pushed them away once more, knocking them both onto the rain-slick ground.

"Wait!" Win shouted from behind them.

"Stay out of this, cowboy!" Jamie jumped to her feet. "This is our responsibility."

Win glanced at Kora.

"Let him try," Kora whispered. "He can't make matters any worse."

Dan was now curled into a ball in the dirt. He'd began shouting names from a roll call long dead.

Win took a deep breath. "Soldier!" he snapped. "Soldier, stand at attention! You're getting the uniform dirty."

To both girls' surprise, Dan slowly stood. His list changed to battle names and numbers dead and wounded.

"Now march!" Winter commanded.

Dan slowly began his walk, circling back to his chair. When he finally sat down, he was silent once more. Kora stepped inside and retrieved a dry blanket as Jamie removed his wet shirt and boots.

Win watched as both women wrapped the spider-thin man tightly in quilts. Once again he was touched by the way they cared for Dan. Win had missed that kind of family, and the sight of them made him feel as if there were a cavern in his heart.

He dried his face at the washstand and almost ran for the privacy of his study. Stripping off his wet clothes, Win wished he could clear his thoughts as easily.

As he pulled on a dry pair of pants, Kora walked into the room. She stood just inside the door looking like a child who'd fallen down the chimney. Her nightgown was spotted in black, her feet muddy, her hair a shambles of ashes and dirt from where she'd fallen in the field.

Win stepped aside and reached for a clean shirt. "You look like you've been riding drag during a mud storm."

She hugged herself and took a step backward. "I just stopped to say thank you before I go clean up."

"Come get warm first," Win said, offering his fire. "And no thanks needed."

Kora moved closer. As she stretched her hands toward the fire, Win pushed a footstool close for her to sit on. "That gown looks ruined," he mumbled from behind her as he rummaged for another shirt. "Why don't you put this on while I get some more wood? You'll catch your death if you go back up to the attic all wet."

Kora slipped out of her gown and into Winter's shirt. The shirttail hung to her knees. She cleaned off mud from her legs and arms using the few clean spots from their damp clothes.

When Win returned, he carried a small tub and a bucket of water. "For your hair," he mumbled awkwardly.

Without a word she knelt and leaned her head over the tub. For a moment Win didn't move, then slowly he dropped to one knee beside her and the water poured over her head. She shook the dirt from her hair and let her fingers run through the tangles as he slowly poured.

When she finished, he handed her a towel he'd brought in over his shoulder. She covered her head and began to rub the water out.

His large hands lightly touched hers, pushing them aside so that he could dry her hair. Kora raised her head and enjoyed the feel of the warm towel moving over her. He worked the towel down, drying all the way to the ends in long, sure strokes. His towel-covered hand returned again and again to her scalp, slowly moving over her hair.

Kora rested her arm against his leg and leaned her cheek on his knee as he continued to stroke. She was almost asleep when he stopped.

"Thank you," she whispered. "No one's ever done that for me before."

He sat, using the footstool to lean his back on, and pulled her against his side. "Thank you," he said more to himself than her. "I enjoyed doing it. Watching your hair turn from warm honey to sunlight as it dried was a pleasure.

"Besides, I should be thanking you for your help. If you hadn't yelled, we might have gotten to the fire a minute later and lost the barn along with several horses stabled there."

"Why would someone do such a thing?" She raised to look at him. "It doesn't make sense."

"Tell me every detail you saw," Win quizzed. "The markings of the horse, how fast he rode, how tall, anything."

As Kora related all she remembered, Win's frown grew deeper.

When she finished, he whispered, "You saw no face?"

Kora shook her head.

Win let out a long breath. "You may have seen just enough to put you in great danger."

He moved his hand slowly over her hair.

"Don't worry." Kora tried to make her voice light. "I can take care of myself and Jamie's always around. After all, it's only till summer."

"Until then"—Win moved his hand into her hair—"with all that's going on, I'd like there to be peace between us."

Kora leaned forward and hugged her knees. ''I'd like that, also,'' she said. ''I've never lived in a place like this. It's not the house so much as the way of life. All the men treat me with such respect, and there is so much to do. I guess I thought life on a ranch would be dull and lonely, but I feel like I'm standing in the center of a swarm of bees.''

Win laughed. ''I feel that way since you moved in. I've been alone for so long, I'd forgotten what it was like to live in a tribe.''

She looked at him. ''Is that what we are, a tribe?''

''Very much so,'' he answered. ''When I was little, I lived with my mother's tribe. Everyone took care of everyone else. I saw that tonight with you and Jamie on the bucket line, and again with Dan. I'll miss it when you're gone.''

Kora turned toward the fire so he couldn't see her face. He'd said he'd miss them, but he hadn't said stay.

FIFTEEN

WINTER LEFT THE SALOON AND HEADED ACROSS THE street to the mercantile. The ranchers' meeting had lasted hours longer than he'd thought it would, and he'd downed several more drinks than he needed to keep his head clear. Most of the men felt they had to have their say, even if they were only repeating an idea someone else had already voiced. Then H. D. Worth, who'd argue with a dead frog, had to counter everyone's speech. And of course Lewis, who'd bet that same frog how high he would jump, felt a need to summarize anything Worth said. All in all, it was a waste of valuable time. They wanted to help, but anyone who knew the land knew Winter's ranch was the one that would be crossed if the cattle moved. It was in the middle of the only practical trail, and it was too big to be missed.

"Afternoon," Kendell, the mercantile owner, said as Winter forced the door shut against a north wind.

Kendell was a man graying into his forties with the thin look of a buzzard about him. He was always pleasant, helpful, and almost too friendly. He'd inherited the business from his father and married his wife by blind luck. Everyone except him seemed to know that his treasure lay in her and not the store. But Kendell valued only things he could keystone and sell for double the price.

"Good afternoon," Win mumbled. "My order ready?"

"You bet. I've got it boxed with the bunkhouse order on the porch, ready to load in your wagon." Kendell glanced at the last box on his counter. "I was just waiting to see if there was anything you'd want to add to the missus' order."

"Shirts," Winter remembered. "She said to throw in three new work shirts for me."

"Yes, sir." Kendell pulled the shirts from the standard stock. "How about something for her?" His eyes widened in hope.

Win frowned at the insanity of the question. How in the hell was he supposed to know what she might want extra? If she'd wanted anything else, she could have added it to her list.

Before he could say no, Kendell grinned, taking Winter's hesitation positively. "I got a pretty brush that came in, or all kinds of new dry goods."

Glancing at the case of pens on the counter, Winter asked, "You have any pen holders and things that go on a lady's desk?"

He reached in his pocket and felt the scrap of paper Kora had used to sign over the house to him. She'd completed her grocery list on the other side. The paper had been poor, but her handwriting smooth. The kind of handwriting that should be on quality paper.

Kendell took a long breath, enjoying the smell of money, and opened the case. "I've got a inkstand with double enameled finish on an iron base and a pen rack on the side. It came all the way from Chicago. Fine, heavy, durable, and worth every nickel."

Win nodded.

Kendell pulled it from the case. "And it's got a pencil box with it that . . ."

Win nodded again.

"A letter opener? It wouldn't be complete without that."

"I'll take the set. Include paper and anything else a woman would need for a writing table." Kora had put the desk in the attic; the least he could do was see it fully stocked.

Win folded Kora's scrap of paper and slid it into his breast pocket. He didn't care that the paper gave the house to him. The house was hers. What mattered was that she'd offered. That made the note valuable.

Kendell quickly slipped the most expensive items from the case and began wrapping them. "This will take me only a minute to total up, if you'd like to look around."

Winter only wanted to get back to his ranch, but he waited. He wandered over to the ladies' corner to say hello to Kendell's wife. Winter had always liked the woman. She was one of the few people he found it easy to talk to in town. Maybe it was because she wasn't afraid of him, or maybe it was because neither expected anything of the other more than friendship.

"Afternoon, Win." She smiled at him over her knitting. "How's the new wife?"

"Fine, Mrs. Kendell," Win said, wishing he could ask the woman a few questions. She was ten years his senior, and he'd always thought Kendell got himself a lady of quality when he married Sarah. She treated every customer as though they'd dropped by for tea. There was an honesty about her Winter liked. He wished she would advise him about how he should treat a wife, but judging from Kendell's example, she might not know.

"I saw you buying her a desk set. She'll like that, Win."

"You think so?"

Sarah Kendell put down her knitting. "I can think of only one thing she might like more."

Winter watched as she moved her hand along the shelves marked LADIES.

"When she was in here the other day, I helped her pick out a few things. She's delightful. I remember her from a few times before, but she always seemed too shy to say much." Sarah looked at him with approval in her gaze. "You've been good for her, Win. I could see it in her eyes."

He didn't see how. Sarah's praise made him shift and want to change the subject. "Didn't she pick up any of the ladies' things when she was in?" He remembered seeing what looked to be a new nightgown and wrapper.

Sarah smiled in understanding of his discomfort. "She chose a few things, but was very conservative in her shopping for personal items. Any woman can always use a few frills, especially when she's a bride."

The woman didn't need to say more. Winter got the point. "Would you mind picking out a few things, Mrs. Kendell? And make sure to add another nightgown."

"I'd be delighted," Sarah answered. "A little lace can go a long way in making a woman feel special."

He was thankful she didn't tell him the price or discuss details. He trusted her judgment, and she knew he could afford whatever she selected.

Win thanked her when she handed him the things wrapped in brown paper and tied with string.

"Tell your wife to stop by and visit a while next time she's in town," Sarah Kendell said. "She's a rare one I think, and I'd like to call her a friend."

"I'll tell her," Winter answered as he left the store and put the bundle on the seat.

As he stepped to climb into the wagon, Mary Anna called

his name, drawing his attention, spooking the horses, and almost making him fall.

"Yes?" he grumbled as he turned.

"Winter, what are you doing in town? I'd think there would be enough to keep you busy on the ranch." She twirled a parasol over her shoulder.

"I'm in kind of a hurry." Win tried to stand still and not be rude. Mary Anna's aunt and uncle were well known in the county. Once her visit was over and she'd returned to south Texas, he didn't want bad blood to remain.

She moved closer. Too close, to his way of thinking. He could smell her perfume thick in the air.

"How is that dear little plain wife of yours?" Mary Anna's eyes widened suddenly, and she covered her mouth with a lace glove. "Oh, my, I didn't mean to say 'plain' out loud!" She looked truly horrified for a moment, then smiled as all beautiful women do who are always forgiven. "I'm sure she tries with what she has."

Win wasn't amused or insulted. Mary Anna was too shallow to affect him. The simple fact that he hadn't noticed before irritated him. "My wife is fine." He couldn't help but compare the over-rouged, overdressed, pampered woman before him to Kora and find the sight standing so near now greatly lacking.

She moved even closer. "You should have married me," she whispered. "We're alike, you and I. We'll both do anything to get what we want. And we both want the same thing."

"No," Win answered without backing up, refusing to allow her to pin him against the wagon. "I want the land. You want what you can take from it."

"You'll regret not getting rid of her and marrying me. She's such a fool, she even offered to give you the house.

Any woman with the sense of a turnip would keep it in her own name.''

''It's over and done,'' Win answered, seeing no point in discussing his marriage with her. ''We're married and the house is hers.''

''No,'' Mary Anna whispered between snarled teeth. ''It may be done, but it's not over. Someday you'll be sorry for making me the laughingstock of this whole town. I told everyone I was riding out to give you another chance. I even ordered clothes for our honeymoon while I was waiting for you to ask again. I wired my father about the marriage just before I came out. You'll be sorry you made me look the fool.''

Win turned his back on the lady, not caring how it might look. He climbed into the wagon and slapped the horses into action, suddenly in a hurry to get home.

Normally, Win didn't like driving a team as much as riding, but it had been practical to pick up supplies if he was coming to town. And today he needed the time to cool off. His teeth hurt from forcing his mouth to remain closed in front of Mary Anna. A hundred replies came to mind. All of which would have caused a stir in the town if he'd voiced them.

On horseback, he would have cut a straight line to his ranch, but by wagon the road was winding and slow. The silence of the afternoon and the boredom offered him time to think. A wife, even one who lied, seemed a far sight better than Mary Anna.

He'd spent hours thinking of Kora these past days and resented most of the time because he felt it had pulled him away from more important duties. But now there was nothing to do. No chores he was neglecting. No men he needed to talk to. No corner of his ranch he should check before dark. Now he could think of Kora and thank his lucky stars that she'd been the one to stand up with him and not Mary Anna.

By the time he reached the ranch house he had several speeches practiced and ready for Kora. He wasn't going to be one of those husbands like Kendell who didn't know the value of a good wife. He'd tell Kora how much he appreciated her. A few tickets to California seemed a small price to pay for all she was doing.

Logan met him and drove the wagon on down to the bunkhouse kitchen. Winter balanced the box under one arm and the package Sarah Kendell had wrapped on the other shoulder. As he kicked open the kitchen door, the sight before him almost made him drop his load.

Jamie, buckskins covered in flour, sat at the table trying to force a ball of dough into a pie pan. The kitchen was a mess with pots and supplies everywhere.

"What are you doing?" Winter asked as he lowered the box beside the pump.

"What does it look like I'm doing, you idiot? I'm cooking supper." She gave the dough a hard punch, and it spread around her fingers. "And I'll tell you the same thing I told that Indian friend of yours. Stay out of my way or I'll shoot the other leg."

Winter picked up Kora's gifts and moved around Jamie, giving her as much room as possible. When he was safely on the other side of the kitchen, he asked, "Where's Kora?"

He prepared to duck as Jamie pried the dough off her fingers and tried to spread it in smaller pieces into the pan. "She's not here. Doc came by a few hours ago and asked her to go with him. He says he's got a man down the road who's got to be operated on or he'll die for sure."

Jamie attacked the pan once more. "He could have asked me, even if I wouldn't have answered him 'cause I'm never going to speak to him again as long as I live. But no! He runs up here like the house is on fire and begs Kora to go with him to the Breaks Settlement.'' Jamie looked up, her eyes dancing with mischief. ''So she leaves me to cook supper for you and Cheyenne.'' Jamie laughed. ''Exciting, ain't it?''

''I'm not hungry.'' Winter wasn't sure he trusted her cooking.

''Me, either!'' Cheyenne yelled from the dining room behind Winter. ''I'd rather eat my own knuckle than your cooking, Jamie.''

''Well, good!'' Jamie yelled back. ''Then all I'll have to make is the gravy.''

Winter waved at Cheyenne and climbed the stairs as they continued to yell at each other. For a moment he remembered when the house was silent and all he had to suffer through was the loneliness. It seemed like a much simpler life.

He straightened the things on Kora's desk without fully taking his gaze from the window and the road beyond. If the doc had any sense, he'd have Kora home before dark. The Breaks Settlement, as everyone called it, was really just a group of drifters and folks down on their luck who lived along the southeast boarder of Winter's ranch. The land wasn't any good for farming or running cattle, so as far as Winter knew, no one owned it, but the uneven hills of rock offered shelter from the wind. Sometime after the War Between the States, men started camping out there when passing through. Buffalo hunters probably built the first shacks, and the place didn't look as if it had been improved upon since. Some of the drifters had stayed, finding work on nearby ranches when they had to, but mostly they just lived off the land.

The sun set without him seeing any sign of her return.

The settlement wasn't the kind of place he liked to think of Kora being after dark. He washed and put on a clean shirt, telling himself that she'd be home when he finished. He'd grown used to supper being ready and her having everything in order when he came home. Even on those late nights, he could sense her near, and just knowing she was upstairs asleep was calming.

But he couldn't feel her presence now. Not even when he went to her dressing area and set the bag of lady's things on the stool. She'd left everything in order. His large hand felt awkward touching her belongings. Almost as if he were touching her.

Finally he went downstairs, knowing he'd waited as long as he could. Jamie and Cheyenne had stopped yelling at each other. In fact, the house was dark except for the kitchen.

When Winter walked into the kitchen, he was surprised for the second time in an hour. Cheyenne stood by the stove frying eggs. He leaned heavily on a wooden crutch, but he managed well. Jamie still sat at the table, the dough no closer to being reincarnated into a pie crust. Dan sat in the corner with his chair turned to face the window.

"Want some eggs?" Cheyenne offered. "I cooked enough for you and Dan."

"No, thanks," Winter answered as he crossed the room. "I'm going to ride out to meet Kora and the doc."

"Good idea." Cheyenne's concern mirrored Winter's. "I'd go with you if I could. You think you can find her in the settlement?"

"If she's still in the settlement, I'll find her."

He heard Jamie saying something about maybe they stopped to look at the stars, but Winter wasn't listening. Suddenly the urgency to find Kora was a hunger he could wait no longer to satisfy.

SIXTEEN

WINTER RODE THROUGH THE NIGHT PUSHING HIS horse faster as he approached the settlement. He was slowed by staying with the road, but he didn't want to take any chance of passing Dr. Gage in the dark. The wind had turned cold and whirled around him, making him think he heard things when nothing was there. Clouds blocked the moon and most of the stars. By the time he saw the lights of the Breaks Settlement, he could taste icy rain in the air. But the moisture did little to cool his anger. This was no place for a lady after dark.

The number of shacks had doubled since he'd last ridden by the area, and several outdoor campfires dotted the uneven land. Breaks Settlement was a deformed town with no businesses or patterns of streets. There were no schools, or churches, or even barns. Most of the horses were corralled in a small boxed canyon near the end of the settlement. Lodgings were as simple as wagons turned on their side against the wind or crude houses made of anything handy, waterproofed with thick layers of sod for warmth.

Win lowered his hat and silently urged his horse to pick his way through the scattering of trash along trails marked by ruts. He fought the urge to raise his bandanna from his throat, for the smell was worse than riding drag on a cattle drive.

Anger toward Gage for bringing Kora to this place began to bubble over in his mind. He liked the young doctor, but the man should have considered Kora's safety if not his own.

He rode among the dwellings looking for any sign of the doc's buggy. But the lights in the shacks were small, and the tiny beams escaping from between cracks offered little help as the night grew darker.

The hollow sound of a mouth harp drifted through the air. Win turned toward what looked to be the largest dwelling. Voices grew from the sounds of the night to human pitch as he came upon a long lean-to rigged with a tarp from a couple of Conestogas.

"Evenin'." The harp music stopped, and a man stood at the edge of the covered area. He was rail thin, and the rags he wore made it seem as if his clothes were fringed in the darkness.

Three tables were set up beneath the covering, and Win could make out a dozen men, maybe more, playing cards. Large jugs of home brew dotted the dirt. Win guessed he'd have to down half a jug of the home brew before he could stomach the smell of unwashed humans and open outhouses.

"Somethin' I can do for you?" The harp player was no more friendly than his music had been cheery.

Win didn't raise his hat as he would have done to talk to someone in town. He wasn't sure it would be wise to let anyone see his face. He recognized two of the men at the closest table as cowhands he'd had to fire a few months back for drinking.

"I come looking for the doc." He kept his voice low, hoping only the harp player would hear it.

"Haven't seen him." The man snorted a laugh. "He ain't a regular around the tables."

Winter clicked at his horse and began to back away. He saw no need to thank the man.

The harp player lifted the wire to his mouth, but just before he played, he added, "If anyone here's in need of a doc, it's probably Miller down by the creek. I heard he got shot a while back."

"Thanks." Win turned his horse toward the creek.

After passing several empty campsites, he spotted the doctor's buggy pulled up to a sod house. The light barely escaped through the oilcloth hanging over the two tiny windows in front, but Win could see that a lamp burned inside.

Just as he leaned forward to swing his leg to the ground, the door of the place opened. Win had his Colt halfway out of its holster before he saw Kora step from the doorway.

Her arms were loaded down with rags, and her hair was as bright as sunshine with the firelight behind her. She dropped the rags in a basket by the door and wiped her forehead with the back of her hand.

"Kora?" He said her name so low he wasn't sure it had passed his lips.

She looked up.

"Kora!" Dr. Gage yelled from inside. "Hurry!"

With only a moment's hesitation, she turned back inside, leaving the door open.

Win swung from the saddle and tied his horse to the doc's buggy. He walked slowly to the doorway, already guessing what he might see.

The cabin was filthy, as he'd expected. It looked more like a rat's nest than a human's home. A man lay in front of the fire on a crude cot made of ropes and logs. Dr. Gage knelt over him working frantically on his chest. His hands were spotted in blood to the elbow, and his face was dripping sweat. Kora stood beside him following rapid-fire orders.

Win watched as his little wife, who shied away from him, helped Dr. Gage like a seasoned nurse. He wanted to be mad because she'd left without telling him, because she'd put herself in danger, because she'd worried him half to death. Because she'd left Jamie to cook. But he couldn't be angry. Not with the pride welling in him.

"I've got it!" the doc yelled as he pulled a hand from halfway inside the man's chest. "The bullet is out."

Kora took a breath and for the first time looked up. If Winter's presence surprised her, she showed no sign of it. She simply smiled that quiet, shy smile of hers and returned to her chores.

Gage glanced at her, then Winter. "Hello, Win," he said without any note of apology. "We're about finished here."

"Take your time," Win mumbled. He leaned against the doorframe and tried to wait patiently as they worked at sewing up the man. Not wanting to watch, Win glanced around the room. His gaze settled on a black duster hanging on a peg. For a few minutes he couldn't think of why it looked so familiar. Then he remembered. The three men in black who'd shot at him and Cheyenne the day Jamie rode with them.

Slowly, almost casually, he walked over to the peg and turned the duster around in the light. Sure enough, there was a bullet hole about gut level, maybe a little higher. This man had been one of the three, but from the looks of him now, he couldn't have sat a horse, much less have ridden in to start the fire.

"How long ago was this man shot?" Win asked over his shoulder.

"Several days," the doc volunteered as he worked. "At

first I thought it was too risky to try and take the bullet out. Then, when he got worse, I figured it would be the only chance to save his life. And it's a slim chance. Yours was the nearest place I could go to get someone I could trust to stay with me through the operation. And Kora did, just like a trooper."

The doc smiled at Kora as he praised, making Win feel a sharp stab of jealousy.

Kora stood and washed her hands as the doc wrapped the wound. "I've no desire to be a nurse, but I'm glad I could help."

Win moved closer to her. "You left Jamie to cook," he whispered.

"I had to." Kora glanced at him as though she couldn't believe how selfish he sounded.

Win cleared his throat. "This is one of the men who shot at Cheyenne and Jamie. He tried to kill us all in that ambush."

Dr. Gage stood. "You think it could be?"

Winter faced Gage. "The men were wearing black dusters and I put a bullet in one's gut and one in another's shoulder."

"Are you sure?"

"That's my bullet you just dug out, Doc."

Gage took a long breath. "Well, this man's not going anywhere for several days. If he makes it through the night, we'll tell the sheriff and let him do the arresting."

Winter frowned. "When the ambush happened, I figured the men were from down south maybe sent to scare us. But if this fellow's here, the other two may be, also. I don't think you should stay in the settlement tonight, Doc."

"I'll be all right." Gage waved them out. "You may have put the bullet in this man, but I might have killed him trying to dig it out. We'll know one way or the other come morning. In the meantime, outlaw or not, I've got to do all I can to keep him alive.'' Gage straightened his tired shoulders. ''Besides, I've got Rae here to protect me.''

Both men laughed. Rae was an old woman who'd lived in the Breaks for years, and she was meaner than any outlaw or drunk in the place.

Kora picked up her shawl, too tired even to ask what the men were laughing about. ''Good night, Doc,'' she said as she walked toward the door. ''I'll go back with Win now.''

Gage waved them away as he made himself comfortable by the fire. ''Thanks again,'' he called. ''Don't worry about me. Rae will be around soon. She'll help if I need someone.''

Win followed Kora out and untied his horse. He could feel her close beside him in the darkness. ''I didn't think about bringing you back alone or I'd have brought a wagon.'' He hesitated, knowing her fear of horses. But from what he knew, the doc wasn't much of a rider, so it wouldn't be fair to leave him the horse and take the buggy. ''You mind riding double?''

''No,'' she answered. ''This could be my first riding lesson.''

He swung up into the saddle and offered her his arm.

There was a moment's hesitation before she slid her fingers over his sleeve and he closed his hand around her forearm, pulling her up in front of him. ''Comfortable?'' he asked, thinking of how light she felt.

She leaned against his chest without answering, but the rapid pounding of her heart told him she was far more frightened of being atop a horse than comfortable. But he couldn't hide his smile. He'd wanted her this close for days.

''Don't worry,'' he whispered. ''I've got you and I promise I won't let go.''

Win guided the horse back over the uneven path of the

settlement. He watched the shadows for any movement and kept his right hand free to reach for his gun. The only advantage to the moonless night was that anyone would have as much trouble seeing him as he did them.

To ease her fears he talked softly in her ear, telling her how to hold the reins and when to trust the horse to pick the path.

When they were away from the campfires and shanties, Kora relaxed slightly as if she, too, had been watching, waiting. ''Thank you,'' she whispered as she leaned against him. ''I'm glad you came to get me.''

If Winter had any plan of yelling at her for disappearing, it vanished. The nearness of her washed over him as it had before, smoothing rough edges that had been a part of him since he could remember. ''I was worried about you,'' he said, rougher than he'd intended.

She didn't seem to notice his tone as her arm slid around his waist. ''When I was about eight, I carried sewing to my mother's customers.'' She kept her voice low, but her grip was strong. ''One winter evening I lost my way and thought I'd never get home. I remember praying my mother would come to find me, but she never did. When I finally made it home, she hadn't even noticed I'd been gone.''

He moved so that she could rest her back against his arm and lowered his head, slightly breathing in her closeness with each breath. ''Don't disappear just so I'll worry, but I'll always come find you.''

Kora laughed. ''Did you worry more about me or having to eat Jamie's cooking?''

''I left Cheyenne to face the cooking.''

''If I know Jamie, there won't be much besides apples to eat tonight.''

Winter joined her in laughter. ''That could be a blessing.''

They rode for a long while, huddling against each other for warmth. In time, their breathing matched as did the rhythm of their hearts. A beat at a time, she was losing her fear both of him and of riding.

When they passed onto even land, Winter circled the reins around the saddle horn and allowed the horse to pace himself. He gently took Kora by the shoulders and turned her slightly.

He felt her stiffen.

"Easy, now, wife," he whispered with his cheek against hers. "I only plan to kiss you if you've no objections."

"You're talking to me in the same tone as you do the horse," she whispered.

"I guess I haven't had much practice talking to women," Winter answered as he touched his first knuckle beneath her chin and lifted her head slightly. "I'll learn, though, Kora. Give me a little time. I'll learn."

"Is a kiss part of the peace between us?"

Win didn't want to talk. He only wanted to kiss the woman. He'd never asked for a kiss in his life, and he wasn't about to start begging now. "No," he mumbled. "It's part of nothing. And it's certainly not something you have to do to play the part of my wife."

He pulled his hat lower as if ending the discussion.

She didn't say a word, but moved her arms around his neck. Slowly she leaned into him and raised her face to his.

"I think I'd like to kiss you," she whispered against his cheek. "For no other reason than I want to." Her mouth moved feather light across his cheek and touched his lips.

At first the kiss was awkward, but after a few moments he pulled her closer and groaned as she melted so softly against him.

He'd kissed a few women in his years, but none tasted like Kora. Her lips were soft and yielding, with just enough hesitancy to fascinate him. He hadn't kissed her since that night in the barn, and now he was surprised at how much he'd missed the taste of her.

As the kiss continued, she moved her fingers over his shoulders and touched the hair at the base of his neck. She was getting used to him, he thought. Accepting him one action at a time.

Her small hands lightly stroked his jawline as her lips brushed against his. She was no longer just accepting his kiss, she was returning it.

He let her set the pace, returning her kisses, without demanding more. Slowly she grew bolder, and he answered her request.

His fingers around her waist gripped tightly as he kissed her again and again. ''You like riding?'' he whispered against her lips.

''I like riding with you,'' she answered.

She straightened, trusting his grip to hold her, as she opened her mouth. The action was bold, but his smile told her of his pleasure. His arms tightened as the kiss deepened. No words could pass between them. No words were needed.

When the horse stopped, Win glanced up in surprise. ''We're home,'' he whispered as his face moved against her hair, loving the clean smell of it.

''Really?'' She sounded as if she didn't believe him. ''The trip seemed shorter on horseback.''

Win laughed as he swung down, then reached for her. His hand slid lightly up her leg to her waist in an action far bolder than he'd ever done. When she didn't pull away, he lowered her slowly, close to his body. ''Maybe it was because we didn't talk much.''

She turned away. He might have thought he'd stepped too far, embarrassing her with his teasing. But her hand lingered on his sleeve, moving along his arm as his hand had covered her leg. The slight touch was a promise.

Cheyenne appeared in the kitchen door before Winter could say anything.

"Win!" Cheyenne yelled as he hobbled onto the back porch. "They found a man shot at dusk on the south rim. Another lookout spotted a rider wearing black moving away from that direction."

Win pressed Kora to the corners of his mind. "I'll ride back for the doc!" He turned to ready his horse.

"No need." Cheyenne stepped off the porch. "The man's dead."

Winter's rage matched the fury of the storm blowing in from the north. He gave Kora a quick nod of goodbye and began issuing orders at his men. By midnight they'd brought in the man's body and prepared it for burial at dawn and doubled the guard in every section. The trouble had finally reached them.

Winter knew killers waited somewhere in the night. He'd reacted when they'd ambushed Cheyenne and him, but now he was planning to act. He couldn't stand by while they picked off his ranch hands one at a time. By dawn he planned to be hunting the men down. He'd start by paying the fellow at Breaks Settlement a visit. If the man was still alive, he might tell who rode with him and who hired them. Then he'd find the other two riders in black and see that they were soon behind bars.

SEVENTEEN

BY FULL SUNUP TWO MORE MEN RODE IN WOUNDED. Both told the same story of being shot at by two men in black dusters. One reported that he had the feeling they were shooting wild, trying to scare more than kill.

Winter organized riders and Kora helped with the wounded. The Winchester Quarantine, as the ranchers were calling it, was working, but no one knew for how long. The riders in black reminded everyone that the trouble was real and could be deadly.

The men lived in their saddles, and Kora worked late each night cooking and nursing. Dr. Gage came almost daily, and on most visits the gambler was with him. Wyatt reported he'd been out of town on a two-day poker game, and in truth, he looked as if he hadn't slept.

Kora watched him talking with Jamie, realizing the man was fascinated by her sister. But there was something dark about him, as if all around him stood in brighter light. He laughed and was always friendly and polite, but Kora didn't miss the wariness in his eyes or the sadness that turned his mouth down when he thought no one was looking. He seemed overly interested in the blockade, and Kora finally decided that he might be trying to fit into this ranching world that seemed to have little use for gamblers except on Saturday night.

Kora did enjoy Steven Gage's company, however, and looked forward to the doctor's visits. He was a kind man whose low voice was as soothing and reassuring as his medicine. Almost from the first, they became the kind of honest friends few people find. She could talk and laugh about almost anything with Steven.

One evening, when everyone had turned in for the night, Steven was still waiting for Wyatt and Jamie to make it back with his buggy. He relaxed in the kitchen with Kora. They talked over coffee and joked about the possibility of Jamie and Wyatt's children.

Just as Kora finished laughing so hard she had to hold her side, she looked up to see Winter in the doorway. He seemed so tall and dark, like a one-man thunderstorm that would wipe out an entire county if it moved.

He was just standing in the doorway staring. His Stetson was low, shading his eyes, and the layer of dust over him reminded her of the way she'd first seen him.

"Winter!" She fought to sober her expression.

He'd been constantly worried about the blockade, and he didn't need her laughter. After his long day he probably only wanted food and sleep.

For a moment he stood as stone, then suddenly turned and vanished. Kora could feel the sparks in the air, rippling through the room like dry lightning.

Steven stood, looking nervous. "I really thought Wyatt and Jamie would be back by now." He paced to the window and back.

Kora stared at the doorway, then at Steven. "I hope nothing's wrong," she said, thinking more of Winter than her sister. Why would he come all the way to the door and not come inside?

The doctor shuffled. "I think I'll make a final check on the wounded. If they're doing all right, they can be moved into the bunkhouse soon. My buggy should be back by the time I'm finished." He almost ran out of the kitchen.

Kora cleaned up the dishes and set Winter's supper out, thinking somehow Winter's dark mood had been caught by Steven. She made Win a plate every night, even though some nights he came in too tired to eat it. At least tonight he made it home in time to say hello before retiring into his study. He reminded her of a clock wound too tight; he seemed to tick off his life in double time.

Win hadn't kissed her again since that night he'd brought her home. Kora couldn't help but wonder if he thought of it as often as she did. Sometimes late at night, when he was sleeping soundly, she'd touch her lips to his, but it wasn't the same as it had been when he'd held her so close.

She waited on the porch for a few minutes, then grew restless. He should have been back from the barn by now. Something was wrong. She could feel it, though she had no idea what it might be. She'd seen the anger in Winter's fast movement. And Steven had felt something, also.

With long quick steps she hurried to the barn, suddenly needing to know what had happened. She couldn't help Win unless she knew what bothered him so. There was no use worrying herself sick alone in the house, when all she had to do was ask Winter.

The barn was dark. When she called his name, no one answered. There seemed a restlessness even in the animal sounds in the barn. Kora folded her arms around her, wishing she'd brought her shawl, though the night was not yet cold.

As she walked out of the barn, Logan stood on the bunkhouse porch smoking a twisted cigarette he'd just finished rolling with equally twisted fingers.

"Evenin'," he mumbled as he played with the cigarette.

"Good evening." She took a step closer to the bunkhouse. "Is something wrong? Has something happened? I saw Win, but now I can't find him."

Logan didn't answer for a moment, leaving Kora to wonder how bad the news might be. Yet all seemed quiet. If something were amiss, shouldn't men be running for their horses or everyone preparing? No more wounded had been brought in. She'd heard no shots. Only Winter's stance had been her gauge.

She took a step closer to Logan. The doc's buggy jingled in the background, but Kora paid little attention to Jamie and Wyatt as they climbed from the buggy and walked hand in hand toward the house.

When Kora was only a few inches from the older man, she whispered, "What is it, Logan? I have to know."

He put out his cigarette and looked up at her. "Win ain't too good at voicing his feelings, but that don't mean he ain't got them." When she didn't answer, he added, "Just because a rabbit can't scream like a hawk, don't mean he ain't hurting."

Kora had no idea what was happening or what Logan was talking about. Winter had never had any trouble telling her what he wanted done. He didn't strike her as a man who was afraid to let the world know how he felt.

"Where is he?" She decided asking Winter might be faster than deciphering Logan's words.

The old man shrugged. "Don't know if he ain't in the house. His horse is in the corral."

Kora turned to walk back to the house. In her mind she rolled through all the breakfast talks they'd had in the past few weeks. It had been mostly about the trouble. He usually asked about her plans for the day. He seemed to enjoy leaning back in his chair and finishing his coffee as she told him. Once, in a moment when no one was around, he'd leaned across the table and touched her hand.

"You might look among those apple trees," Logan mumbled, as if he were thinking to himself and not giving advice. "I've seen him go there when he's worried."

She glanced back, but Logan had already turned into the bunkhouse.

"Thanks," she whispered to no one.

Halfway across the yard, she waved to Steven and the gambler as they climbed into the buggy for the drive back to town. There was something about the way the gambler raised his left arm high to wave that reminded her of the fire, and she picked up her pace. If something else had happened, she needed to know.

The doctor and Wyatt drove off. She thought of returning for a lantern but didn't want to waste the time. The sky was clear, offering enough light to walk by. If she went back to the house, Jamie might decide to go with her, and Kora wanted to talk to Winter alone.

"Win?" she whispered as she moved into the trees.

Suddenly branches darkened her path. She walked slowly through the orchard, trying to remember the way she'd seen the trees placed. They seemed to have no pattern. She could almost see Win as a boy planting them after dark in a pattern only he knew. The wind became a breeze, and the first blossoms of spring made the air smell wonderful. Kora closed her eyes as she moved, enjoying the feel of the soft flowers along the branches, gently buffering her from the hard wood of the tree. The ground was uneven with roots. As she moved, the trees seem to close in around her, sheltering her, blocking all starlight, hovering.

Kora opened her eyes to blackness, suddenly afraid. A

root almost made her fall. A dead branch scraped along her arm, pulling at her sleeve.

The perfume of the blossoms robbed her breath. Twisted branches seemed to reach toward her from all directions. A fallen trunk blocked her path.

"Win!" she cried.

Before she could call again, he was there, pushing the branches aside, enfolding her in his arms.

Kora clung to him tightly, loving the way she could huddle against him and feel cocooned by his warmth. For a long while she didn't say anything, but simply held him, letting her breathing slow to normal.

"Are you all right?" he whispered against her hair.

"Yes," she answered. "I got turned around. Suddenly it seemed like the trees were closing in around me."

"What are you doing out here? You could have gotten hurt stumbling through this place in the dark." As always his voice was low, angry.

"I came to look for you." Kora raised her head, trying to see his face, but the shadows made it impossible.

"Why?" he asked. "You seemed to be having a grand time with the doc."

"I was." Kora pulled an inch away. "He's becoming a great friend."

She felt his body stiffen, but Win didn't say a word.

"He was waiting for his buggy. Wyatt and Jamie took it for a little ride after supper." Kora wasn't sure why she was explaining. Gage sitting in her kitchen didn't seem anything unusual. And everyone, including Kora, had given up on trying to discourage Jamie from her rides with the gambler.

Winter was silent for so long, she didn't know if he was going to say anything. Finally he let out a long breath. "I never heard you laugh like that."

In the darkness Kora felt like a light flashed on in her mind. Suddenly she knew what she'd never thought to guess. Win was jealous.

The knowledge made her feel powerful and cherished for the first time in her life. He wasn't angry about the ranch, or at anyone.

It was time to put her shyness aside. The darkness became her ally, allowing her to do what she might never do in the light. She'd been the outsider, looking in all her life, and she couldn't stand the thought that Win felt like that now.

She slid her fingers down his arm and closed her hand around his. "We need to talk," she whispered as she led him the few feet to a fallen tree trunk.

Win was silent, but she could feel his body tensing for a fight.

"Sit," she ordered as she put her hands on his shoulders.

Slowly he lowered to the log. Now she was almost a head taller than him. Kora moved between his knees, trapping him. She pulled off his hat and laid it beside him.

"Steven is a friend, but you are my husband. That night we talked on the porch, the morning you washed my hair, when I rode with you—all those were times I let you closer than I've ever allowed another person. And I did it not because I signed some paper and made an agreement for six months, but because I wanted to."

Kora rested her hands on his shoulders. "I could never feel about him the way I feel about you." How could she explain that laughter was shallow compared to the way Winter made her whole body react just by being in the same room? Could he really have been so close and not know what he did to her? "I did those things and more. Every night I kiss you when you're asleep. Not because I'm playing the part of your wife, but because I want you.'' Kora surprised herself with her boldness.

She lowered her lips to his and lightly kissed him. He pulled away at the unexpected act, so she repeated her action more slowly.

''And you,'' she whispered against his mouth, ''want me.''

He returned her kiss, but didn't respond otherwise, leaving Kora to wonder if she'd been wrong. He was the first man she'd ever wanted to touch her. Could it be possible that he didn't feel the same?

Moving her fingers into his hair, Kora held his head in her hands as she lowered her lips once more for a longer kiss. She had to make him believe how much his nearness meant to her. She didn't want him to feel like an outsider any longer.

When she straightened, he moaned slightly, but didn't reach for her.

''You know I was never in mourning, but I still needed time. But since that night you held me all the way back from the settlement, I thought you'd come up to our room if only to sleep beside me. It's the way of husbands and wives. But you haven't.''

''I was waiting to be invited.'' Winter moved his hands gently around her waist. ''Is that what you're offering now?''

''You're my husband, if only for a while,'' she whispered against his hair. ''You don't need an invitation to your own bedroom. How can I get used to you if I only see you a few minutes at breakfast each morning? If you don't climb the stairs, how would we ever find a minute alone together?''

''I have a lot on my mind.'' Win moved his hands along

her sides. ''Though I'm having trouble remembering any of it at the moment.''

Kora moved closer until his head rested against her chest. ''We don't need much time, only a little to get to know each other.''

She knew she was being bold. He might shove her away and think her foolish. Except for a few times when he'd kissed her, Win had shown little interest in wanting her. But she'd seen the way he looked at her and was willing to bet a desire was building in him as it had been in her since that first night.

Running her fingers deep into his hair, she tugged until he leaned his head back. She kissed him lightly on his mouth and stepped a few inches away. ''I'm not sure how this works since my first husband was dead on arrival, but I think I want you to touch me.''

Win couldn't believe what she was saying. This shy mouse of a woman he'd married was starting to roar. ''Where?'' he asked.

''All over,'' she answered. ''I'll not undress outside my bedroom, but I'd like not to jump when you touch me. So I think it would be a good place to start if you put your hands on me.'' She swallowed. ''Anywhere you like.''

Placing her fingers on his shoulders, she straightened in front of him. ''Isn't that how people who want to know each other better start getting used to each other?''

Win laughed. ''Not in any civilization I know of. But I'm not about to ask Logan or argue with your plan. Are you sure you want me to touch you, really touch you?''

Kora lifted her chin. ''Yes.''

''Why?'' he whispered as his large hands moved to her waist.

''Because . . .'' She swallowed. How could she put it into words? She admired him more than she had any man. Not because he owned this ranch, or was strong and honest. Not because he'd stayed with their bargain when any other man would have thrown her out. Not because, despite all his armor, he was as lonely as she. She wanted him to touch her because he made her feel like she belonged in the circle of his arms. He was gentle and kind and tender beyond anything she'd ever dreamed a man could be. "When I'm gone," she whispered, "I want to remember your touch."

For a long while he didn't move. Kora could feel her heart trying to break through her chest, but she couldn't say more. She'd made the offer; now she'd wait.

Finally he raised his hand to her throat. Slowly he moved his fingers over the material of her cotton blouse. She could feel him hesitate as if he thought she might pull away. But she didn't move.

His hands glided along her arms, then to her waist. The layers of material kept her from feeling the warmth of his touch as his fingers moved lower over her hips. Then slowly he slid his hands back to her middle and up until he passed over her breasts. The action was slow, calculated, almost impersonal.

He repeated the action.

Kora let out a sound as she felt the weight of his palms over her breasts. The cotton barred his warmth. She hoped he couldn't feel her trembling, but she wanted to grow accustomed to his touch . . . anywhere on her body. It seemed only reasonable if she was planning to sleep beside him. And sleep with him she would before she left for California. Jamie might be destined to have many lovers in her life, but Kora would have only one. This one.

But the feel of a man's hand was something she never thought she'd experience. For some reason fate had given her this one good chance, and she planned to play it out.

''Again, please,'' she whispered, knowing that in the years to come she'd need this memory.

''Are you sure, Kora?''

''I'm sure,'' she answered. ''Move your hands over me once more.'' She thought she'd find the action unpleasant, but she didn't in the least.

He slid his hands into her hair and pulled the strands free of pins. He watched her hair fall, then brushed over it lightly as it fell over her shoulders and back.

''More?'' he questioned, his voice now very low.

''Please,'' she answered.

With a sudden impatience he pulled her mouth down to his. The kiss was warm, hungry. He pushed her mouth open and tasted her, shocking her with his boldness.

When she shook with near panic, he held her head with one hand and stroked her back with the other. But he didn't lighten the kiss. He seemed starved for the taste of her, and now that she offered, no reins would be pulled. He was free to let her see just how deeply he longed to touch her.

As she finally relaxed and accepted his kiss, he moved his hand through her hair, gently turning her head to fill his desire. The strokes along her back grew longer until he covered her hips with each passing. When his hands formed over her hips, his kiss grew bold and fiery with need, taking his pleasure, giving her a hunger for more.

Kora felt herself shake with sudden passion. She'd never dreamed a kiss could be so consuming. He moved his fingers along her jaw and tugged her mouth open wider. The more he tasted, the more his longing seemed to grow. Bracing herself against his shoulders, she took the full wave of his desire, feeling as though she were swimming in fire.

He was all she'd ever know of passion. And all she ever wanted. When she'd begged to be touched, she had no idea that his touch, or his kiss, could be so complete.

''More,'' she whispered, suddenly wanting to know how deep this well of passion in him was.

He didn't answer with words, but with action.

For a while she was so lost in the kiss that she didn't feel his hands caressing her body once more. Warming her though the layers. They grew bolder, more sure of their path, as his fingers gently slid over the worn cotton of her dress.

She whispered his name within the kiss as he pulled her hard against him. The smell of leather and dust and Winter surrounded her. She could feel his need for her even through their clothing. His strong hands rocked her against him as his mouth devoured her. She could taste the passion and longing he had for her, and the knowledge excited her even more. This strong powerful man filled with so much passion had waited to be invited.

When he ended the kiss suddenly, Kora leaned back, drinking in air. Her mind was whirling, and a fever seemed to be pulsing though her, making her feel more alive than she'd ever felt.

''Is that what you wanted?''

''Yes,'' she answered, suddenly realizing it was far more than she even thought to want. ''And you?''

''No,'' he whispered. ''I need more.''

''The invitation's open,'' she whispered.

He pulled her back to him, only now he buried his face between her breasts. His hands ventured up her sides, pressing her mounds against his face, seeming to need to feel her with more than just his hands.

When she sighed in pleasure, he raised his head in question.

A slow smile spread across his face as their eyes met.

Without a word he kissed her again. Now she leaned into him as his mouth moved softly over her tender lips and his hands slowly opened and closed around her breasts. His passionate kisses before had made her mouth feel raw, sensitive so that now even the light kisses were wildly felt. He gently pulled her bottom lip into his mouth and tasted it, and she knew she would deny this man nothing.

His hands crossed over her as if they'd always had the right to do so. His tongue touched the corner of her mouth until she smiled, opening her lips to his kiss. And kiss her he did, soft and hard, gentle and rough, fast and slow.

Finally he turned her in his embrace and wrapped his arms around her while pulling her full length against him.

"Are you accustomed to my touch now?" he whispered into her hair.

Kora couldn't answer. Nothing had ever prepared her for how he'd touched her. Nothing had prepared her for how she'd reacted. When she'd asked him to touch her, she'd expected a light brushing of his fingers over her, maybe an embrace, but nothing like what he'd done to her.

"I'm trying to go slow, but God, woman, your body's not making it easy." He ran his hand along her side. "All day I tell myself I've got other things to think about, but I keep remembering the way you move and wishing I could touch you. Then, tonight, you walk up and ask me to do the very thing I've been wanting to do every hour I've been with you since we met."

He moved one hand low, over her tummy and down. She arched her back against his shoulder as she felt his hand press hard through the layers. Panic flooded her mind once more. He was touching her where no one had ever dared. Covering his hand with her own, she tried to pull his fingers away. But his strength didn't seem to feel her action as he stroked boldly.

His teeth bit gently into the flesh of her neck as his fingers explored. She pressed against his hand, suddenly needing his touch. Her back shifted against his shoulder as his hand roamed freely over her, dipping again and again between her legs. Each time his actions grew bolder, stronger. Her reaction matched his. She heard herself let out little sighs as his warm mouth moved along the pulsing in her throat.

He twisted his hand into her hair and pulled her around once more to face him. This time when his mouth found hers, his kiss was light. "Don't pull away from me, Kora," he whispered. "I need you so desperately."

"I won't," she answered, knowing that her fear was of the unknown and not of him. "Touch me, taste me all you like."

Hesitantly she spread her hands over his shirt. The rock wall of his chest was there as always, but she could feel the heat of him through the material. As she kissed him, she glided her hands along his chest to his belt and then back up.

As her hands passed over his chest, his kisses deepened. Suddenly he stood, pulling her off the ground in his embrace, and kissed her wildly as his arms tightened around her.

Kora couldn't breathe. She tried to break the kiss, then her hands turned from touching to pushing. Finally, in panic, she slammed her fist into his chest as hard as she could.

Win broke the kiss immediately and lowered her to the ground. For a moment he didn't want to let go, but Kora pushed free.

"Stop!" Her voice was shaking as she took in quick breaths. "You were holding me too tightly. You were hurting me."

Winter turned away and slammed his fist so hard against the tree trunk that a shower of blossoms fell around her like huge snowflakes. He swore in his low voice.

Kora felt as if she'd been on a runaway train. Her emotions were raw, out of control for the first time in her life. She lowered to the ground as silently as the flowers had fallen. The solid earth felt good as she leaned back, her body drained of all energy.

After a long silence Winter looked over his shoulder. For a moment he thought she'd vanished as quickly as she'd appeared tonight. Then he saw her lying on the ground with tiny flowers all around her. Her hair was wild and he thought she looked like something not quite of this earth. Maybe an angel, or a fairy.

All the anger left him as it always did when he looked at her. Logan had been wrong about her being invisible; she was magic. She was all he could see, even when he closed his eyes.

He knelt beside her and gently lifted her. For a moment she didn't open her eyes, and a fear stabbed at him that he might have really hurt her by holding too tightly.

"Kora?" he asked as he moved the long golden strands away from her face.

She opened her eyes and surprised him with a smile. "I'm sorry," she whispered. "I was afraid I couldn't breathe. I panicked. I pulled away when I said I wouldn't."

"No . . ." Winter couldn't believe she was the one apologizing. "My hold is too strong. I'll have to learn to be careful. Dear God, I'd never want to hurt you."

He leaned back against the tree trunk and gathered her gently against his chest. "This is no justification for what I did, but there's never been anything soft in my life. I don't know much about women, and the women I've known have been hard and fast. I've seen men lightly holding a woman's arm, or gently patting her hand like it might break at any moment, but I never considered myself one of those dandies. Everything I've ever wanted in this world

I've had to fight for to win and to hold. Nothing's ever come easy to me except finding you to marry."

"But you didn't want me when you offered marriage." Kora rested her head against his chest, listening to the steady pounding of his heart. "Not the way you did tonight."

"I didn't want a wife and I fought it as long as I could. But I wouldn't give up the house, so I married. At first I told myself we'd made a fair bargain, nothing more, and I could forget you were there. But I was wrong. Every time I see you, I've had to fight a stronger urge to reach for you."

He lifted her shoulders so that she faced him only an inch away. "I want you, Kora. I want you like I never wanted anyone in my life. Not just to touch, but to hold all night long."

"I want you, too," she answered honestly. "But you don't have to hold so tightly. I'll try not to pull away again."

EIGHTEEN

KORA MOVED AS SILENTLY AS SHE COULD UP THE stairs to the attic. She sensed Winter following a step behind. The soft jingle of his spurs echoed his movements. Everyone in the house, Cheyenne, the two wounded cowhands, Jamie, and Dan, was asleep, and Kora was surprised the rapid pounding of her heart didn't wake them all. She couldn't believe that she was about to sleep with a man. And not just any man—Winter McQuillen. He was big and powerful and frightening when he roared. He only knew one speed, full gallop, when he wanted something, and tonight, he wanted her.

But that wasn't the reason she was interested. The fact he owned the ranch didn't matter. Or that he wielded more power with his low voice than most men did with a yell. Even the knowledge that he was her husband hadn't been her motivation.

Kora wanted only the man. He thought he was so hard, but she'd seen the gentleness in the way he looked at her, and tonight she'd felt it in his touch. The very wildness that worried him excited her. She'd never thought she'd marry. She liked everything calm and in order. His world was filled with clutter and danger. But his was a chaos that made her blood rush. She didn't know what it was like to sleep with a man, but it was about time she found out. And there was no other man she wanted to show her except Winter.

Without a word Kora slipped behind the divider and undressed. Her fingers trembled as she buttoned her nightgown. She thought of all the things he'd never said. Like that she was beautiful, or that he loved her. Those words might matter to other women, but Kora told herself they didn't matter to her. He'd said more important things, like the house would always be hers and that he needed her help. His words weren't the words of love, but they were honest words.

When she stepped out from behind the thin wall, Winter was standing next to his washstand. He'd removed everything except his jeans, and they were open at the first button. He'd managed to spill most of the water and nicked himself shaving, making Kora smile.

She moved across the room and touched the tiny spot of blood. He looked down at her with dark eyes afire with need, but he didn't touch her as she lifted his towel and patted his chin.

"We'd better go to bed," he whispered, as if they were words he'd said every night since their marriage.

Without touching her, he moved to his side of the bed and pulled back the covers.

Panic climbed up Kora's spine. In the trees when he'd kissed her it had been dark. When she'd told him she was ready, she'd still been warm from the passion of his kisses. Now he was standing before her silently waiting for her to share his bed, and she wasn't sure she could. Maybe she didn't have what it took. She'd never even been interested in any man this way except him.

She backed away.

For a moment Winter looked concerned, then confused, then he seemed to understand. Without a word he leaned over and put out the light.

Now the only illumination was from the moonlight and stars. Still she hesitated.

With a quick jerk, he pulled the covers from the bed and spread them on one of the rugs. ''Are you afraid of me,'' he asked, ''or the bed?''

He dropped to his knees on the blankets. ''If you won't sleep with me on the mattress, I'll join you on the floor.''

She smiled and moved toward him. When she was only a few feet away, he gently put his hands on her waist and pulled her to him, resting his head at her middle.

Kora touched his hair and felt the excitement that she had before. Slowly she lowered to her knees. Without a word, he kissed her gently as he lowered her to the blankets and spread out beside her. The night was cool, but his nearness kept her warm.

Her head rested on his arm as he leaned above her, kissing her gently. ''Are you sure you want this?'' he whispered between kisses. ''I still have enough reason left that I could go to the study. I promised you I wouldn't force this role on you.''

Kora wasn't sure at all. What if he got carried away and held her too tightly again? She wasn't even sure what she was agreeing to. She'd heard many women say it was something every wife had to endure. But if it was like Winter's kisses, making love would be easy to become accustomed to. And his touch had been a taste of heaven.

His fiery need for her excited her.

''I'm sure,'' she lied.

On his side, with her pressed close, Winter watched her face in the moonlight as his hand lowered to the center of her gown. He spread his fingers out over her abdomen and felt the warmth of her flesh beneath the thin layer of cotton. He wanted to feel her skin but didn't want to frighten her. *Move slow*, he kept reminding himself. *Move slow.* He knew she was unsure, but she was looking at him like he knew what he was doing. Win wasn't about to tell her how little he knew of loving. Surely it couldn't be all that difficult. He knew the basics. He'd learn.

He kissed her on the forehead. When she closed her eyes, he lightly touched his lips to her eyelids and felt her lashes tickle his mouth.

When he reached her lips, they were full and ready for him. Opening without having to be encouraged. The knowledge that she was learning and responding to the way he liked to love made his blood warm, and awkward movements became smooth. Her mouth had the feel and taste of soft, warm honey. She remained still as he felt and tasted her mouth.

His kisses were no longer hard, almost bruising, as they had been in the orchard, but still a fire coursed through her. The feel of his hand across her abdomen moving slightly, pressing gently, made her long for him to touch her as he had.

For a long while he seemed content to kiss her. She timidly raised her hand and touched his bare shoulder. With her touch she knew that his wild, maddening need was being held at bay.

His fingers stroked her face and hair as his lips brushed hers.

Kora liked the pleasure he brought, but she wanted the passion. If she was to drink tonight, she wanted the full glass. She raised her hand and stroked his chest, trailing her fingers over his warm skin.

The kiss deepened.

She continued to explore the wall of flesh over muscle.

She liked the way his body tightened with her touch and rippled beneath her hand. The sun's warmth seemed baked into his skin.

Winter was fighting all his passion to go slowly, and she seemed to be fanning the fire with kerosene. When her fingers tickled their way down the center of his chest to the spot just below his waist where his pants were open, he couldn't hold back a groan.

Kora laughed softly against his ear and repeated her action, loving the way she could make him react.

The third time she broke the hold on his reserve, and they began galloping at full speed. His kiss turned to liquid desire, and his hands moved over her in bold strokes. At first he'd been content to rest his hand on her; now he longed to touch her all at once.

When his fingers captured her full breast, Kora arched her back, offering more. His hold was tight as his thumb found her peak and rubbed across it back and forth with maddening pressure. The thin layer of cotton offered nothing to protect her as the layers of cloth had in the orchard. She took passion's wave and moved, begging for more.

He no longer kissed her as he continued to explore her body, but allowed her to sigh and cry out softly in pleasure. But he couldn't live without the taste of her. He left his mission only long enough to unbutton the buttons at her throat. When his hand returned to her breasts, he loved the way she sighed and rocked her fullness into his embrace as though welcoming him home. The roughness of his hands seemed to excite her.

With her gown undone, he could fully taste her throat. She rolled her head aside, offering him her neck from the sensitive area he'd found just below her ear to where the material parted, revealing the rise of one breast. For a moment, he stopped, unable to do anything but stare at the beauty she offered him so easily, so freely. The sight of her lying on her back with her eyes sparkling with starlight and her gown open made him feel as if his brain were exploding. He pulled the material away slightly until he saw the swell of both breasts and the inviting valley between them.

Her breasts were fuller than he'd expected, with creamy skin that begged to be touched. His gaze locked on hers as he brushed two fingers down the center of her gown's opening, applying pressure to each breast.

Moving restlessly she silently begged to be touched. He closed his hand over the cotton covering one mound, enjoying the way she cried softly in pleasure as her eyes darkened to velvet blue. His hand molded around her, taking slow pleasure as his grip tightened over the mound.

Her lips parted in whispered cries of pleasure. He leaned over her and kissed her deep and completely.

When he rolled back beside her, she moved restlessly and her leg brushed against his need. He covered her ripe breast with his hand once more, enjoying the way she responded by moving again and once again, brushing against his jeans. He knew he could open her gown farther, but he wanted to ration out perfection. The feel of her was enough tonight, later he'd undress her completely. He brushed the thin cotton covering her peak, and her lips parted, begging him for more.

Her eyes were wide with passion and need and uncertainty. His thumb crossed her peak again as his fingers tightened around her. Her eyes turned a darker blue and her mouth opened with a sigh. He'd never dreamed she'd respond to him so, and the knowledge drove him mad. This shy woman wasn't going to just take his loving; she was feeling his every touch with a passion that rocked him.

He answered her with a deep, full kiss. As she relaxed

in his arms, he spread his hand out and felt the rise and fall of her chest.

Then his mouth lowered to her throat as one arm encircled her. She responded as she had before, allowing him free rein over her body. Her back arched as his hand pulled demandingly against her virgin flesh. His grip tightened and she cried once more with pleasure, whispering his name.

His fingers became bolder, pulling, molding as his thumb once more circled her peak roughly, then held her tightly as her body shook with pleasure. He leaned into her, wanting to feel her responding. The pleasure he brought her burned him with deeper passion.

She didn't disappoint him. Each time his hand circled and tightened, she moved. Each time his kiss grew bolder, she trembled with a need he knew was building inside her as well.

Curling against him, she began to swim in the fire of passion, losing all her mind except the desire, the need, the longing for more. His touch was gentle one moment, begging for her, and demanding the next, taking all he wanted of the feel and taste of her.

Suddenly he placed one hand on her hip and pulled her closer against him so that he could feel her with the length of his body. His mouth returned to hers, silencing her cries of pleasure as his fingers continued to travel along her legs and over her hips. When he returned to her breasts, each touch was like the first, making her bolt with fire and need. Only now her peaks were sensitive from his first rough touch and responded to even his slightest brush.

''More,'' she whispered against his mouth. ''More!'' He'd created an addiction within her.

Win smiled. She was made for loving, his loving.

The kiss deepened as he moved above her. The wall of his chest pressed into her, giving her the pleasure his hand had. Only now the pressure was doubled. Kora moved wildly beneath him, loving the feel of him above her.

She wasn't aware that he'd lifted her gown until she felt his knee pry her legs apart. He raised above her for a moment, and she closed her eyes against the sudden cold without him. Blindly she reached for him and pulled him to her.

His chest pressed into her breasts as his mouth covered hers with a kiss that was almost savage with need. She was vaguely aware of his hands gliding over her legs, pulling them open with rough hurried movements. He pushed into her so suddenly she felt like she'd been struck by lightning.

She jerked wildly as pain shot through her body and her scream was caught in his mouth. He pushed again and again before she could think enough to react. The ceiling began to spin as he continued, driving deeper with each advance. Passion gave way to pain. Weakly Kora began to fight, but he didn't stop.

Finally he shoved one last time with even more force than he'd used before. He broke their kiss as he let out a sound like none she'd ever heard. A heartbeat later her scream filled his ears as completion emptied his body of all energy.

Winter rolled to his side. He reached for her, but she rolled away. For a few breaths he couldn't think of anything but how wonderful it had felt to be inside her. Then her soft crying reached his passion-drugged mind.

Lifting to one elbow, he looked at her. Kora was curled in a ball, pulling the covers around her as she cried.

"Kora," he whispered. "Kora, are you all right?"

She didn't answer. He didn't even think she heard him. When he touched her shoulder, she pulled away.

Then he saw it. Blood. A spot on the blanket and another on the back of her gown.

Winter fell back and swore to the heavens. A virgin! Of

course she'd been a virgin. Andrews hadn't even known her until Win said her name; how could the man have slept with her? No other man had ever kissed Kora, much less touched her.

She'd come to him a virgin, and he'd taken her like she was a whore.

NINETEEN

WINTER STOOD AND PULLED ON HIS JEANS. ALL HIS life he'd thought of himself as strong and hard. He'd work hours longer than any man and was justly proud of what he accomplished. He'd stand to the death for something he believed in. He never backed down when he knew he was right.

But tonight for the first time, Winter hated himself. He hated himself more than he'd ever hated anyone since he'd learned Custer's soldiers killed his mother.

He walked over to the pitcher of water on his washstand. Grabbing his discarded shirt, he soaked it in cold water and crossed back to Kora.

She didn't move when he knelt on the floor beside her. The sound of her crying ripped his heart apart.

"Kora?" he whispered as he gently touched her cheek.

To his surprise she didn't pull away, but seemed frozen in place. Maybe she figured he'd done as much damage as he possibly could for one night. She stared up, but didn't seem to see him.

He brushed her hair out of her face and saw the bruises already beginning along her throat where he'd tasted her flesh. He hadn't meant to leave passion marks on her, but the proof was clear.

Winter swore to himself. He'd have killed any man for doing this to her. He'd never seen such marks on respectable women, only on those who liked to be passed around. "I'm sorry" was too lame an excuse for what he'd done. "I'm sorry" wasn't even worth voicing.

She didn't move as he slowly pulled the covers away. He wasn't sure if she was too afraid to react or if she'd lost all feeling.

Her gown was still at her waist. With shaking hands, he wiped the blood away from her thigh, then placed the wet shirt between her legs, hoping to cool any more pain. He gently pulled her gown down and wrapped her in the quilts. She'd stopped crying and her eyes were closed, but he doubted she was asleep.

He lifted her in his arms and carried her to bed. Before he lowered her, he buried his face in her hair and fought down a curse. Her unvoiced cry rocked through him all the way to his soul. He'd crushed the only gentleness that had ever come into his life.

"Kora?" he whispered from above her, wishing she'd say something, anything, but she didn't answer.

Win felt so helpless. He wanted to lie down next to her and hold her all night, but her scream haunted his mind. It had been a cry of pure terror. He knew she wouldn't welcome him near tonight or probably any night for the rest of their time together. From this point on she'd count the days until she was on the train to California.

He paced the room for a few minutes, then went downstairs. Maybe if she took a little brandy she could sleep? Maybe tomorrow the pain wouldn't be so bad? Maybe she'd not hate him? He'd swear never to touch her again. It had been hard never reaching for her before tonight, but after what they'd shared, it would be torture.

She'd felt so good in his arms. She'd been so soft and willing, she trusted him completely. Until the last. Until she'd screamed.

He reached the study and was headed back to the stairs when he thought of tea. Kora always liked to drink a hot cup of tea each night. He'd watched her pass the study, carrying it to bed with her. But tonight they hadn't stopped in the kitchen on their way to the bedroom.

Win had little idea how to make tea. He boiled some water and scalded his fingers pouring it into a cup. He misjudged how many tea leaves to drop in and frowned when the liquid turned to mud. With the cup in one hand and the brandy in the other, he started back through the darkness toward the stairs.

At the second-floor landing Jamie stepped in his path, making him splash tea onto his hand for the second time.

"What are you doing up at this hour?" she demanded as if she were the night watchman.

"I was getting Kora a cup of tea and myself a drink." Win tried to sound calm.

"Something wake you up, too?" Jamie leaned on her door frame. "I was sound asleep and swear I heard a scream."

Win was glad it was dark. "I heard it, too." A lie wouldn't set easy on him.

Jamie shrugged. "I looked around but didn't find anything amiss. I figure it must have been one of those wounded men. Doc's got them pretty full of pain medicine. I checked on them, but they were both sleeping like babies by the time I got my buckskins on."

Win didn't answer. He shifted, waiting for her to move out of his way.

"Kora's all right, isn't she?" Jamie asked suddenly.

''It's not like her to let someone else wait on her.''

''I wanted to.'' Win fought the knowledge that Kora wasn't all right and it was his fault.

''You'd better be good to her,'' Jamie began.

''I know!'' Win snapped. ''Or you'll cut me up in little pieces.'' He might as well buy her a good knife, because when Kora woke up in the morning, Jamie was bound to find out how cruel he'd been.

''Well, getting her tea is a start in the right direction, cowboy.'' Jamie disappeared in her room. ''Night!'' she yelled just as the door closed.

Win walked up the next flight of stairs and across to the bed. First he lit the lamp, then laced the tea with a good portion of brandy. Kora was silent now, but he guessed she wasn't asleep.

''Kora,'' he whispered as he sat on the edge of the bed and pulled her, blankets and all, toward him.

He could feel her stiffen, but she didn't answer.

''Drink this, darling,'' he whispered as he cradled her beneath his arm.

She had a death grip on the covers around her, so he touched the cup to her lips. Even in the shadowy light he could tell her lips were swollen slightly.

She made a face as she drank, but she swallowed half the cup of tea. The warm liquid seemed to help her body relax slightly. A thousand apologies came to Winter, but he didn't know where to start.

Win lowered her head to the pillow and added another blanket over her.

''Good night,'' he whispered as he put out the light and walked out of the bedroom.

He spread out on the study couch and tried to sleep, but it was impossible. He thought of ways he could make it up to Kora, but all of them seemed shallow. In the beginning she'd wanted him, he was sure of it. At one point he knew she was loving his touch as much as he was enjoying touching her. But at some point it all changed. Thinking back, he remembered the glory of entering her. How wonderful she'd felt beneath him. Her breasts pressing against his chest. The silk of her legs as he parted them. She'd opened her mouth wider when he'd entered her. She'd raised her breasts against his chest.

Or had she? Had she been moving with him, or against him?

Winter fell asleep near dawn without an answer.

Win awoke with a sudden jerk as he almost tumbled off the couch. The smell of bacon frying and biscuits cooking was thick in the air. Every muscle seemed stiff and contrary, rebelling to his movements. He dressed as fast as he could and followed the voices to the kitchen. He might as well face whatever happened. There was nowhere to run and he'd offer no defense. He wasn't even sure he'd bother to dodge if Jamie's knives started flying.

Cheyenne and Jamie were sitting at the kitchen table arguing. Kora had her back to him as she stood at the stove. She had on a new dress, and he couldn't help but notice the collar was higher than her other dresses. She also wore her hair down. Usually by now she'd combed it up for the day.

Her hair reminded him of how she'd looked on the blankets when he'd unbuttoned part of her nightgown. She'd been so beautiful. She'd taken his breath away.

"You look like death crawled up from six feet under." Jamie laughed as she spotted her brother-in-law.

Winter didn't even glance at her. He couldn't take his gaze from Kora as she turned around. She looked as though nothing had happened. He studied her face. Except for a slight swelling of her bottom lip nothing was amiss. The lady was as proper as always.

"I said—"

"I heard you," he answered Jamie without taking his gaze off Kora. "I had a little trouble sleeping last night."

"So did I after I heard something." Jamie started telling Cheyenne all about the scream she'd heard.

Winter crossed the room and stepped out on the porch. He dumped a pitcher of icy water over his head and shook hard like an animal. He grabbed the towel and dried off his hair as he walked to the edge of the porch, trying to get his mind awake enough so that he could deal with Kora in the daylight.

There, ten feet away from the corner of the porch, was the washtub filled with water. He saw a patch of a blanket, his shirt, and what might have been a white nightgown soaking in the tub.

For a moment he just looked at them. How like Kora to straighten everything up. She'd have them clean and hanging by full sunup. Too bad he couldn't put the relationship they'd started back together as easily.

"Coffee?" Kora whispered from just behind him.

Winter turned slowly, very much aware that their conversation could be overhead from the kitchen.

"Thanks," he said as he took the cup from her hand. Blue eyes stared up at him. They were the color of a clear evening sky, and he wondered why he hadn't noticed them before. He couldn't look away. She was almost close enough to touch, almost.

He didn't know the words to say. Not even as he watched her beautiful eyes brim with tears. She was waiting for the right words, and he'd say them gladly if he could figure out what they were.

''Be careful,'' she finally said softly and looked away. ''The coffee's hot.''

He took a swallow, not caring. Here she was standing in front of him as though nothing was wrong . . . as though nothing had happened.

''Kora, I . . .''

Kora touched his mouth with her fingertips. She glanced toward the open kitchen door. Raising to her tiptoes, she whispered close to his ear, ''We'll talk later.''

Then, to Winter's total shock, she kissed him on the cheek and hurried back to her cooking. For a while he forgot to breathe.

When he walked back in the kitchen a few minutes later, no one seemed to notice him. Jamie had told Cheyenne about the gambler's shoulder, and Cheyenne was suggesting that maybe Wyatt had been shot dealing a crooked hand.

No one noticed Winter as he sat down and drank his coffee without taking his gaze from Kora, while she served breakfast. When she pulled her apron off to join them at the table, Winter did something he'd never done. He stood and pulled out her chair.

Cheyenne and Jamie continued arguing as Winter and Kora ate in silence. Winter didn't even listen to the conversation until Kora touched his hand. ''Win,'' she whispered, ''Wyatt was hurt the same day Cheyenne was shot.''

The knowledge fell into a slot he hadn't even thought existed.

''And,'' Kora continued while Jamie and Cheyenne talked to each other, ''the man with the torch. I remember thinking it odd that he held the reins in his right hand and tossed the fire with his left. As he rode away the reins were still in his right hand. Wouldn't a man hold a horse with his best grip, the same grip he'd use for throwing?''

Winter glanced up at Kora and realized he'd had the same idea. "He would unless his right shoulder was hurt."

"When Wyatt waved last night from the buggy, he lifted his left arm. I remember thinking how the movement looked familiar somehow."

"You think he's one of our men in black?" Win mumbled.

"I don't know." Kora shook her head. "I like the man. I wouldn't want to accuse him or anyone falsely."

Win leaned close to her. "I'll do some checking and let you know what I find out."

Kora smiled at the way he included her. He was acting as if they were in this maze of trouble together.

Downing the last of his breakfast, Win stood. "I have to make a trip into town this morning," he said too loudly to sound casual. "I'll bring back anything you need, Kora."

Kora also stood and acted as if she and Win weren't up to something. "I'll make a list," she said, as if reading lines from a badly written play.

Cheyenne leaned heavily on his crutch. "If you'll hitch a buggy, I'll ride along with you." His voice was casual, but his eyes said much more. Win and Kora weren't fooling him.

"Are you up to it?"

Cheyenne nodded. "It couldn't be any more painful than listening to Jamie all day. Besides, I'd like to ask the doc something."

Win nodded, knowing just the questions he'd also like to ask the doc. He left and hitched a team to the buggy while Kora made a list of supplies she needed and Jamie helped Cheyenne outside.

Jamie insisted on him riding on a pillow, even threatening to shoot him if he tossed it out along the way. Cheyenne grumbled beneath her mothering, but he took the pillow.

While Jamie pampered Cheyenne, Kora handed Win the list. He leaned slowly and brushed her cheek with his lips, returning her kiss as awkwardly as she'd kissed him earlier. Anyone watching would never guess how they'd kissed last night. "Is there anything I can do?" he whispered. "Anything?"

His hand lightly brushed her collar, knowing the bruises were beneath the lace. He wished she could name a price for his penance. He'd do whatever she asked. Never step foot in the house. Buy her whatever she wanted. Allow Kora her own account to travel as far away from him as she liked.

She looked up at him with those wonderful blue eyes. He thought he saw a touch of fear, a touch of worry, and to his surprise, a touch of understanding.

"Come back safe," she whispered, brushing his jaw with her fingertips.

If he stayed a moment longer, he'd make a fool of himself. Winter climbed in the buggy and slapped the horses into action.

Jamie was still yelling at Cheyenne when they drove off.

"I'll never understand that girl," Cheyenne grumbled, uncharacteristically unaware of what was happening to Winter.

"I think Jamie's starting to like you." Win laughed, suddenly feeling like the sun had come up after a very long night.

"That fact could be the death of me," Cheyenne moaned. "If I have to stay cooped up with her another day, she'll drive me to drink. You've got to find her a husband fast, Win. Some good man who would take her away and teach her about being a lady."

Winter lowered his hat against the sun. ''True, but it doesn't look good when I'm heading to her most likely choice, and I'm not planning a social visit.'' He told Cheyenne about Kora putting a few pieces together that they hadn't thought about.

''Too bad the man in the Breaks Settlement died before he could tell us anything.'' Cheyenne swore as he tried to find a comfortable position on the pillow. ''Kora's guesses are a long shot, but it seems to be the only lead we have at present.''

An hour later both men were standing in front of Wyatt as he dealt solitaire to an empty table. Cheyenne had left his crutch in the buggy, refusing to use it in town.

''Morning, gentlemen. It's a little early for a game, but I'm ready if you are.'' Wyatt's gaze darted between the men in a nervous action, though his smile was friendly.

Winter sat on one side of him, Cheyenne the other.

''Morning, Wyatt.'' Winter waved the bartender to bring a few drinks. ''We didn't come to play cards.'' His voice was casual and low, letting the few people in the saloon think that the three men were merely passing the time of day.

''We'd like to talk to you alone,'' Winter said as he downed his drink and waited for the bartender to walk away. ''How about the back room?''

The gambler did the unthinkable in his business. He dropped a card. ''All right,'' he said slowly. ''I'll have Charlie bring us another drink.''

''Don't bother,'' Winter said as he watched Wyatt stand. ''This isn't a social call.''

They walked to the back room and Winter closed the door. Cheyenne moved in front of it, as always, the guard.

''What's this about, gentlemen? If it's about Jamie, I assure you I've never—''

"It's not about Jamie," Winter interrupted.

Wyatt took a breath. "I'm glad. I think a lot of the girl, but I said from the first I'm not the marrying kind."

"I'd like to take a look at that shoulder of yours, gambler." Winter moved toward the smaller man.

"I appreciate your concern, but it's fine. I've had the doc look at it a few times."

"Take off your shirt!" Winter ordered.

"Now, wait just a minute. You may think you can boss everyone around, but I don't work for you."

Winter thought of fighting the man. He could have used the release from all the tension he'd felt lately, but in truth, he liked Wyatt despite the man's poor taste in women and obvious dishonesty. He might be short on character, but his personality made him easy to tolerate at least. Also, both Kora and Jamie would be fighting mad if he beat the man up and the poor gambler turned out to be innocent.

"You can show me now, or after I get the sheriff." Win waited. "He might be interested in knowing the time you received your injury."

Frustrated, Wyatt pulled his string tie and unbuttoned his collar, then his shirt. "All right. I don't see what the fuss is about. It's only a scar. And as for the sheriff, he already knows about it."

Cheyenne and Winter watched as Wyatt turned his shoulder to them. True to his word, a scar still red from healing dotted his shoulder. Both men had seen enough bullet wounds to know one.

"How'd you get that?" Win asked.

"I was shot," Wyatt answered, frustrated at having to explain the obvious. "The same day Cheyenne was. That's why I was in the doc's office the night your men came to get him."

Wyatt was being too straightforward to be lying, even

for a gambler, Win guessed. "Who shot you?"

"Hell if I know. Some farmer who bet away all his money, I guess. I tried to find out, but it was only a scratch compared to Cheyenne's. Plus, the sheriff had all he could handle with the blockade trouble without worrying about a gambler who got nicked."

Win glanced at Cheyenne, then back at Wyatt. "Sorry to have bothered you, but we're checking out every man in the county who's been shot lately to see if they're related in some way. No offense."

Wyatt buttoned up his shirt. "None taken. I guess if I was in your shoes, I'd be turning over every rock I thought might lead me somewhere." He walked toward the door, then turned back to Winter. "But think about it, Mr. McQuillen, if I were going to shoot you, I've had plenty of chances. And if I was one of the men running the blockade, you'd be my first target. Take you out of the fight and the other ranchers will fall like dominoes." Wyatt flashed his teeth. "If I were you, Mr. McQuillen, I'd watch my back. And the next time I'd shoot all three riders in black, not just two."

He walked out of the room.

Cheyenne lowered his voice. "You never mentioned you thought he might have shot at you."

"No," Winter answered. "And I don't remember telling him I shot a second ambusher that day you were hit."

"Think he's one of the black riders?"

"He might be. Or he might just have overheard folks talking," Winter answered. "Let's keep him close a few days so we can keep an eye on him. He might be spying. What better disguise than being a gambler with no interest in cattle? And Jamie gives him an excuse to come out to the ranch."

Cheyenne nodded. "If he's a snake, we're bound to hear the rattler eventually."

On their way out of the saloon, Winter stopped and apologized once more for inconveniencing Wyatt. Then he casually invited the gambler to dinner. When Wyatt accepted, Win added an invitation to spend the night on the ranch.

When the gambler took the bait, Win knew the ante raised and what was at stake came to far more than money. His ranch—his life—was on the line.

TWENTY

THE SKY TURNED DARK WITH BOILING CLOUDS ALONG the horizon as Winter rode home on a borrowed horse behind the buggy he'd driven to town. They'd spent far longer in town than he'd planned and accomplished nothing. The sheriff couldn't remember talking to Wyatt the night Cheyenne had been shot. After waiting on the doc for hours, he'd been able to shed little light on Wyatt's injury. He also reported hearing the man at Breaks Settlement mumbling about gunfire, but the doc said his words didn't make any sense. Mixed in with the screams of being shot was talk of a woman whose aim was deadly. The only woman there that day, Win told the doc, had been Kora, and she hadn't carried a gun. The dying man must have been mixing nightmares.

Winter was beginning to think he was on the wrong track accusing the gambler. It appeared Wyatt knew nothing and Winter's only lead was dead. But it wouldn't hurt to keep Wyatt close a few days and watch his behavior. If the cattlemen were moving a herd north, they'd do it soon. The weather was right and market prices high. If the gambler was involved, they wouldn't have long to wait.

Winter could hear Wyatt spinning some long tale to Cheyenne as the two rode side by side in the buggy. Winter smiled. Men who talked a lot eventually said too much.

Kicking his horse, Win pulled beside the buggy. ''We'll be lucky to make it in before the rain.'' He was ready to be home, and he imagined Cheyenne was tired of the chatter.

Wyatt slapped the horses into a trot, and Cheyenne swore in pain. They managed to reach the barn just as huge raindrops fell, turning the dry, tan earth to a dark brown.

Winter waved the gambler and Cheyenne inside and took the buggy along with his horse to the barn. He took his time unsaddling the horse and brushing down the animals, not because they needed extra care, but because it was one way he could delay before going in the house. Being home was one thing, facing Kora was another.

He'd racked his brain all day and was no closer to thinking of what he should say to Kora. He'd gone from hating himself to being angry at her for not warning him. She should have reminded him she was a virgin. She should have made him go slower. She shouldn't have made him so half-mad from kissing her that he wasn't thinking.

He was no lovesick cowhand who hadn't seen a woman in months. She was driving him crazy with her soft manner and gentle ways. And after all, she'd been the one who came looking for him in the orchard with her soft plea for him to touch her. The more he thought about it, the more he saw this whole mess as her doing.

He'd told her from the first he would never love her, Win thought. He'd been honest about wanting to share her bed. So she better not come crying and complaining now. The way he saw it, all he'd done was keep his word.

Win marched at full attack across the yard toward the house. ''She got what she asked for and agreed to,'' he mumbled, figuring there was no need for him to say a word about last night. What happened to her happened to every wife.

As he stomped in the kitchen primed for a fight, the smell of home cooking was all that greeted him. He loved the smell of cinnamon and apples baking. Since she'd been here the aromas always washed over him when he came home, making him forget most of his problems.

Win frowned. Maybe her revenge would be to fatten him up. If he kept downing half a pie at a time, he wouldn't be able to sit a horse come next fall.

Voices drifted from the dining room. Win tossed his hat and coat on the rack and moved across the room. He ran his hand over his gunbelt. He knew Kora wanted him to remove it before sitting down at the table, but tonight he refused. Maybe that was another thing she'd just have to get used to. She was married to a rancher, and the Colt strapped to his leg was a part of his life. He hadn't married her under any false pretenses, and if she thought she was going to change him, she'd better start thinking again.

He advanced into the dining room and took his seat, but if anyone noticed his dark mood, they gave it no credit. Wyatt was in the middle of a story, and Kora seemed far too occupied slicing meat to greet him. He joined the group and ate silently without anyone making a comment about his late arrival. Kora sat at the opposite end of the table between Wyatt and Cheyenne. Both men complimented her meal but gave most of their attention to Jamie.

When the meal was over, Jamie helped Kora clear the dishes. Win nodded to Wyatt and Cheyenne, then disappeared into his study, saying he had work to do. He was suddenly sick of talking to people, and most of all to himself.

He tried first to work, then to read, but pacing was the

only thing he could do with any ability. Win thought of going out to the barn, but with the rain, all he could do there was think. Also it was not his habit to return to the barn. Win had a feeling Logan would notice and comment come morning.

Logan would mutiny if he thought Win and Kora were having trouble. The old man would be on Kora's side before he even heard what was wrong. Not that he, or anyone else, would ever hear a word about last night. What happened was driving Win mad, and no one seemed to notice, including Kora.

Over and over in his mind he retraced the uneventful evening. The way Kora hardly looked at him. The way everyone talked around him. He might as well be Dan. No one noticed him, and he was starting to pick up his brother-in-law's habit of walking. It was only a matter of time before he and Dan would both be circling the house nightly. Who knows? Maybe it hadn't been the war but a wife somewhere who'd made poor old Dan the way he was.

Why couldn't Kora have yelled at him about the Colt, or about being late to the table, or about the mud he'd tracked all over her kitchen? Why'd she have to act like nothing was wrong when he knew she must hate him? But, hell, the woman even passed him the first piece of pie. That was about as far as he'd be pushed, he'd almost exploded.

Win could stand the study's confinement no longer. He almost jerked the door from its hinges as he bolted out of the room and down the hall to the kitchen. He would allow her to drive him mad no longer. It was time she faced him and had her say. How was he supposed to defend himself if she didn't take a swing at him? She'd probably thought out this strategy of kindness just to drive him insane. Well, he would stand for it no more.

The kitchen was dark except for the glowing fire in the

corner and the flashes of lightning from the windows.

Win stormed back down the hall and up a flight of stairs. If she'd gone to bed without a word, it would be the last straw.

But when he touched the railing to the final staircase, he hesitated. What if she were packing? What if she'd already left him despite the rain?

Jamie opened her bedroom door only a few feet from where Winter stood. "Evening, brother. I figured you went over with Wyatt and Cheyenne to the bunkhouse for a game of cards." She looked pouty. "They made it plain I wasn't invited."

"I didn't go." Winter looked up the stairs toward his bedroom. "I was working in the study and finally decided it was time to turn in."

Jamie laughed. "I never know if you're going up or down. I figured you were sleeping downstairs again. You're worse than a yo-yo. I've seen bedbugs stake claims longer than you do, cowboy. She kick you out again?"

Winter frowned. "No." He wished he'd managed to sound more definite. "I just had some work I needed to do in the study first."

"Well, try to stay up there all night this time. You wake me up always tromping down these stairs." She leaned against the door facing. "I could give you some advice."

"I don't need any!" Winter snapped. "I'm doing fine on my own."

He took the stairs two at a time, wishing his words were true. Kora probably hated him more than she had ever hated anyone. For all he knew, she'd blockaded herself in the room or would toss him out in the rain. But not without a fight. If that was what she wanted, he'd give her one.

When he reached the top of the stairs, the warm glow of several lamps greeted him. Kora was curled in a blanket in an overstuffed chair she'd set next to the bookshelves. She glanced over at him, and he saw the fear in her eyes. Raw, childlike fear.

Winter almost turned around, but he wasn't sure he could stand another day of arguing with himself. He took a step toward her.

"Win," she whispered, and in one sudden movement she was up from the chair and running toward him.

He caught her in midair as her arms wrapped around his neck with such force, for a moment he wasn't sure if she was hugging or attacking.

"I was wrong about the room!" she cried. "It's frightening up here."

Her words didn't register. The feel of her against him, the smell of her surrounding him, the light dancing in her hair was all he could take in.

"What?" he said as he held her.

Kora pulled away. "The lightning looks like it will hit the house at any moment, and the thunder rattles the glass. I don't like this place anymore. Maybe we can both sleep in the study tonight? Up here, it's like being in the middle of a thundercloud."

Winter smiled and lifted her off the floor in his arms. She wasn't frightened of him; she was frightened of the storm. "It's all right," he whispered as he carried her back to the chair.

He sat down and pulled the blanket over them both. "The captain told me once that he ordered the glass for these windows all the way from Chicago. He said the wood in the frame will split before the glass will break. The house has stood for fifty years without a storm taking it down, and I think it will be all right tonight. But if the storm bothers you, I could have shutters put up for nights like this."

She cuddled into his lap, leaning her head on his shoulder. ''I'm sorry to be such a fool. I usually don't let storms bother me. It doesn't seem so bad now that you're here.'' She placed her hand over his heart. ''Jamie would make fun of me for being so childish. I like to see the sky, but when it's stormy I feel closed in. Shutters might be a good idea.''

Win thought of all the things he'd considered saying to her. How he'd argued with himself for hours. In his mind he'd apologized, blamed her, and organized his strategies all day. But now, with her curled in his arms, he couldn't remember what he'd been going to say.

''Kora,'' he finally whispered as his hand moved comfortingly along her back. ''About last night.''

She raised her head and looked at him, blue eyes full of question. ''I forgot to thank you for placing your shirt where you did.'' She paused and looked down, embarrassed at the memory. ''It helped ease the pain considerably.''

Win leaned his head back and closed his eyes. She wasn't holding up her half of the discussion he'd planned. But he'd already prepared his reply and it jumped from his mouth before he could stop the words. ''Well, don't expect me to apologize for taking what's mine.'' He knew he sounded rough. That hadn't been the way he'd meant to say it. ''You should have reminded me you were a virgin and to slow down some. I may not be as experienced in these matters as you seem to think. You can't expect me to slow down in the middle of a stampede.''

Kora straightened in his arms and moved to face him. ''I didn't ask you to apologize.'' Each word rose in anger. ''And I didn't think you were so dense that I'd have to remind you I was a virgin. And you don't have to tell me you aren't an overactive lover. I think I figured that out on my own last night.''

He steadied her back as she squirmed in his lap. It was one thing for him to express his lack of female partners in bed, and quite another for her to comment on the fact.

Before he could think of anything to say, she attacked. "I don't know what I have to do to convince you I'm not some fragile doll made of china that will break. I can take all the bedding you want to give, but I'll not be taken like a whore, and that's final."

She stood and faced him with her hands on her hips. Her anger rivaled the storm outside. "The act of mating hurt me far more than I thought it would, but I survived. Last night when I finished crying, I realized I'm your wife, not because of some bargain we made or because you bedded me, but because I *want* to be. And if you weren't so stubborn and bullheaded, you'd realize the same thing. We'll share a bed as married folks do, but we'll only do the act when both of us are willing. So don't go thinking you were taking when I was the one giving."

Winter felt the anger in him building. She wasn't saying any of the things he'd thought she would, but she'd obviously practiced for this discussion as he had. She wasn't crying or throwing him out, or even running from him like a frightened rabbit. "Are you saying you'll sleep with me again?"

"I am," Kora answered directly. "But there will be no more bedding until the bruises heal. You'll not touch me until then. And you'll never leave a mark on me again."

"Like hell." Win pulled her back into his lap with a sudden jerk. "I'll try never to bruise you again, but I'm not waiting to touch you. Last night in the orchard you said I could touch you whenever I liked."

Before she could protest, his lips covered hers. All the worry and anger vanished as he tasted her again. He groaned when she only hesitated a moment before opening her mouth to his. She was right about one thing. He knew he was her husband and would be until the day he died. Not because of any bargain or last night, but because he wanted to be.

When he finally lifted his head, she made no move to leave his arms.

''I've been waiting all day to taste you again.'' He brushed her cheek with his knuckles. ''I like the way your mouth looks when it's been kissed.''

She cuddled into his arms, resting her head on his shoulder. The kiss had cooled her anger as well and reminded her of the part of last night that she'd enjoyed greatly.

''I didn't intend to hurt you last night,'' he whispered as he stroked her hair. ''I've spent my life working hard and, when the need came, fighting hard. You're the first person in my life who ever made me want to soften my touch. I didn't think about it much, but I figured even if you hadn't slept with Adams, at your age you'd have already had a few lovers.''

Kora straightened slightly. ''I'm not the kind of woman men notice. I've seen men fall all over themselves to open the door for a lady in front of me and let the door close in my face without even noticing.''

Win laughed. ''I find that hard to believe.'' But he remembered the way Logan had first described her and how he'd thought he was marrying a shadow to live in his house. ''There was no one?'' Win watched her closely.

Kora smiled. ''When I was ten there was a boy who lived next door to a basement room we rented. He kissed me once.''

''So I'm not the first?''

''No,'' Kora answered. ''And what of you, Win?''

Win frowned. ''Men don't talk about the women in their past.''

Kora's bottom lip came out. "I told you."

Win fought to keep from kissing her. "All right," he finally answered. "The first time I was man enough to handle a cattle drive the captain bought me a woman when we reached Dodge. I'd had so much to drink I don't remember much except she'd earned her money and was gone before I finished the bottle."

"And the others?"

Win took a long breath, debating how much to tell her. "There was an Indian girl in Wichita Falls I used to see now and then. She was nice and friendly. She wasn't seeing anyone else that I know of and didn't do it for the money, but she didn't mind if I made a few months' payments on her house while I was passing through town. I think I thought that with her I could go home, back to my past. But every time she left me feeling hollow. Like somehow I was muddying the past with what I was doing. I stopped visiting and later heard she'd married the local blacksmith."

"And the others?"

"There were no others," Win said. "I was too busy with the ranch to have time to go courting, and the women for hire were like cheap whiskey. I knew I'd regret it come morning."

"And then there was me," Kora whispered. "Did you regret bedding me?"

"No," he answered honestly. "But I regret hurting you."

"I know," she answered as she wiped the hair from his forehead and kissed his cheek lightly. They sat silently for a while, then she whispered, "I like the way you kiss me. I never thought a kiss could be like that. And when you asked me if I was sure, I said yes, so it wasn't all your fault." She leaned against him. Her voice was so low, it passed between them as almost a thought. "I'll try not to scream the next time you open my legs."

Her words cooled his building passion. Suddenly he didn't want to just bed her, he wanted there to be more between them, much more. She enjoyed his kisses and even his touch. He'd slow down. He'd give her all the time she needed. She was right, she was stronger than he gave her credit for being. By the time she climbed on the train to California she'd know what it was like to enjoy being loved.

Gently he rose with her in his arms and carried her to the bed. While she curled beneath the covers, he stripped and joined her. He kissed her forehead lightly as she rested her head on his shoulder and fell asleep. He guessed she'd slept little last night and probably worried as much about what she'd say to him as he had. Now, in his arms, she relaxed.

All night, Win slept with her next to him. He was always aware of her movements. The feel of her hips pressing against his leg. The warmth of her breath against his throat. The softness of her breast resting on his arm.

Deep into the night, with his mind heavy in dreams, he closed his hand over her breast. She moaned softly in her sleep. He stroked the mound, thinking it might be tender from last night, but she didn't roll from his touch. She'd accepted his touch, and he still saw it as a dream.

She was his, he thought as he gently moved his fingers over her, knowing he could touch her now wherever he liked. This wonderful creature was his to caress all night. She hadn't argued when he'd reminded her she'd given him the right. He moved his fingers over her gown, feeling the peak of each breast and the rise and fall of her breathing. She was his to touch until sunup. He tasted her lips and spread his hand wide over her abdomen. She was his if only for a while.

The smell of her hair filled his senses as he moved his fingers over her hips, stroking her back. He loved the feel of her soft yielding curves. She stretched like a lazy cat and moved her arm around his neck. With only a gentle tug, he pulled her against the length of him so that he could feel her length with his body while his hand moved over the small of her back and down across her hips. She made no protest, but relaxed against him, unaware of the pleasure she brought him while she slept.

He tried to sleep himself, but with each breath her breasts pressed softly against him. Win fought the urge to unbutton her gown. She was sleeping so soundly, she might not awaken, and even if she did, he didn't think she'd stop him. As illogical as it sounded, she'd made it plain that she was his wife and that he was welcome. She'd even asked him to touch her. Last night, when they'd made love, she'd never stopped him from taking all he'd wanted.

And now, tonight, he wanted her more than he had last night. He wanted to see her body, not just feel it. He wanted to taste her breasts, drawing each deep into his mouth. He wanted to caress her until she was ready and would welcome him inside with a cry of pleasure and not pain. But she'd said they'd wait until they both were ready. She'd said not until the bruises healed.

Suddenly the truth dawned on him, shaking him full awake. This was her revenge. Why scream and cry and kick him out when she could torture him like this? She wasn't his, he was hers. She'd drawn every need he'd ever felt out until all he could think of was her. He wanted to pull away and tell her to go to hell, that no woman would ever own or control him. But her soft arm was a chain, her body a magnet he couldn't pull free of.

This small woman with her soft ways and gentle voice would take her revenge all night, and Winter knew he would do nothing but endure the torture.

TWENTY-ONE

KORA AWOKE SLOWLY WITH FIRST LIGHT. SHE COULD feel Winter's body along the length of her, keeping her warm. His arm rested across her waist and his slow steady breathing brushed the nape of her neck. She thought of what a fool she'd made of herself over the storm. It seemed she'd spent a month convincing him she wasn't some frightened child who was intimidated by him, and now she'd acted like one.

But, she smiled, he hadn't seemed to mind. She liked the way he'd lifted her in his arms and carried her back to the chair. Sometimes this strong man reminded her of a little boy. Since almost the first he seemed to be expecting her to pull away from him. He didn't want her to matter to him, but she could see the cracks in the wall between them.

Kora slipped from the bed and moved to her dressing area. She'd found the undergarments wrapped in brown paper yesterday but hadn't put them away. At first she told herself that maybe they weren't hers or that Win would mention them. But he hadn't said a word. It only made sense that he'd bought them for her, then probably forgotten to say anything.

Unfolding the camisole, she slipped it on, loving the soft silk against her skin. She'd never owned anything so grand with lace and ribbons no one would even see. Laughter bubbled from her. He was a strange husband, buying such things for her and never saying anything. Almost as if he didn't want his kindness to show. As always, it was the things he didn't say that told her so much.

Covering the new garments with her worn dress, Kora ran her hand down to her waist remembering the way he'd touched her. Win was a good man, strong and fair. In time, if she stayed long enough, she'd learn to take his bedding. It was a small price to pay. The world might see him as a bear, but she saw another side. A side that was full of longing and sadness. A side she wanted to hold and understand.

The thought of Andrew Adams crossed her mind. Kora flinched. She couldn't imagine allowing Adams to touch her, and the thought of kissing him made her almost gag. He'd given her up for a few dollars, something Win would never do. For the first time, Kora was valued, and that one thought mattered more than the house or the ranch or all the money in all the banks in Texas. She could see it in the hunger of Win's eyes when he looked at her.

Maybe the world had settled and her bad luck had passed. Maybe she could stay here and make a home for Dan and Jamie.

She hurried down the stairs knowing there was much to be done before the rest of the house awakened. Both of the wounded cowhands would return to the bunkhouse today. She had to clean the rooms and be ready. Everyone spoke of trouble as though they could already see the storm coming. They spoke of "when," not "if." But she'd seen no sign of anything happening.

"It won't come this time," she whispered, trying to convince herself as she worked. "I won't let it."

Jamie stumbled into the kitchen about the time the coffee boiled. She hadn't bothered to wash or comb her hair. She grumbled about how Wyatt hadn't returned from the game even to say good night.

Before Kora could offer any excuse for the gambler, Winter walked through the kitchen looking as out of sorts as always. He stepped out onto the porch and turned the icy pitcher of water over his head. The women could hear him swearing when the water hit him.

Jamie griped about the wild man her sister married, but Kora only touched the lace of her camisole. He could be as moody as he liked; he wasn't going to frighten her away by growling. She acted as if she didn't notice him as he reached in and took one of her new kitchen towels to dry his hair without saying a word to her.

"Men!" Jamie snorted. "They're a plague on this earth, that's what they are! Worse than the curse and more irritating than fleas. I'm finished with the lot."

"I thought you liked Wyatt." Kora readied the stove.

"I hate him. He talks real pretty, but he hardly notices me. I'll probably be married and have four younguns before it dawns on him to wonder what happened to me."

Winter stormed back through the kitchen.

"Morning, cowboy," Jamie chimed. "Get up on the wrong side of the bed this morning? That is if you ever found your bed last night."

"Quiet," he mumbled, rubbing his forehead.

"Don't try to boss me around." Jamie grew louder. "I'm not the one who gets up in such a foul mood every morning. You know, cowboy, I'm starting to think I'm worrying about the wrong person in this marriage of yours. Kora gets up all dressed and ready for life every morning, and you look like you've been cactus-drug all night."

Winter stormed out of the room without a word.

Jamie jumped from her chair and crossed to Kora. ''I'm right.'' She stared at Kora. ''You *are* torturing the poor man. All this time I was worried about you, and *he*'s the one who's aging every night. By the time I start liking having a brother-in-law, he'll be near dead. Tell me, dear sister, what are you doing that makes his life such a living hell? What does he have to endure each night that takes ice water to shatter the memories of it at dawn?''

''Stop it, Jamie.'' Kora didn't meet her sister's gaze. ''He just doesn't wake up in a good mood, that's all.'' She handed Jamie Dan's tray. ''Take your brother his breakfast.''

Jamie left, promising she'd learn Kora's secret about how to torment men. As soon as she'd gone, Kora filled a mug.

Winter was pulling on a clean shirt when she appeared on the stairs. ''Thanks,'' he said, taking the coffee from her hand.

''Is something wrong?'' Kora watched him closely while he drank. ''Am I somehow torturing you, as Jamie said?''

Winter took a step closer as he sipped his coffee. With his free hand he touched her throat. She didn't move when his fingers slid along her shoulder and arm, finally resting on her waist.

''You come so easy to me,'' he whispered. ''I never expected that. If that's torture, it's sweet indeed.''

Kora didn't know what to say. She wasn't sure his words were praise. Surely he didn't expect his wife to protest?

''Unbutton your collar,'' he ordered, watching her closely over the rim of his cup.

Straightening slightly, she slipped the first few buttons free. She saw no reason to deny his request.

''Another,'' he said.

Kora felt her cheeks warm beneath his gaze, but she slipped the next button free. When he waited, she moved to the next and the next until the top of her new camisole showed.

He opened her collar, exposing her throat. ''The bruises look lighter today,'' he whispered as his fingers slid over her skin.

Kora relaxed when his touch continued to brush her throat. Despite his rough talk, he was only worried about her. If only Jamie could see him now, she'd think him kind, not hard.

She closed her eyes and sighed as he lowered his lips to the bruises. His mouth was warm and he smelled of soap and coffee.

His hand worked another button free. Then another until the front of her blouse was open.

Kora didn't move. She knew all she had to do was take a step back and she'd be free. No arms bound her.

He pulled a few inches away, his gaze meeting hers as his fingers shoved the material away to reveal her underclothing.

''I touched you last night while you were sleeping,'' he whispered as his gaze lowered.

''I know,'' she answered, feeling her skin warm to his stare. ''I said I didn't mind.''

''And now?'' He moved his fingers lightly over the silk of her camisole. ''Do you mind now?''

''No,'' she answered as she closed her eyes and took a deep breath.

''I'm glad,'' he whispered. His hand moved maddeningly light over her. ''You'd think I'd have had my fill after holding you all night, but it wasn't near enough. Not even close.''

He pushed one strap gently off her shoulder. The silk

slipped lower. He slowly pushed the other strap down. The silk dropped so that he saw the swell of each breast and the hardened peaks just beneath the lace. "I won't be sleeping in the study again." He brushed his fingers over her. "I want your body within reach all night."

"All right," she whispered as she leaned her head back, enjoying the pleasure of his touch.

Slowly his hands slid to her waist, then began the climb upward, buttoning her blouse. Each button seemed a struggle, and his fingers fumbled across the lace. Finally, when he reached her throat, he raised his eyes to hers. "I have to go," he whispered as his fingers brushed her chin. "With you standing before me like this it makes leaving you difficult."

Kora forced her thoughts to the problems of the ranch and not the memory of his touch. "Have you learned anything?"

"Nothing," Win's voice was still thick with passion. "But I told Cheyenne to let you in on every detail. You have a mind for reason inside that body that drove me mad last night."

"I'll keep an eye on Wyatt. I still think he may know more than he's saying."

She smiled a smile that almost made him forget what they were talking about. Their attraction for each other seemed to be sharpening her mind and dulling his, Win thought.

"I'll be here when you get back tonight," she promised and saw the moment of doubt in his eyes.

"Stay buttoned up until I get home." He kissed her lightly. "I'll tell you everything that happens today over supper, then I want to undress you."

"I'll keep supper warm until you return." She smiled. "If you like."

His hand tighted at her waist. "I like what I see and what I feel very much, Kora. What about you? Would you enjoy me undressing you completely tonight?"

She closed her eyes. "Yes," she whispered. "I think I'd like that very much."

"I won't hurt you," he promised as his fingers lightly circled over her back. "I never wanted to hurt you."

"I know." She slowly moved her hands to his shoulders. "I'll be waiting for you tonight."

He bent and touched his mouth to her lips. A shock seemed to vibrate through his body. With one mighty sweep, he pulled her off the floor and into his arms.

She could taste the hunger in him as his lips pressed against hers and the kiss turned to fire between them.

Then, as quickly as he'd held her, he set her down and was gone. Kora felt light-headed. Slowly, with trembling hands, she checked the buttons of her dress, knowing she'd open it again tonight when he asked. His hunger for her made her feel all warm inside. She felt beautiful and cherished and desired. He might never say the words, but for the first time in her life, she felt loved.

The fire in his eyes fascinated her, and his slight touch had made her want to give him anything he asked. He was a man who seemed to need nothing . . . except her.

She hurried to the kitchen, knowing Winter would be back as soon as he saddled up. He made a habit of always stopping in before riding out. Always a second goodbye. He'd say nothing, but she'd meet his eyes and they'd both know he wanted to touch her once more.

As Kora worked, Jamie still complained about Wyatt ignoring her. Kora also paid little attention to her sister. She could still taste Winter's lips on hers and her cheeks were warm from his touch.

"Mornin'!" Wyatt yelled from the doorway. "Win says you got coffee ready."

He stepped into the kitchen with Cheyenne a few feet behind. The Indian was leaning heavily on his crutch, indicating yesterday's trip had not come without a price.

"Win said he's going to cover the south rim again today," Wyatt announced, "but I think I'll stay around and keep you ladies and Cheyenne company, at least until the riders who were out all night come in. Then I might wander down to the settlement and look for a game." The gambler tossed a gold coin in the air and winked at Jamie. "That is, if I can think of nothing else to do."

Jamie walked past Wyatt as if he were invisible and she heard nothing. "Morning, Cheyenne," she said in a voice laced with honey.

Before Cheyenne could answer, Jamie stood on her tiptoes and kissed him hard on the mouth. She wrapped her arms around his neck vise-tight.

Kora and Wyatt stared.

Jamie broke the kiss suddenly and walked out of the room, leaving Wyatt staring after her with his mouth open and fire in his eyes.

Cheyenne wiped his mouth hard with the back of his hand. "I'd like that coffee if it's ready." He limped to the table as if nothing needed to be said about what happened.

"I'd like to kill her!" Wyatt stormed.

Kora poured the coffee. "She's just upset about last night."

"Well, she didn't have to take it out on me!" Wyatt snapped.

"On me, you mean," Cheyenne answered without emotion.

Wyatt wasn't listening. "I've hardly spoken to another girl since we've been stepping out. She knows how I feel about her.'' He paced the kitchen. ''First she looks at the stars with the doc and now this. I don't know how much more I can take.''

''Maybe you should marry the girl, Wyatt. Then at least she'd leave me out of the fight.''

''I'm not the marrying kind.'' Wyatt stared at the door where she'd exited. ''But I'm not going to stand for this. She knows she's my girl and it's time she started acting like it.''

When he stormed out of the room, Kora glanced at Cheyenne. ''Do you think I should call Win in to try and stop him?''

''You mean before Wyatt gets himself killed?'' Cheyenne laughed. ''No, I never was too crazy about the gambler anyway. I'll pick up the body parts she throws over the banister after I've had my coffee.''

Winter returned to a silent kitchen. As he reached for his hat, he heard something crash from the floor above. He glanced in question at Kora and Cheyenne, but neither of them moved. ''What's wrong?''

''Nothing,'' they both said, grinning.

Cheyenne cleared his throat. ''The gambler just might be asking for Jamie's hand. By tonight we'll either have a wedding or a funeral. My money's on the funeral.''

Though Win nodded, his mind was on something else. He grabbed Kora's hand and pulled her out of the kitchen without another word. On the porch he let go of her fingers and faced her. ''Remember,'' he whispered. ''No matter how late, wait up.''

Kora smiled. ''I'll stay dressed.'' She draped her arms around his shoulders and kissed him soundly, even though they both knew half the ranch could be watching.

''You're awfully bold, woman.'' He smiled when she let him go.

She raised an eyebrow. "Do you mind?"

"Not a chance," he answered as he walked away.

Riding south, Winter began at the corner of his land and rode toward Break's Settlement. He'd moved most of his cattle to the north pastures, but a small herd of longhorns still roamed among the uneven ground by the south edge.

He'd always liked the sturdy longhorns. They were powerful animals with their long curved horns and ornery dispositions. But they were survivors. He'd brought other lines in working on improving his herd, but it was always the longhorns who survived the hard winters and hot summers.

About midafternoon he saw a cow low in the draw, stuck in a muddy creek. For a moment he watched her struggling, thinking how strange that the animal would get herself in such a mess. She was far deeper in the water than she would have needed to go to get a drink.

Unhooking his rope, he moved down the rocky incline toward her. If he didn't take the time to pull her out, the coyotes would get her before morning.

Just as he threw his lasso, he realized he wasn't alone. Three men, almost completely hidden behind the cottonwoods, were watching him.

They were close enough to have gotten off a shot, but they hadn't. He glanced over the muddy ground and realized the cow had been driven into the water.

As he worked, he kept his hand close to his Colt, expecting to hear a shot any moment. But the men stayed well back, only outlines among the trees.

Winter struggled for a few more minutes to free the cow, then saw them moving toward him. They were men he'd seen around, but couldn't put a name to any face.

"Afternoon, Mr. McQuillen!" one yelled. "We was just riding along and saw you might need a little help."

Winter knew they were lying, but he was also curious about what they might want. If they'd been ambushers, they would have fired from safety.

One of the men was playing with his rope while the others circled Win's horse. "I'll give you a hand." He tried to sound casual.

The drifter on Win's left began to work his lasso, also. Win shifted in the saddle. The cow on the other end of his rope kept him rooted; otherwise he'd have backed away from the strangers.

Just as the first man swung his rope, not toward the cow, but at Win, another swung a rifle butt toward Win's head.

With his hands caught in his own rope, Win twisted violently to avoid the blow and got snared in the other stranger's loop. A second later he hit the mud, rolling and fighting to reach his gun. Another rope circled his arm and pulled it tightly behind him.

Win fought to free himself as the men laughed and backed their horses until the ropes were tight. The man with the rifle slid from his saddle and moved cautiously toward Win.

"We figure you took a blow to the head when you fell, mister. So here's the blow." The drifter swung twice before the wood of his rifle cracked against Win's skull.

Though the world went dark, Win's body still fought to pull free.

"Drag him over to that nest of water moccasins, boys. We want this to look like an accident!" one of the men yelled. "The way he's thrashing around, he'll take a dozen bites, maybe more, before we can pull him out."

The ropes tightened around his shoulder and arm as Win slid across the mud and water. He fought wildly but couldn't free himself.

"Keep the ropes tight while the snakes bite!" the leader

yelled again. ''We don't want him getting lucky and drowning. We want to take him back alive so we'll be heroes. Then when the poison seeps in, it'll look like we done our best to save him. While they're mourning, we'll follow the rest of the plan.''

Water rushed over Winter, barely deep enough to cover him before he felt them. Snakes, thin and fast moving over him, curling around his legs, crossing over his chest.

Water moccasins. Winter's mind drifted back to when he was a boy living among his mother's people.

''How many bites would kill me?'' he asked his mother once as they watched the olive-brown snake slide across the water with his head up slightly.

''With the wet snake be it little or long, it's not how many, but how long you have left. One, two, three . . . a man can take, but after that he doesn't need to count the snakes . . . only the hours of pain he has left.''

TWENTY-TWO

THE SUN HAD A WAY OF LYING DOWN ALONG THE horizon and dying a slow brilliant death. Kora sat on the porch and watched, smiling at her memories of last night. Fate had given her a chance to be a wife, and she planned to enjoy the role as long as it lasted. All her life she'd wondered how it would feel to be cherished. Winter might frighten half the folks around here, but he was gentle with her. He thought she was special. She could see desire in his eyes, and his passion proved his longing for her. He was also talking to her of the problems of the ranch, which made her feel like she belonged, she was truly family.

Three riders appeared far to the south. Kora watched them approach, trying to see if one was Win. She shook her head. None of them had the height.

Jamie slammed the screen door as she joined her sister. "I'm bored." She pouted. "I wish I'd gone with Win. Since Cheyenne is still hobbling around here, I could have riden backup. Now I'm stuck here bored out of my mind."

Kora knew the mood had more to do with Wyatt leaving after their fight than with Jamie's lack of anything to do. Cheyenne had been wrong when he'd predicted the gambler would propose. Wyatt wanted a girl, but not a wife, it seemed. And Jamie wanted no strings on her as well.

Leaning against the porch railing, Jamie added, "Maybe it's about time we moved on before the witchin' luck catches up to us."

Kora didn't say a word. She didn't want to think about her mother's pet name for the bad luck that always followed them.

"I don't want to leave this time," Kora whispered more to herself than Jamie. "I like it here and Dan hasn't coughed in days. He's growing stronger with regular meals and clean air." She knew Jamie loved the adventure, but Kora had longed for roots. "I thought we'd stay till summer." She'd been wondering how she'd tell Jamie that her marriage to Win was only temporary. Even with all that had happened, Win had never said a word about her not leaving. "Then we might finally head to California." She tried to sound excited.

Her sister wasn't listening. As she spotted the riders, Jamie bolted like a shot from her perch and ran toward the yard. "Logan! Cheyenne! Come quick!"

"What is it?" The air seemed to pop with excitement around Kora. "Jamie, what's wrong?" All she could see was three riders, one leading a horse, the other two riding a few yards ahead. Nothing seemed unusual, yet Jamie was dancing around wildly.

Logan and Cheyenne appeared at the barn entrance as Jamie shouted, "That's Win's horse they're pulling behind them!"

Cheyenne was in the saddle in a heartbeat riding toward the men at full gallop despite his injury. Logan disappeared back into the barn. He stepped out a few seconds later with a rifle in his hands.

"Best get in the house, ladies, until we know something.'' He moved toward the center of the yard. Other rifles slid out the doors and windows behind him. '' 'Pears trouble finally found us.''

''No,'' Kora answered, standing beside her sister in the center of the yard. ''I'm not leaving.''

The riders drew closer. They were hard men with the look of a drifter about each. All three needed haircuts and shaves, and their clothes were so layered in dust and sweat Kora couldn't even guess what color the fabric had once been.

Just as Cheyenne reached the riders, she saw a body tied over Win's horse.

Kora screamed as Cheyenne jumped from his mount at full gallop and drew his blade. He slit the ropes holding Win and pulled his friend into his arms. With great effort, he lifted Win on the saddle and climbed up behind him. He kicked the horse into action and rode toward home.

All the blood seemed to drain from her as Kora watched Cheyenne bring Win the last hundred yards. She couldn't move. Her husband's body was covered in mud and soaking wet. And lifeless.

Logan shouted orders as the riders came in, but all Kora could do was stare. They lowered Win to the dirt while the three strangers climbed down from their saddles.

''We found him in the water,'' one said.

''Snake bit. They was crawling all over him.''

''We know you'd want us to bring him home for the time he has left,'' another mumbled.

Kora glanced at Jamie. Neither said a word, but both were thinking the same thing. Witchin' luck had struck again. They hadn't left this place soon enough. Misfortune had found them.

Kora felt her flesh turn to stone. She'd known from the first that nothing good lasted. How long did she think she could stay in this daydream that she could live happily as Winter's wife? People like her and Jamie and Dan were never meant to be happy. They were never supposed to stay in one place.

"Take him inside!" she ordered. "All the way to our bedroom."

The men did as she asked, marching in a funeral procession up the stairs.

Kora hardly noticed the mud they tracked across her floor or the dirt that scarred the walls as the men scraped against them. All she saw was Winter's lips, white and swollen, and his body limp and twisted awkwardly by several pairs of hands.

The strangers who brought him in were the only ones talking.

"He's been bit several times."

"I counted six on his arms and legs."

"Ain't never known anyone to live with more than three or four."

"Your boss will never see another sunrise."

Kora wanted to grab Win's Colt and shoot all three of them. But they were only the bearers of bad news and not the villains. "Thank you for bringing him home," she managed to say. "Please come in and rest while I see to my husband."

The three men smiled and began thanking her, but Kora was no longer listening. She followed the men upstairs never stopping the string of orders to first Logan, then Jamie, then several of the hands. She couldn't explain why, but danger still seemed heavy in the air. Maybe she was just seeing Dan's ghosts, but something seemed wrong. When she had time she'd reason each clue out, but for now she'd protect them.

Cheyenne unstrapped Win's gunbelt and laid it on the

floor. "I'll help you get him out of these clothes first, then we can take a look at the bites. With water moccasins there's no use sending for the doc. He'll either be better or dead before the doc could get here."

Kora lifted the wet gunbelt from the floor and strapped it around her waist not caring that the mud stained her dress. The weapon hung low over her full skirt. She pulled the Colt from its nest. "Will it fire?"

Logan stopped helping Cheyenne long enough to answer. "No, ma'am."

"Then clean it when you have time and load it for me. I'll wear it until he's up and able to do so again." She left no room for discussion as she laid down the useless gun and began ripping away Win's shirt, it was one of his new shirts.

Just as they spread a clean quilt over him, Jamie entered the room with a tray loaded down with supplies Kora had asked for.

"How is he?" she whispered.

Both men were silent. They'd counted six deep bites and maybe a dozen scratches that might not have released much poison.

"He's going to make it," Kora said without blinking. "But until he's up and on his feet, we've got to be on guard. Something's not right." She mixed the water with a handful of baking soda. "I don't care what those men downstairs said, Win would not fall into a nest of snakes."

Cheyenne's head snapped up as if someone had hit him hard in the jaw. "She's right," he whispered. "Win's no fool. He's known about water moccasins since he could walk. His mother's tribe believes in living with them, not killing them."

A silence fell between the four people standing around the bed. Words were not needed. Win hadn't suffered an accident; someone had tried to kill him and might very well have succeeded. And the most likely villains were downstairs in the kitchen right now.

"I'll kill whoever did this," Jamie mumbled. "It must have been a gang because no man could take my brother-in-law down alone."

Kora pulled the quilt to his waist and began washing the bites with a rag soaked in baking soda. "Force a drink of whiskey down his throat," she ordered as she worked. "Jamie, you may be right. Go downstairs and give the strangers all the leftovers we have in the cool box." Before Jamie could question she added, "And don't miss a word they say."

"I'll only make a quick stop at my room. I only have two knives on me and I may need three." Jamie disappeared to do as ordered.

Kora slid down the quilt and began soaking the red dots on Win's legs. The thought crossed her mind that for a girl who hated Win, Jamie was sure fighting mad at him being hurt.

"That won't help." Logan's voice was thick with sadness. "Nothing will, that I know of."

"We've got to try and pull the poison out," Kora answered in almost a cry. "Give me your knife, Cheyenne. Logan, open the windows."

Cheyenne did as she asked without question.

"If he's cold, maybe the poison will move slower." Kora told them. "Cheyenne, keep one eye on the stairs. No one but the four of us is getting any closer to Win tonight. Logan, spread the word that if anyone comes up here, he'll be shot on sight."

"Yes, ma'am." Logan moved to the stairs, but before he went down, he added, "The boss would be real proud of you. If he makes it through this, I plan on telling him what a lucky man he is."

Kora nodded her thank-you and went back to work. With tears rolling unchecked down her cheeks, she cut each bite from fang mark to fang mark, making the swollen flesh bleed.

Cheyenne forced more whiskey down Win, then held his head as convulsions shook Win's body and he began to throw up. He vomited until there was nothing left in his stomach, then Cheyenne poured more whiskey down him.

Kora forced each bite mark to continue bleeding, spilling a great deal of Winter's blood along with a tiny bit of the yellow venom.

When Win finally stopped shaking and throwing up, Cheyenne made him take another swallow of whiskey, then covered him. "Let him rest. We've done all we can for now."

Kora gently wrapped each of his wounds, thankful that none of the bites had been on his face or neck.

"He might just make it," Cheyenne said as he moved to where he had a clear view of the staircase. "All the bites were on his arms and legs, and none looked to be as deep as I've seen some. The bigger the man, the more poison he can take in his blood without dying. Win's got a good chance, Kora."

For the first time Kora noticed Cheyenne's limp, much more pronounced than it had been earlier. "You're hurt?" she whispered. "The ride out to him must have been painful."

"I can live with it," Cheyenne answered.

The hours passed. The night grew colder. But Win didn't move. She tried every poultice she'd ever heard of, even having Jamie heat coal and spread it over the wounds. Nothing seemed to work. Win's breathing was so light she had to listen for his heartbeat to tell if he was still alive.

"Don't die on me," she whispered once in anger.

"Don't die on me just when I started believing in us."

Cheyenne brought in a root he said his people used for the bites. When they rubbed it on the wounds, it did seem to help the redness some. They brewed a tea from it and made Win drink, but he didn't keep much of it down.

While Logan went down to talk to the men, Jamie took up guard by the stairs. She badgered Cheyenne until he sat down, resting his injury for a while. "You'll reopen the wound and end up sitting around here another month," she complained.

"I'm fine," Cheyenne insisted, but he took the offered chair.

Finally, when Kora had done everything she could think of to do, she curled next to Win's still body and lay her arm over his chest. His breathing was now deep and regular, giving her hope.

They'd sent for the doctor, but the rider had only left a note on his door. The doctor was out somewhere on call. Anything they did, they'd have to do alone.

TWENTY-THREE

AN HOUR LATER, WHEN LOGAN RETURNED WITH THE story of how the drifters had just happened on Win, Kora was convinced the men were lying. They claimed he'd been floating in the shallow water with his horse only a few feet away. One suggested the mount must have thrown him. Kora glanced from Cheyenne to Logan. *Impossible*, she thought.

Kora barely noticed Jamie silently slip from the room as Logan went over every detail of the men's story for the third time.

While the others talked, Jamie tiptoed down the stairs and approached the dining room. The three men were whispering at the far end of the table. She crawled on her belly until she slipped under the tablecloth and crept to the center of the table, her body within inches of their legs.

"Well, how do you like the old guy? He offers us a place to sleep in the bunkhouse. You'd think we'd get to stay in the main house after what we did bringing the boss in and all."

"Shut up, Miller. We ain't got time to sleep. If McQuillen ain't dead yet, he just might pull through, and where is that going to leave us? I knew we should have left him in a little longer until he took a few more bites.''

''We held him till he stopped jerking. That should have been long enough.'' The man called Miller added, ''We'd best hightail it out of here. I ain't dealing with a man six cottonmouths can't kill.''

''No,'' the third man, smaller than the others, interrupted. ''We've been paid by the lady to get Win McQuillen off the blockade line by tomorrow night. 'Whatever it takes,' she said. If this don't work, we'll have to find another way.''

''But how?'' Miller whined. ''I'm not charging up those stairs with that Indian and that wild girl standing guard. Even the wife wears a gun. These folks aren't going to let us just kill him.''

''No''—the little man giggled—''there's a way he won't be thinking of minding the blockade even if he wakes up. And we don't have to kill anyone.''

''How's that? I only went along with the snakes 'cause I wouldn't have to do the killin'. I'll do just about anything, but killin's where I draw the line.''

''Since when did you get religion, Miller?''

''I ain't got religion. My dad used to tell me no matter what I did, don't do nothing that would get my neck stretched. He said a man can always break out of a prison, but there ain't much you can do to survive when you're dangling from the end of a noose.''

''Hush up, Miller. We ain't got time,'' the third man whispered. ''What's the plan, Al?''

''When the wife comes down, we take her for a little ride. She'll have every man on the place looking for her, and we can probably drive a herd within sight of the house. She ain't more than a snip of a girl. It shouldn't be too much trouble to collect her and drop her off at the hideout."

Jamie pulled back, biting her knuckle to keep from screaming and charging out and killing all the men. She crawled away as they went to refill their coffee.

Cheyenne met her on the landing. He'd been sitting in the blackness, waiting. She almost bumped into him before she saw him.

A frightened scream died in her throat as she took an angry swing at him. "You scared me to death!" she whispered. "What are you doing here?"

"I wanted to know what the men said. I could tell they were scheming with their heads all together, but I couldn't hear anything. Then I see you sliding from beneath the tablecloth."

Jamie debated telling him. The chances were good he wouldn't believe her. But he was her one hope. He might irritate her to the breaking point, but for once they had a common goal, to keep Win alive. She leaned close beside him in the darkness.

"They've been hired by some woman to make sure Win isn't watching tomorrow night. She must be the one planning to run the cattle past. Since the snakes failed, the only other plan those three toads can come up with is to kidnap Kora."

Jamie placed her hand on Cheyenne's leg to keep him from reacting. "Settle down. I already thought of killing them in the kitchen. It would just make a mess."

He relaxed slightly, but his breathing grew rapid with fury.

"If we kill them, we're no closer to knowing who's behind this than we were before. The woman who hired them may not be the boss but just a hired hand like those three downstairs. If we're going to help Win, we need to find out who is behind all this trouble."

"So what do you suggest?" Cheyenne asked. "We let them kidnap Kora?"

"Exactly." Jamie didn't let go of his leg for fear he'd bolt. "Only it won't be Kora. It'll be me."

Cheyenne's breathing stopped.

Jamie leaned closer, frantically pleading her case. "We don't have time to get the sheriff and let them spend a few days in jail before they decide to talk. One man said a herd will pass through here tomorrow night. If we don't know who wants to stop Win by then, we won't know who to trust. Our men will be sitting ducks all along the blockade."

"But they won't take you instead of Kora," Cheyenne whispered.

"Not dressed like this. But if I put on a dress and tie my hair back, I'd pass for her in poor light."

"No, it's too dangerous."

"Give me some credit! I've spent my life running with the boys. Some towns we lived in, the neighbors thought I *was* a boy because I could whip anyone close to my size. I'm able to take care of myself, and I'll have a few surprises tucked away in the folds of my dress." She could tell he wasn't convinced. "Plus, you'll be watching and following me. Once they take us to their camp, you can barge in and the two of us can fight our way out."

Cheyenne groaned. "It's a lame plan." He removed her hand that was resting on his leg, putting her plan aside as easily as he did her touch.

"Well, I've got a lame partner." Jamie laughed as she patted his leg, discovering how much her touch bothered him. "I've waited all my life to pay Kora back for all the sacrifices she's made for me. Now's my chance. I can save her and Win's ranch."

"We'll probably both be killed."

"Got any other ideas? Anyone else we get involved will be pulling men off the guard. Logan will be here to protect Win and Kora." Jamie rested her hand on his leg, rooting her fingers into his flesh so she wouldn't be so easy to cast off again. "It's just you and me."

Cheyenne was silent for a long moment. "All right. But don't do anything foolish. Once you're in their camp, just play the frightened woman. I'll find a way to get in and save you, maybe without having to fight our way out."

Jamie nodded. "I'll go get dressed and then start making myself an easy catch." She patted his leg once more before disappearing.

Cheyenne slowly climbed the stairs, shaking his head. It was a crazy plan that would probably get them both killed, but Jamie was right. It was the only one they could think of. Win had told him to talk anything new over with Kora, but he wasn't about to tell her what Jamie was planning. Kora would never go along with it, and if he had any sense left, he wouldn't, either.

Kora sat beside the bed as Cheyenne entered. "He's better," she whispered. "He mumbled my name a few minutes ago and asked for water. He's pulling out."

Cheyenne stood over the bed, staring down at Winter.

He'd do anything for Win, even die, and Win would never know why. The time had come to tell someone in case he didn't come back and Kora was the one. "When Win's village was attacked years ago," Cheyenne began more to himself than Kora, "I was away with several of the older boys training to be a 'dog soldier.' I wasn't there to help my mother or her tribe. The soldiers killed her without even knowing that she'd been a white woman, raising her sons among their father's people."

Kora listened, knowing the Indian was speaking words long in his heart.

"I returned to find only bodies, mostly women and children. My mother and two little brothers were among the dead. My father lived the night, but didn't want to face dawn without my mother. I was holding him in my arms when he just stopped breathing.

"A few of the tribe's children had managed to run and hide. When they returned to camp weeks later, the leader of our people made a little half-breed named Winter go back to the white man's world. All my family was dead, so I followed Winter. I guess I figured since we were both of mixed blood, we were the same somehow. He looks like his father from the white man's world and I look more like my father from the Indian world, but we are the same inside. A part of no world."

Silently he drew his knife and cut the bandage on Win's arm. Without hesitation, he then slit into his own wrist.

Kora made a little sound but didn't move as Cheyenne lowered his bloody wrist over Winter's open wound. The Indian didn't explain, he didn't have to. Kora knew he was offering his own blood to Winter.

After a few minutes Kora gently lifted Cheyenne's arm and bandaged his wrist. He didn't make any speeches by telling her he'd die for Win, or how much Win meant to him. He'd proved his point with the action.

As she finished wrapping the cut, Logan stepped into the attic. "I thought I'd relieve you on guard. Our three guests are preparing to leave. They said they'd like to pay their respects to Mrs. McQuillen before they go."

Kora glanced at Winter. "I don't want to leave Win."

"You stay," Cheyenne volunteered. "I'll see them off."

He took a few steps, then looked back. "Promise you'll stay up here."

"Of course." She smiled. "Where else?"

She sat back down beside the bed.

Cheyenne hurried out of the room. He met Jamie at the bottom of the attic stairs.

"How do I look?" Jamie asked as she spun in her dress. Her bun was not as smooth as Kora made and her boots showed from beneath the hem, but in a poor light it would be hard to tell them apart.

"You'll pass. Same hair, same size, but try to move in smaller steps like Kora."

"I know what to do!" Jamie scolded. "You just make sure you follow. If I have to kill those three fellows, I don't want to have to walk back here in this dress."

Cheyenne nodded. "Logan says the men are saddling up now. I'll move out and get my horse ready, then wait behind the barn. You go stand on the porch. The light is dim there. And don't do anything foolish like fight when they grab you."

"This is my idea, remember." Jamie poked him in the chest with her finger. "I know what I'm doing."

"I'll remember that when this plan falls apart," Cheyenne answered.

Jamie turned to go, but his hand on her shoulder stopped her. "One more thing," he said as he closed the distance between them. "Before you get yourself killed, I want to give you back something."

Before she could react, he kissed her hard on the mouth like she'd kissed him that morning.

When he released her, Jamie's eyes stung, her lips tingled, and her heart raced. She felt the kiss all the way to her toes. "How dare you!" she stormed, more angry that he had such an effect on her than that he'd kissed her.

Cheyenne moved toward the front door. "I'll take it back if we live through this."

He was gone before she could answer that she'd make sure he did.

TWENTY-FOUR

THE WIND WHIPPED AROUND, CONFUSING THE DIRECtion of sounds. Cheyenne crept in the blackness of the night until he could see the lights from the house. He'd saddled his horse and now all he had to do was wait.

Jamie stepped off the porch just as the three strangers emerged from the barn. They were talking among themselves. One pointed in Jamie's direction while the other two huddled around him.

Cheyenne saw her walk toward the well, a bucket swinging at her side. Good, he thought, look natural. She was doing a great job of shortening her step to act more like Kora. In the dress he could almost believe she was a lady. Before the three men had moved more than a few feet, a blackness passed between Cheyenne and Jamie. One second she'd been walking toward the well, the next she vanished as though the moonless night had swallowed her whole.

Cheyenne twisted uneasily. There were too many black spots in the yard. He couldn't see her. The three men were still standing by the barn door mumbling. They seemed to be arguing about something as they tossed a blanket between them like children playing hot potato.

Somewhere in the shadows at the side of the main house, Cheyenne heard the jingle of a harness and the groan of a wagon beginning to roll out. The lonely sound of a harmonica drifted from the bunkhouse, and the cook yelled from the kitchen, reminding Cheyenne that the ranch was still very much alive, though Win was near death.

Cheyenne searched the darkness once more, fear climbing up his spine. Something was wrong, very wrong.

Then he saw Jamie step off the porch once more. She was safe! He'd worried for nothing.

She walked slowly toward the trees as though just out for a stroll. Since earlier, she'd grown restless. Her steps were jerky, not nearly as smooth. Cheyenne reminded himself she was young, and despite her bravado, games like this one were new to her. He hoped she wouldn't panic and run before the men could kidnap her. If they were going through with this plan, everything had to go right. Her life was the ante.

The three strangers finally took the bait. They were in the saddle and heading toward her before she had time to turn around. Cheyenne heard her muffled scream as one man tossed a blanket over her head and another lifted her off the ground and onto the front of his saddle.

Somewhere in the darkness a guard sounded the alarm. Men hurried from the bunkhouse pulling weapons ready as they moved. Cheyenne raised into the saddle, allowing the strangers enough lead not to know they were being followed.

But Jamie's reaction was too natural to be forgotten as planned. She fought wildly, kicking and screaming. Her actions frightened the poorly trained horse, who began circling instead of running. She kicked violently, knocking the man from his horse and landing on top of him. The two others slapped their animals into action without staying to help the downed man. Jamie was on her feet whirling a knife at her captor even before she could pull the blanket from her face.

Suddenly she realized what she'd done. "What kind of kidnapper are you?" She stormed at the injured man, kicking him hard in both legs and banging him on the head with her fist as though he were a drum. "Can't you even stay in the saddle?" She booted him again and continued her pounding beat against his ears. "Don't you even know how to grab someone and hold on? I should kill you for not even knowing how to hold a frightened mount!"

Cheyenne grabbed her around the waist from behind before she could deliver another blow to the poor man balled on the ground.

"Stop it!" Cheyenne shouted in her ear. "Don't kill him before he answers a few questions."

"Keep her off me!" the man yelled.

"Where are your friends going?" Cheyenne asked as he struggled to hold Jamie.

The man hesitated. Cheyenne lowered a still kicking, fighting Jamie to the ground.

"I'll tell." The man held up his hand. "Just don't let her at me."

Cheyenne pulled her back against his side. "Then you'd better talk fast, because as you know, she's hard to hold."

"They're heading for the Breaks Settlement. We was just going to keep her there for a day or two. We weren't going to hurt her none, I swear."

"Who's paying you?" Cheyenne fired the next question as other men came running from the barn.

"I don't know. I swear. I just saw a woman on horseback bring the money. She told us to make sure Win McQuillen was busy for a few days. I don't know nothing else."

''What'd she look like?'' Cheyenne shouted over Jamie's death threats.

''I couldn't tell.'' The man crawled away a few feet. ''I couldn't tell nothing. It was night and she had on a black duster.''

Several ranch hands reached them, pulling the man to his feet and removing his weapons.

''Tie him up.'' Cheyenne let go of Jamie. ''I'll follow the others.'' He grabbed his reins, when a single fact froze him in place.

The woman heading toward the well earlier had carried the bucket in her left hand!

TWENTY-FIVE

CHEYENNE TOOK THE STAIRS IN DOUBLE TIME WITH Jamie just behind him. They stormed into the attic bedroom as the first hint of daylight touched the horizon.

"Where's Kora?" Cheyenne asked Logan.

Jamie bumped into him from behind and swore at his sudden stop.

Logan stood from the chair by the bed. "She's gone down to check on Dan. Almost forgot him, she did, with all that's been going on."

Cheyenne turned and trudged down the stairs. The sick feeling he had in his gut grew worse.

"What is it?" Jamie was right behind him. "What's wrong?"

"I've got to find Kora!" He left unsaid what he feared.

They stopped at the kitchen first, then covered the downstairs. Cheyenne's worry was contagious. Jamie ran up to the bedrooms on the second floor while Cheyenne checked the barn. By the time they reached the orchard, they were both yelling Kora's name.

"Where is she?" Jamie demanded. "She's usually around the house. By dawn she's always cooking breakfast.

She couldn't have disappeared. She wouldn't have left us.''

''I don't know about leaving you,'' Cheyenne responded. ''But she wouldn't leave Winter any longer than needed. In the blackness just before sunup, I thought I saw you by the well, then you vanished.''

Concern turned to panic in Jamie's eyes. ''I never walked toward the well. I stayed on the porch until I knew you were in place, then I walked toward the orchard. Do you think one of the two men who got away grabbed Kora?''

''No,'' he answered. ''They had no time. Besides, they rode out alone.''

''Well, if they didn't take her, she must be somewhere around here.'' Jamie kicked at her skirts.

''Was Dan in bed?''

''No,'' Jamie answered. ''He's probably started his walk by now.''

Cheyenne rubbed his forehead, trying to get the pieces to fit after a long night of no sleep. ''You look for him. I've got to talk to Winter. If the snakes didn't kill him, Kora's kidnapping might.''

''Kidnapping!'' Jamie screamed as she followed him back into the house.

Win came awake inch by painful inch. His limbs throbbed, his stomach felt as if it were gnawing away at his backbone, and his head pounded war drums.

''Kora,'' he whispered as he rolled over and reached for her.

''Win?'' someone said. ''Win, can you hear me?''

Reluctantly he opened one eye. Kora was several feet away by the window. Cheyenne and Logan were on either side of his bed.

''Water,'' Win whispered, feeling as though he'd die if he didn't have a drink soon.

Logan placed his hand on the back of Win's head as Win downed several swallows before the old man pulled the cup away as if rationing.

Leaning back, Win let his gaze rest on Kora. She was looking out the window, her hair catching the morning sun. He opened and closed his fingers, wishing he could touch her. All through the night he'd been fighting his way to Kora, reaching for her, trying to hold her. But the wind kept whirling her around, blowing her away from him.

Logan offered him another drink.

This time Win closed his hand around the cup so it wouldn't be pulled away.

The old man laughed. "He's going to be fine. He's fighting me for the water."

Slowly the room came into focus. It was late morning, maybe early afternoon. For some reason he was still in bed.

As Win's mind cleared, he looked down at his arms, bandaged in several places. Without inspection he could feel bandages on his legs, also. "What happened?" he mumbled. "The last thing I remember I was pulling a cow out of the mud."

Winter closed his eyes. Memory came back in flashes, like stills flipping through a stereoscope. Three men offering help. The ropes. The snakes. The ride home. The blackness.

Logan interrupted Win's thoughts. "Three men brought you back snake bit."

"I was—"

"We know," Logan said. "It wasn't an accident."

"Kora." Win tried not to let his frustration show that she hadn't even bothered to turn from the window.

Slowly she twisted. It took a moment for Win to take in the woman before him. It wasn't Kora, it was Jamie, and tears were streaming down her face.

"I'm sorry, Win!" Jamie cried. "I wish it were me and not her."

"Kora," he whispered and let the black of sleep melt over him once more.

Logan looked across the bed at Cheyenne. "What do we do?"

"We save the ranch. If they're planning to move the cattle tonight, we must have every hand in the saddle and well armed. Kora's kidnappers will find us, we don't have to go looking for them. I'm surprised we haven't had word yet of the terms. Until we do, we think of the ranch."

"No!" Jamie cried. "We save my sister."

Cheyenne shook his head. "The ranch has always been the most important thing in Win's life. We have no idea where she is. We can't have men everywhere looking for her. We've got to save the ranch."

"But whoever has her might hurt her."

"If infected cattle cross this land, thousands of head are going to die and that will hurt a lot of people. Win can bury his dead beef and burn the grassland and survive, but it will spread to the smaller ranches. It could mean their farms and ranches being bankrupted. Families having to move or going hungry."

Jamie ran to the stairs. "Then I'll find her myself. She must be near crazy with fright by now. She's always had me around, you know."

Cheyenne was a step behind her. He grabbed her by the arm. "You don't understand. Someone has to stay here and guard the ranch, look after Winter. At least until the doc gets here."

Jamie jerked free of his grasp. "No, *you* don't understand. *Someone* has to find my sister!"

• • •

Kora sat at the table, trying not to breathe. The smell of dirt was so thick in the air she could almost feel it coating her lungs each time she inhaled. Closing her eyes, she tried to picture her bedroom with Win, the clean air, the sunlight, the warmth of his arms about her.

Andrew Adams rattled around the kitchen area, tossing empty cans aside that he hadn't bothered to throw out.

She knew she should probably be afraid of him, but all she felt was angry and irritated. "Untie me!" she demanded.

"Shut up!" Andrew Adams yelled back. "I have to think." He pulled a bottle from the empty flour can.

They'd been in the tiny dugout for a long while. She wasn't sure of the time. He'd tied her hands and gagged her before tossing her in the wagon loaded down with hay and old blankets. As soon as he'd gotten her to the dugout, he'd sat her in the only unbroken chair. She guessed that he'd never thought of the kidnapping succeeding, for he seemed to have no plan of what to do with her now that she was here in his home.

"Let me go," she tried for the hundreth time. "You'll only get in trouble with the law for kidnapping. If you let me go, I won't tell anyone."

Andrew Adams drank his nervousness away while he packed his things. At first he'd been so flustered he'd ignored all her requests, but now he was willing to talk to her. "They don't arrest a man for taking his own wife. I only took what was mine. I didn't do nothing wrong."

"I'm not your wife."

He downed another swallow and moved toward her. "Maybe you think you're not because the high-and-mighty Win McQuillen paid what you took from me. Or maybe because the lawyer in town said the proxy's no good. But the way I figure it, you owe me. I wouldn't have headed to Bryan and been shot if I hadn't thought I was going after a wife. All I came back with was a bag of hurt and a woman who hadn't even stayed for my funeral."

"But I wasn't the one you came for." Kora pulled at her ropes.

"No, but you was the one who signed the paper." Andrew Adams took another drink. "So I figure that makes you my wife."

He moved across the room and squeezed her shoulder. "You ain't much in size. I like my women a little fluffier, but I guess you'll do. I had me a wife once several years ago. Ever'thing was good for me then. So I figured it was time for me to start over. A woman in the house gives a man something to come home to."

Kora could see his eyes darken in hope. "Win will kill you for taking me," she whispered. "I'm his *wife*."

"McQuillen's already dead." Andrew looked sorry for her as he sat at the table across from her. "So you might as well live with the fact. Men don't survive six snakebites. I was at the settlement, and the minute I heard it, I headed over and hid out in the dark. I've made enough deliveries to that place to find my way drunk or sober."

He took another drink. "I figured while everyone was waiting for him to pass on, I'd just wait for you to come out. Then I'd snatch you up and bring you home where you belong. After the funeral, we'll move back into that big house. Since the law thinks you're his bride, you'll get everything. By the time he's cold, you'll be mine in the eyes of the Lord. I can promise you that."

Kora pulled at the ropes. "He's not dead."

Andrew wasn't listening. "We need a better place to hide until you come to your senses. I wouldn't want anyone finding us until you wise up. You liked me enough once to marry me. I figure it'll just be a matter of time until you do again.''

''Let me go!'' Kora screamed, her patience at an end. The man was insane if he thought time would change anything. ''I'm not, nor will I ever be, your wife!''

Andrew gulped a long swallow of whiskey. He leaned across the table and slapped her hard.

Kora felt her ears ring and her eyes blur.

''I didn't want to do that,'' he said almost in tears, ''but you got to come to your senses and realize you still belong to me.''

She could feel his whiskey breath only inches away as his hand doubled back and struck her again.

''You got to see the facts, girl,'' he mumbled as he grabbed his bottle and moved away from her. ''I got to do whatever it takes to make you realize I'm your husband. I got to.''

Kora was silent as her head rocked forward.

TWENTY-SIX

KORA KNEW IT HAD TO BE MIDAFTERNOON. THE DUG-out was warm with streams of light shooting through tiny cracks in the roof. Dust danced playfully in the sunbeams, as if nothing was wrong with the world.

No one from Winter's ranch had come for her. Could it be possible they didn't know she was missing? Something was delaying them. The range war Win always talked about might have started, or Win may have grown worse. A hundred thoughts came to mind.

Cramps in her legs made her muscles twitch. Her wrists were raw from trying to free her hands. The rope around her waist kept her from breathing deeply, and the wooden back of the chair seemed to be cutting into her spine.

Andrew Adams had finally drunk himself into a deep sleep. He'd wandered over several times during the morning to slap her and then spent time telling her how much he hated doing it. After each cruelty came a sermon. Kora hated the sermons worse than the blows. He mumbled on and on about having parents who'd known right from wrong and that they had finally beat rules into him. Now he saw it as his duty to make her see the error of her ways.

The last time he'd tried to convince her of how important it was for her to listen to him, he'd been so drunk he'd missed when he'd tried to hit her. The action had infuriated him, sending him headlong into a drinking binge.

Since the first slap, Kora remained silent. She knew the only thing he wanted to hear, and he'd have to beat her to death before she'd claim to be his wife. The whiskey changed him into a different man. But whether he was a sober coward or a drunken bully made no difference in her conviction to be free of him.

She was exhausted from having no sleep the night before. Her body ached, but she didn't dare close her eyes.

Andrew lay across a filthy bed. His bags were packed by the door. He was waiting until nightfall to take her away. His plan was to disappear until she'd grown accustomed to him, then return to claim Win's land. If someone didn't get here soon, it would be too late to find her.

An hour passed, then another. Kora tried to move so that she was comfortable. Just as she felt her eyes closing, the door slowly opened.

"Winter," she whispered, thinking her prayers had been answered. Somehow he'd recovered from the bites and found her.

But to her shock, Dan walked through the door. He moved in his slow way to the fireplace and sat down on the ground in the dark corner where his chair had once been. His thin body folded into the shadows, almost disappearing.

"Dan," she whispered, knowing he'd never hear her. "Dan, please help me."

But he didn't move.

Kora whispered his name again, realizing somehow he'd climbed into the wagon last night to sleep and Andrew hadn't seen him before dawn. Knowing he was here added responsibility, but no comfort.

Dan didn't budge as she whispered his name again. She had to look closely even to be sure he was there.

"Dan!" she begged. "Please hear me!"

She was trying to cross twenty years of not listening. Somewhere along the line Dan had stopped hearing, and he couldn't be pulled back now. The war had killed a part of him, and all her calling couldn't bring him back.

"Dan! Please! Hear me!" He was her only hope of getting free. If he could just help they could be gone before Andrew Adams woke up. "Dan, it's Kora."

Andrew mumbled in his sleep and rolled over. "What?" he yelled.

Kora looked down, trying to act as if she were asleep in the chair. Her hair fell over her eyes, making a curtain she could barely see through.

Andrew rubbed his face and stumbled forward. "Did you call me, girl?"

Kora fought back the fear. She had to do something fast to get both herself and Dan out of here. She could wait no longer for someone to save her.

"I've decided you're right, Andrew. I am your wife." Kora bit back her lie.

He glared at her with bloodshot eyes.

Kora forced the words. "I've been remembering all those things you said in your letters. You're right, I was your wife first and that's the way it should be. If you'll untie me, I'd like to cook supper. I'm really hungry."

Though he stood staring at her, he was still just drunk enough to believe her. "And you ain't mad at me for smacking you? 'Cause you know I didn't want to have to do that, but you wouldn't listen."

''I'm not mad,'' Kora lied. ''You did what you had to do.''

''That's the truth.'' He straightened, proud that she'd seen the light. ''I knew you couldn't be happy with that half-breed no matter how rich he is. Folks say he's the hardest man in the county.'' He looked down at his feet. ''Since we're starting out, I want to tell you somethin'. I didn't write those letters, but they was my thoughts. I ain't never learned about writing.''

Kora couldn't bring herself to say anything against Win. ''I belong here, with you,'' she answered. ''Whether you wrote the letters or not.''

''That's right, you do.'' Andrew smiled a yellowed grin. ''All I want is a woman to work around the place and warm my bed at night. I won't even smack you around if you behave yourself. In time you'll settle in just fine.''

Kora studied him, feeling sorry for him. He was a little man who seemed to be shrinking before her eyes.

''You will warm my bed tonight, won't you, girl?'' he asked.

''All right,'' she forced herself to say. ''Now, untie me.''

He pulled out a long hunting knife from his boot and slit the cord he'd used to tie her to the chair. Leaning, forward, he untied her hands. ''I don't want no trouble. I only want a wife,'' he mumbled. ''I never wanted any trouble, but a man can't just let somebody take what's his without doing something.''

He tossed the knife on the table and staggered toward the door, swelling in victory. ''But don't get any ideas about running off again or I'll beat you, yes, I will.'' Puffing up his chest and straightening his belt, he said with pride, ''My pa used to have to beat my ma ever' now and again, but I never heard her complain. After the beatings, she was always real nice to him.''

He opened the door. ''In another hour it'll be dark enough for us to move. I know places over by the settlement where we can hide. An army couldn't find us there, so you don't have to worry about McQuillen's men bothering us. We'll take all the time you need to get to know one another.''

She stood slowly and moved about the kitchen she'd once tried to keep clean. There wasn't much, a few half-rotted potatoes, a can of peaches, some rancid lard. She only hoped the chickens were still laying. ''I'll cook you something before we go,'' she said hoping to stall for time.

He closed the door and moved up behind her. His voice grew low and thick. ''It's been a long time since I had me a woman.''

He reached for her and Kora stepped away.

''Go over by the bed, girl.'' He tried to make his words sound like an order, but he seemed a man unaccustomed to having authority over anyone.

Kora faced him. ''Why?''

'' 'Cause I want a taste of what my nights are going to be like since you're staying. There's no use waiting. Now go on over and lift them skirts. It won't take long.''

''No.'' Kora swallowed hard and forced herself to smile. ''There will be none of that until bedtime.'' She tried to sound determined, yet not angry.

To her relief, Andrew shrugged and backed down. ''All right. That's the same way my other wife felt. She used to say only whores do it before full dark. I figured you was more of a whore after sleeping with McQuillen, but maybe you got some respectable left in you.''

Kora busied herself at the sink and waited for her chance. She had no plans of still being around come nightfall. Somehow, now that she was untied, she'd get Dan and herself out of this place.

"I'll go get the wagon ready." He patted her on the hip as he passed her, as if trying to reshift the power between them. "I can tell I'm not going to have to beat you much at all, girl. You'll be hardworking and respectable in the daytime and still at night. A man can't ask for much more."

His fingers squeezed hard, suddenly making her jump.

There was no place to run. He was behind her and the counter was in front of her. Kora leaned far into the counter while his palm rubbed over her bruised hip. He was close behind her, daring her to try and run.

She had to let him prove who had control. Now was not the time to make a stand. She had to make herself remain still.

He spread his hand once more over her rounded hip and squeezed again, laughing at the way she took his advance without a word.

A sound of pain escaped her lips as she forced herself not to move. Andrew patted the twice-bruised flesh. "I figure you'll be a fine wife. You'll be still while I take my right, won't you? I always hate it when a woman fights and wiggles."

Pawing at her flesh, he tried to hurt her through the layers of material. "Won't you?" he whispered from just behind her.

"Yes," she answered, closing her eyes, fighting back the tears.

He pressed his fingers into the flesh of her hip as if to hurt her once more. "You sure you want to stay? You wouldn't be just fooling me now, would you?"

Kora couldn't breathe as she waited for his hand to tighten. "I'm sure," she whispered. "I'll stay and I'll be still if that's what you want."

Straightening behind her, he laughed with victory. "I'll

treat you real good,'' he promised. ''I forgot how a woman felt.''

Relaxing his fingers, he rubbed his palm along her thigh, as he slowly leaned into her with his body. His hot breath was at her neck as his hands circled her waist and he pushed against her backside.

''I have to cook supper,'' she managed to whisper.

Andrew laughed. ''All right. But it'll be dark in an hour and the waiting will be over. I'll have that dress stripped off you in no time. Then you'll never forget you're mine.'' He pushed her harder against the counter. ''Say it.''

''Say what?''

''Say you're mine, will you? I want to hear it.'' He rocked his body slightly as his hands pulled at her waist.

Kora whispered, ''I'm yours.''

''Again,'' he said as he rocked against her.

''I'm yours.'' She fought back the tears.

Andrew backed away slowly. ''Bringing you around wasn't the work I thought it might be. We're getting along fine. I'll be back in a few minutes for my supper.''

The moment he was out the door, Kora ran to Dan. ''Help me,'' she whispered as she shook her brother. ''Please, Dan, help me!'' She couldn't endure another second of Andrew touching her. The lie she'd just told him made her mouth taste bitter, and his touch left her flesh feeling as if something slimy had crawled across it. But she'd convinced him. Now all she had to do was get away.

Dan only stared past her. He wouldn't, or couldn't, help her.

Kora looked around the room for a weapon. The old rifle that didn't fire still leaned against the fireplace. Winter's gunbelt she'd worn lay beneath the table, but the Colt was missing.

As Kora heard the door, she stepped away from Dan and

grabbed the rifle. He wouldn't touch her again. She'd taken all she could.

"What the hell?" Andrew shouted as his eyes adjusted to the poor light. "Stop pointing that thing at me."

Kora turned the rifle like a club. "Stay away from me!" The memory of his body pressing against her drove her tired mind to the edge. She'd endured his advances to save Dan, and her brother didn't even care. She was alone, totally alone.

Swinging wildly, she stormed forward. Andrew rolled beneath the table. "Stop that, girl, or you'll be sorry!"

Kora swung again, catching one of his legs. He yelped like a dog.

"Don't ever touch me again!" she yelled. The thought that Andrew, and not Winter, might be undressing her was more than she could take. She swung again.

Andrew grabbed the gunbelt and tried to fight back. But his first swing missed, and Kora clipped his shoulder with the rifle butt. When he grabbed his shoulder in pain, she hit him in the knee, almost toppling him.

He began snorting like a bull and, swinging the belt full force, stormed toward her in rage.

Out of the corner of her eye, Kora saw Dan stand and move toward the door, as though nothing were going on in the room. She tried to rotate so that Andrew wouldn't see Dan, but Andrew's wild swinging kept her still. The gunbelt made a whistling sound as it sailed through the air at steam-engine speed.

Dan stepped in the way before Andrew even saw him. Her brother wasn't looking their direction when the belt hit him full in the face. The buckle ripped across his forehead like a knife.

"Dan!" Kora screamed and dropped the rifle.

"Dan?" Andrew staggered back.

Without a sound, Dan let the power behind the hit turn him. The belt wrapped around his throat as he whirled. Blood from his forehead splattered the walls as he slowly crumbled across the bed.

Kora ran toward her brother, almost catching him. ''Dan! Dan!'' she screamed.

Andrew recovered slowly. ''Who is he? What's he doing here? It wasn't my fault.''

Kora looked up at Andrew. First, she'd felt sorry for him, then she'd feared him, now she hated him. ''He's my brother, and if you've killed him, I'll shoot you. I swear I will.''

There was something so certain in her tone, Andrew tried to blink away his own fear. ''I didn't kill him. He stepped in my way. I just cut his forehead. It'll bleed a lot, head wounds always do. But he won't die.''

Kora took her shawl and wrapped it around Dan's head. ''We've got to get him to a doctor. He's been ill. If it bleeds much, he might die.''

''No,'' Andrew said. ''I ain't going near no doctors. The last one I saw had me in the grave. I woke up arguing with the undertaker.''

''Then leave us here and go. Someone will help us. Just go.''

Andrew rubbed his face, trying to think. ''No. I'm not leaving you. You're my wife. You're coming with me.''

''I'm not leaving Dan.'' Kora crossed to the shelf and lifted down a box of clean rags she'd left there a lifetime ago. While Andrew tried to decide what to do, she slipped the knife he'd used to cut her ropes from the table and into her pocket. She wasn't sure she could kill Andrew for kidnapping her, but she knew she wouldn't hesitate to do whatever she must to protect her brother.

He was motionless as she knelt by the bed and removed

her bloody shawl. She wrapped the wound as tightly as she dared. "He needs stitches badly."

"All right!" Andrew yelled suddenly, as if the room were full of screaming people. "We'll go and take your brother."

Andrew was sobering up. Drunk, he might try a great many things, but sober he was far more of a coward. "I ain't taking you or him to town, but there's an old woman, name of Rae, at the Breaks who'll look after him."

"I'll go to the settlement with you. It's closer than town," Kora agreed. "But that's all. I'm not going anywhere else with you."

Andrew looked at her. He opened his mouth as though about to argue, then closed it again. "We'll talk about it later. You're just upset."

Kora touched the knife in her pocket. Now that she wasn't tied up and helpless, or worried about Andrew seeing Dan, Andrew didn't seem near as frightening.

Suddenly she realized something. In the time she'd known Winter, she'd grown stronger. She'd do whatever she had to do. Jamie might be right, they might just be weeds in the garden, but she was ready to fight for her right to live. All her life all she'd ever thought of was running, but now she knew she was strong enough to stand and fight if she must.

Fighting his way back to the light, Win opened his eyes and blinked away the glow of a candle only a foot from his face.

"Win?" someone said.

"What?" he grumbled and turned to find Doc Gage sitting by his bed. For a moment he thought he might be in some kind of strange dream. But the doc was too real, just like the pain in his head.

"Can you see me? You've been out quite a while."

"How long?"

"All day."

"Kora?"

"How's the head?" Gage asked as he offered Win a drink.

Accepting the water, Win leaned forward on one elbow. He felt weak, as if he were moving in water.

"The ranch. Has anything happened?"

"No," Gage answered. "Cheyenne says all is so quiet it's spooky on the range."

"Where's Kora?"

Gage looked uncomfortable. "You're still very weak. You'll need at least another twenty-four hours in bed for the poison to work its way out."

Win's tone hardened. "Where's Kora?"

"Tell him the truth!" Logan snapped from the landing. "Even half dead, he can face whatever he has to."

Gage nodded. "We think she was kidnapped this morning before dawn. Jamie heard some men talking about ways to get you off guard. One was to take Kora. But Cheyenne had tracked down the men who were talking, and they weren't the ones who took her."

"Hand me my clothes!" Win ordered.

"No, Win." The doc held his hands up, as if the barrier would stop Win. "You're far too weak. I know how you must feel, but we're doing everything that can be done."

Logan moved to the chair and handed Win his trousers. "I've kept a buggy waiting. Cheyenne spotted the trail almost an hour ago. He and Jamie have gone ahead."

"But . . ." Gage looked frustrated that no one was listening to him. "Win, you could black out at any moment. You're in no shape to sit up, much less travel."

Win jammed his pants on, gritting his teeth at the pain.

He wasn't sure he could stay conscious, but he wasn't waiting. ''You have no idea how I feel, Doc. If you did, you'd be helping me.''

Gage picked up his bag. ''Well, I'm coming along. I have a feeling before this night's over, someone's going to need me.''

TWENTY-SEVEN

JAMIE RODE SILENTLY BESIDE CHEYENNE ACROSS THE open land. He followed a trail only he saw, but at least they had a direction. She'd wasted most of the day riding first one way then another while he'd checked on the ranch and looked for clues. By midafternoon she'd been near hysterics from worry. Kora might think she was the oldest and the leader of their family, but Jamie had always been there to protect her. To make sure she was safe. To prevent anyone from hurting her.

Finally, when Jamie had nowhere else to turn, Cheyenne told her he'd found a trail of wagon tracks and planned to follow them as long as daylight held. Now, not only darkness threatened, but also rain. The clouds were as dark as her mood. If he hurried, he might lose the trail. But if he didn't hurry, the rain would wash it out before they could find her sister. With each passing minute Kora could be farther away.

After riding beside him an hour, Jamie wasn't sure he'd been telling the truth, for she could see no trail even though Cheyenne kept watching the ground and moving slowly. Kora had vanished. Even with all her plans and the guards watching, somehow she'd vanished. Jamie knew the men who'd brought Winter home hadn't taken Kora, so who had?

Jamie glanced around her. Far into the distance she saw two hills that looked familiar. It took her tired mind a minute to figure out where she'd seen them.

Suddenly they registered. "Saddleback! The farm. Andrew Adams!" She'd completely forgotten about the weasel of a first husband. "Of course, he's taken Kora!" One of the guards had even mentioned seeing his freight wagon crossing Win's land.

Kicking her horse, Jamie knew exactly where the tracks led. Cheyenne yelled at her to slow down, but she wasn't listening.

She reached the rundown farm a few lengths ahead of Cheyenne. After jumping off her horse, she ran through the open door with a gun in one hand and her knife in the other. She'd teach Andrew Adams a thing or two.

Cheyenne was only a few feet behind her. What they saw froze them both in place. Blood was everywhere—on the table, the bed, even the door. The once-neat little cabin was a mess with empty bottles, cans, and boxes littering the floor. The home looked more like a battlefield.

As Cheyenne knelt and lifted Winter's gunbelt, blood dripped off the leather. Jamie saw Kora's shawl in a puddle of crimson by the bed. Bloody footprints crisscrossed the dirt floor.

"Kora!" she screamed. "Kora! I'm too late." She should have made Kora leave; they both knew the "witchin' luck" would catch up to them. Jamie should have packed Kora and Dan up as soon as the trouble started.

"The blood's still warm," Cheyenne said as he studied

the dirt floor as though reading a map. "We couldn't have missed them by more than ten minutes."

"I'll kill him!" Jamie cried. "If he murdered Kora, I'll cut his heart out before it has time to stop pounding. I'll tie him behind my horse and drag him back to the ranch, then I'll hang him."

Cheyenne grabbed her arm and swung her around. "It may not be Kora's blood, but she was here with what looks like two men." He shook Jamie hard. "Jamie, listen to me. It may not be Kora's blood! The two men could have been fighting, or Kora may have been the one swinging Win's gunbelt. Don't fall apart until we know."

Before they could say more, they heard a buggy. Cheyenne reached for his gun, then glanced through the open doorway and recognized both the doc and Win. He let the pain in his face show. There was nothing he could do to soften the blow for his friend.

The doctor and Win walked into the shadowy cabin. The doc struck a light, but Win was still. The smell of blood was thick around him. He didn't need a light to know disaster had struck.

Winter's face was stone just like always when he was hurt or angry. He moved around the room studying the signs. If the others hadn't known him, they would have thought he was unaffected by the sight. He lifted her shawl, twisting it in his fist, then he picked up the gunbelt. The muscles across his jaw moved, tightening, hardening against all expression but anger. The pain in his body was working with him now, fighting down the rage so he could think.

Jamie buried her face against the wall and cried uncontrollably.

Win walked slowly over to her and pulled her beneath

his arm. He held her tightly as she sobbed tears he could never cry.

''It's all my fault,'' Jamie whimpered. ''I should have been close enough to help Kora.''

''No,'' Win said as he rocked her in a brotherly hug. ''It wasn't your fault. We'll find her.''

Looking over her head at Cheyenne, he ordered, ''Find her and the men. Pull every man off the blockade if you have too, but find her.'' He couldn't bring himself to say *dead or alive.*

Kora watched as an old woman, mumbling to herself, leaned over Dan. She lived in one of the few shacks that looked strong enough to face the wind in this place. Steven Gage had mentioned her when they'd come here before to take the bullet out of a man. He'd said he thought Rae used to be one of the buffalo hunters' women. Her man must have died, leaving her stranded out here. She survived by boiling root stew and selling it to men too lazy to cook, and by doing some doctoring.

''I can sew him up.'' The old woman wiped her hands on her skirt. ''But it'll cost you a dollar.''

''What?'' Andrew shouted. ''I don't even know the fellow. I'm not paying you a dollar.''

Kora had lived among these kind of people long enough to know the game. ''Sew him up.'' She stepped from the shadows and faced Rae. ''And I'll see you get a bushel of apples twice a year.''

The old woman laughed. ''Sure you will.'' Then Kora seemed to catch her interest, for she leaned closer, looking Kora over carefully.

''I'll leave this hunting knife here until the first bushel is delivered.'' Kora pulled her only weapon from her pocket. ''That and my word is all I have to bargain with.''

"Now, wait just a minute." Andrew turned on Kora and attempted to take the knife. "That's my good knife."

"No," she countered, whirling the blade an inch from his gut. "If you say another word, it'll be you that needs stitching up."

Andrew backed down. The woman took the knife and shoved it into her pocket. "Are you willing to help me?" The question seemed to be more than a simple request.

Andrew hurried to the door. "Not me. I need a drink." He glanced at Kora. "I'll be right outside when you're finished, girl, so don't go thinking of leaving without me. We're together now. As soon as the old hag's finished, you and me got some settling up to do."

He rubbed the leg she'd hit. Kora thought she saw the first sign of doubt that his plan was a good one as he limped out.

"I'll help you," Kora answered Rae and ignored Andrew. Now that she'd stood up to him, he seemed no more than a gnat bothering her. "What can I do?"

For the next hour Kora worked beside the old woman. Though her hands were wrinkled with age, she did a fine job.

When they were wrapping the wound, the old hag whispered, "You're Mrs. McQuillen, ain't you?"

Kora let out a long breath. "Yes."

The old woman giggled. "I seen you that night you were here with the doc. You're a good woman, everyone says so. I reckon your helping now proved it. Most of us didn't believe a rich lady like yourself would come down here to help the doc. The women who come here are mostly bad. But you done a good job helping, even if the rat you were working on died."

"Thank you," Kora answered, wondering why the old woman would suddenly be so talkative.

"So why you with the likes of that trash?" She pointed with her head toward the door where Andrew waited on the porch. He'd been nursing a bottle for most of the time, and now Kora knew the drunk would replace the coward.

Kora wasn't sure what to say. It would take too long to tell the whole story, and she didn't like the idea of facing the drunk Andrew without a weapon. Maybe Rae could help. "I don't want to be," she answered. "I have to get away."

Rae raised an eyebrow that looked evil in flight. "I figured as much. I've heard talk of the trouble your man's been having from that woman and her kin." She slipped the knife from her pocket and gave it back to Kora. "You keep this with you until you get back to your man. I'll trust you about the apples. If you have to use the blade on the likes of him, aim for the middle. You won't cut him bad enough to kill him, but I'll make sure he doesn't recover too quickly. You just run."

"I can't leave," Kora said. "Dan is my brother. I can't just abandon him." She twisted a leftover piece of bandage around her finger, needing to talk to someone. "I'm not sure I should go back to Win, either. I've been nothing but bad luck to him."

"I'll take good care of your brother. You get back to that man of yours. I've seen him many a time. He's something. The kind of man that could make a woman real happy if he took a liking to her. Everybody around here thinks he's hard and mean, but one winter years ago when most of the drifters had moved on, he rode up here delivering food 'cause he knew we was snowed in. I never did thank him for that, so I'd like to repay him now."

She moved to the back of her shack and pulled a blanket from across a small opening. "You go back to him and tell him the old woman from the settlement helped you. He'll know who you mean. Bad luck or good don't got nothing to do with loving—you belong with each other."

Kora knelt to crawl through. "Thank you," she whispered. "I promise I'll repay you."

"I know you will. I'll be showing up some night for dinner at that big house of yours like I was Sunday company." Rae giggled again. "And I expect to be treated to the best."

"I promise," Kora whispered.

"And one other thing," the woman whispered. "Tell Win not to misjudge the woman. She's deadly."

"What woman?" Kora asked.

But Dan made a noise and the old woman almost shoved her through the opening without answering.

Kora ran along a path slick with rain. She wasn't sure where to go. She only remembered that the night Winter had carried her home, they'd followed the river until they cleared the shacks, then turned north.

She almost fell into a tarp stretched across what looked like a cave opening. Several horses waited in the rain as men inside seemed to be arguing. At first she thought of asking one of them to take her home, but she wasn't sure. Win had said he had many enemies among the residents of the Breaks.

Moving against the corner of the tarp, she tried to find shelter from the rain without being seen. She could wait here, then, when the storm passed, walk home.

Voices rose from within.

"Now's the time to move." A woman's voice startled Kora. "We could have the cattle across McQuillen's land by daybreak."

"It's too risky in this weather. I wouldn't mind the rain, but this storm is bad. A bolt of lightning could spook the whole herd and they'd scatter for miles. We'd all be dead men if we got caught rounding them up."

"It's too risky to wait!" the woman shouted above the others. "My father's cattle are dying every day down below the caprock."

"All right," a second man, with an age-rusted voice, said. "My daughter's right, but we have no choice. If the rain lets up a bit, be ready. But I'm not moving them in a storm."

"Storm's not letting up!" someone yelled. "It'll pour like this till daybreak. Always does in early spring around here." Metal clanged against metal. "Pass the coffeepot. We're here till dawn."

"We'll give it an hour to let up," the older voice ordered. "If not, we'll wait until tomorrow night." He lowered his voice slightly. "Want some coffee, darlin'?"

"Not out of one of those filthy mugs." The woman's words were almost lost in the movement.

The men made plans and drank as Kora tried not to shiver. She couldn't wait for the rain to let up. She had to get home now. Win had to know what was planned. And if he was still too weak, she'd discuss what to do with Cheyenne and Logan.

Carefully taking one step away from the back of the tent, she walked straight into the black wall of a man's coat.

His hands circled around her like iron as he pushed her back against the blackness surrounding the tent.

She opened her mouth to scream a moment before his fingers gagged her. He leaned close against her and whispered, "Quiet, Kora, or we're both dead!"

"Wyatt!" Kora mumbled as he folded her into his slicker and pulled her away from the tent. "What are you doing here?"

He ran, half carrying her, half dragging her for several yards.

"Did Win send you?" Kora asked as she ran.

"No," Wyatt answered. "I know these men, but I'm not like them. Cattle are not worth a war."

"But . . ."

He found a horse hidden in the trees and tossed Kora roughly up. "I haven't time to explain!" he shouted above the rain. "If you're found here with me, we're probably both goners. If they find out I've helped you, I won't be seeing daylight. So be careful and ride!"

As he said the last word, he slapped the rump of the horse, and Kora leaned close to the neck to hold on as the animal took off. Rain blinded her to the little the moonless night would have allowed her to see. She let the horse find its way as she held on.

Finally, when she was well away from the campfires, she managed to grab the reins. "North," she whispered as if the horse might know his directions. "I have to go north."

Kora closed her eyes and buried her head in the horse's mane. The animal kept moving, galloping across the open land as though he'd understood.

For a while, all she heard was the steady thumping of the hooves and the rain, but slowly she heard another sound.

Kora straightened as two riders came out of the night in front of her. They circled wide around her and flanked her. Fear made her shiver uncontrollably. Their horses were too powerful to belong to Andrew, and their slickers and hats made it impossible to see their faces. If they were the men Wyatt had been with, she might very well be signing her own death certificate as well as Wyatt's.

She thought of trying to outrun them, but she was having

enough trouble just holding on and they seemed seasoned horseman.

"Kora!" Jamie shouted above the storm as her hand crossed the distance between the mounts and touched Kora's arm. "We'll see you home."

Kora glanced to the left and saw Cheyenne tip his hat slightly, spilling rain as he did. "Hold on tight!" he yelled. "Jamie, let's ride."

"Home," Kora whispered, finding it hard to believe it had only been hours since she'd seen Win and not days.

Win paced the attic room. His head was swimming, his body ached, and he knew he needed to lie down, but he couldn't stop. Kora was gone. How many times had she told him she didn't believe anything lasted? Had she been fearing this time, predicting it, or planning it?

He walked over to her dressing area. Nothing was missing. She'd been kidnapped, he was sure of it.

Then he remembered how she'd cried out when they'd made love. Maybe she'd just been waiting for her chance to run. The snakes had given her that opportunity, and she wanted nothing of his to take with her.

Win slammed his fist against the dressing table in anger. The blow shattered the thin board and sent the perfume bottle flying. It hit the windowsill and broke, the thin blue glass still held in place by the decorative metal frame.

Win ignored the destruction he'd caused and knelt beside the window. He picked up the broken bottle and stared at it as the perfume dripped through his fingers.

Like the bottle, if Kora was gone, he was only a shell, broken inside and empty. Somehow, with her quiet gentle ways, she'd crawled into his heart, leaving it open for a pain he swore he'd never allow himself to feel again.

TWENTY-EIGHT

KORA CLIMBED THE STAIRS WITH BARELY ENOUGH EN-ergy to lift her rain-soaked skirt. Jamie had offered to help her, but she wanted to face Win alone. She needed to be with him for a while, even if he were already asleep. She had several things she had to tell him, but with the rain growing worse, Kora knew she had little time.

The attic room was bathed in moonlight. Kora crossed slowly to the bed with its twisted quilts. Her wrapper lay over the chair where she'd left it, as though nothing had changed since dawn. She looked around the room, fighting down the tears. Win was gone. All day she'd struggled to get back to him. It was a relief that he must feel well enough to be out of bed, but little comfort. She needed his arms around her.

Pulling off her wet dress, Kora tossed it over the wooden panel. Without bothering to remove her damp underclothes, she slipped into her wrapper and struck a single light at Win's washstand. Lifting his comb, she pulled it through her damp hair, letting the stress of the day pass away with the tangles. Somehow, she'd done the impossible. She'd made it back.

Silently Kora tiptoed down the stairs to the kitchen, trying not to let her disappointment show. Jamie and Cheyenne sat across from each other drinking coffee. For once they weren't yelling, but talking as they sliced cheese and bread from a large platter. While Kora waited for her tea, she sipped a glass of milk, and listened.

"We'll hitch a wagon and go after Dan tomorrow," Cheyenne said as he pushed Jamie's hand off his arm. "The rain looks like it's getting worse tonight. He'll be more comfortable with the old woman than caught in the storm."

"But what about the plans I overheard?" Kora asked as she leaned against the counter so she could easily see both doors in case Win returned.

"Nothing is moving tonight," Cheyenne reasoned. "It would be suicide to move cattle in this storm. We'll be lucky if the storm's over by morning."

Jamie put her forearm on his shoulder and leaned against him. "I'll go with you tomorrow. I know how to handle Dan."

"You didn't even notice he was missing." Cheyenne shrugged her arm away. He'd done the action so often it was starting to look like a twitch he'd developed. "And the settlement's no place for a lady."

"Good," Jamie chimed. "Then I'll fit right in."

Cheyenne did his best to growl at her. "Some of my people believe folks take their personalities from animals. If so, yours would be a leech."

Jamie stood and walked her fingers across his shoulders as she moved behind him. "Yours would be a bear."

She jumped away as he swung behind him as if swatting a fly.

"Stop pestering him, Jamie!" Kora scolded, then glanced at the door. "When do you think Win will be back?" she asked. "I thought he'd still be in bed."

Cheyenne looked at her closely, like he was trying to read something she hadn't said. "He's in the study." His words came slowly. "I talked to him when we came in. I told him what happened to you and assured him you were fine. I figured he'd have found you by now, but maybe Gage talked him into having his dressing changed first."

"The study door was closed when I came down the stairs." Kora lifted her cup and stood, trying not to let her worry show. "I must have missed him."

She set her cup on the counter and hurried out of the room, trying to imagine why Winter wouldn't have found her if he knew she was home. Maybe he was too weak? Maybe he didn't want her to see the wounds?

Steven Gage was in the foyer putting on his coat when she rounded the hallway.

"He must be hell to live with," Gage mumbled when he saw Kora. "All I want to do is change the bandage. He said I'd best get my doctoring done when he's out cold, because if he's conscious, he's well enough to take care of himself."

"What needs doing?" Kora asked.

"I left the bandages and ointment in the study. Each of the bites needs washing and wrapping with clean cloth." Gage fitted his hat. "I've got to get going. There's a baby about to be born that may not wait until this storm clears."

Kora tapped on the study door.

"Go away!" Win shouted.

Gage shook his head. "He's feeling pretty bad. If he doesn't die, send for me when he lets you in."

Without another word, the doc stepped into the rain.

Kora knocked again.

"Go away!"

Cheyenne appeared in the opening from the kitchen. He didn't seemed surprised by Win's behavior. "He doesn't want you to see him hurting,'' Cheyenne whispered. ''We'll have to wait until he unlocks the door. Ten men couldn't knock it down, and there's only one key. The one on the other side of the door. That's the way the captain liked it, and I figure Win plans on continuing the custom.''

Kora whirled and ran up the stairs. In a few minutes she was back down. She lifted a gold key. ''Will you stop me?'' she asked, knowing Cheyenne guarded Win as if he were the king's royal guard.

''No, ma'am,'' he answered. ''It's your house. Boss said you could do anything you wanted to in this house, and no one was to ever stop you. Mind my asking how you made that key appear?''

''I found it,'' Kora answered. ''And it's mine.''

Cheyenne smiled. ''Anything you say.''

Silently she unlocked the study door and slipped inside. The windows were open to the storm and a fire roared in the fireplace. The room was in shadows except for occasional blinks of lightning.

Kora tiptoed farther inside, feeling Win's nearness more than seeing him. From the first, this room had been his, she reminded herself. Only, she had a key.

Halfway across the floor, she saw him sitting in the tall wingback chair by the fireplace, his legs stretched out long in front of him.

''Win?'' she whispered as she ventured closer.

He didn't move. His head was back, his eyes closed.

Without a word, she crossed to the desk where the doctor had everything ready. She soaked a rag in warm water and picked up the scissors. Slowly she knelt by Win's side and began cutting away the bandage on his arm, allowing the rag to soak into the places where blood had dried, holding the stained cloth to Win's flesh.

He looked at her with angry eyes. ''What do you think you're doing?''

''I'm going to rebandage the bites and put salve on them.'' She didn't stop working. ''You can help by removing your clothes, or I can cut them off.''

Win remained stone. She wasn't sure how he'd react, but she'd faced kidnapping, assaults, and riding a half wild horse today. She wasn't in any mood to be crossed.

Without a word she unbuttoned his shirt and set to work on the second wound.

When she'd finished, she motioned for him to undress as she resoaked the rag.

Standing slowly, he removed his shirt. ''I locked the door for a reason.'' His voice seemed to rumble around the room like a mirror of the storm outside.

''And I unlocked it for a reason.'' Kora waited for him to sit back down. ''Why did you shut me out?''

Win plopped back in the chair and allowed her to resume. ''I didn't want you to see me like this.''

''Like what? Tired? Hurt? Stupid?''

Win smiled. ''That does feel better,'' he admitted as she rubbed salve across the third wound.

''Then sit back and let me work,'' she ordered. ''And while I work, I'll tell you what I've learned.''

Win leaned his head back and relaxed. He listened as she told him the discussion she'd heard at the settlement. As before, he found himself asking her questions as she reasoned through all she'd learned.

''You could have been killed if Wyatt hadn't been the one to find you.'' Win frowned. ''I'm not sure why he was there. But he helped you and that stacks the deck in his favor.''

Winter rubbed his forehead. ''I'll think about it in the morning. Right now all that matters is you're safe.''

"And you're alive," Kora countered.

Win winked at her. "How'd you get in here anyway? Jamie pick the lock?"

"No, I have my own key."

"There's always been only one key. The captain used to lock the place up sometimes so he could drink. Even Miss Allie couldn't get in."

"So he may have thought." Kora moved the rag over his swollen skin. "But there was a key hanging on the inside of one of the wardrobes. I'd never noticed any of the doors locked, so I didn't know what it fit until tonight."

"So the captain wasn't safe from Miss Allie any more than I am from you."

"Do you want to be?" Kora looked up suddenly. The thought had never occurred to her that he might really not want her around.

"No," Win answered. "But I'm hard enough to live with on a good day. On a bad day like this, I'm not much for company. Once I knew you were safe, I figured it would be better for me to stay away until the pain eased."

Kora wrapped the third bite mark. "Is it easing now?"

"Much better," he whispered. "God, how I missed you, woman."

Kora leaned over him and lightly touched her lips to his. The warmth of his mouth spread through her. From the very first she'd thought about what he'd be like to kiss and he hadn't disappointed her. All day her only sanity had been the thought of getting back to his arms.

He didn't kiss her back, but only accepted her offering, which excited her. When she ended the kiss and moved away, she felt in control. No matter how much she longed to kiss him again, she had work to do first.

She pulled him once more to his feet and helped him with his trousers. Then she doctored the other bites as he relaxed. Gage had cut off Win's drawers, making him seem as if he had on a pair of short pants. When she finished, he stood and carefully redressed.

"You should be in bed," she whispered as she watched the muscles of his arms move. "It's late."

Win poured himself a taste of brandy and leaned back in the huge wingback chair. "I wasn't sure I could make it up the stairs before, but the pain is much better now."

"What else can I do to help?" She moved her fingers into his hair. Even weak from the bites, he still had a power about him. The need to touch him was like a craving. She leaned forward and let the front of her wrapper brush against his arm as she lightly kissed his cheek.

"What you're doing is nice." He didn't move.

Kora kissed him again. Slowly moving along his face until she brushed his lips.

This time he responded.

When she straightened and broke the kiss, he whispered, "It's good to have you home." His hand moved gently along her side. "Were you hurt?"

"No," Kora answered. "I was worried about you."

"I'm fine, now you're here." Win tugged at her belt and pulled her closer. "I never thought I needed a wife, or that I'd miss a woman, but I missed you. I didn't like waking up and not having you near."

He tugged again and she sat on the arm of the chair. "Pull the drapes and lock the door. I want to use the last of my energy looking at you, not climbing the stairs."

"But don't you want to go to sleep?"

"I want the rest of the world to go away," he grumbled. "For a few hours in our marriage, I want to see and think of nothing but you."

TWENTY-NINE

KORA STOOD AND CLOSED THE STUDY DOOR AND pulled the curtains. She knew he was still weak and she should probably insist he sleep, but she wanted to be alone with Win tonight.

When she returned to his chair, he motioned for her to stand between him and the fire. "I need to look at you, Kora. Do you mind?"

"No," she whispered, unsure of his meaning. She didn't know if her cheeks burned from blushing or the fire's warmth. How could he want to look at her? Didn't he know she'd always been invisible? She'd heard the way folks talked about some women, the way boys talked of girls. That they were pretty or beautiful, or grand. No one ever said things like that about her. They usually only commented on how they hadn't noticed her.

He didn't say a word as she leaned her hair back, letting the heat dry it. He just stared as she stood before him. The fire danced in his eyes as a slow smile spread across his lips.

"Are you warm enough?" he finally whispered.

Kora felt his words were touching her somehow across

the space between them. "Yes," she answered.

"Then take off the wrapper." His voice was low, a little rough as always, but she wasn't the least afraid.

Slowly she pulled the belt free and let the wrapper slip from her shoulders. The camisole she wore was bound at the waist by her muslin underskirt. The skirt pulled the silk tight over her breasts.

She reached behind her and pulled the ribbons of the skirt. It tumbled, joining her wrapper. Her underdrawers were damp from the rain and clung to her knees.

For a long while, Win was silent, but she could feel him watching her. Devouring her with his gaze. With the firelight behind her, he could see the outline of her body clearly through the thin clothing. His change in breathing confirmed her theory. Kora smiled and turned slowly.

Finally he offered his hand and she moved to him, sitting on the arm of his huge chair as she had before.

"I'll never get over how easy you come to me," he whispered. His fingers brushed her throat as though he were touching velvet. "Even when I hurt you, you come back to me. I didn't have to win your hand, or promise you foolish things like love. I don't have to flatter, or give you things, or pamper you. You just come to me. You're like a rainbow that follows my stormy life."

It was the first time he'd ever said such things. Kora knew it by the awkwardness in his voice.

"I'd think of you all soft, but when Cheyenne came in earlier, he told me you threatened to kill Andrew Adams." Win laughed. "Did you really hit him with that old rifle and threaten to slit him open with a knife?"

"I did," Kora answered. "I think he was afraid of me by the time we got to the settlement. He's probably glad to be rid of me."

"Well, I'm glad to have you back." He pulled her across

his lap and kissed her as she'd wanted him to when she first got home.

Kora sighed and relaxed against him. "Am I hurting you?" She would have sat up, but his hand on her shoulder held her in place.

"No," he said. "Be still, Kora. You're where you belong."

As he stroked her hair, he asked, "Do you think Andrew is a part of moving the cattle across my land?"

"No. He would be if he were smart enough, but the man has no idea that my kidnapping was just what they wanted. He thought he was just getting a wife and if he kept me around a few days I'd decide to stay."

"And would you have?"

Kora opened her eyes and stared at him. "No," she answered. "I'd have died first. I'd have killed him if he'd tried to bed me. Just his touch made me shiver."

Win could hear the anger in her voice. Cheyenne might have told him the facts, but Kora provided the emotion. "Tell me every detail," he asked. "From the time he kidnapped you until Cheyenne and Jamie found you. Let every detail out, and then we'll never have to speak of it again."

Kora looked down. "I'm not sure I can," she whispered.

"Everything," he answered. "You're safe in my arms now."

Slowly she began to talk. She told of the pain of being tied to the chair and how Andrew slapped her. She shivered when she spoke of the way he'd grabbed her hip and tried to hurt her. Of how he demanded she promise to be still when he bedded her that night. She related meeting Rae and how the woman had helped her.

While she talked Win stroked her gently, wiping away a tear, moving his hands along her arms, silently washing away the pain.

When she finished, Win was right, she let go of the anger. She stretched and relaxed as his hands moved gently over her.

"What about my touch?" he whispered against her ear.

"I love your touch," she answered.

"Then, darling, I'm going to touch you tonight."

She wanted Win close, closer than she'd ever allowed anyone. Somehow it had always felt right to let him touch her. And tonight it felt like heaven.

Win's fingers spread over her camisole, molding the silk to her warm flesh. Slowly he pulled the ribbons free, but he seemed in no hurry to part her garment. He ran his fingers from her throat to her waist, feeling the sides of each breast before bringing it into view.

His hands were large and rough from hard work, but the way he touched her made her feel valued and beautiful. He brushed his fingertips over the lace, pushing it slightly down until the camisole barely covered each peak. He moved the back of his fingers over her sides, sliding along the material, pressing gently so that the valley between her breasts deepened.

The firelight sparkled in his dark eyes, telling her of his pleasure as words never could. He took his time exploring her body gently so that he could touch her wherever he liked and see all he wanted. His palm slid up her leg and pushed her drawers high, then he tugged suddenly, pulling the waist until her bare skin showed and the garment clung to her hips. As he had with the top, he pushed it lower and lower, a fraction of an inch at a time.

His large hand circled her exposed abdomen, pushing the camisole higher and the underwear lower. Then he stopped, one hand at her waist, the other in her hair, and looked at her.

"Do you mind this?" he finally asked, as if expecting

her to say yes. "I've heard some women do."

"No," she whispered.

"And if I touch you like this every night?"

"I wouldn't object," she answered as she stirred slightly in his lap, stretching, knowing the thin garments revealed more with each move. "I like it a great deal."

He rewarded her by sliding his fingers more boldly over her warm flesh. He cupped her head and raised her lips to his. The kiss was long and searching, leaving her lips pouty and her mouth hungry for more. He'd break the kiss to stare at her, watching her thinly covered chest rise and fall until her breathing grew regular once more. Then he'd pull her mouth to his again.

Slowly Kora's tired muscles relaxed. She matched his kiss with equal longing, and when he released her lips, she rested in his arms, loving the way he stared at her. His fingertips would trail between her breasts in long lazy strokes, then the hunger would return and he'd raise her mouth to his again.

When he finally pushed the silk aside, she was begging for his touch. Her breasts felt full and hard with need.

He shifted her, pulling her up in his lap.

"Relax, darling," he whispered. "I'm not going to hurt you."

She leaned her head against the side of the wingback chair as his mouth traveled down her throat.

"Shhh," he mumbled as he moved his hands to her back and pulled her to him, capturing her breast in his mouth.

Kora stiffened at the sudden flood of sensations and tried to push away as her soft flesh was pulled farther into his warm mouth and he began to taste her fully. But she didn't make a sound as he held her fast, ignoring her efforts to pull away. His grip was strong and his hunger grew as he continued to feast on her. Finally her jerky movements slowed and she stopped trying to move away. She settled into his arms and allowed him to taste.

When she'd settled against him, he raised his head. As he stared into her eyes, he cupped her wet breast with his hand and fondled it gently. She knew he was giving her time to object, but she didn't say a word. With a slow smile, he leaned over her and kissed her.

"That was wonderful," he mumbled against her lips. "Now turn, darling, and let me taste the other. I'll have my fill of you tonight."

She hesitated, still feeling the warmth of his mouth on her skin and the taste of him on her tongue. His breath was warm against her throat as he waited.

Slowly she turned, offering him the other virgin breast. He took it as he had the first, hungrily. She jerked again at the sudden feel of his mouth, but he held her close, not allowing her to break free. As he had before, he made her flesh his, and as he did, she relaxed in his arms.

When he finished tasting, he leaned his head back and took a deep breath, one hand resting on her back, the other covering one tender breast.

"You taste so wonderful," he whispered. "Like a wine I'll always crave."

His thumb moved in lazy circles over the point of one nipple. Kora sighed in pleasure. His touch was spreading a warmth through her body. She couldn't believe she'd first pulled away, for now she longed for more.

He lowered his mouth for another taste, only this time he didn't hold her. She could pull away at any time. Yet, she remained. When he raised his head, she shifted, offering him the other. Her skin was sensitive now, flushed with warmth, wet from his kiss.

Slowly she accepted his touch, his mouth, his tongue all along her body. Slowly she relaxed, allowing him to move her, and mold her, and taste her wherever he liked. Slowly the silk disappeared completely and flesh touched flesh. She was lost in the beauty of being cherished.

When she was long drunk on his touch, he stood and pulled her to the couch. He lifted a blanket and wrapped it over her bare shoulders, then lowered her to the cushions. Kneeling beside her, he kissed her until the room filled with stars and she stretched contentedly.

He no longer had to tease her mouth open. With the touch of his lips on hers, she freely opened, giving him what she knew he hungered for. Her body responded to his hands, warm and soft and willing.

Without a word, he opened the front of the blanket and traveled down her throat. Now she cried in pleasure, feeling a bolt tingle through her. As he nibbled, she began to move slightly from side to side.

His hand slid down her body, opening the blanket. Pressing his palm gently against her abdomen, his mouth moved back up to her lips with his kiss.

"Relax, my love," he whispered. "Come easy to me now. I'm not going to hurt you."

She smiled and opened her mouth to his exploration. His hand inched down between her legs and began to softly brush across her as the kiss deepened.

Again she began to rock, only now his hand between her legs moved with her. She told herself she was giving him what he wanted, but she knew it was a lie. She was taking all the pleasure she could endure. She cried out softly with pure joy, and he increased the pressure between her legs.

Passion's river flowed over her once more. Only now there was no pain, only pleasure. She felt him touching her, satisfying her, making love to her.

She moved faster, feeling her body shaking with desire. Now she was rocking from side to side against the soft cushions, wanting more. All the blood in her body, all the heat, seemed to be moving to where he stroked. As his fingers pressed deeper into her, he twisted his free hand around her hair and pulled her head back as he covered her mouth with his own.

This time when the scream came it was one of pleasure, exploding within her, and not of pain. He tasted her climax in his kiss and felt her press against his hand in uncontrollable movements.

She drifted back to shallow waters with his kisses light across her face. Now his touch was a part of her, as casual as breathing. There was no shyness, only an overwhelming feeling of being loved.

He wrapped her in the blanket and lay beside her.

''That was . . .'' She circled her arms around his neck. ''That was so . . .''

Win laughed against her hair. ''I know.''

His voice was rough, but his hands gentle as they caressed beneath the blanket. ''Go to sleep now, wife. I plan on touching you all night long even while I'm sleeping.''

And he did. Kora woke twice to find him kneeling beside her, once more setting her body afire as his hands pulled her into the deep waters of passion. He'd please her until her body shook with desire, then he'd hold her again as she slipped back into sleep. He was learning to be gentle, she was learning to be his.

By first light she felt as if she'd slept soundly for a week. She stretched and opened her eyes to find Win staring down at her. He was fully dressed in clean clothes and held a cup of coffee in his hand.

''Did you sleep well?'' he asked as he hid his smile with a swallow of coffee.

''Yes.'' Kora pulled the blanket over her shoulders, embarrassed at the memories of what he'd done. She'd never dreamed a man could touch a woman so. And to do it again and again.

He offered her his cup. "Drink this," he ordered. "It's still raining and there's a chill in the air."

Kora swallowed several gulps, feeling not only thirsty, but hungry. "Thank you." She returned the cup, trying to be formal without allowing the blanket to slip. "I'll get dressed and cook breakfast." As she moved, her body ached slightly. He'd touched her all over, and kissed her where she thought no one would ever kiss. He'd made her feel beautiful.

Win just stared at her as she picked up her things and pulled on her wrapper. She could feel him following her movements but guessed he couldn't think of any more to say than she could. The night seemed a dream away. Something they'd never speak of in the light. She folded the blanket and moved slowly to the door.

Just as she touched the knob, he said in his usual gruff voice, "Lock the door again, darlin'."

She turned toward him and smiled. Without a word she turned the key.

THIRTY

JAMIE LEANED AGAINST THE PORCH RAILING AND watched the rain as she sipped her third cup of coffee. "I can't go get Dan yet," she complained to Cheyenne. "He'll catch his death if he gets soaked. He's better off with that old woman Kora told us about in the settlement."

"Wait until the storm lets up and I get back before you even think of heading out." Cheyenne stood a few feet away. "I don't want you going after Dan alone."

"I can make it," she said angrily. "I don't remember signing up to take orders from you. Kora and I make out fine seeing after him."

"Where is Kora, anyway?" Cheyenne tried to change the subject. "She's usually up by now."

"I don't know where she is." Jamie shrugged. "Win came in about half an hour ago. He fixed himself a cup of coffee and walked out without so much as saying 'morning.' I swear the man doesn't have a good side—only grumpy and grumpier." Jamie lifted the corner of her mouth in a half smile. "If I didn't like the man so much, I'd complain."

"Maybe he had something on his mind and didn't want

to be bothered with small talk.'' Cheyenne walked to the porch railing on the other side of the steps. ''As soon as this rain stops, we're going to have another shower of trouble.''

''Maybe not,'' Jamie offered. ''Maybe whatever is causing the trouble will disappear.'' She didn't add, maybe she and Kora would disappear as well. After being up most of the night thinking, she'd come to one conclusion. The only way this ranch would settle down would be if they left. Weeds have short roots anyway. It was time for them to tumble on.

Cheyenne cocked his head and looked at her. ''Do you know something I don't?''

Jamie walked slowly toward him and leaned on the railing so closely that their thighs brushed. ''I just know how life works.'' She raised her cup and let her elbow brush his ribs.

He shifted away.

She smiled at the game they played, moving close again until she just touched him.

''Stop it!'' He set his coffee down on the railing and folded his arms as though determined not to allow her to affect him. ''You'd think in a state this size there would be room enough so that we didn't have to share the same porch railing.''

''Why not? It could be interesting.''

''Because I don't like you so close. And I don't like you touching me! Or brushing against me! Or patting on me!''

When she reached for him, he stepped backward into the downpour.

''The hell you don't,'' she said as he walked away.

''Hell, I don't!'' he answered without turning around to look at her.

She laughed and yelled, "You keep this up and you're going to be irresistible!"

He turned then, full of rage and soaked with rain. "You keep this up and I'll—"

"You'll what? You'll kiss me? Am I scared? Like I haven't never been kissed. I've been kissed more'n—"

"I know!" he yelled back. "Your mouth's been tasted by more men than the church hall will hold. Well, maybe I don't want to be part of the congregation!" He shoved the hair from his face. "With you the invitation's always open to anyone. Come on down and have a feel of Jamie!"

"What are you saying? If I'd turn down a few men, you'd be more interested in me now?"

"I'd be more interested if you turned down *any*," he answered. "But there may not be many left to refuse. You do tend to make the rounds."

Jamie picked up her coffee mug and threw it at him.

He dodged her mug, but his flew a moment later and smacked him on the arm.

"You can go to the devil!" she shouted.

"Well, at least I'll be going alone and not with you hanging on me!" he countered as he disappeared into the sheets of rain.

Jamie lifted the pot and swung it around in a circle, letting the handle go so that the pot sailed toward where Cheyenne had stood. When she didn't hear a yelp, she swore loudly, knowing she'd missed him.

The screen door slammed.

"Guess we're out of coffee," Win said from behind her.

"Yes, we are." Jamie stormed past him. "And that's all I can cook."

She let the door slam once more, but Win hardly noticed, he was laughing so hard.

Kora joined him. She'd dressed and combed her hair,

turning from the woman he'd craved all night into his proper little wife. Without a word, she moved beneath his arm and they watched the rain.

He leaned down and kissed her lightly, wondering how one woman could make him feel so complete. With her near he felt whole for the first time in his life. She wasn't fancy, or high-spirited, or showy. She was soft-spoken and shy, but in a thousand little ways she had changed his world. When they talked, just talked, she enchanted him. When they touched, she enslaved him.

She smiled and he couldn't help kissing her again, enjoying the way her lips seemed fuller and velvety from having been kissed all night.

The rain allowed them the privacy they needed. She slid her arms around his neck and pressed against him, making him groan in pleasure.

"I'm already hungry for you again," he whispered against her ear as his hands moved along her sides. "I can't get enough. I'd like to undress you right here on the porch."

Kora laughed and snuggled closer, as if daring him.

Win fought to keep his hands from being too bold along the soft curves he'd grown to know so well during the night. "As soon as things settle down, I'm building a door to our bedroom with a lock on it."

"To lock me in or out?" Kora rolled against him as his hands came dangerously close to covering her breasts.

The slight action might have gone unnoticed by someone watching them, but it reminded Win of all he'd held only minutes before. When she locked the study door and came back to him this morning, she'd come as a woman who knew what she wanted. And he'd pleased her.

"To lock the world out," he whispered, remembering the way she'd lain nude before the fire and allowed him to stroke her. ''With a lock on our door, I can touch you not only at night, but in the daytime. Maybe all day and all night. I'll make you cry my name over and over with passion.''

She laughed. ''We'll starve.''

''I don't care,'' he mumbled.

She parted her lips and knew he'd take the invitation.

He kissed her, pulling her close until her breasts flattened against his chest.

When he finally raised his head, he tried to make himself remember where he was. ''I've always hated the rain,'' he said, even though all he could think of was pulling her back to the study so they could be alone. ''Even though I know I need it.'' He moved away slightly, trying to slow his breathing. ''I usually feel like I've lost a day's work when it rains.'' He kissed her lightly, very properly. ''Right now I wouldn't mind if it rained for a week.''

''Thank you''—she fought back the tears—''for the most wonderful night of my life.''

''There will be other nights. Better nights.'' He pulled her lightly against him, allowing his words to caress her. ''You'll move as you did to my touch this morning, only I'll be inside you next time.'' He felt her stiffen. ''Relax,'' he whispered. ''I'm never going to hurt you again. I practiced most of the night.''

She hid her tears against his chest. He was the only good thing that had ever happened in her life. And he wanted her. Not just as any man wants any woman, but as one man needs one woman. She could tell it in the way he touched her, as though branding her, forever making her his. And in the way he kissed her as if he'd hungered for her for years and now that he'd finally found her he planned to have his fill.

Win slowly pulled away, letting his fingers brush her as

long as possible. "I have to talk with Cheyenne."

"Jamie said he's a dead man when I passed her in the hall." Kora laughed. "She plans to kill him if she ever sees him again."

Win nodded. "Murder by coffeepot. It's a common way to die these days. For his safety, I'd better meet him in the barn."

"I'll cook breakfast."

"And I'll be back. I promise you I'll never leave you without saying goodbye twice."

"I'd rather you not say goodbye at all"—Kora moved toward the door—"then you'd never leave me."

Win pulled on his slicker. "The thought has crossed my mind."

Kora watched as he moved away. "A dream," she whispered as she turned into the kitchen. "I must be living a dream."

As she watched Win disappear in his light brown duster, she remember something from last night. Wyatt had worn a black one.

She yelled Win's name, but he was too far into the downpour to hear her. She'd have to wait until breakfast.

Jamie stood at the other side of the room with her arms folded in anger. "We're in the middle of a nightmare, not a dream, sister. A nightmare I'm about ready to wake up from."

"You're just mad at Cheyenne," Kora answered as she started breakfast.

"No," Jamie said. "It's more than that. Can't you see it, Kora? The trouble. Witchin' luck has struck again. It's time to travel on. You know the pattern. Once the trouble starts, we need to be packing."

"I can't." Kora looked at her sister and said the one thing that had been on her mind for days. "I love him too much. I'm staying this time.'' Kora closed her eyes, remembering that the last time Win talked of her leaving had been the night Andrew Adams had first shown up. Win had said simply that she could stay the six months, but he wanted her gone as soon as the time was up.

He'd never taken those words back. And if he didn't, no matter what happened between them, she'd have to leave.

Jamie moved closer and lowered her voice. ''If you love him, leave him before someone gets killed.''

Kora couldn't answer. Outside, thunder seemed to echo Jamie's warning and lightning split the sky. She couldn't remember the exact moment she'd known she loved him, but she couldn't tell him when he'd never said the words to her. In fact, he'd made it very plain that he'd never love any one woman.

An hour later, when the rain stopped, a sense of doom passed over her. The sun might be coming out, but her world was dying. How could she live with him until summer and then leave him? How could she tell him she wanted to stay forever when he'd never asked her?

Jamie shoved her things into a bag. ''I was just starting to get used to this place,'' she mumbled. ''Another ten years or so, I think Cheyenne would warm up to me.''

Kora watched her from the door. Jamie had exchanged her buckskins for Kora's best dress. ''What are you doing?''

Jamie handed her a note. ''A rider brought this to me a few minutes ago. It's from Wyatt. He says it's urgent that he talk with me.''

''But why are you packing?''

''I'm planning to go up to the settlement after Dan, but if Wyatt asks the question I think he will, I may be leaving with him.''

"But are you sure? Do you love Wyatt?" Kora couldn't believe Jamie was planning to leave.

"I don't know. I guess. Much as I love any man." She looked at her older sister. "I'm ready for some excitement. If you'd leave, that would be fine, but I can't wait around forever for you to make up your mind. The cowboy you married is crazy about you. I'm not even sure he'd let you go."

"But all the men are saddling up. They figured after what I heard at the settlement, today is the day. You can't leave now."

Jamie carried her bag down the stairs and out the back door with Kora following only a step behind. "Maybe not"—she shrugged—"but I got to be ready. If Wyatt asks me to leave with him, I'm going. I can't stay around here and watch the two of you falling wildly in love."

As Win walked his horse out of the barn, Kora turned toward him.

"See what I mean." Jamie pouted. "Another week of this and I'll vanish completely from your view."

"No, never," Kora answered Jamie as Win crossed to the house to say goodbye again. He looked strong and healthy; only Kora noticed the tightness of his jaw. He'd live with the pain. It was his way. But she wasn't sure she could live without him.

Jamie moved around to climb in the wagon.

"Jamie, promise you won't go today. Promise we'll talk first," Kora whispered.

"I'll pick up Dan and hear what Wyatt has to say," Jamie answered. "Then we'll talk before I leave. I promise."

Win walked to the corner of the porch. "It's going to be a long day," he said as he removed his hat. "I'm not sure how much trouble will come our way. Stay prepared here."

"I'll be fine." Kora fought back the tears. Unless she could talk her sister out of her crazy plan, she might never see her again. "I'm riding with Jamie to get Dan."

Suddenly Win flung his leg over the railing and stepped back on the porch. He pulled her to him. "If I asked you not to go, would you stay here?"

"No," Kora answered. "I have to go get my brother."

Win nodded in understanding. "Then take Logan as guard," he compromised.

Kora thought of all she'd learned from him about loving. "Take care," she whispered back. "And never forget, I love you."

Win's hold tightened, but he didn't speak. For a long moment he held her, then he turned and left without a word.

His silence should have made her angry, or think he didn't care about her. But she understood. He'd shown her he loved her all night. If he couldn't say the words in daylight, it didn't matter. No man would ever make her feel so cherished.

Kora watched the yard. Jamie was saying something to Cheyenne, and for once she didn't look as if she was going to tackle him. Logan stood close to Win, making last-minute plans.

"I can't leave," Kora whispered as her vision blurred. "Win's right. Folks make their own luck in this life. We can fight it together. This time I don't have to run." She glanced at Jamie. "If only I could convince Jamie," Kora whispered as she saw Jamie fight back the anger when she waved at Cheyenne and he didn't even bother to look back at her.

Win rode south with a dozen of his men, crisscrossing his land, making sure all was calm. The sky was still cloudy, but it had been clearing all afternoon. If the cattle were just below the caprock, it wouldn't be long before they were moving across his land.

He knew he should have nothing on his mind except the ranch, but Kora's words kept resounding in his brain. She'd said she loved him as easily as if she'd always said the words. He'd never known her to be so foolish.

They had a bargain, nothing more. She didn't have to say she loved him. He'd given her little enough reason to care about him. Win hadn't missed Jamie's comments about his shortcomings. Except for a few things from the store, he'd bought her nothing, not even a wedding band. He'd never taken her anywhere, or offered to. Hell, most women got a few days' honeymoon. He hadn't even stayed home the first night. Most of the time he didn't say a handful of words to her a day. And the first time he'd made love to her, he'd hurt her so badly she'd screamed.

Win frowned. It made no sense that she loved him.

Yet she took care, not only of his house, but of him. From the very first, she kissed him good night as though it was something important for her to do. She'd forgiven him for their first time together as if it had been her fault and not his. And last night she'd let him touch her like he'd never thought a lady would allow. Then she'd welcomed him again and again. Offering him whatever he wanted, moving so he could see her undressed, raising her arms to allow him freedom to touch her, spreading her legs . . .

"Hell!" he swore beneath his breath. He didn't have time to think about her. There were more important things to consider. Only all he could focus on, all he could hear, was the way she'd softly said she loved him.

Win grumbled. She wasn't doing what they agreed on.

She was doing far more than just acting like a wife in exchange for his house. The little woman he thought would be almost invisible in his home had gotten into his blood. She was the lover he'd never even dreamed of having. Her body was alive with passion when he touched her, begging for more. The taste of her was habit forming.

Tonight, he'd hold her again. He'd remove her clothes slowly, enjoying each view. Then he'd lay her in the middle of their bed and begin his feast at her throat. He'd make love to her and she'd cry his name as she had last night in passion. And when she had relaxed and fell asleep, he'd continue to touch her. He didn't need to teach her to please him; everything she did pleased him. Last night she'd awakened already warm from his touch, ready for more. She'd do so again tonight.

It might take days, maybe weeks, but he'd make love to her until he got her out of his mind and could think of other things, more important things. Win frowned. On second thought, it might take years.

"You hear that?" Cheyenne straightened in his saddle, listening.

"What?" Win shook his head, trying to get back to reality.

"Cattle!" Cheyenne motioned for the men to follow as they reached the south corner of Win's ranch. Here, for miles, the land was broken by steep inclines where the land jutted up suddenly to higher ground known as the caprock. The pasture below always seemed milder, less windy. Above, the range was cooler, wilder. This steep incline was where Win marked the end of his spread.

Sure enough, just below the rim of the caprock, cattle grazed as far as Win could see. They'd been boxed in by the wall, but all the herders had to do was begin pushing them up the trails, climbing the rim one beef at a time.

Along the south edge of Win's ranch were several places where they could move the herd easily up on higher ground.

One of Win's men was stationed at each opening. One fired a shot of warning. Another followed. Then another and another.

This is it, Win thought. The standoff he'd dreaded. But he had the high ground, and with the caprock wall's help, he'd hold them back. He didn't want to kill the cattle. Let the ranchers keep them below. The strong ones would survive. But, no, they wanted to get them to market without having to suffer any loss.

He studied the border, watching, waiting. Cheyenne rode at his side.

"It looks like they're spreading the herd out, planning to push them all at once."

"If they do, several will break their legs trying to climb up rough trails. Any cow that falls will be trampled." Win didn't want to think what the sight might be like if they stampeded.

"They're hoping we don't have enough men to cover every trail."

Win watched closely. "Do we?" he asked more to himself than Cheyenne.

A man Win recognized as one of the fellows he'd seen in the settlement the night he'd gone after Kora, rode through the pass with his hands high.

"Mr. McQuillen!" he yelled. "I just want to talk."

"That's close enough!" Win shouted back. "Tell your boss to turn them around. They'll not cross my land."

"But the next crossing is a hundred miles away," the man tried to reason. "If you'll let us cross in one place, my boss is willing to pay you. He'll even leave men to help burn the grass his cattle move over."

"No," Win answered. "I can't take the risk!" He knew

burning the grass would prevent the sickness from spreading. But with a herd this size, all it would take was one calf getting away from the others, and all his cattle would be infected within days. He'd be risking all he had, all he'd worked for.

"Not even for money?" the man exclaimed. "Name your price."

"No," Win answered, knowing he wouldn't compromise. How could he put a price on his ranch?

"We could run them through. You haven't got enough men to stop the entire herd."

"I said no!" Win shouted. "And we will stop every last beef."

The man turned his horse around as if to leave. "How about to save your wife?" he queried over his shoulder.

THIRTY-ONE

THE SETTLEMENT SEEMED DESERTED AS JAMIE MOVED the team toward Rae's shack. In daylight the place was even worse than it had been at night.

Jamie jumped out of the wagon and tied the team while Logan slowly climbed down from the back.

"I'm going to talk to Wyatt." Jamie smoothed down the wrinkles on her borrowed dress. "You and Logan can handle Dan."

"But the note didn't say where to find him. And he said this afternoon. He may not be here for an hour yet," Kora answered. "Wait a few minutes and we'll all go with you."

"No way." Jamie started moving away. "I have to go alone for the same reason I wore a dress. He might just be asking me to run away with him. So a girl's got to look her best and a man has to ask when they're alone."

Kora opened her mouth to argue, but her sister was already several yards away.

Rae came to the door as Jamie disappeared between two tents. "Mornin'," she mumbled. "Where's the girl running off to?"

"Wyatt sent a note for her to meet him here," Kora

answered as she moved into the cabin. "How's Dan?"

"He's fine. We've had a grand time." Rae laughed, patting Dan on the arm. "We stayed up late talking."

"You did?"

"Sure, he told me how much he loves his sisters and how grateful he is for all they do for him."

Kora looked shocked for a moment, then she caught Rae winking at Logan. "What else did he say?" she asked, enjoying the old woman's lie.

"He told me he loves you very much and that if you were the one lost inside your own head, he'd be there to take care of you."

Kora straightened Dan's collar as he stared at a crack in the cabin that allowed a sliver of sunshine in. "I think he would," she whispered. "During this conversation, did you tell him I loved him?"

Rae smiled. "I didn't have to. He knows."

Kora took Dan's hand and slowly guided him from the cabin. "Did you have any trouble with Andrew after I left?"

"No." Rae giggled. "I was handling drunks before he could grow chest hair. I sent him on his way."

When they reached the wagon, Rae glanced in the direction Jamie had gone. "Your sister's gonna have a problem finding that gambler, Wyatt. Him and all his kind left out of here as soon as the storm broke, and I haven't heard none come back."

As Kora helped Logan lift Dan into the wagon, she glanced at the old man and saw worry in his eyes.

"You're sure Wyatt isn't here?"

Rae scratched her tumbleweed hair. "I ain't seen nobody but those two drifters who found Win in the snake pit. They asked when you was coming to get your brother, and I told them it ain't none of their concern and they'd better be in the next state before you see them.''

While Logan helped Kora down from the wagon, a scream shattered the morning air from just beyond the trees.

''Stay with Dan!'' Logan shouted as he pulled his gun. ''I'll go see about Jamie.''

Kora covered Dan with a blanket as he lay down in the wagon bed filled with hay. She reached for the rifle beneath the seat and waited.

Rae grabbed a knife from her cabin and stood beside her.

Silence. Nothing but silence. Logan and Jamie were both gone, leaving Kora alone with an old woman and Dan. Alone and in the open, for she'd not put her rifle down to help Dan back inside. Alone with the feeling that someone was moving slowly through the brush toward her.

Win narrowed his gaze and lowered his hat against the afternoon sun as rays bounced off the barrel of his Winchester.

All the years of burying his emotions, of hiding his tears, of refusing to allow any feelings to surface exploded into one eruption of anger. He drew his rifle and took aim at the man in the center of the pass.

Cheyenne was at his side. ''Wait!'' he whispered. ''Let's hear what he has to say. They're bluffing. You and I both know Kora is safe with both Logan and Jamie watching over her.''

''I'm not so sure. After all, that drunk Adams didn't have any trouble stealing her from under our noses.'' Win didn't take his attention from the stranger in the pass. ''I'll kill them all if they try to use Kora as bait.''

''I'll help you,'' Cheyenne agreed. ''But my guess is they're lying.''

Nodding slowly, Win turned and yelled down at the man in the pass. "Leave my wife out of this!"

"I'd like to, Mr. McQuillen. We don't want to hurt her. All we want to do is get our cattle to market. But the boss has given orders to move north no matter what we have to do."

"Not across my land!" Win answered.

"We'll give you an hour to think about it. Then we'll show you that wife of yours for the last time unless the cattle start moving through this pass."

Win watched the man disappear below the caprock. Reason told him that they couldn't have Kora. But his heart argued, what if they did? He pulled back out of sight and signaled his men to move closer.

They formed a campsite far enough away to be safe and rotated guard. In a few hours it would be dark and not a man would ride for home. Win climbed down from his horse and began to pace. There wasn't time to send someone to check on Kora, so he had to accept the possibility that they had her. But these weren't murderers. They were ranchers. Running cattle was one thing; killing a woman seemed quite another. Something beyond profits from the herds must be driving them.

"Rider coming in!" one of Win's hands yelled as a rider galloped in from the west.

Win looked up as a stranger, traveling fast, kicked his horse toward them. For a moment he looked familiar. All he needed was a dark duster.

But as he rode closer, Win recognized the gambler. He'd shed his black suit and string tie in favor of chaps and cotton.

"Wyatt," he whispered to Cheyenne. Both men rested their hands on the handle of their Colts.

Wyatt jumped from his mount without slowing. "Wait!"

he shouted. "Don't start shooting. They've got your wife!"

"What?" Win grabbed Wyatt by the collar. "How do you know?"

The gambler knocked Win's hand away with surprising strength. "I know because I've been watching them for weeks now." He straightened before them, looking far less of a dandy than he had before. "An hour ago I saw two men riding near the settlement with your wife across one man's saddle. She was screaming and kicking, but alive."

"Are you sure?"

"She had on that same blue dress she wore the last time I visited your place."

Win studied him closely. The pieces had never fit with Wyatt. He rode too well to be a man who spent his days at a gaming table. He disappeared and reappeared whenever trouble boiled. "The only reason you're alive is because of what you did to help my wife at the settlement. But don't bank too heavy on one action. You've got some explaining to do."

Wyatt let out a breath, as if tired of holding it. His eyes darted to the left, then the right. "I was sent in to keep a lid on this war you people are trying to start over a few head of cattle. I'm a ranger stationed at Fort Elliot."

"Sure you are," Cheyenne whispered.

Glancing at Cheyenne, Wyatt shouted, "I don't care if you believe me or not!"

"I don't," the Indian said simply.

"Look, I'm here to help. I know these people. They aren't here to murder, just move cattle. Let them through. You'll recover in a year or so. Let them pass and end this blockade tonight. You don't have a prayer of winning anyway. If they stampede the cattle toward the ridge, they'll come up from too many directions for your men to stop them all. A few will get through your web and infect your cattle. They'll lose the herd and you'll lose half, maybe more of yours. No one wins.''

Win didn't answer.

Wyatt moved closer, pressing his case. ''The trail boss will listen to reason. He'll let Kora go if you give your promise. But you'd best do it fast. Most of his offspring are bloodthirsty, and if you hesitate you'll be giving them the chance they're looking for to kill. I've never met a woman like the oldest daughter, all sweet one minute and deadly the next. It's more than money with her. She's out for blood. Let me talk to them. I can bluff my way through this.''

''All right.'' Win hesitated for only a moment, realizing he had nothing to lose.

The gambler relaxed for the first time. ''Before I go I have to know how far you're willing to play the hand.''

Win didn't blink. ''If they don't have Kora and it's only a bluff, I'll shoot the beef as they try to cross. My word stands.''

''And if they do have her?''

''Tell them to turn her loose and they can cross my ranch.''

Wyatt looked surprised. ''You'd bet the entire ranch against her life?''

''I would,'' Win answered. ''And more.''

Wyatt nodded and swung back into the saddle. ''Someday I'll sit down and explain my part in all this,'' he said. ''But until then, it wouldn't hurt to trust me a little. When this is over, we might even become friends, or maybe even family.''

''Yeah,'' Cheyenne interrupted. ''When you come up with a story we'll believe.''

Wyatt glared at Cheyenne silently, the look promising a

reckoning in the future. Then the gambler rode off into the pass with his hands high and in plain sight.

"He's lying," Cheyenne said.

"I know," Win agreed. "Only I can't figure out why."

"The hour is up!" A man shouted from the entrance to the pass. "Do we move the cattle?"

Win shifted to where he could watch the pass. He hadn't heard a word from Wyatt. He'd either joined them, or they'd killed him. Neither would come as a surprise.

"Where's my wife?" All the McQuillen guns were pointed at the long rock-walled vee that marked one of the larger gateways to Win's land.

Slowly two men walked up from below, dragging a woman between them. Her hands were tied to a rope in front of her as if she'd been led. A bandanna covered her eyes and most of her face. Another dug into the sides of her mouth muffling her screams.

Her hair was long and almost white in the afternoon sun. Win felt his stomach tighten as he saw her dress, dirty and torn. She'd put up quite a fight. He remembered the first time he'd seen her. He'd wondered then how such a tiny creature, so fragile, had survived. He wondered the same now and his heart ached.

"Turn her loose!" He fought to keep from moving down the pass. Her life depended on his remaining calm. "I'll give you whatever you want."

Both of the drifters stood tall, proud of themselves for capturing her. They might have failed the first time, but she'd almost stumbled right into their camp this morning.

Wyatt rode from below to where the men stood holding Kora. He looked none the worse for wear. "I told them you would!" he yelled at Win, then glanced to the men. "Untie her, boys, and I'll take her to him."

As they worked, Wyatt turned his attention back to Win. ''All they want is to cross your land.'' He didn't have to say more. Everyone watching knew what the action would cost. ''She's free when we have your word.''

''You have it.'' Win stared at Kora as she kicked at the men untying her. ''As soon as they've crossed, I'll burn my own ranch to keep the fever from spreading.'' All he cared about was the woman below.

As the men pulled the bandanna from their captive's eyes and mouth, one word echoed across the space between Wyatt and Win. ''Jamie!''

Cheyenne was in the saddle and riding down the incline before anyone else could move.

The kidnappers suddenly realized they'd captured the wrong woman. They tried to pull her back, but she kicked and screamed like a wildcat.

No one was sure who opened fire first, but all at once the air rained bullets. They ricocheted off the stone walls, echoing certain death. The men in the pass who'd been holding Jamie scrambled for cover. The men above lowered their aim.

''Wyatt! Please!'' Jamie lifted her still-tied hands to him. ''Wyatt!''

He fought to close the ten feet between them, but bullets splattered the ground around him. His mount danced in the flying dirt, wild with fear. Wyatt fought for control as the men above shot at the men below and the men below returned fire.

With a sudden turn Wyatt pulled his horse back from the center of the passage and rode up toward Win, leaving Jamie standing alone in a circle of gunfire.

Win kept a steady stream of bullets aimed at the rocks behind the pass as he saw Cheyenne approaching Jamie at full speed. Like a wild warrior from another time, Cheyenne rode into the fire and swept Jamie up. Unlike the men who'd tried to kidnap her at the ranch, Cheyenne could hold her in balance and control his powerful horse.

By the time Win reloaded, Cheyenne was out of trouble and riding at gale speed toward the safety of the camp.

Jamie was bouncing and swearing as she lay across his saddle. But she was alive.

The gunfire died down. There was no one left in the pass. Win motioned for his men to stay ready. Nothing or no one would cross now and live. All bargaining was over.

THIRTY-TWO

CHEYENNE RODE BEHIND A BANK OF ROCKS TO THE campsite and dropped a screaming Jamie to the ground a few yards from Wyatt. She fell onto her backside as he swung from the saddle and pulled his knife.

But before he could cut her free, she whirled and turned on the gambler like a skillet-warmed rattlesnake. ''You left me!''

''I tried to reach you,'' Wyatt said, looking like a man who'd faced death and had no stomach for the sight. ''If I'd stayed longer, we both would have been killed.'' He crossed his arms in front of him to keep his hands from shaking.

Jamie doubled her bound fists together and swung, knocking the gambler down with one mighty blow that almost toppled her. ''One of us may be killed yet!'' she screamed. ''Stand up so I can hit you again.''

Wyatt remained on the ground.

Cheyenne walked up behind Jamie and circled his arm around her waist. The action was becoming a habit. He lifted her just high enough so that her feet left the ground.

''Let me go!'' Jamie shouted and twisted against his side.

He moved several yards away from Wyatt and the others. "Don't make me sorry I rode down after you," Cheyenne said calmly as he set her down and tried to untie her. "Be still, or I'll leave you bound."

Jamie straightened, offering her hands before his blade. "Don't expect me to be grateful. It's not one of my traits."

"I imagine I'll come to regret what I did." Cheyenne smiled. "Sooner or later." His knife sliced through the ropes.

She looked at him then, truly looked at him, for the first time. A portion of her anger passed as the realization of what he'd done sank into her frightened brain. "Thank you," she said. "No one else would have risked his life for me like you did." Jamie offered her hand.

Cheyenne closed his grip around her fingers and held tightly as he pulled her a step closer. "You'd have done the same for me," he mumbled, but his eyes seemed to say so much more. His thumb moved across the back of her hand in almost a caress.

"I tried to reach you, Jamie," Wyatt interrupted. "In fact, when I rode away from you, you were safer because everyone was shooting at me. I'm probably the reason Cheyenne didn't get hit when he rode in."

Jamie glanced in Wyatt's direction without turning loose of Cheyenne's hand. "Then I guess I should thank you, too." Her gaze came back to Cheyenne. "You never know what someone will do until under fire."

She moved beneath Cheyenne's arm, and he let her close for once. His hold was strong, but not an embrace.

"You've got some explaining to do, Wyatt." Cheyenne stared at the man. "You're no ranger and you're no gambler, but you've been trying real hard to straddle the fence. Didn't anyone ever tell you that the man who sits the fence makes the easiest target?"

Wyatt lowered his head, unable to stare at Cheyenne. "I was a ranger for a while, and I fancy myself a gambler."

"But that's not all."

"Maybe it is." Wyatt looked dissatisfied with himself. "And somehow it's not enough. Whatever I am, whatever I do, never seems to be right, or enough to measure up."

He lifted his hand to touch Jamie, but lowered it before he reached her. "I sent you the note hoping you'd meet me and run away from this mess. But they got to you first."

A wagon rattled up to the campsite, drawing everyone's attention and ending the conversation.

Kora jumped out and ran toward them. "Jamie! Are you all right?"

Jamie pulled away from Cheyenne. "Sure. No problem now. You missed all the excitement."

"We heard your scream, and Logan went to look for you," Kora announced as she hugged her sister. "Some men hit Logan in the back of the head and rode off with you before I could stop them. Rae was very upset, even trying to get men to follow."

"I'm fine now thanks to Cheyenne . . . and Wyatt," Jamie added. "How's Logan?"

"Rae's looking after him. He's hurting, but we got him back to Rae's place and doctored up. He told me to ride along the south border and I'd find help. I was so frightened. I pushed the team as hard as I could with Dan asleep in the back."

Win climbed over the cluster of six-foot-high rocks and slid down the incline to the camp. He was issuing orders as he approached, but when he saw Kora, he froze. Slowly he straightened and faced her directly as though forgetting all else. "What are you doing here?" His voice was low. "And why did you bring Dan?"

"I was worried about Jamie," she answered, no longer bothered by his gruffness. "There was no time to get Dan out of the wagon. He's sleeping like a baby. I couldn't leave him with Rae. She had her hands full with Logan."

"Jamie's out of harm's way, for the moment." He seemed to be fighting to keep his voice calm. "Take her back to the house and wait this out there." He started moving toward the wagon. "Is Logan hurt bad?"

"No, just a headache and a two-inch cut. He'll be fine."

Kora followed, but didn't step forward when he offered to help her onto the seat. "Are you coming back?" She touched Win's sleeve gently as she always did.

"No. I've work to do here," he answered, looking irritated that she wasn't already on her way but not pulling his arm away. "But you'll be safe back at the house."

Kora took a step backward. "If you're not going, I'm staying."

Everyone in the campsite was silent, not even breathing as they waited for Winter's reaction.

Win knew he could reach down and lift her into the wagon. Or he could raise his voice and frighten her with his anger. If it had been Jamie, he'd already be yelling at her.

But Kora didn't even look afraid. He didn't know whether to be proud of himself for being so convincing that he'd never hurt her or proud of her for being so brave.

She raised her hand and gently laid it over his heart.

"I'm a rancher's wife. I belong here." Her words were only a whisper.

"But we may be here all night," Win began. He'd just offered his entire ranch for her safety; he couldn't hurt her by arguing now. And no matter how much he wanted her safe, he wasn't sure he could turn her away.

"It doesn't matter," she answered. "I'll stay with you."

Leaning, Win propped his rifle against the wagon wheel. Then, without a word, he unbuckled his gunbelt.

No one moved. Jamie started to move toward her sister, but Cheyenne's hand on her shoulder stopped her.

Win knelt on one knee and wrapped the belt around Kora's waist. ''If you're staying, you may need this.''

Everyone in the site let out a breath at the same time.

Win adjusted the gunbelt. ''Promise me you'll follow orders. There may not be time to talk things over.''

Kora nodded. ''What can I do?''

He stood beside her and pointed toward a cluster of cottonwoods. ''You could use the wagon and bring as much wood up as you can. By dark I'd like several fires going just back from the rim. With enough wood at each to keep it burning all night.''

Win reached for his rifle. When he rose, he met Kora's eyes. For a moment all the trouble didn't seem so bad. All he'd asked for was a woman to marry him so he wouldn't lose the house, and he'd gotten all he'd ever imagined a woman could be in the bargain. She'd even said she loved him once, and if she never said it again, once was enough.

Kora climbed into the wagon as men within hearing distance tried to act as if they hadn't been listening. ''I'll make a bed for Dan under the trees. He'll be safe there while I move the wood.''

Jamie ran to the other side of the wagon and jumped in. ''I'll help, 'cause I'm staying, too. I don't want to miss the fun.''

''But, Jamie!'' Wyatt ran to her side of the wagon. ''What about us? My offer still stands. Run away with me now, and I promise you a wild time.''

Jamie shook her head. ''I'm sorry, Wyatt. I have to turn you down. I'm not sure what you're looking for, but it's not me.''

Wyatt tipped his hat as though she'd turned him down for a dance. His lack of sorrow made it plain to everyone that she was just an extra and not a staple in his life.

As the women moved away toward the cottonwoods, Win said to Cheyenne, "Take a man and ride as fast as you can back to the house for supplies. We may be here for the night, and I don't want Kora hungry or cold."

Cheyenne nodded. "And I'll pick up your extra Colt. You want me to take Dan back?"

Win smiled, thinking of where his gunbelt was resting around Kora's waist and wishing his arm could do the same. "No, she wants her family close."

Win leaned closer to Cheyenne. "You still got that deed I bought from the bank and Andrew Adams?"

"I picked it up this morning before I rode out here to join you," Cheyenne said. "Andrews couldn't believe you were paying him double for his share. But it was a smart investment. That's a pretty spread, but it will never be farmland."

"Put the deed in the safe when you get back." Win watched the pass between the rocks. "And put Jamie's name on it."

"What?" Cheyenne questioned as if he didn't hear Winter correctly.

"I don't want her ever feeling she has to run off with drifters and gamblers just because she doesn't feel like she has a place to stay."

"All right," Cheyenne said as he walked away. "You're the boss. But you sure picked a hell of a time to be passing out land."

THIRTY-THREE

TIME PASSED SLOWLY UNTIL SUNSET. KORA AND JAMIE made several trips to the cottonwoods and brought back firewood. The men helped them unload and build fires all along the ridge where the cattle below might come through.

Winter didn't say another word to Kora, but he looked for her each time he rode past the camp.

At dusk Cheyenne returned with supplies and Dan's chair. He helped Jamie tie it to the bed of the wagon, both knowing that Dan would climb into the wagon before full dark and not budge no matter what happened.

Win worked with his men, giving instructions and advice like a general preparing for battle.

When Cheyenne walked beside his boss, he said, "If they stampede that large a herd and we spread the fires out, there will be no place for the herd to turn except in on itself."

"I know," Win whispered.

"It'll be a slaughter. Some of their men may be caught in the middle. A man down in that size a herd would be dead within seconds."

"I thought of that," Win agreed again. "I've always

depended on you being my right hand. But tonight, if the shooting starts, I want you to leave. Take Kora and Jamie and travel north toward the settlement. With my men busy fighting, we may not be able to stop the fire once it starts. The folks at the settlement will need warning. From there, take the women and Dan back to the house."

Winter had made sure months ago that the house was surrounded by a breaker against grass fires. The stream on one third, the corrals on another. Plowed ground void of grass on a third. It made the grounds muddy when it rained, but it acted as a breaker. Cheyenne would have time to knock the corral posts down. With Kora and Jamie keeping watch, the headquarters would be safe. The stark plainness of his ranch headquarters that Mary Anna had complained about once would be the very thing that saved it from burning.

"What if Kora won't go?" Cheyenne asked. "Do I drag them off screaming and fighting?"

"Tell her the house is in danger."

Cheyenne shook his head. "She won't go."

Win frowned. "Tell her Dan and Jamie are in danger. She'll do anything to help her family."

"Even leave you here to fight alone?" Cheyenne asked.

"Even leave me," Win repeated. He figured one "I love you" would never outweigh a lifetime of caring for her brother and sister.

Darkness moved across the prairie, but the men kept the vigil. In one-hour shifts they stood guard at every location where cattle might climb. Win remained in the saddle, moving from one location to the other, waiting.

Wyatt restlessly circled the campfire where Kora and Jamie sat. He'd flirted with Jamie until nightfall, but she'd turned him down cold. Yellow never aroused her passion, and he seemed dipped in it. He'd pleaded his case better than a big-city lawyer could have, but she was no longer interested.

"Rider coming in!" one of the men on post yelled.

Win and Cheyenne stepped into the glow of the campfire as a rider cleared the pass and rode toward the light.

All guns were drawn as the rider dismounted. "I've come with a message!" he shouted. "For McQuillen."

"I'm McQuillen." Win moved forward. "What is it?"

"One of my boss's daughters wants to talk to you. She wants to try and make peace one last time. She said to meet her in the pass alone in ten minutes." The drover looked nervous. "She says if you do, it'll all be solved."

"I'll be there," Win stated and raised his hand to allow the messenger to return unbothered.

"Don't go," Cheyenne whispered. "It's a trap."

"For once I agree with Cheyenne," Wyatt said. "The woman is mean and self-centered. Whatever she wants will only serve her own interest. I think she's probably the one responsible for the lookouts being shot."

"Maybe she doesn't want to see her father killed," Kora offered. "Maybe she's trying to help."

Wyatt lifted the coat Win had been wearing. "She's deadly. She always has been," he whispered. "I'll talk to her."

Win studied him closely. A man doesn't get many chances to prove his courage. Wyatt looked near to being shattered. He might be playing both sides of the fence, but he had nothing to gain by this action. "All right," Win said, giving the man an opportunity for no reason other than he needed one. "I'll be right behind you. But when we get back, you've got some talking to do and it better be the truth."

Tension thickened the air as the minutes ticked by. Wyatt put on Winter's coat and hat in silence. Win moved to the wagon and removed his spurs, then began blackening his face and hands with ashes.

"What are you doing?" Kora asked from just behind him.

Win smiled, enjoying the sound of her voice. "I'll be moving in silently, a part of the night. No one will even know I'm there, unless Wyatt gets himself into trouble."

"Be careful," she whispered. She watched him slide a knife into his belt. "Do you want your gun back?"

"No." Win leaned and kissed her cheek. "You keep it for me. A shot that far into the pass might set off the cattle below."

Kora wanted a moment alone with him. All day she'd been longing to have him hold her, or whisper something only for her ears. But there was no time and no place.

"Ready?" Wyatt asked.

"Ready," Win answered. As he passed Kora, he touched her cheek. "See you in a few minutes, darlin'."

Kora couldn't speak for the lump in her throat.

Win crossed into the blackness with Wyatt. They walked toward the opening. "You don't have to do this for me," Win said.

"Yes, I do, but not for you. For me." Wyatt squared his shoulders. "I've been dodging this problem all my life."

Win slowed as they moved into the narrow space and began to descend into a natural hallway that joined the low lands with the higher ground. It was too rocky for a wagon to move through, but a man on horseback, or cattle, would have no problem.

Halfway down a female voice echoed off the walls. "That's far enough, McQuillen."

Wyatt stopped and Win moved into the blackness a few feet behind him.

"Aren't you even going to say hello to your first love?"

The woman took a step closer. She was dressed in a red riding suit with white lace at the collar and cuffs, reflecting the moonlight.

The gambler remained silent, his hat down hiding his face.

Fighting down the reaction to her voice, Win moved closer. Mary Anna! Of course, she was the woman Rae warned Kora about. Her family were ranchers in the south, and she'd been here visiting since before the trouble started.

"You could have made it so easy. Marry me and I'd have had you on a honeymoon while my father moved the cattle. But I guess I waited too long expecting you to crawl. You panicked and married another."

Wyatt remained stone as she thought she was talking to Win before her.

Mary Anna took a step closer. "I told Papa from the first I'd take care of the problem called McQuillen. He promised me Wyatt's share of the profits. My loser of a brother's been no help at all. He doesn't deserve any part of what will be Papa's greatest year if he can just get the cattle to market. Wyatt rode with us in black dusters, but he'd always shoot high. But not me. I almost killed that shadow of yours, Cheyenne, and I would have killed you if Wyatt hadn't demanded we take cover."

Win fought down his rage as he took a step closer and pulled his knife. He was alone in the passage with two of the siblings someone had told him were deadly. Sweet, beautiful Mary Anna sounded as if she was capable of anything, and Wyatt might turn on him, or run at any moment.

But the brother remained motionless with his head down.

"The time has come for me to keep my word to my father. Your little wife is about to become a widow once more." Mary Anna lifted a small derringer from her pocket.

"No!" Winter shouted. He rushed forward, trying to

push Wyatt aside. The knife in his hand clanged among the rocks as he dived toward the man wearing his coat.

The gun fired just as she caught a glimpse of Win coming from the shadows. Wyatt lifted his face to his sister as he crumbled.

"Wyatt!" Mary Anna screamed when Win knocked the gun from her hand.

He blocked her path, but Wyatt's groan of pain drew his attention. Mary Anna backed away yelling to no one that it wasn't her fault.

Win lifted the gambler's arm over his shoulder to help him to his feet. They both stared at the silhouette of Mary Anna running down the path. The shot had spooked the cattle, and they were moving about restlessly below. Her sudden descent sent tiny rocks showering and started the cattle nearby trying to move away. But hundreds of head pinned them in. The herd seemed to churn below her, stomping up dirt and making low sounds.

Mary Anna suddenly lost her footing and screamed as she fell among them. Several men on horseback moved toward her, but they were too far away. Her body was trampled before her scream could die in the air.

Win turned and moved up the passage half carrying Wyatt at his side. There was nothing he could do to save Mary Anna, but Wyatt was still alive.

When he walked back into camp carrying Wyatt, everyone gathered round to help. They placed him in the wagon bed near the firelight. Win explained what had happened while Kora took a look at the wound on Wyatt's side.

"I'm all right," Wyatt said as he fought back the pain. "The bullet just grazed me. She never could shoot a handgun worth a darn."

Kora bandaged the wound as best she could. "You need to see a doctor."

Wyatt nodded as he sat up. ''First, I have to tell my father what happened. Mary Anna was always more the son he wanted than me.'' He glanced at Win. ''Get me my horse, would you?''

''Take mine.'' Win understood the gambler's need to find his father. ''Thanks for saving my life.''

''No.'' Wyatt smiled. ''It's time to tell the truth. If you hadn't jumped in when you did, she might not have missed. You saved mine.'' He pulled off Win's coat. ''And if you don't mind, I'll take my own horse. I wouldn't want to be mistaken for you twice tonight.''

Wyatt stood slowly. ''I may not be back, but I'll see my father's anger isn't turned toward you.''

''You're welcome anytime.''

The gambler glanced at Jamie.

''As a friend,'' she answered his unasked question. ''You're always welcome as a friend.''

Wyatt touched his fingers to his hat and gingerly climbed atop his horse. He moved into the night without another word.

Kora slid beneath Win's arm. ''Is it over?''

''If our luck holds, we'll know by morning.'' He held her tight.

The camp settled down for the night. Men still rode in changing shifts, but no one heard a word from below. Kora and Jamie climbed into the bed of the wagon and tried to sleep on either side of Dan's chair, but both were too excited.

Just after dawn Winter drew everyone's attention with a sudden resounding shot. They all scrambled to see what he'd shot at.

''That's far enough!'' Win shouted as he raised his rifle and pointed toward the passage. ''Another foot and the bullet won't just dance in the dirt at your feet.''

A man in his fifties slowly raised his hands. ''All right. I'm not going to try anything. I'm not armed.''

Win didn't lower his rifle. Kora pulled the Winchester from the wagon and joined her husband. Cheyenne did the same, taking only a moment to shove Jamie down out of sight as he passed her.

She glared at him, but didn't stand back up.

''What do you want?'' Win asked the man below.

''Name's Randell Monroe. I've come to say I've had enough. I quit. You win. I never planned on pushing so hard. Wyatt told me you saved his life last night. Thanks for that. I don't know if I could survive losing two children in one night.''

''Mary Anna's dead then?'' Win asked, even though he knew she would be.

The old man nodded. ''She never could stand not getting her way. And I always spoiled her, so the blame of what she tried to do is more mine than hers. Wyatt tried to stop me from herding the cattle, but all I saw was how much money I'd lose if I didn't try.''

Win didn't say a word, but he found himself admiring the man in the passage for his honesty.

Randell removed his hat and pushed his silver hair back. ''We're already turning the herd for home. I'll bury my daughter and suffer my losses, but I'll not try to cross your land.''

Win lowered his rifle. Randell Monroe looked like a proud man. He wasn't sure if he felt more sorry for him for losing Mary Anna or for having lost control of what was right.

''We'll burn the grassland behind you,'' Win said as he stood.

''I figured you would,'' Randell said, then turned slowly

around. "Give us a day's start. We should reach the river by then."

"No more," Win answered, knowing they'd have to drive the cattle hard to stay ahead of a brush fire. The grazing would be burned for miles across the rocky land no one claimed, but in a month with a few good rains, the growth would come back.

Winter watched the man walk back down the pass, his head high. He looked older than he had when he'd climbed the ledge.

"Will he have enough years left to start over?" Kora whispered.

"Maybe he'll turn the ranch over to Wyatt," Win answered.

"How many men do you want to leave on guard?" Cheyenne asked.

"It doesn't matter. I have a feeling Randell Monroe will stop any trouble from reaching us."

"So do I," Kora added.

They left a half dozen men camped on the ridge and headed home. Kora wanted to ride double with Win, but he didn't offer and she wasn't about to ask. They were all exhausted. Kora and Jamie headed toward the settlement to pick up Logan while Win and Cheyenne rode with the men toward home.

As they crossed Win's land, Jamie sat beside her sister in the wagon.

"Cheyenne's not speaking to me again," she mumbled. "I swear, why'd he bother to save me if he's not going to notice I'm alive? I hate him with every bone in my body."

Kora didn't comment. She couldn't force Cheyenne to like her sister. The man had a right to his own opinion.

"Maybe Wyatt will come back," Kora finally said, hoping to change the subject. "Win said he'd send a man south next spring to offer to help restock his herd.''

''I don't care if his does.'' Jamie pulled her skirts up above her knees. ''Right now I don't care about much of anything but a bath and a bed.''

Jamie slapped the team into action. They circled by the settlement, picked up a grumpy Logan, and headed slowly home. When they reached the main house, no one was around, but there were signs that someone had been. The bunkhouse cook had put out a spread of food. He said Win had hit home issuing orders like someone special was coming to visit. He wanted a meal on the table and about a hundred other things done before Kora returned, then he up and disappeared riding toward town.

''I wish he'd told me where he was going, or when to expect him back.'' Kora knew her words sounded like a complaint, but she was too tired to remain silent.

''What?'' Jamie chimed. ''And break a perfect record? I may stay around a while longer just to see you whip him into shape. He's not overly friendly, but he does grow on a person. At least he's brave and honest and never goes back on his word. But I'm not promising to stay long.''

''For a while then.'' Kora smiled.

THIRTY-FOUR

KORA STEPPED INTO THE SUNNY WARMTH OF HER COLorful bedroom. After a night of trying to sleep in a wagon bed, the space looked like a slice of heaven. The quilts welcomed her as they shone in the sunlight. In the center of the room awaited a hip tub already filled with water. Her robe and a towel lay over the chair by her writing table.

Smiling with delight, she stripped off her dirty clothes and sank into the cool water.

''He does care,'' she whispered, knowing Win had set the bath up for her. Most of the time he might seem to think only of the ranch, but he had made several trips getting this ready for her.

After washing her body and hair, she barely had enough energy left to slip into her undergarments before she curled atop the quilt that covered their bed and fell asleep.

It was late afternoon when she felt someone touching her hand. Opening her eyes, she saw Win standing by the bed. He held one of her hands in both of his.

''Hello,'' she whispered, noticing his hair was still wet from being washed. ''You look like my husband, but you can't be. My husband smells like trail dust most of the time.''

"You look like my wife, but my wife would never be so lazy as to sleep during the day." He lifted her hand. "But you must be her, because you're wearing a wedding band that matches mine."

Kora leaned up suddenly and pulled her hand from his. Sure enough, on her left hand was a wide gold band that matched the shiny gold one on his finger.

"You didn't have to—" she started.

"I know, it wasn't part of the bargain." He rolled into bed beside her. "But then neither was the way we make love."

He moved his fingers gently down her back and over the silk covering her hips. "Did you enjoy your bath?" His hand continued to stroke her.

She relaxed to his touch. "Yes," she whispered as she stretched beside him, allowing him to move her arms and legs as he continued to touch her.

"I wish I'd made it back in time to watch," he mumbled between light kisses.

Gently he rolled her to face him, and moved her leg around his waist, pulling her close against him at the waist. Then he leaned her head back over pillows. For a long moment he watched her, then lightly he traced his fingers down her throat.

Kora closed her eyes as his hand slid over the silk of her camisole, touching her breasts, circling along her abdomen, and gently moving between her open legs.

"You come to me so easy, Kora," he whispered as he repeated the action. "You drive me mad with need."

She arched her back, pressing against him with her legs and straining the silk across her breasts.

He slid his hands up her thighs and pulled her tighter against him, fitting her to his need. Then he lowered his mouth and tasted her full breasts through the silk. As always, at first his hunger was rough, pulling against her tender flesh, demanding, starving.

She sighed and tried to roll away from the tidal wave of passion and need. But his hands on her legs held her to him and his mouth tasted full of her flesh. Then, slowly, like a hungry man who'd reached the banquet, he slowed, enjoying each touch.

"Don't pull away from me, darlin'," he whispered. "I want all of my wife tonight."

She relaxed once more as his touch turned tender. He slowly unlaced her undergarments one ribbon at a time so that he could enjoy her slowly. He stopped for a long while, enjoying the sight of her camisole open to her waist and pulled wide enough apart that only the peaks of each breast were covered. Her underpants were pushed low over her hips so that his hand could cross back and forth in wide strokes below her waist, then circle back to caress her hips.

"I love watching you like this," he whispered as his fingers brushed the silk completely from her breasts. "I thought of it all last night and all day today."

She could feel his wedding band sliding along her skin as he pushed the garment aside.

Now his hands roamed over her, molding her with his need. He covered her hips with his touch and pulled her against him, rocking her to him as he kissed her throat. She hadn't said a word, his silent wife; she didn't have to. She brought him all the beauty and passion he could hold.

She felt her body growing warm, alive with feeling. Sighing softly, she leaned back, allowing him to lower his mouth once more to her chest.

His hand moved down as he kissed her. She felt his fingers slide inside her.

When she tried to pull away, he held her tightly, not

removing his hand. "Easy," he whispered against her skin. "I'm not going to hurt you, darlin'."

Without another word he kissed her again, drawing her into passion as she opened her mouth. His hand moved once more between her legs, and this time she didn't try to pull away.

The third time he touched her, he was kissing her lightly on her waiting lips, but he wasn't holding her to him at all. She could have pulled away from his probing hand, but she remained still.

He rewarded her with a deep kiss while his hand circled her breast. By the time he pulled away she was afire with desire and moving slightly against him, begging for more.

Laughing, he gave her what she wanted. Kissing her in all the places he'd tasted her the night in the study, driving her beyond all reason, pulling her into passion's deep water.

Slowly, in the warm afternoon glow of sunlight, he made love to her. As he had in the study, his hands moved over her, touching each part of her body, readying it to be tasted. And as she had before, she set no boundaries.

There were no words of love, no whispered endearments, no promises voiced. Only the loving, pure and silent, as wave after wave of passion passed over her. When he entered her, he did so slowly, allowing her to accept him without pain.

She moved her hands over his shoulders, loving the feel of him above her, loving the way he made her feel all warm and protected and afire.

The pleasure she brought him was doubled when he felt her passion explode. She held tightly to him and whispered his name as he brought her back down to earth.

Then, without a word, they cuddled in each other's arms and fell asleep.

• • •

Kora awoke to the night sky. Something Jamie said had haunted her dreams. Jamie had made the point that Winter never went back on his word. He'd never said he loved her. He'd never told her to stay forever. But he had told her he wouldn't try and stop her if she wanted to leave. He had said he wanted her gone when the six months was up. He had told her over and over that he'd never love any woman. But he called her his wife. He'd given her a ring.

She dressed and tiptoed down to Jamie's room. "Jamie?" she whispered as she opened the door. "Are you asleep?"

Jamie stretched and sat up in bed. "Why would I be doing a fool thing like that?"

"I have to talk to you."

Jamie moved over. "All right. I've been waiting all my life for you to come to me for advice. I'm a sage, you know."

Kora smiled. "All right, tell me what to do."

Jamie rubbed her eyes. "Shoot."

"I love Win, but I'm not even sure if he'd follow me if I left here."

Jamie didn't waste any time thinking. "Then let's leave and see."

"What!"

"Trust me, Sis." Jamie jumped out of bed with a loud thud. "Go up and get your coat and I'll get the wagon. We'll take Dan for a ride."

Kora thought this was probably the dumbest idea she'd ever heard, but maybe Jamie was right for once. At best, Win might miss her. At worst no one would notice them gone and they would have had a little drive in the middle of the night.

Jamie stomped into her shoes and opened her door. "Go

on and pack,'' she said too loudly. ''It's time we were moving on.''

Kora went upstairs for her coat, wondering why Jamie was acting as if they were leaving for good. As she walked down the darkened stairway, she wondered why she was even bothering to listen to Jamie.

A chair from the study blocked her path at the opening of the foyer. Kora circled it and found Win, wearing only his jeans, sitting in the wing back chair with his feet stretched out on one of the stair's steps.

''I said I wouldn't say a word if you decided to leave.''

His words were cold as they drifted across the darkness to her. ''But I lied.''

''If I just rode off one night,'' Kora tested him, ''you could have the house.''

''I don't want the house. I want you to stand by our bargain.'' He wasn't saying the words that would make her stay, and they both knew it. ''I was working in the study and couldn't help but hear Jamie shouting you were leaving.''

''But I'm bad luck. Look at all that has happened since I've been here.''

Win was silent for so long she wasn't sure he'd say anything.

Just as she turned, he whispered, ''You're the only luck I've ever had.''

''Then tell me why you want me to stay, Win,'' Kora whispered.

''We had an agreement. The six months is not up yet. I need a wife.''

Kora fought back the tears. She'd been wrong—she did need to hear words of love, but he wasn't saying them. How could he have made love to her so completely and not voice the words?

"Why else?" She had to give him another chance.

"I've never felt the way I feel when I'm with you. I've a hunger for you that may never be filled from a lifetime of sleeping with you." He was trying, but she was asking him to speak a language he'd never had the time to learn.

Kora held her breath, waiting for the words. Three words that even this strong, powerful man should be able to say. In the final hour the decision wasn't hers, but his. She suddenly realized that if he couldn't say he loved her, she couldn't stay.

The door swung open and Jamie stepped through with a lantern swinging at her side. "Kora," she whispered, without seeing Win sitting in the chair. "I've put Dan's chair in the wagon twice, and Dan keeps taking it out."

"Maybe he doesn't want to go," Cheyenne said, making everyone jump. He rounded the doorway with his arms folded as though he'd been on the porch for a while.

"No one asked you." Jamie set the lantern down on the stairs. "I'll put the chair in again. And don't you dare call the alarm or try to stop us."

"If you're leaving, I'll be glad to help load the wagon," Cheyenne offered.

Before Kora could join them, Win's voice stopped her. "I want it back," he whispered.

"What?" she asked, saddened that he hadn't attempted to stop her. When Jamie had suggested the wild plan, she'd never thought that she might really be leaving. She never should have tried to force Win's hand. He wasn't the kind of man to be pushed into saying something just because she thought she needed to hear the words.

"The ring!" he demanded.

Kora sat on the step with the lantern and pulled the band from her finger. She placed it in her palm and held it up to him. In the end all he was worried about was the ring, not her. What difference did it make if she left now or a few months from now? She was only a temporary wife anyway.

The light reflected off the gold, sparkling the metal into a ring of tiny shooting stars. Kora stared at it, marveling at how beautiful it looked.

Something caught her eye and she turned the ring to the light. Letters were carved deep into the gold on the inside. She turned it, slowly reading the words aloud. "For Kora, my love, my life, Win."

Tears bubbled onto her cheeks. "Am I?" she whispered. "Am I your love?"

Win stood then and knelt on the stairs beside her. "No," he whispered, forcing each word out. "You're more, much more. You're all the beauty I've ever known. You're my heart, my soul. You're worth more than all I own or will ever have. If you leave, you'll take the only key that can keep my heart beating."

Tears streamed down Kora's face as she lifted her arms, and he pulled her against him.

"Well, I'll be!" Jamie squealed from the foyer. "Damned if you didn't finally say the right thing, cowboy. I was about to think I'd have to hog-tie you and beat it into you."

Win held Kora tightly as he faced Jamie. "You pushed me as far as you could, didn't you? When I heard you upstairs, I guessed why you were talking so loud. But when Kora came down those stairs, I couldn't think of anything but that she might leave me. You planned it that way."

"Right again, cowboy. I didn't want my sister marrying because of some bargain. I wanted her to be loved and appreciated like she ought to be . . . like a smart man would appreciate me."

Cheyenne stood behind Jamie. "Dan's out of the wagon

again,'' he complained. ''Moved his chair back to the porch.''

Jamie winked at Win and turned to the Indian. ''Stop trying to slow me down, Cheyenne. I'm leaving.''

''Slow you down! I'm doing all I can to help you along.''

''Sure you are.'' She followed him onto the porch, patting his bottom as they moved. ''I know how you really feel about me.''

Cheyenne took long strides away. ''I can't wait until you're out of my life!''

Jamie was right behind him, yelling what a liar he was and that maybe she'd decided she'd stay around a while just to prove it.

Win and Kora laughed as they heard Jamie and Cheyenne arguing all the way to the barn. Then Win turned Kora in his arms and kissed her soundly.

''We'd better go back to bed, darlin','' Win whispered.

Kora smiled up at him. ''How far were you willing to go to make me stay?''

''As far as it takes,'' he said as he lifted her in his arms. ''Even if it means having to say I love you every day and night of my life.''

Kora smiled. ''That's the price.''

Win kissed her. ''Then, darlin', it's a bargain.''

EPILOGUE

"MOVE THE TABLES OUT UNDER THE TREES!" JAMIE yelled at several men. "Hurry, she's on her way."

Kora carried out plates and a linen tablecloth.

"Remember," she whispered to Jamie as she passed, "only the best of my new china."

Jamie grumbled. "All right, but it don't make much sense setting such a table under the trees."

"It's too hot in the house. I want her to be comfortable."

Ten minutes later Kora, Jamie, and Win stood on the front porch and watched Cheyenne pull Kora's new buggy up to the front steps.

Win moved forward and offered the special guest his hand. "Welcome, Miss Rae," he said. "We've been waiting for you to join us for dinner."

The old lady from the settlement smiled as she stepped out into the late afternoon sunshine. Her ragged clothes were clean, and she'd tried to comb her hair, but several strands had bindweed mentality among the strawlike gray tumbleweed.

"Why, thank you, Mr. McQuillen. I'm mightly glad you sent your *mute* to get me."

Cheyenne grumbled and Win laughed. Cheyenne never talked to anyone much, except Jamie, whom he yelled at regularly.

Kora took Rae's arm and led her through the house. "I thought we'd have a glass of apple wine first. If you've got the time, I'd love to show you some of the things Win and I brought back from Dallas."

Rae nodded as though she might pick up some decorating tips.

Win watched as Kora treated her guest with all the respect and charm she would have a queen. The cowhands joining them took their lead from Kora, and soon everyone was on their best behavior. As they sat beneath the trees, Dan carried his chair from the porch and moved it in between Rae and Logan. Jamie looked surprised, but Rae never missed a step. She began talking with Dan as though the man would answer her.

To Win's surprise, everyone enjoyed dinner, and by the time dessert was served, the atmosphere seemed more of a party.

As the men left to have their cigars, Jamie caught Win by the arm. "Did you mean what you said about making any man who got me with child marry me?"

Everyone including Kora froze.

Win raised an eyebrow. "I did."

"Well, I'm going to have a child, and the father is right here."

Cheyenne swore, Logan swallowed his tobacco, and several of the men looked at one another trying to guess who the unlucky man might be.

"Oh, no!" Kora cried as she moved to Jamie's side.

"Name the father and I'll get my gun." Win's face was hard. "Any man who did this to you will be a husband or dead by morning."

Jamie smiled as if all her problems were solved.

Everyone waited silently for her to speak. Jamie lowered her head. When she looked up, she had eyes only for Cheyenne.

Cheyenne looked confused, then angry. He slammed his napkin on the table and bolted from his chair. "This is the limit, Jamie. You know damn well I'm not the father of any baby you're carrying."

Kora saw the confusion in Win's eyes. He couldn't go back on his word, and he couldn't shoot his best friend. She suddenly became more worried about Win than Jamie or Cheyenne.

"Are you sure?" Rae laughed as she took the reins of the mess before her as if it were after-dinner entertainment.

"Am I sure! Am I sure! It's not something I'd likely forget happening!" Cheyenne shouted.

"So you never thought of Jamie in that way?" Rae folded her arms over her stomach.

Cheyenne opened his mouth and closed it three times before he could get a word to come out. "Sure I've thought of her in that way, but thinking and doing are two different things."

"Do you love her?" Rae became the judge.

"No!" Cheyenne answered. "I hate most every ornery bone in her body. She's just saying this now because she's run out of anything to badger me about. The woman has considered it her life's calling to pester me since the night she showed up here."

"Well, there's only one way to know for sure," Rae said, as if she'd read the cure in a book somewhere. "Kiss her."

"What!"

"Kiss her. I can always tell if a man cares about a woman by the way he kisses her."

Cheyenne took a step away. "I made that mistake once, and she won't stop touching me since."

Kora slipped her hand into Win's and tightened her grip. She wanted him to know that no matter what he had to do tonight, she would stand beside him.

"Best follow Rae's advice," Win said. "If Jamie's lying, we'll all know soon enough."

Jamie frowned at Win, seemingly unhappy at even the thought that she might be lying.

"Of course she's lying—her mouth is moving, isn't it?"

"If Rae says kiss her, you'd best follow her advice." Win ordered.

Cheyenne stormed to Jamie like a man charging a grizzly bear. He grabbed her arm and pulled her roughly against him and lowered his mouth.

Win took a step to help Jamie, but Kora held him back.

Cheyenne lifted her off the ground in a hug as Jamie's arms circled his neck.

Everyone waited . . . and waited . . . and waited.

Rae made a sound like she was bored and glanced at Kora. "I'll help you clear the table."

"Shouldn't we do something?" Win asked.

Rae chuckled. "They're already doing it."

When the dishes were clear and men had brought the table inside, Jamie and Cheyenne were still locked in each other's arms.

"Well," Rae said as she circled her ragged shawl around her neck. "I guess we got our answer."

"He's the father," Win mumbled.

Both Rae and Kora laughed.

"No," Rae snorted. "Jamie ain't pregnant. She was fibbing flat out. It's obvious. But that don't mean she won't be by morning."

The old woman climbed into the buggy. Logan had been

appointed to take her home. Before he could adjust the reins, Dan walked off the porch and climbed in the back without looking at anyone.

As the buggy pulled away, Win drew Kora under his arm and kissed her hair. ''I don't understand,'' he whispered as he moved to her cheek. ''How was it so obvious that Jamie was the one lying?''

Kora raised her lips to his. His kiss was loving and warm with promise. ''Because,'' Kora whispered against his cheek. ''He was starving.''

Win lifted her into his arms. ''I'm feeling a little starved myself. Even though that was a wonderful six-month anniversary dinner.''

''Thank you,'' she whispered as she moved her hand into his hair.

''Have I told you how much I love you today?'' Win asked as he started up the stairs.

''Yes.'' She laughed. ''Twice already today.''

''I must be gettin' old. I can't remember and Jamie's behavior makes no sense.''

''It seemed plain from the first that she was bluffing,'' Kora whispered as he opened their bedroom door and carried her into the starlit room. ''Besides, everyone knows I'm the one who's pregnant.''

Win felt the heart he'd spent most of his life swearing he didn't have explode with joy. He'd found where he belonged. He'd found his tribe.